"They all think you're sweet, don't they?" he murmured.

"Everyone assumes you're just a good girl who does what she's supposed to."

"I am." Tate smiled as she snuggled against his lean hard body.

"Hmm… I overheard your discussion of *Story of O*, remember? And I know *exactly* how you feel about that steamy scene in *The Big Easy*. You might have been on the phone with Sara, but you were really talking to me."

"Oh, God," she said, burying her head in the pillow so he couldn't see her blush. "Was I that obvious?"

"Yes. You were." He was grinning now.

It was just the kind of scene she'd dreamed of, in her bed, alone, in the dark. Everything about him was perfect. The situation was wonderful, like something out of a Nora Ephron movie. Except for the danger that hovered a whisper away.

She groaned.

"Hey, I liked it. I like you."

Tate shook her head, not wanting to believe. She knew he was just trying to distract her so she wouldn't be scared.

He leaned down so his mouth was close to her ear. "I used to go home and stroke myself to the memory of your sexy voice…"

you someplace,
...id.

Bec... ...an't manage more than a mute nod. She didn't bother to ask where they were going or how long they'd be there. As long as she was with Max, she was happy.

When he lifted her, it seemed the most natural thing in the world to wrap her arms around his neck – and her legs around his waist. He carried her through the empty lounge and over to the baby grand concealed behind the decorative metal screen. Kicking the bench aside, he sat her down atop the piano's glossy hood.

He stepped between her parted legs and bent to brush kisses along her knee. "You're beautiful. So beautiful."

Bracing herself on her palms, Becky leaned back on the cool surface and let the heat the man was stirring within her wash over her like a warm, sexy wave.

Then Max's hands were on her thighs, pushing her dress up and out of the way and Becky forgot everything else…

STROKES OF MIDNIGHT

BY
HOPE TARR

&

KIDNAPPED!

BY
JO LEIGH

MILLS & BOON®
Pure reading pleasure™

First published in Great Britain 2008
by Harlequin Mills & Boon Limited,
Eton House, 18-24 Paradise Road, Richmond, Surrey TW9 1SR

Strokes of Midnight © Hope Tarr 2007
Kidnapped! © Jolie Kramer 2007

ISBN: 978 0 263 86727 5

14-1208

Harlequin Mills & Boon policy is to use papers that are natural, renewable and recyclable products and made from wood grown in sustainable forests. The logging and manufacturing processes conform to the legal environmental regulations of the country of origin.

Printed and bound in Spain
by Litografia Rosés S.A., Barcelona

STROKES OF
MIDNIGHT

BY
HOPE TARR

Dear Reader,

Strokes of Midnight is my second winter holiday book for Blaze® and my first contribution to its WRONG BED series.

Bound for New York on New Year's Eve, romance novelist Becky Stone, aka Rebecca St Claire, feels certain her horoscope forecasting a new year of "fresh starts" and "dazzling opportunities" is about to come true. Instead, Becky learns she has no choice but to co-author her next book with bestselling action-adventure novelist Adam Maxwell if she's going to save her career.

The tall, blue-eyed hunk Becky bumps into in Midtown seems straight out of a fairy tale. With the stroke of midnight fast approaching, a sexy one-night stand seems the perfect way to ring in the New Year. Besides, it's not as if she has to ever see him again – right?

Wrong. Her perfect stranger is Adam Maxwell, and as writing partners they are going to be seeing each other day – and night – for the next several months. Can these two accidental lovers craft the perfect plotline and still fall head over heels in love?

Wishing you a holiday season filled with magical moments and sexy surprises…

Hope Tarr

www.hopetarr.com

HOPE TARR

is an award-winning author of multiple contemporary and historical romance novels. *Strokes of Midnight* is her third book for Blaze® and her first contribution to its WRONG BED series. When not writing, Hope indulges her passions for feline rescue and historic preservation.

To enter Hope's monthly contest, visit her online at www.hopetarr.com.

To my friends, Barbara Casana and
Susan Shaver, for seeing me through yet
another of life's not so little challenges
with wit, wisdom and laughter.

Also, to my wonderful editor, Brenda Chin,
for her keen insights and patience in helping
me bring Max and Becky's story to
life on the printed page.

Prologue

Train bound for New York City
December 31st, 10:30 a.m. (give or take)

"So, HAVE you started celebrating your big book deal yet? I expected to hear champagne corks popping in the background." Sharon's voice, sounding as excited as Becky felt, faded in and out amidst the cell phone static.

Holding the phone more snugly against her ear, Becky Stone, soon-to-be bestselling romance novelist Rebecca St. Claire, didn't bother to strip the smile from her voice. "It might be New Year's Eve, but I'd better hold off on the celebrating at least until we make Manhattan."

In another few hours, Becky expected she'd be kicking up her four-inch high heels and celebrating in earnest—and not because of the holiday. The day before, her editor, Pat, had called to say she had important news to share, news with far-reaching ramifications for Becky's career, and could Becky make it up to Manhattan in the next few days so they could chat over lunch? The busy New York editor generally preferred communicating by e-mail. An actual phone call requesting an in-person meeting meant something big must have happened or was about to. Becky had immediately booked a first-class seat on an express train that would get her from Washington, D.C.'s Union Station to New York's Penn Station in less than three hours. Thinking of her fellow New York-bound holiday travelers packed like sardines into the coach and business-class cars, the splurge struck her as money well spent.

Pat's impromptu call could only mean one thing. Becky's latest Angelina Talbot novel must have sold out its print run, or close to it. The genre-bending mystery erotica series seemed to have struck a chord with her female readers that her previous historical romances had somehow missed. Who knew? But maybe the book had even made one of the bestseller lists—if not the *New York Times* then certainly *USA Today*. Why else would Pat make such a huge deal about meeting face-to-face right before the biggest party night of the year?

Becky's year-end horoscope for Libras predicting a fabulous new year chockfull of "fresh starts" and "dazzling opportunities" in her houses of career and love wasn't only coming true—she had hit some sort of astrological jackpot.

Sharon's voice pulled Becky back into the present. "Don't go too overboard on the shoe shopping, at least not until the ink dries on that megabucks multibook deal. Oh, and call me as soon as your victory lunch wraps. I want to hear all about it."

"I will." The increasing static had Becky looking out the window to the tunnel they were coming up on. "We're about to go under the Hudson River. I'd better sign off before I lose you. Thanks for calling to wish me luck. Love you, girlfriend."

"Love you, too, Becks, and Happy New Year."

Becky opened her mouth to return the holiday felicitation but the cell cut out. She clicked the phone closed and dropped it into her Kate Spade tote bag, exchanging it for her latest Angelina Talbot release. Smoothing a loving hand over the paperback's glossy-finish cover, she had to admit the art department folks had pulled out all the stops on this one. The sleek, raven-haired cover model embodied her British bombshell heroine down to her chic, body-conscious black minidress, smoking pistol and shiny black do-me stilettos. The footwear was an attitude statement, not a necessity. Becky might only stand a piddling five foot one inches sans her beloved designer high heels, but her fictional creation towered at five foot ten, tall enough to look other women and most men in the eye with or without shoes on. Along with the height she'd always coveted, Becky had blessed Angelina with a Mensa member's mind, a Playboy Bunny's libido and a Victoria's Secret model's killer curves. Talk about a complete package.

But the best part of the cover was the review from *Publishers Weekly*. Printed below the gold-embossed title, the coveted blurb proclaimed Becky "a fresh, innovative voice" and "an up-and-coming talent to watch."

An up-and-coming talent to watch... Becky slipped the book back into her bag and eased into her extrawide seat with a satisfied sigh. Stretching out her legs, she cast a fond downward glance to her Manolo Blahnik chocolate-brown Napa-leather knee boots. Growing up the middle child in a family of five in Dundalk, Maryland, designer shoes had seemed about as obtainable as Cinderella's glass slippers. Even her Barbie dolls had gone barefoot. Now she was wearing Manolo Blahniks while traveling first class. Some dreams at least did come true.

Things definitely looked brighter than they had at

Christmas the week before. She'd celebrated the eve of the holiday home alone with her tiger-striped tabby cat, Daisy Bud, Thai takeout (for her) and a can of albacore tuna (for the cat). In honor of the so-called season of hope, she'd made a wish list of all the things she wanted to do—make that *would* do—in the coming year. Become bestselling author. Take trip to Ireland. Go on motorcycle ride. Go to animal shelter and find feline friend for cat. Save up down payment for house. Meet man of dreams and fall in love…

Since her ex-boyfriend, Elliot, had dumped her for a twentysomething twit the year before, she'd been pretty cautious—okay, scared shitless—about getting involved again. Romantic intimacy played great on paper, but in real life it was damned hard to achieve. In her case, she'd been so sure the former federal agent turned media commentator was The One. After two decades of dating, starting with locking lips and orthodontics retainers with her ninth-grade boyfriend in the back of the Uptown Theater, she'd thought she was a pretty good judge of the male psyche, but her ex had played her as only an A-list player could. Looking back, the red flags popped like a neon-lit roadmap—his spurts of phone calls followed by sudden silences, his plans with her that never seemed to make it beyond the talking phase, the fact that the only address she had for him was an e-mail one. And yet she'd stayed with him, believed in him, even taken his advice to quit her day job. Talk about piss-poor judgment. Forget trusting a man again. When it came to love, how could she ever trust herself?

"Next stop, New York Penn Station."

The conductor's voice blaring over the intercom had her turning her head to look out the window just as the train emerged from the tunnel, bringing the Manhattan skyline into view like the Emerald City—distant but within reach, not unlike her dreams. Lying boyfriends and tepid book sales and money worries in general were all a part of her past. For once, *this* once, luck—and the Universe—seemed to be lining up squarely on her side.

Still thirteen and a half hours to a new year, and already it was shaping up to be 365 days of "fresh starts and dazzling opportunities"—and Becky was more than ready to let the good times roll.

1

"Turnabout is fair play, Falco, or hadn't you heard? Now where are the bloody plans?"

Dressed in dominatrix black leather down to her spiked heels, Angelina trained the subcompact Beretta on the silver-haired man lying in the center of the mussed bed. Red silk scarves lashed his wrists to the bedposts, and sweat from the long, rough ride she'd just given him rolled down his taut neck and leanly muscled torso.

The year before, the double agent had seduced her and then stolen the missile plans from her flat while she lay wrapped in silken sheets and the afterglow of his expert lovemaking. To add insult to injury, he had then turned over the plans to a twenty-two-year-old blonde for a ridiculously small sum. Rumor had it the plans were once again for sale on the black market—and that Falco knew exactly who the latest purchaser was.

Falco's deep-set dark eyes met hers from across the room. "Angelina, love, you wouldn't shoot me, not after that incredible shag we just shared. Now be a good girl and let me loose."

His cocky self-assurance made her palms itch to

slap his handsome lying face—again. "Don't flatter yourself. I would have shot you when I first spotted you at the embassy ball earlier tonight, only my gown was vintage Valentino and I hated to ruin it with the splatter."

"THE BOOK tanked, Becky. I'm sorry."

Pat punctuated her pronouncement by upending the bottle of ketchup over her burger. The bright red glob landing atop the plump, midrare patty might as well have been Becky's career lifeblood.

Eyes watering, Becky took a moment to recover from the sip of champagne she'd just aspirated. Hearing the word *tanked* in the context of her hoped-for bestseller was like watching the New Year's ball drop over Times Square—and then detonate. "I'm uh…sorry, I must have misheard you. It sounded like you said—"

"Tanked, bit the dust, bought the big one—take your pick." Pat slapped the top of her bun back on, picked up the burger and sank her teeth in for a sloppy bite. "Publishing is a tough business and, as the saying goes, 'them's the breaks.'"

Oh, God. Becky felt as though the Grinch had stolen her Christmas, not just the tree but all the trimmings, including her favorite Christmas carols and her goodwill toward men. "B-but…the sales on the launch book were solid and the reviews on this book were all—"

"Raves," Pat finished for her, ketchup dribbling down the side of her mouth. The senior editor slid her side plate of crispy thin fries toward Becky. "Try a *pomme frite*. They're delish with this Dijon mayonnaise."

Becky resisted the urge to slap a hand over her forehead, which had begun pounding like a bad hip-hop beat. As if a strip of deep-fried potato with a fancy French name could possibly make her feel better. "Thanks, but I'll pass."

Pat picked up a fry and stabbed it into the space between them. "Know what differentiates my star authors from midlist schmucks? It's not talent, though sure, talent helps. It's not looks, though those don't hurt, either. It's moxie, balls, perseverance—take your pick. Today's bestsellers, Becky, are all writers who've persevered, who've done whatever it took to claw their way back to the top of the industry heap. You have to reinvent yourself. Who was that silent film actress who said 'failure isn't the falling down but the staying down.' It's time to make like the Nike ads and just do it."

The slogan-packed pep talk had Becky feeling more panicked than inspired. "Okay, I'll reinvent myself, but how? I mean, I thought that's what I was doing by blending romantic erotica with a mystery element."

Pat nodded, her sprayed-in-place platinum hair reminiscent of Meryl Streep's in *The Devil Wore Prada*. "And it was high-concept, very high-concept—for its time."

For...its...time. The gale force of those three chilling words knocked Becky back against the booth seat. The point was, she was dated, she was done. Pat might as well pull a miniature bugle out of her Fendi shoulder bag, play some taps and make it official.

"The problem is the mainstream market for genre fiction has been shrinking steadily. It's only the established star authors who've managed to hold on to their spots. Midlist up-and-comers like you are getting squeezed out. You came on the scene a few years too late to break in. Under the circumstances, I can't offer you another multibook contract. The fact is, I can't offer you a contract at all."

So much for those forecasted fresh starts and dazzling opportunities. With no regular paycheck to fall back on, she'd been counting on her advance to pay the bills for the coming year. "But I thought you said—"

"That was before the feedback from the reader poll we ran from our Web site rolled in. Readers are burned out on Angelina's bed-hopping lifestyle."

Feeling queasy, Becky pushed her salad entrée away. "But I thought her willingness to put herself out there sexually was what they liked about her?"

Pat passed a bright-pink thumbnail over her front teeth and shook her head. "Not anymore they don't. They want to see her meet her match and settle down with a sexy male counterpart."

Becky couldn't believe what she was hearing. "Are you saying readers want Angelina to be *monogamous?*"

Pat frowned, the deep crease in her brow hinting it must be time for her next Botox treatment. Ordinarily the fifty-something's face was as tight as a twenty-year-old's and as immobile as a mannequin's. "Don't say it like it's a four-letter word. Monogamy is very hip right now. Even if it's serial monogamy, readers like to see one guy and one girl at a time."

Becky laid a hand alongside her temple where the pounding had segued into thousands of tiny needles jabbing away. "But Angelina doesn't stay in any one place long enough to form long-term relationships, romantic or otherwise. That's the glamour of her job as a crime-solving secret agent. She's always on the go."

"And she can still be on the go, only instead of just designer luggage she'll travel with a sexy partner." Pat dusted crumbs from her fingers and leaned in as though to share a confidence. "Angelina needs a man who's not just another pretty face but who's her match in every way. A man's man but not a Neanderthal, an American version of James Bond sans the tuxedo and the shaken-not-stirred martini, a guy's guy who's also sexy, gutsy, smart and sophisticated—but not so sophisticated he comes off as a wimp."

Relief flooded Becky. Her editor hadn't written her off. Pat was still on her side, still in there pitching for her. Her career wasn't dead. She was just experiencing one of those annoying setbacks most writers cycled through at some point in their careers. Like a bad menstrual period or a zit that took extra-extra long to clear, eventually this, too, would pass.

"Gotcha!" Buzzing on adrenaline, she nodded profusely and slipped to the edge of her seat. "I'll get to work on writing him ASAP. You'll have the revised proposal early next week."

Was it her admittedly overactive imagination at work or did Pat suddenly look the tiniest bit uncomfortable? "That's the best part. You don't have to create him. He's, uh…already created."

Becky was feeling more confused by the minute. "Already created? But how…"

Dropping her gaze, Pat played with the lone fry left on her plate. "Ever read any of Adam Maxwell's 'Drake's Adventures' books?"

The sucker punch hit Becky dead-on, a direct shot to the solar plexus that again had her choking on her champagne. "Adam Maxwell. *The* Adam Maxwell! If you're suggesting what I think you are, my answer is no, no way. Not on your life—or mine."

Of all the writers to propose teaming her with, Adam

Maxwell was the very worst Pat could have come up with. The reclusive author rarely ventured forth from his home in New Hampshire's White Mountains, but Becky couldn't fault him for that. Introversion was a forgivable failing, particularly among writers. When you spent the majority of your waking hours creating splendid, larger-than-life fictional characters, finding real flesh-and-blood human beings to measure up was no small feat. Occupation aside, Maxwell was a native New Englander and New Englanders had a reputation for keeping to themselves. No, if Adam Maxwell had stuck with banging out his bestsellers from behind bolted cabin doors, Becky would have no beef with him.

It was the outlandish things he said when he did venture out into the public eye that set her blood boiling. In the interview he'd given just after his second book hit the bestseller lists, he'd shown himself to be a chauvinistic jerk. A year later, his remark likening romance novels to "housewife porn" still stuck in Becky's craw. Ever since reading that quote in the *New Yorker,* she and her fellow romance writer buddies had voted Maxwell the still-living white male novelist they could feel good about hating. Who was he to judge another writer's work, anyway? He penned action-adventure novels. It's not like he was friggin' Hemingway.

Pat dropped the fry and looked up. "I love your writing, Becky, you know I do, but with these disappointing numbers, I can't sell you upstairs. Teaming you with Adam Maxwell would be a way to keep you in the game, maybe even boost you into the bestseller league. What do you say?"

Their pretty blond server sidled up, saving Becky from having to answer. "Can I bring you any coffee or dessert?"

Becky opened her mouth to ask what decadent desserts

they might have on the menu—in some cultures, chocolate was considered medicine, after all—but Pat cut her off, handing over her credit card. "Go ahead and run this, and please put a move on—or *vite vite* as they say in Paris."

"Whatever." The girl rolled her eyes and sped away as only a tall girl wearing comfortably flat shoes could.

Pat turned back to the table, gaze dropping to the Dolce & Gabbana lizard-embossed print bangle watch cuffing her right wrist. "Sorry, doll, but I really have to dash. I have a meeting across town with another author and catching a cab this time of day is going to be murder."

Fighting the sinking sense she'd just had the publishing equivalent of the Last Supper, or in this case, Last Lunch, Becky nodded. "That's okay. I need to think things over anyway."

The waitress returned in record time. Pat signed, snapped the vinyl bill holder shut and dropped the receipt into her purse. "The office will be closed tomorrow for the holiday but call me on my cell before you head back to D.C." Pulling on her hot-pink trench coat, she slid out of the booth. "Remember, there's a jungle filled with hungry young writers salivating for the chance to snag your spot and be the next Rebecca St. Claire."

Elbows sinking onto the table, Becky watched the older woman head out the door, the warning words ringing in her ears like a blast of New Year's noisemakers. She was a good writer, a *damned* good writer, but in a business as fickle as publishing no one was so good they couldn't be replaced.

The waitress returned to clear the table and pick up the check. She glanced over at Becky's untouched lunch. "You want a box for that?"

"No, thanks." Becky felt certain the smell of lime vinaigrette and grilled shrimp would forever be paired in her memory with the gut-wrenching feeling of failure.

Handing over the salad, she caught herself studying the girl's fresh face, mane of shiny, straight, blond hair and model svelte body—and felt the sinking sense of insecurity she'd spent the past year and a small fortune in self-help books trying to get over.

Shoving the vinyl folder into her change apron, the server asked, "Can I get you anything else?"

Becky hesitated. She did want something else, and in this case it wasn't a cellulite-free ass, straight blond hair or even the extra vertical inches that made it okay to wear sensible flats instead of nosebleed-high heels. If faced with a similar state of emergency, her fictional heroine, Angelina Talbot wouldn't hesitate to soothe herself with her signature cocktail.

"As a matter of fact, I'd like a double Bombay Sapphire martini, straight up with an olive, not a twist. Oh, and make it shaken, not stirred."

She might not be a British bombshell sniffing out kidnappers and murderous foreign agents, but it had turned out to be one roller-coaster ride of a day.

"TEAMING ME with a romance writer is your idea of a career jump start? You've got to be joking." Adam Maxwell—Max—stared at his editor, her latest editorial "suggestion" spearing the space between them like a stingray's barbed whiptail.

"It's no joke, Max." Seated across from him in the Hotel Chelsea's Serena Bar and Lounge, Pat reached for her drink, the Serena specialty cocktail known as the Pink

Bitch. Under the circumstances, the beverage struck Max as remarkably apropos. "My instincts are telling me that pairing your Drake Dundee with Rebecca St. Claire's Angelina Talbot may just be the marketing move that takes both your careers to the next level."

Glancing at the glass in his hand, Max half wondered if the single sip of Macallan single-malt Scotch he'd taken might have aversely affected his hearing. "Sometimes the next level is down."

Pat leaned over and picked at the appetizer plate of hummus, pita bread triangles and spiced olives sitting on the circular chrome cocktail table between them. Popping an olive into her mouth, she said, "I want you to do this book with Rebecca St. Claire. Think of it as a creative experiment. One book is all I'm asking."

Max shook his head. "I don't care if it's one book or a hundred and one books, the answer is still no. There's a reason I've never had a writing partner—I've never wanted one. I'm a solo act—period."

That wasn't entirely true. When Elaina was alive and still reasonably well, they'd sit up nights over an open bottle of wine or freshly brewed pot of coffee and brainstorm. Playing the "what if" game, she'd called it. Trust his wife to turn plotting a book into recreation rather than work.

He'd lost her to cancer the year before on New Year's Day, and he still hadn't gotten used to cooking dinner for one or sleeping alone or coming home to an empty house. If it wasn't for writing, he wasn't sure how he would have gotten through the past twelve months. Creating a fictional universe of colorful, noisy characters made it easier to block out the deafening silence. Once he'd forced himself to start working again, he'd quickly finished the book he'd set aside and then fired off two more in rapid succession. His adventuring Aussie hero, Drake Dundee, was too busy blazing new trails and tracking new treasure to stop long enough to feel much beyond an explorer's thrill of discovery. Bringing a fictional love interest—and a real-life romance writer—into the picture promised to seriously mess with Max's formula, not to mention his head.

Pat leaned back in her seat, the lifting of one pencil-shaded brow bringing to mind Cruella De Vil. "A sixty-percent sell-through would be considered respectable for a first book, but for a veteran author, it's pretty disappointing. Either we come up with a plan to bring your sales back up or you can expect to see your print run on the next book slashed to smithereens, and the marketing budget right along with it."

So Pat wanted to play hardball, did she? The prospect of losing control over both Drake's destiny, as well as the real life he'd spent the past year pulling back together had him lashing out.

"I've worked too damned hard building up the Adam Maxwell brand to blow it because the sales numbers for one book came in on the low end."

Drake had started off his adventures married to a tall, lovely Greek-American cryptologist, Isabel. The character was a thinly veiled version of Elaina. After her death, Max had killed off Isabel. A curare-laced arrow hit her in the left breast, the spot where Elaina's first cancerous lump was found. Giving Drake a new love interest would be a betrayal of his wife's memory. It was out of the question.

Pat picked up a pita point and dipped it in the hummus. Nibbling the edge, she said, "The Angelina Talbot books are genre benders, a blending of romantic erotica and mystery. Folding the romance and mystery elements into an action-adventure scenario could boost sales for both series. Who knows what the commercial potential might be? And I'm not just talking books. It's not unheard of for a movie screenplay to be based on a blockbuster novel."

Pat must be under some big-time pressure from her boss to sign him up because she was really putting on the razzle-dazzle. Feeling as though he was on the receiving end of an exploded bag of New Year's confetti—annoying, unnecessary and damned messy to clean up—Max shook his head. "Being a novelist and writing the best damned book I possibly can has always been a big enough dream for me."

Sticking a liver-spotted hand inside her suitcase-size pink purse, Pat pulled out a mass market paperback and handed it over. "Before you decide, give Beck—give Rebecca's work a read. This is her latest. It's gotten rave reviews, including *Publishers Weekly* and a nice write-up in the *Chicago Tribune,* too."

Max glanced at the book, not bothering to hide his distaste. The campy cover featured a slender, dark-haired female wearing a low-cut black dress, her perfect breasts standing out in silhouette along with the smoking pistol she pointed. A cone of light framed in rifle crosshairs suggested an unseen target. Talk about clichéd.

"I don't care if the woman's books are the best god-damned things to come off the printing press since Gutenberg invented it, my answer of no still stands."

Pat frowned. "I wouldn't be so sure about that. You have a multibook contract with us and, as you may or may not recall, the final book of that contract is written as 'blind,' meaning it's anything we want it to be—and we want it to be this."

Like the fictional Drake, in real life Max didn't take kindly to threats, veiled or otherwise. "I won't do the co-write. If that means we part our professional ways, then so be it. Yours isn't the only publishing house in New York and ever since 9/11, action-adventure is a huge share of the fiction market. If need be, I'll take my chances."

"We have a contract, Max, a legally binding document. Maybe you should have a talk with your agent before you burn any bridges."

Max slammed the paperback on the table and shot to his feet. He shoved a hand into his wallet and threw a wad of money down on the table. Pissed off as he was, he wasn't about to stick a woman with the bar tab even if that woman did represent the global publishing enterprise hell-bent on destroying his brand and his career.

Pat stood, as well. "Max, don't leave like this. We need to talk things over."

Max had had just about all the talking he could stomach for one afternoon. It was high time he tore a page from Drake's book, or rather *his* books, and took action instead.

"I'm going to have that little talk with my agent you recommended. You can expect to hear from him by close of business today—along with my lawyer."

HALFWAY through her martini, Becky was beginning to feel a little maudlin, as well as a little numb. Some fabulous start to the new year—not! Just that morning she'd felt as though she was standing on top of the world and now she felt as though she'd plummeted to, if not exactly rock bottom then certainly some substrata of inner earth.

Maybe I have bad restaurant karma.

The final episode with Elliot had taken place in a restaurant, too. She and Sharon were sitting down to dinner at Coppi Vignorelli in Becky's Northwest, D.C. neighborhood of Woodley Park. Within steps of Becky's apartment, the Italian bistro was her and Elliot's special place when he came into town. They'd just started in on their pasta when Elliot had strolled into the dining room, the distinctive metal studding on his deconstructed Mark Nason Italian "strummer" loafers catching Becky's eye like a lighthouse beacon.

Her heart leapt and then landed, the thrill of seeing him clashing with confusion over why he hadn't told her he was coming into town. She was pretty sure he was supposed to be in L.A. that week and New York the next. Given his bi-coastal lifestyle, they only saw each other once a month, but Becky was too head over heels to press for more, especially now that he'd started talking about her moving in with him. In the picture he painted, she'd spend her days lounging poolside with her laptop in L.A. or soaking up the artistic vibe of some hip Manhattan coffee bar. He'd even urged her to quit her regular nine-to-five job. She'd hesitated at first, but he'd seemed so sincere that she'd finally set aside her misgivings and given her notice. Evaluating federally funded literacy programs was a paycheck, not a dream job, the kind of steady career that justified her master's degree and the thousands of dollars she'd racked up in student loans. For Elliot, though, money obviously wasn't a consideration. Other than his running shoes she'd never seen him wear anything actually manufactured in America.

Ignoring the uneasy feeling settling into her stomach, she nudged Sharon. "Hey, that's Elliot, the guy I've been telling you about. I can't believe he's here. He must have missed seeing me when he walked in. Come on, I'll introduce you." She started up from the seat.

Sharon's hand clamped over hers, anchoring her to the booth. Face wearing a funny look, she leaned in and whispered, "Becky, don't look over there right now but he's… he's with someone."

Becky sank back into her seat, the few bites of rigatoni she'd taken threatening to come up. Following Sharon's nod, she saw his dinner date bounce over to their table, all white-toothed smile and sun-bronzed skin and long, shiny blond hair. Wearing a tight black tank top and a pair of skinny jeans with zippers at the ankles, she looked twenty-two, twenty-three tops.

But even worse than seeing her lover with a woman almost young enough to be his daughter—forget the *almost,* he *was* pushing forty-five—was the moment when Becky looked over and caught his eye. Instead of sending her an apologetic smile or a guilty wave, some recognition that she was alive, that she was there, he met her gaze head-on—and looked straight through her. Straight through her as if she didn't exist, as if she were made of see-through glass, with no more sentience than the wooden booths or the framed photographs lining the walls.

She reached beneath the table and found Sharon's hand. "Oh…God…this hurts. This *really* hurts." She squeezed as hard and tight as she could, as though Sharon was her anchor to everything that could still be counted on to be honest and safe and real.

Sharon squeezed back, whispering commiserating words—"Oh, Becky, I'm so sorry," and, "This is brutal, the worst," and finally, "I'm getting the check and getting you the hell out of here."

Feeling frantic, Becky shook her head. "No, we can't. I mean, *I* can't. I'm not going to give him the satisfaction."

And she hadn't. For the next thirty minutes or so she'd sat pushing pasta around on her plate and keeping up a show of cheerful chatter while bit by bit her heart withered and shriveled and finally died on the vine of her happily-ever-after dreams.

On the bright side, the Dark Night of the Soul had sparked a career epiphany. The next morning when she'd crawled out of bed, dredging up an evening's worth of Oreo cookie crumbs and wadded-up tissues, she knew she couldn't stomach writing period pieces about twentysomething heroines any longer. She'd called Pat and told her she had an idea kicking around in her brain for a contemporary novel that pushed the boundaries of traditional romance fiction. By the time she'd finished pitching the proposal her editor had given her a verbal green light and sworn that if the draft was even half as good as the pitch, there'd be a contract coming her way for a whole series.

Enter her alter ego, Angelina Talbot. Unlike Becky, Angelina could eat chocolate trifle without getting fat and knock back double martinis without getting toasted—and have sex with men without falling in love. Sales for the launch book had been brisk, the word-of-mouth buzz spreading like a California brush fire. Even with Elliot out of the picture, that first fat royalty check made quitting her job seem like an okay decision after all. But more than financial security, it was having created a thirtysomething heroine readers obviously loved that had helped her shake off the bad vibe from the Elliot episode—sort of.

She'd based the character of Falco, Angelina's nemesis and former lover, almost entirely on Elliot. Forget "entirely," Falco *was* Elliot down to his wavy silver hair, sexy full mouth and lean, hard, to-die-for body. She kept promising herself she'd kill him off soon but two books into the series she still hadn't been able to let him go.

But cluttering her head with a fictional character who was the alter ego of her ex was a small problem compared to the decision looming. Did she team with the publishing industry's answer to Bill O'Reilly and sign herself up for months of literary head butting or did she turn down the deal and hope another publisher would pick her up before she maxed out her credit cards and drained her small savings?

Torn, Becky reached for her drink, then realized the tip of her nose had gone numb. She popped the last fat green olive into her mouth and slid the glass away. For sure, sitting around in an empty restaurant moping over her martini wasn't bringing her any closer to those "fresh starts" and "dazzling opportunities" her horoscope had forecast, let alone to an answer to her Big Decision. Before she sank any lower into the self-pity slough, she needed to channel the Zen of her personal happy place—and in Becky's case, that meant Manhattan's Fifth Avenue shopping corridor.

She slipped on her coat, shouldered her tote and rose from the restaurant seat. Spending money was the very last thing a potentially out-of-work writer should do but then again they didn't call it retail *therapy* for nothing. This was no time to scrimp. Her career and her character's very existence were in danger of fading away. If she and Angelina couldn't go out in a blaze of glory, at least they could go out in a splash of high style.

2

Drake's Code: Never turn your back on a friend.
Never turn your back on an enemy.
Never take shit from either.

AFTER LEAVING Pat in the bar, Max stopped in at his rooftop suite to pick up his winter coat. Slow elevator notwithstanding, he still made it from his hotel to Harry Goldblatt's midtown Manhattan office in record time. Hot as he was around the collar from his meeting with Pat, the windy walk down the Avenue of the Americas did little to cool him off. Harry had represented him since pulling his first novel out of the slush. If Max could count on anyone to cover his back, it was his agent.

The first suspicion that something was wrong hit him when the purple-haired receptionist didn't seem at all surprised to see him. Like an off-Broadway actress stumbling through badly memorized lines, she looked up from her *People* and suggested he take a seat until Mr. Goldblatt got off from "a very important call." The fifteen-minute wait along with the "very important call" cinched it in Max's mind. He was being set up. While he sat sipping canned soda and gnashing his teeth, Harry was inside his office selling Max out.

He slammed the can on the glass-topped coffee table, blew by the receptionist's desk, and stormed into his agent's corner office without knocking. "Goddamn it Harry, I don't know what you're up to, but I need to talk to you—*now.*"

The receptionist hurried inside after him. Tugging her leather miniskirt down over chunky thighs, she faced the slope-shouldered sixtysomething seated behind the big chrome desk. "Mr. Goldblatt, I'm so sorry. I told him you were on the phone but—"

Covering the receiver with his hand, Harry gestured for her to go. "That's all right, Janice, I can handle this." One eye on Max, he returned to his call. "Yes, Patricia, he's here. I'll have to call you back. *Ciao,* baby." Replacing the cordless in its cradle, he smiled and said, "Why, Maxie, this is a surprise."

Eyeing the copy of the St. Claire woman's book lying on Harry's desk blotter, Max exploded. "Like hell it is. I don't know what scheme you and Pat have cooked up, but I've spent too damned many years building my brand to let some smut writer come in as coauthor."

Harry fingered his few threads of silvered hair. He'd given up the comb-over a few years back and since seeing Jack Nicholson's cue-ball head on the televised Oscars, he'd been seriously considering shaving the whole damn thing. "Max, I'm sensing some anger on your part. Have a seat and let's discuss this like rational human beings." He gestured to the pair of leather chairs set before the desk.

"There's nothing to discuss. It's not happening, do you hear me?"

"Loud and clear, Maxie, but I'm starting to ask myself if maybe all the listening isn't going one-way. All Patricia is asking is that you give the coauthorship a chance. One book with Rebecca St. Claire—is that really so much to ask?"

Max didn't hesitate. "Hell, yes! My readers are predominantly men. Men are visual. If we want raunch, we rent a movie or buy a magazine, but never a novel. Besides, Drake isn't some pretty-boy cover model with a waxed chest and a spray-on tan. He's a real guy, a man's man."

Harry let out a sigh. Pushing sixty-two, he'd been in the industry forty years. Knowing when to coddle an author and when to get tough was part science and part art. Max's bullshit barometer was a lot lower than most of Harry's top-selling clients. He didn't need ego-stroking from his agent, his editor or anyone else. Like his fictional bounty hunter, Drake, he was a man's man who appreciated it when you played it straight.

And yet everyone, including Max, had a weak spot.

"It's time for a reality check, Maxie, and the reality is the sales numbers on your last royalty statement don't look so good."

Max shrugged, though he felt far from nonchalant. A few years back he'd sold his family's regional newspaper business for a minor mint, but writing novels was his first love, his dream job ever since he could remember. The income earned from his books was a secondary reward to the joy of sharing his stories with readers around the globe.

"Everybody's numbers are down. It's a tough market. Unless you're Michael Crichton or Dean Koontz, you're bound to take a hit."

Harry mustered a sympathetic look, but Max detected a certain smugness lurking beneath. "It's a shrinking market, no doubt about it, and it's shrinking more all the time. First Generation X, then Generation Y and now Generation Echo and each cohort of kids reads less than the one before it. By the time you reach my age, you'll be writing your books as blurbs and posting them on a Myspace page, the attention spans will be that goddamn short."

Max stuffed his hands in his coat pocket if only to keep them from his agent's throat. "Come to the point."

"Gladly. My point is this—our entertainment-glutted society has created a survival-of-the-fittest publishing market. Only the toughest authors survive. These days toughness means tenacity and tenacity, Maxie, means flexibility. Look at this collaboration as your golden opportunity to grow your readership. Women are the number-one consumers in this country. Whether the product is a book or a car tire, they drive the purchase decisions, not men."

The old buzzard was playing him, no doubt about it. Determined to stand his ground, Max shot back with, "I didn't become a writer to churn out trash I wouldn't read myself."

Harry bobbed a vigorous nod. "Of course, of course, *quality* is our watchword, but this Rebecca St. Claire is supposed to be very good." To Max's chagrin, Harry picked up the paperback and tapped a finger to the quote on the cover. "Her latest received a very favorable review from *Publishers Weekly*. Pat tells me she has quite a following. Why not look at collaboration as an opportunity not only to broaden your readership but give Drake a little action between the sheets for a change? The poor bastard's been living like a monk for the past two books now."

The remark hit home. Drake wasn't the only one who'd been living like a monk. Over the past year, well-meaning friends had foisted one woman after another on him, begging him to start dating, start *living* again. The trouble was, Max wasn't interested in dating. His ten-year marriage hadn't been perfect, no marriage was, but it had been damn close to it. It might not be macho to admit it, but Max had *liked* being married. Still, he couldn't see himself taking that step with just anyone, and Elaina was one hell of a tough act to follow. At thirty-nine, he'd more or less resigned himself to living out the second half of his life solo. If he wasn't exactly a confirmed bachelor, he was well on his way to becoming a confirmed curmudgeon.

Harry clucked his tongue. "Your personal life is affecting your writing and not in a good way. Killing off Drake's wife at the beginning of the second book wasn't the smartest marketing move."

Writing Isabel out of the story hadn't been about marketing. It had been about survival—Max's. When Elaina lost her battle with cancer, the second "Drake's Adventures" book had existed only as a rough draft. It had taken Max months before he'd been able to look at it again. When he had, he'd known there was no way he could carry his wife's fictional persona into future books, just as in real life there was no way he could imagine another woman ever filling her shoes.

Harry's voice pulled him back to the present. "I hate to bring this up, I know it is a sensitive subject, but the clause in your last contract—a clause you willingly signed off on—states that the last novel is a blind book, meaning the publisher, not you, calls the shots on content. If they want you to write a comic strip or pulp fiction, you are legally bound to do so. It could always be worse."

His hopes sinking like the *Titanic,* Max doubted it.

Pressing his advantage, Harry added, "If it doesn't work out, I give you my personal guarantee I'll find a way to break the contract."

Max folded his arms across his chest, adrenaline firing his blood like rocket fuel. "In that case, find a way now."

"It's not that easy."

Max stabbed his index finger into the air. "If it were easy, I wouldn't be forking over fifteen percent for your commission. There has to be some loophole, and I expect you to find it."

Harry pressed a hand over his heart. "Now after all we've been through together, that hurts me, Maxie. When I discovered you, you were lucky if you could—"

Max held up a silencing hand, in no mood to hear yet again how Harry had pulled his unsolicited manuscript from the slush pile of submissions and generously overlooked his shaky sentence construction and typo-riddled prose to focus on the star quality blazing beneath. Certainly Max was grateful for all Harry had done to build him into a name, but loyalty had its limits. If the coauthored book with the St. Claire woman tanked, Harry wouldn't hesitate to toss him out like a week-old deli sandwich discovered at the back of the office fridge.

Harry waved a hand. "Okay, okay, you win. I'll get our literary attorney to look into it but I'm making no promises. In the meantime, do me a favor and at least make it look like you're complying. Pat tells me Rebecca St. Claire is in town overnight. Why not invite her out for drinks, or better yet, buy her dinner? It is New Year's Eve after all and something tells me you don't exactly have big plans."

Max's biggest plan for the evening was to catch a drink and light dinner at his hotel and turn in early. If he did stay up to see the ball drop over Times Square, it would be on a television screen. Still, he shook his head. "No way."

Pretending not to hear him, Harry held out the paperback. "Here, take her book with you. Skim a couple of chapters and be sure to tell her how much you admire her work, yada yada. Remember, Maxie, in life you win more flies with honey than vinegar."

Though Max hadn't ever met her, Rebecca St. Claire was already turning out to be a fly in the ointment and a pain in his ass. He grabbed the novel out of Harry's hand. "You're full of good advice. Too bad none of it's free." Jamming the book in his coat pocket, he made a mental note to leave it for the hotel maid along with the tip when he checked out in the morning.

Harry took off his glasses and scoured his forehead with the back of his hand. "You don't pay me to lie to you. You pay me to tell it like it is. You're not going to win this one, Maxie. This time you really don't have a choice."

The last time Max had been told he was powerless to turn a bad situation around he'd been sitting in the oncologist's office with Elaina. Despite a scathing protocol of high-dose chemotherapy, a strict macrobiotic diet and the best doctors money could buy, his wife's cancer had not only come back but had spread. There was nothing anyone, including him, could do beyond making her last months as pain-free as possible.

Remembering how helpless he'd felt then, how angry at everyone and everything, he punched a fist into the empty air. "No choice, huh?" Fisting his hands at his sides, he stormed to the door, shaking his head. "We'll see about that, Harry. We'll just see."

CHOICES, choices. Standing in stocking feet in the shoe department of Saks, Becky did her best to ignore the captive salesman's foot-tapping and throat-clearing. No doubt he was impatient to clock out for the night and get started celebrating the new year, but she had a big decision to make, and she couldn't afford any distractions. Should she take the fun and flirty Manolo Blahnik black leather ballet pumps with the adorable little bow on the vamp, or the ultrasvelte Jimmy Choo red satin sling backs topped off with stunning black and red crystal-encrusted brooches? The Jimmys cost almost twice as much as the Manolos, but then they were special-occasion shoes, which meant they'd last a lot longer. On the other hand, the pumps were a lot more practical. Solid black, they could easily double as day and evening wear, so she'd really be getting two pairs of shoes for the price of one—way too sweet a deal for a savvy shopper such as herself to pass on.

It was a case of apples and oranges—or more appropriately, Cristal and Dom Perignon. Each shoe was so stylishly distinctive and yet so seductively hip, it was impossible to pick. For someone with Becky's sweet tooth for designer foot candy, there was only one conceivable course of action.

She dug out her wallet, surrendered her credit card, and uttered the words she would undoubtedly live to regret. "I'll take them both."

What the hell, I'll be the best-shod woman in the shelter.

On her way out of the store, she picked up a Roberto Cavalli beaded bracelet bag from the accessories department and a red lipstick from the Clinique counter, both to go with the shoes. Wrists rimmed in shopping bag handles, she stepped out onto the Avenue. Across the street, the bronze doors of St. Patrick's Cathedral offered a portal to a calmer state of mind. She hesitated, thinking about going in, but shuffling through the sanctuary with shopping bags didn't strike her as particularly respectful. Instead she

made her way over to Forty-ninth Street. Skirting Rockefeller Center, she headed toward the Avenue of the
Americas. Given the number of large hotels in close proximity, she should have better luck catching a cab there.

Several whizzed by, either already occupied or with
their roof lights turned off. By the time she came up on the
New York Hilton, the pointed toes of her boots were
rubbing her feet raw and the wind had picked up, pulling
the pins from her hair and sending rogue strands streaming over her face. Seeing a taxi that looked as if it might
be slowing down, she shot a hand up into the air, hoping
to catch the driver's attention before he headed for the
hotel pull-up.

She was in luck. The cab skidded to a stop a half block
up the street, tourists pouring out of the rear passenger
door. Arms raised, she raced to catch it before someone
else beat her to the punch.

"Taxi. Taxi! Hey, wait up...oomph!"

She hit the pavement hard, bags flying. Pulling herself
up on bruised elbows, she blinked. Damn, but she was
smack dab in the middle of a moveable feast of footwear,
everything from top-tier designer shoes like the ones in her
bags to sock-clad feet stuck into leather sandals so limp
and scuffed they might have been left over from the seventies. Wow, a lot of people had really bad foot-care habits.

"You walked right into me. Are you all right?" The deep
New England-accented male voice apparently went with
the pair of pebbled-leather penny loafers parked in front
of her. The classic shoes badly needed a good polishing.

"I...I think so. Oh...shit." Eying a pair of muddy Nikes
coming on at a brisk clip, she grabbed the tissue-wrapped
Cavalli purse and tossed it back in the bag.

Mr. Loafers swooped down beside her. "Here, let me help you."

Becky looked up and caught her breath, feeling as though the wind had been knocked out of her a second time. Blond and blue-eyed, her hunky Good Samaritan was probably in his mid- to late-thirties—and certifiably hot. Stealing a glance at his broad shoulders, she was pretty sure his khaki-colored trench coat was Burberry, not London Fog.

"That's all right. I think I've got—"

A breath-stealing whip of wind ripped through, and Becky felt the snap of cold air on her crotch. *Uh-oh.* Looking down, she saw her caramel-colored knit dress was bunched at her waist, her peach-colored Victoria's Secret panties on display for all to see. *Oh...my...God.* She snapped her legs closed, yanked down her dress, and grabbed hold of his arm as if it was a lifeline.

Taken by surprise, Max brought the woman to her feet, amazed at how tiny she was, how light. Even wearing high-heeled boots, she barely reached his breastbone.

Brushing herself off, she glanced down at their feet. "Oh, look, you dropped your book." Before he could stop her, she picked up Rebecca St. Claire's paperback and handed it to him. "You read romance novels?"

Max knew his burning cheeks had nothing to do with the wind. "Not really. Not yet, anyway. A...friend passed it on and said it was worth having a look at. I'm not sure whether I will or not."

She pushed back her hair and looked up at him, and Max forgot all about the damn book. He felt the breath leave his lungs as though *he'd* just hit the pavement. Talk about a knockout. In one sweeping glance, he took in her wide-set brown eyes, porcelain-perfect skin and delicate features—delicate except for her full pink lips. An image of her head of maple-colored curls buried between his thighs, those luscious lips slipping over his cock, burst into his thoughts and he felt his erection rising like a sail caught in a stiff breeze.

"Well, you should give it a try. You might be surprised. You might even enjoy it." Was it his writer's imagination at work or had her expressive brown eyes narrowed ever so slightly?

Pocketing the book, he said, "Thanks, maybe I will." Taking up her packages in one hand, he laid the other on her elbow and steered her away from the busy sidewalk to a public bench fronting a snow-covered patch of urban park. Setting the packages on the seat, he turned back to her. "You fell pretty hard. Are you sure you didn't hurt yourself?"

"Mostly my pride." She reached behind to brush off her bottom. "I didn't think this day could get any worse, but this brings it to a whole new level."

So she'd had a shitty day, too. That was interesting. Running his gaze over her, he decided she definitely wasn't a tourist—too well-dressed and too obviously at home in the city. He could see her if not in Tribeca or Soho then certainly in one of the trendy up-and-coming neighborhoods in Brooklyn or the Bronx. Wherever she was going, she'd squeezed in a little shopping before heading there. He shifted his eyes to the two heavy Saks bags. Make that a *lot* of shopping.

"Sometimes the next level really is down," Max said, thinking of the book in his coat pocket.

She nodded. "You can say that again." She turned her attention to rearranging her jumbled purchases, maple-syrup curls blowing about her face.

Max knew he should probably be on his way, but curiosity kept him hanging around. Gaze gliding over her, he found himself wondering what she wore beneath her three-quarter-length camel-colored coat—aside from peach panties, that is. The coat's belted waist suggested a trim torso and softly curved hips, but beyond her small size it was hard to get a sense of her body beneath the outerwear.

For whatever reason, he found himself confiding, "I haven't had the best of days myself."

Her brown eyes stole a quick sidelong glance at his face. "If you don't mind my asking, what sign are you?"

Feeling himself harden—thank God for overcoats—Max wondered what the hell was going on with him. Since his first book had hit the bestseller lists, he'd come into contact with any number of women, from attractive news reporters to bikini-clad Playboy Bunnies, the latter when his book was excerpted in the magazine. Despite numerous opportunities, he hadn't had sex in more than a year, closer to two. His need for release was something he'd gotten used to taking care of himself when Elaina was ill. After she'd passed, going to bed with another woman hadn't even entered his thoughts.

So why was he so completely turned-on by a shopaholic stranger?

Catching her curious stare, he realized he hadn't answered her question. At times like this, he'd give a lot for Drake's smooth-talking tongue. "Taurus."

"The sign of the bull." She gave a sage nod. "That makes sense." Sexy lips pursed, she studied him as though he was a *New York Times* crossword puzzle she'd just begun figuring out. "What does your horoscope say?"

He hesitated. "My horoscope? I…I don't know. I never

read it." He considered astrology to be a bunch of New Age crap but since he'd probably pissed off his quota of people for one day, he held back from saying so.

Expressive brown eyes settled on his face, bringing a funny fluttery feeling to Max's stomach—and a warm sensation over the vicinity of his heart. "Well, I read mine every day online, the monthly and daily forecasts and then the end-of-year predictions. I suppose you could say it's my guilty pleasure, only I don't really feel guilty about it." Slender shoulders lifted in a hint of a shrug. "I figure it's free, so why not? I'm a Libra—you know, the scales, the eternal search for balance and justice and…well, partnership." When she came to *partnership,* her breezy tone seemed to falter. "January is supposed to be bringing me fresh starts and dazzling opportunities in my houses of career and love. Transportation is another area apparently not going so well for me." She shifted to look around his shoulder. "I guess I lost out on that cab, huh?"

Bedazzled, it took Max a moment to absorb that last bit of information. He looked back over his shoulder, past a cluster of young people, tourists judging from their I Love New York baseball caps, sweatshirts and windbreakers, to the empty curb. "Looks like it." Turning back to her, he realized he was fresh out of excuses to linger. "Well, I guess I should be getting on—"

"Oh, no. No!" She stuck a hand inside the open shopping bag and brought out a tissue-wrapped red satin high-heeled shoe.

Staring at the shoe and then back at her stricken face, Max asked, "What's wrong?"

"I'm missing a shoe. The mate must have rolled out when I fell." She unfurled the shoe from the paper and held it up for him to see, the sparkly beaded medallion on the top winking in the waning winter light. "What am I going to do? I can't take them back like this, and I can't go around wearing one shoe."

"I don't know about that. It worked for Cinderella." He couldn't remember the last time he'd cracked a joke, but even if his attempt was pretty lame, it still felt good, damn good.

"Very funny." Her frown told him she found it anything but. "If you knew how much these cost me, you wouldn't be laughing, either."

He made a show of sobering. "Designer stuff, huh?"

She answered with a guilty nod. "Yeah, I really splurged."

Max might not be much of a talker but like his creation, Drake, he was a man of action. "In that case, Cinderella, hold the carriage horses. I'll be right back."

Leaving her standing by the bench, he went to scavenge the sidewalk where she'd fallen. It was a long shot but then it didn't hurt to try. After peering beneath a hot pretzel cart, the sneakers of a twentysomething kid handing out free passes to a nearby comedy club, and the paws of a trio of leashed French poodles, he was close to giving up when he spotted a flutter of white in the curbside gutter. At first he thought it must be one of the city's ubiquitous pigeons but bending closer, he saw it was tissue paper—tissue paper with a slender red heel sticking out.

He scooped up the shoe in the nick of time, seconds before the wheel of an oncoming taxi sent frozen mud splashing up. Brushing it off on his coat, he brought it over to her, proudly presenting it like his dog, Scout, dropping his retrieved rawhide in a guest's lap. "If the shoe fits…"

Her smile rapturous, she took it from him. "Thank you, thank you! Look, it didn't even get messed up. The sales clerk wrapped it really well and then used the Saks sticker seal to hold the tissue in place. I love Saks, and I absolutely *love* these shoes." Holding the shoe to her heart, she looked up at him with shining eyes.

Max felt as though his six-foot-three frame had just shot to a full ten feet. Eyeing the four-inch heel, he shook his head. "You really walk in those things?" Balancing on stilts like those might send her the podiatrist sooner rather than later.

She shrugged. "I'm used to it." She laid the shoe in the box beside its mate with loving care, replaced the lid, and picked up her packages. "Well, uh, thanks for all your help."

Max realized he wasn't ready to let her walk out of his life, not yet anyway. Stalling until he could come up with some way to ask her name without seeming like a stalker, he said, "Red shoes always remind me of that Brothers Grimm fairy tale."

"Excuse me?"

Shit. Judging from her startled look she didn't think he was a stalker but instead a stalker with a foot fetish. *Great going Maxwell*—not!

"You know, the children's story about the match girl who covets the pair of fancy red slippers. Once she puts them on, though, they take over and won't let her stop dancing, and she ends up begging a woodsman to cut off her feet to be free."

Though she'd never been much into shoes or fashion, period, Elaina's classic copy of the children's book had been one of her cherished childhood possessions. He still had it on his bookshelves somewhere, unable to part with it when he'd boxed up the rest of her stuff. Still, that didn't explain what he was doing standing around in the middle of midtown spouting a story by the mid-nineteenth century's answer to Stephen King. Back in his hometown of Hadley, New Hampshire, he scarcely said hello to people he'd known all his life.

"And I thought I had a bad shoe habit." Instead of freaking out, she shook her head and smiled. "I think you mean Hans Christian Andersen, though."

Caught up in that delightful smile, it took a moment for her comment to sink in. "Sorry?"

"Hans Christian Andersen wrote 'The Red Shoes,' not the Brothers Grimm."

Max thought for a moment. Damned if she wasn't right. "I stand corrected." Sexy, sophisticated and smart, she was appealing to him more by the minute—minutes that were rapidly slipping by.

"I do know my shoes if you hadn't already guessed." She shot him a wink, and he saw her eyes had little flecks of gold rimming the pupils. "Well, thanks again for all your help." She stepped around him, shopping bags swinging. "Sorry again for running into you."

Cinderella brushed by and started up the street, brisk strides carrying her quickly away. Max hesitated, asking himself what his alter ego would do were he standing in Max's loafers in the middle of Manhattan instead of in his cowboy boots in the Australian Outback. The answer was a given.

Drake would go after the girl.

"Hey, wait up."

Threading through the foot traffic, Max dodged several baby strollers, a homeless man's shopping cart and a trio of Japanese tourists pausing for a photo op.

He caught up with her just before the next crosswalk.

She stopped and turned around, looking puzzled. "Did I leave behind more shoes?"

Feeling like a high-school kid stumbling through his first ask out, he caught his breath and shook his head. "I was thinking maybe we could share a cab. Better yet, why not let me buy you a cup of coffee? We could go inside somewhere and warm up and…" He let the rest of the clumsy sentence die.

She hesitated, biting her full bottom lip, her pretty top teeth coming into view, then the tip of her tongue darting out to moisten the plump pink flesh. Watching the machinations of that amazing mouth, he felt telltale heat pooling in his groin.

The streetlight changed and a wave of pedestrians poured into the crosswalk and headed toward them. Max felt the spell break—and the moment slip away.

"I can't," she finally said, dashing all his hopes with those two regrettable words. Though she shook her head, he was pretty sure he saw real regret in her eyes. "I really have to be…getting back. It was nice meeting you." Again that hint of hesitation that had him hoping. "Have a happy New Year."

Feeling like a dolt, Max watched her walk away, sexy hips swaying. Of course she had to be on her way. It was New Year's Eve, after all, the biggest date night of the year after Valentine's. Women who looked, spoke and *moved* like that didn't stay home alone on New Year's Eve.

He thought of the lucky guy who'd be kissing her come midnight, the one for whom she'd be wearing those sexy red shoes, and felt a jolt of jealousy. Mentally putting himself in the man's place, he imagined the sexy little black dress she'd slip into to go with the stilettos. By the time the fantasy progressed to the dress lying in a puddle on the floor, her clothing winnowed to a pair of black garters banding the slender white thighs he'd ogled earlier, and of course those red shoes, his semierection had rocketed to a full-throttle hard-on.

"Hey, buddy, watch where you're goin'."

Max looked into the scowling face of the falafel vendor whose cart he'd apparently just stumbled into. "Sorry."

He walked back to his hotel in a sort of semiconscious daze. By the time he reached The Chelsea's neon-lit marquee, it was dark outside. He couldn't remember how he'd gotten there or what he might have passed along the way. It didn't matter. Despite being turned down, he was in a "New York State of Mind," not to mention one hell of a good mood.

Humming the Billy Joel song beneath his breath, he stepped inside the lobby elevator. The doors closed, the scent of rosemary and mint filling his nose. At first he thought it must be air freshener but after a few more whiffs he realized it clung to his clothes. It was *her* scent, so fresh and wholesome and altogether clean he couldn't think of it as perfume. With her maple-colored curls, warm brown eyes and the light brown coat wrapping her petite figure, she reminded him of a tightly rolled caramel confection, sweet but not too sweet, satisfyingly rich, sumptuously delicious. There was no chance of sampling her now, but those magical few moments on Sixth Avenue had certainly sweetened his outlook on the year ahead. For the first time in a long time, he felt alive.

Alive—he'd almost forgotten what a good feeling that could be.

The elevator doors closed, the polished metal reflecting Max's smile.

3

Drake walked into the outback bar, ordered a Foster's lager, and slid onto the stool. Restless after concluding his latest adventure, he took a long pull of the beer and glanced across the wood-paneled room hoping for some distraction. A long, tall drink of water with waist-length black hair, a body-hugging black dress and red do-me pumps stepped inside the door. Crikey, what a beaut. But more than the woman's stunning face and killer body, it was her confident carriage as she made her way over to the bar that brought the blood pounding through his veins. She reminded him of the sleek thoroughbred filly not yet broken to the saddle stabled back on his ranch. She'd let you ride her but only bareback—and only on her terms.

Ever ready to rise to a challenge, Drake slid back his stool, got up and rounded the bar. "Goodday, love." He sidled over to the woman, head filling with wild images of all the ways he might go about taming her. Looking into her slanted green eyes, he lifted his beer bottle and gently slid the glass rim over the seam of her full, luscious lips. "Fancy a drink?"

BECKY CAUGHT a cab at Forty-sixth Street, not far from where she'd left the handsome, helpful stranger. Maybe it was just wishful thinking, but she swore she felt the burn of those blue eyes following her all the way up the boulevard.

Climbing inside the taxi's stale-smelling interior, she said, "The Hotel Chelsea, please. That's 222 West Twenty-third between—"

"Between Seventh and Eighth, yeah, I know." The cabbie pulled out into traffic, cutting off an oncoming car and flipping the driver the bird.

Becky settled herself and her packages on the cracked vinyl seat, asking herself why on earth she'd just turned down the hottest man to cross her path in…well, forever. There'd been nothing remotely creepy about him, no bad vibe or warning facial tick. Just the opposite—he'd had charming manners and a sexy smile and the absolute longest eyelashes she'd ever seen on a man. He'd even stuck around to help her up and then gone on a quest for her missing slipper like a modern-day Prince Charming. Come to think of it, he *had* called her Cinderella.

And she'd liked his classic clothes, or more to the point, the totally casual, totally sexy way he wore them, as though he'd thrown on whatever and ended up looking fabulous by sheer accident. Even his lame attempt to impress her with his knowledge of classic children's literature struck her as endearingly sweet.

It was his eyes she kept coming back to, though. They were cerulean-blue, Jude-Law-blue, Prince-Charming-blue, but beyond that so soulful and so sad she'd had to dole out the time she spent looking into them for fear that, like the classic Cure song, "Just Like Heaven," she might fall in and drown deep inside of him.

Had she accepted his coffee invitation, they would have found a Starbucks or some other perfectly acceptable public place, shed their coats and settled in with white porcelain mugs and maybe a shared snack. Afterward they would have split a cab or parted ways on the street, exchanged phone numbers or not depending on how the conversation and chemistry had flowed. It could have been just a lovely interlude or one of those "fresh starts" and "dazzling opportunities" her horoscope had predicted, a prelude to the kind of happily-ever-after ending she used to love writing for her Regency romance heroines but had yet to find for herself. Either way, it would have meant breaking what she'd come to think of as her five-years-and-running curse, by having a date on New Year's Eve.

"Damn, I really blew it this time."

She caught the driver staring at her in the rearview mirror. "You say somethin'?"

"I was just uh…talking to myself. It's a writer thing," she added because a) it really was, for this writer at least and b) she didn't want him to think he was ferrying around a psycho.

He shrugged and turned his attention back to the bumper-to-bumper traffic. In a city the size of New York, apparently talking to oneself was a normal level of crazy.

Thoughts circling back to her latest lost opportunity, she admitted she hadn't turned her sexy stranger down because she was worried about getting robbed or raped or otherwise jeopardizing her physical safety. She'd played it safe, too safe, because deep down she was afraid of trusting her heart and getting badly hurt—again.

The driver skidded to a stop in front of her hotel. "That'll be $7.50."

She handed him a ten, retrieved her purse and shopping bags, and stepped out onto the street. Standing curbside, she looked up to the modest redbrick hotel, the neon sign for Hotel Chelsea welcoming her like an old friend's smile. Formerly home to the likes of Bob Dylan, Janis Joplin and Leonard Cohen, the campy old hotel had hosted its share of suicides, drug overdoses and artistic spats. But even sans its colorful past and celebrity cache, Becky still would have wanted to stay there. With its smaller, more intimate scale and comfortably worn interior, the Chelsea always made her feel welcomed and at home in a way the big, impersonal chains never quite could.

She bypassed the front desk and cut through the art gallerylike lobby on the lookout for celebrities. Half the fun of staying at the Chelsea was never knowing who you might see, be it a Hollywood legend like Peter O'Toole who had a suite named after him, or an under-thirty brat packer like Christina Ricci, or…a handsome blue-eyed stranger with a penchant for classic clothes and classic fairy tales?

Get real, Becky. How many times could she expect the universe to drop a tall, broad-shouldered hunk into her path? In this case, she hadn't just let "dazzling opportunity" pass her by. She'd turned tail and run from it.

Wishing she could rewrite the episode on the street as easily as a scene in her book, she stepped inside the elevator and pressed the button for the third floor. Room 324 was spare and smallish but at only $200 a night, it was a bargain by Manhattan standards. She hung up her coat in the tiny closet and offloaded her shopping bags onto the bed. Sitting down on the side of the mattress, she bent to take off her boots, belatedly realizing her butt was feeling pretty tender.

Crossing her right leg over her left, she massaged her cramped arch and took stock of her blisters. Since quitting her consulting job, her power lunches with Pat provided one of her few chances to step into the shoes—literally—of a glamorous romance heroine like Angelina. Pat telling her to call her on a holiday, even one largely devoted to football and loafing around the house, still amounted to a huge deal. Depending on what answer Becky gave her editor, today's lunch might be their last.

Switching legs, she rubbed her left foot back to life and considered what to do with her evening. Usually after an afternoon immersed in the Manhattan mayhem, including a soul-satisfying shopping spree, she was content to order room service and hunker down to write, but tonight was New Year's Eve. Even if it had been a regular night, until she decided what to do about her career, writing anything would be tantamount to spinning her wheels.

Picking herself up off the bed, she shuffled into the small bathroom, switched on the light, and took stock of the damage in the chipped wall mirror. *God, I'm a mess.* Worse than a mess, she looked like hell, or at least like a bat recently flown out of it. Her hair was down around her shoulders with one side sticking out like porcupine bristles, and her lipstick had worn off, along with most of her mascara. To add insult to injury, when she slipped off her dress and underwear, she saw that her right butt cheek was sore with good reason. It looked like a hippie's tie-dyed T-shirt, a mottling of black, green and blue bruises.

She turned around to face her reflection and gave her naked self a good long look. Barring her bruised backside and sad lack of a tropical tan, for thirty-four—okay, almost thirty-five—hers was not a bad body. Forget the thirty-four-almost-thirty-five part. Not a bad body *period*. Sure, it would be nice to be a little taller—okay, a *lot* taller— but then again that was why some gay European fashion designer, bless his soul, had invented the stiletto. And yes, she supposed if she were the shallow type, she might wish her breasts were a bit bigger—okay, a *lot* bigger—but thanks to the invention of various bras with words like *miracle* and *wonder* in the name, she could at least fake filling up her A-cup. On the upside, her waist was small, her hips were trim, and when it wasn't swollen from kissing the sidewalk, her butt was tight enough that other women in her aerobics class still laid claim to hating her. If that wasn't positive confirmation, what was?

She turned back to the counter with a sigh and looked for the small travel-size hair brush that would fit into the new Cavalli purse. In no mood to hunt, she upended her toiletry bag. A year's worth of beauty supplies spilled out—along with three shiny gold foil packets.

Condoms. She must have had them in her bag for over a year, packed and ready to go for that L.A. trip that had never materialized. She started to toss them in the trash but something stopped her. How long did condoms stay…*fresh* anyway? She picked up one of the packets and read the ex- piration date. Sturdy little devils, they didn't expire for another whole year—a year supposedly chockfull of fresh starts and dazzling opportunities, at that.

Becky hesitated. Maybe it was her horoscope-inspired optimism or just her ingrained dislike of wastefulness from growing up in a big family, but instead of dropping per- fectly good prophylactics into the garbage, she dropped them into her evening purse instead.

Manhattan was a magical place. She'd always thought

so and after that day's midtown encounter, she was more convinced of it than ever. When you were in a city that never slept, you never knew who you might…*bump* into. From now on there would be no more hiding behind her laptop screen and definitely no more tossing sexy blue-eyed strangers back into the single sea (no wedding ring—she'd checked), at least not without first testing the waters. It was New Year's Eve, after all, the holiday for embracing the boundless possibility of 365 days of yet-to-be-written-upon blank pages.

If there were fresh starts and dazzling opportunities to be found out there, by God, Becky was going to find them.

MAX'S GOOD MOOD lasted until he got back to his rooftop suite and saw the phone's message light blinking. There was a voice message from Pat and another from Harry, no big surprises there. Both said about the same thing, the wording close enough to make him wonder if his editor and agent weren't practicing a little collaboration of their own.

Harry's voice mail was slightly more detailed. "As I may have mentioned earlier, Rebecca St. Claire is in town for just the one night. As a gesture of good will, why not meet her for drinks or better yet, dinner? Flies and honey, Maxie, flies and honey. Her number is…"

Max caught the 202 area code but let the other seven digits slide by. There was only one woman he was interested in meeting, and he'd let her get away with her glass slipper without leaving behind so much as a business card or a cell phone number. Disgusted with himself for not trying harder, he punched the delete key and headed into the bathroom for a shower—a cold one.

Ten minutes later he stepped out, wrapped a towel around his waist, and walked up to the vanity mirror. He ran the back of his hand over the five o'clock shadow on his cheek, debating whether to shave or let it go until morning. Other than shaving, he couldn't remember the last time he'd given his face more than a passing glance. Studying it now, he searched for anything that might have scared off his skittish Cinderella. Sure there were some lines on his forehead and creases at the corners of his eyes and a few grays in his beard, but she didn't strike him as someone looking for a twentysomething boy toy. The way she'd lifted her eyes and met his without looking away, he'd gotten the distinct impression she liked what she was seeing.

He dressed in jeans, a collared shirt and a sports jacket, and then spent the next hour checking e-mail and channel-surfing—and negating the benefit of the ice-cold shower he'd taken by conjuring steamy images of peach-colored panties and red high-heeled shoes and slender legs that would look absolutely killer in black garters and silk stockings until the spacious suite might as well have been the close confines of a sauna.

Around eight he couldn't take it any longer. Leaving his room, he took the hallway elevator down to the basement-level lounge, which he was coming to think of as the scene of the crime. Normally his overnights in New York ended with him sitting in his hotel's lounge for hours, noshing on appetizers and sipping Scotch and writing amidst a backdrop buzz of noise. Entering the quiet, nearly empty bar, he felt a sense of letdown. A campy old hotel must not count as a New Year's Eve hot spot. If he was honest with himself, he'd admit he set up the meeting with Pat for New Year's Eve because he hadn't wanted to spend the first-year anniversary of Elaina's death home alone. To get through the night, he needed bodies around him, and it didn't really matter that he'd be looking on from the sidelines rather than joining in. Crazy as it was, he almost wished he'd saved Harry's message with Rebecca St. Claire's phone number just so he wouldn't have to eat alone. But that was desperation talking. It wasn't the romance novelist with whom he was interested in ringing in the new year but his sexy shoe-shopping Cinderella.

The bartender recognized him from that afternoon and poured a generous measure of Macallan Scotch over a single ice cube without having to be told. Max took a sip of his drink and looked around. "When I checked in this morning, the desk clerk mentioned something about a piano in the lounge."

The bartender nodded toward the back of the room. "We just got it in today."

Max hesitated. The only keys he'd touched over the past year were on his computer keyboard. Like his flirting skills, he expected his piano-playing would be embarrassingly rusty. Still, a few bars of "Stormy Weather" might settle his mind, and it wasn't like there was a big crowd to hiss and boo. If nothing else, playing would fill the empty silence.

"Mind if I play?"

The bartender shrugged. "Help yourself."

Max pushed back his stool and got up. Scratch "Stormy Weather." Thinking back to his midtown encounter, he decided he was more in a "New York State of Mind."

ALL DRESSED UP with nowhere to go, Becky stood in the hotel lobby, her black cashmere coat draped over one bare arm.

Like Dorothy in *The Wizard of Oz,* she wished she could click her ruby heels three times and be, if not transported back home to D.C., then certainly somewhere other than alone in an almost-empty hotel lobby on New Year's Eve.

Their lack of magical properties aside, the red satin slippers were hands-down hot, and the black and red crystal detailing made her feel a lot more like a cosmopolitan Cinderella than a jumper-wearing Dorothy. The shoes also went beautifully with the Valentino black tie-waist cocktail dress she'd brought from home "just in case." She'd bought the dress when she'd still been seeing Elliot, and he'd been doing a lot of talking about all the great places he was going to take her once she moved out to L.A. with him. This was the first time she'd had it on her body since she'd tried it on in the Neiman Marcus fitting room. Fortunately it still fit—perfectly, as a matter of fact. The side zipper had rolled up without a hitch and the deep V neckline and banded Empire waist actually gave her the illusion of having boobs. Her hair had turned out pretty good, too. Instead of pinning the wild curls into her normal tight twist or bun, she'd let them fall loosely around her shoulders.

Too bad her hunky Prince Charming wasn't here to see her. He might not recognize the bedraggled klutz who'd barreled into him—and yet, even then he'd somehow seen past her wrecked hair, mussed makeup and torn pantyhose and asked her out anyway. Mentally kicking herself yet again for turning him down, she wandered over to the concierge's desk to look over the tourist pamphlets for some clue of where to go.

"Do you need dinner reservations?"

Becky snapped up her head from the brochure for Madame Tussaud's she was pretending to read. "Excuse me?"

The dark-suited concierge looked at her expectantly, phone in hand. "How many are in your party?"

Becky froze. She opened her mouth to answer "Party of one," but the words stuck in her throat. Somehow dining alone on New Year's Eve didn't measure up to the fresh start or dazzling opportunity she was looking for, not with a heart full of sinking hopes—and an evening bag full of condoms.

She shook her head, brain unfreezing—and racing toward meltdown. "I'm, uh…waiting for someone. She…I mean *he* should be along any time. Yep, any second now, he should be walking through that door…" Remembering her writer's stagecraft, she played it big by peering out into the lobby entrance. "Darn, he's late again. I think I'll have a glass of wine downstairs while I er…wait…for him." *Smooth, Becky, really smooth*—not!

He put the phone back in its cradle and nodded. "What does he look like?"

"Look like?" The echoed question came out somewhere between a squawk and a squeak.

He nodded. "I'll flag him when he comes in and tell him to meet you in the lounge."

Oh, shit. Just when she'd given up complaining about the sorry state of the service industry, she got an overachiever. "He's uh…" A mental picture of her sexy stranger flashed into her brain, and she relaxed. "Well, he's very good-looking. Tall—definitely over six feet—short blond hair, a high forehead but not too high. Oh, and he has the most beautiful blue eyes."

The concierge stared at her, a smirk on his face. He was probably thinking she needed to go back upstairs and stick herself beneath a cold shower—and he was probably right. "I'll send him down when he comes in, miss."

"Great, thanks."

She shoved the brochure back on the rack and dashed to the elevator. Taking it down to the basement level, she asked herself why she'd made such a big deal of being alone. It wasn't like being single was some kind of social disease. Angelina wouldn't think twice about going out solo. Just the opposite, the brainy British bombshell would totally groove on being the center of attention, especially if it was male. She'd sidle up to the bar and order her signature dirty Bombay Sapphire martini while holding the eye of every man in the room. Maybe it was time Becky channeled some of her character's chutzpah in real life.

Piano music greeted her as she stepped off the elevator. She'd been in the Serena a couple of times before but she didn't remember there being live music. Looking around, she decided it was too bad there weren't many live customers to enjoy it. A few lounge tables were occupied, but otherwise the place was deserted. Brad Pitt, George Clooney and Matthew McConaughey must all be making the New Year's scene elsewhere along with the other million-and-a-half Manhattanites. So much for those dazzling new opportunities.…

Determined to channel her inner Angelina, Becky strolled up to the bar, folded her coat over an empty stool, and slipped onto the seat, careful of her bruised bottom. Catching the bartender's eye, she said, "You have a pianist, but I don't see the piano."

He looked up from the glass he was dunking in the double sink and nodded toward the back of the room. "Behind that metal screen."

"Well, it's a nice touch. Live music always adds something." God, she was babbling like a lonely little old lady on a subway bench—so much for playing it Angelina cool.

He set the clean glass on the shelf and wiped his hands on a towel before turning to face her. "The guy playing is a guest in the hotel. Since it's a slow night, I told him to go ahead and play if he felt like it."

"Well, he's very good. That's 'New York State of Mind,' isn't it?" She knew full well it was, but already the silence was getting on her last nerve.

He blew out a breath. "Yeah, I guess. What can I get you?"

"I'm not sure. What do you recommend?"

Shit, she'd just sat down and already she'd blown it. Angelina would never under any circumstances solicit a man's opinion about a cocktail or anything else. Among her many stellar qualities, the Brit was a woman who knew her own mind—and owned her feminine power. She would have captured the bartender in the thrall of her sexy, slanted green-eyed gaze and ordered her signature Bombay Sapphire martini dirty—make that *extra* dirty.

The bartender rolled his eyes and shoved a drink menu at her, his reaction reminding her that in Manhattan an out-of-towner chatting up the waitstaff made the list of Seven Deadly Sins. "I can make anything you want, but these are our specialty drinks."

"Thanks, I'll take a look." Face warm, she opened the menu and made a show of studying it.

She ended up ordering one of the house martinis, a raspberry Cosmo with a float of champagne dubbed the Flirtini. Champagne was the official beverage of New Year's Eve and, like the red shoes on her feet, the cocktail's name seemed symbolic of the sexier, bolder self she was resolving to bring out of the closet.

"New York State of Mind" segued into "Stormy Weather." Sipping her drink, Becky considered making a request when the music ended midsong. She hadn't realized how much company the unseen pianist was providing until he stopped. Feeling all alone again, she was about to call over the scowling bartender to place an appetizer order when a warm hand settled on her shoulder.

"Mind if I join you…Cinderella?"

4

Three hours and several rounds of drinks later, Drake leaned in to the beautiful Brit and lifted a strand of long black hair from her neck. Covering the delicate shell of her ear with his mouth, he said, "Love, I'm mad for you. Come back to my room and let me make love to you. What do you say?"

For one of the few times in her thirty-odd years, Angelina hesitated. The Aussie bloke was definitely rough around the edges, not at all what she thought of as her type, but then again there was something about his deep blue eyes, strapping body and blunt speech that warmed her from the inside out. Unlike Falco, he didn't mince words—or play games. Regardless, she needed him to complete her mission. But first she had to determine whether or not he was trustworthy.

Capturing his blue-eyed gaze, she slid her hand down his hard-muscled torso to the telltale bulge below his silver and turquoise belt buckle. Cupping him with an expert touch, she moistened her lips and tipped her face up to his until their lips all but brushed. "I'll go back with you to your room, but mind I have two rules. No regrets—and no names."

THE SEXY New England baritone sent Becky swiveling in her seat—and swimming in twin pools of deep blue eyes. Her sexy stranger, her Prince Charming from midtown, stood at the bar beside her. Becky couldn't believe her eyes. She blinked, expecting him to disappear, a wishful daydream, a few seconds' tricked-out fantasy. When he didn't, she half wondered if the bartender had spiked her drink with something a lot stronger than alcohol. Two chance meetings in the same day in a city the size of New York couldn't be a coincidence—could it?

Finding her voice, she asked, "Was that you playing?"

He nodded. "Yeah, I'm pretty rusty."

"I thought you sounded great, very professional. I was just about to make a request." She sent him her best take on a sultry Angelina-like smile.

His gaze never left hers, the intensity of his stare doing funny, fluttery things to her stomach. "I'll do anything you want," he said and somehow she didn't think he was talking about playing—at least not the piano. "What did you have in mind?"

A moment ago, Becky had had several songs in mind but the heat in his eyes had her forgetting every single one. Even if she had remembered, the look on his face assured her he wasn't really referring to song titles. Surprised at his forwardness—until asking her out for coffee, he'd seemed a little shy on the street—she answered honestly, "I…I don't remember."

Rather than press her, he glanced over to the next stool. "May I?"

"Oh, God, yes…I mean, please." She shifted over to make room for him.

"Thanks." He set his drink on the bar and settled in

beside her. "The coffee here isn't much, so you're going to have to let me buy you a cocktail instead." He glanced at her half-finished martini. "What is it you're drinking?"

Becky hesitated. "I'm having the, uh...Flirtini." *Geez, what a name for a drink.* She felt her face warming and reminded herself that the Angelinas of the world never ever blushed.

"Flirtini, huh?" His smile widened. "I'll take that over a Pink Bitch any day."

She pulled back. "Excuse me?"

"The Pink Bitch. It's another of their house drinks."

"Oh, right. I think I saw it on the menu." *Lame, Becky, so lame.*

He hailed the bartender and ordered them another round. Turning back to her, he held out his hand. "I'm Max, by the way."

Becky glanced down, the fluttery feeling in her lower abdomen morphing into a steady thrumming. Sliding her hand into his broad-backed one, imagining all the wonderful things his long, thick fingers might do to her, she felt his warmth soaking through to her skin, sending her sex-starved brain spinning salacious fantasies like Rumpelstiltskin spinning gold.

"And your name is...or should I stick to calling you Cinderella?"

Becky hesitated. Had the universe just sent her a golden, maybe even a dazzling opportunity to escape being boring Becky for one sexy night? For a second or two she actually considered answering "Angelina" but held back, thinking that would be definitely over the top. On the off chance he'd taken her advice and skimmed her book, he might start to wonder at the coincidence.

Speaking of coincidences, how weird was it that his name was Max? Here she'd been fretting all afternoon over the coauthorship deal with Adam Maxwell, and it turned out her midtown Prince Charming had a similar name.

"Cinderella it is, then." His voice pulled her back to the present, reminding her she'd yet to answer.

Looking over his shoulder, Becky noticed the single roses in bud vases decorating the lounge tables. "I'm Rose." Actually Rose was her mother's name, which, while a little freaky, should make it easy to remember.

He gave back her hand, but his eyes still held hers. "That's a pretty name for a pretty lady." He glanced down at her legs, and Becky resisted the urge to yank down her shorter-than-usual skirt. "I see you're wearing the shoes."

"Yes, well, after all that trouble, I figured I might as well take them out for a test drive. It is New Year's Eve after all."

"Yes, it is," he answered, and a shadow passed over his face. "You must be on your way out, then?" She thought she detected disappointment lacing his tone but couldn't trust herself to tell.

"I was but…my plans changed at the last minute." That part was no less than the truth. She hadn't planned on meeting him in the first place and certainly not again. Her planets must be aligning in a major way.

"You're a guest at the hotel, too?"

Becky might not be Angelina Talbot, but even she wasn't so out of touch she didn't recognize the question as code for "your room or mine?" Remembering the condoms in her purse, she met his gaze head-on and asked herself, *Can I really do this?* followed by, *Why the hell not?* Unlike

Angelina, she'd never had sex with a stranger, but there was a first time for everything. She'd never coauthored an action-adventure novel with a chauvinist pig, either, and it was shaping up to look as though she'd be doing that soon, too.

"You don't have to answer that, by the way."

His teasing tone set her once more at ease. She nodded, drawn to the warmth of his eyes and his smile. "I always stay here when I'm in town. The big chains just don't do it for me."

"Me, either. They're too impersonal, too noisy and too damned big."

Becky nodded. Not only was he tall, well-built and gorgeous but it seemed he was a kindred spirit when it came to travel, too. "I feel the same way. Whenever I walk into the lobby of the Hilton in midtown, I feel like I'm being sucked into some kind of sound vortex."

He threw back his head and chuckled and Becky couldn't help wondering if his closely cropped hair felt as silken as it looked. If the night stayed on its current sexy course, she just might be finding out sooner than later.

Swiping the back of his hand across his eyes, he said, "That's quite a vivid imagination you've got. You ever do any writing?"

Becky hesitated. Biting her bottom lip, she wondered how many more lies she'd be telling before the night was over. "Some."

Their drinks arrived, saving her from having to say more. Max lifted his glass of Macallan Scotch. "To those fresh starts and dazzling opportunities your horoscope predicted."

Becky had only mentioned her horoscope in passing. She touched her glass to his, surprised and pleased he'd apparently paid such close attention during their short sidewalk conversation. "I have a feeling this may be my year after all."

The evening flew by. Max quickly showed himself to be charming, courteous and funny, as well as amazingly well-traveled. Other than the bartender, soon they were the only two people left in the bar, but Becky was beginning to feel as though they were the only two people in the world. She couldn't remember the last time she'd felt so comfortable with a man—or so incredibly turned-on. She was starting to regret not giving him her real name. Once again she'd been a coward and played it safe.

"Travel has always been a passion of mine," Max was saying. "I've been to thirty countries in all, but Australia and New Zealand are the ones I keep going back to." He opened his mouth as if to say more but instead reached for a pita triangle from the hummus platter, one of several appetizers he'd ordered for them to share.

Becky held in a sigh. Angelina's globetrotting had grown out of her creator's frustrated travel bug. Growing up, she had dreamed of traveling the world, but an annual beach trip to Ocean City, Maryland, was about as far afield as her family ventured. Come to think of it, that probably explained why she'd started out writing historical romances set in England. Once she'd made the career switch to contemporary books, she'd gotten her Anglophile fix by making Angelina a Brit. In real life, though, her international travels were limited to a few trips to Canada. She wasn't sure why but the older she got, the easier it was to get stuck in place. Whether it was bills to be paid or a sick parent who needed her or back-to-back book deadlines, there was always some obstacle to breaking away.

Part of the fallout from the bad lunchtime news was she'd be tabling any vacation plans yet again.

"Do you travel a lot for work?" she asked. As a program consultant, her trips to evaluate federally funded literacy projects had all been domestic and largely limited to the west and midwest. Paris, Texas, was a far cultural cry from its namesake city.

He hesitated and she wondered if she hadn't over-stepped her bounds. Stranger sex relied on knowing nothing or next to nothing about the other person.

Reaching for his drink, he answered, "I'm a travel writer."

A writer! No wonder they'd seemed to have so much in common. Talk about a coincidence-packed day, not to mention a small world. Then again they were in Manhattan, the publishing epicenter of the U.S., perhaps the world.

"What do you do?" he asked.

Taken off guard—so few men thought to ask a woman about *her* career—she almost blurted out she was a writer, too but caught herself in time. This was her chance to escape being Becky for one night. She wasn't ashamed of writing romance fiction by any means, but she also wasn't up for mounting a defense of the genre—or getting into a discussion of such libido-busting subjects as declining book sales and competing entertainment markets.

"I'm a program consultant."

Not really a lie. That had been her day job until a year ago. As the middle kid in a blue-collar family, she'd felt an obligation to get a degree in a field that was practical rather than creative. Her bachelor's in sociology and her master's in statistics had put her in line for any number of decent-paying if boring government positions. Though she'd been good at her job, that was one shoe that had never really fit.

He tossed back the last sip of Scotch and set the glass aside. "That sounds interesting. What kind of programs do you consult on?"

She waved a hand in the air. "Oh, it's boring. I'd much rather hear about what it's like to be a writer. I'll bet anything you're in town for meetings with your editor or agent."

He smiled but this time the expression didn't reach his eyes. "Actually I had meetings with them both." Judging from the frown furrowing his forehead, neither meeting had gone particularly well. "I head home tomorrow morning."

He was leaving in the morning. How great was this! Talk about a made-to-order one-night stand.

"What about you?" The smile he shot her was so blindingly sexy she almost slipped off the stool for her second tumble of the day.

Becky decided there was no harm in telling him her general geographic location. Washington was almost as easy to get lost in as New York. "I live in Washington— the city, not the state. I'm leaving tomorrow, too."

She caught him staring at her hand, which she'd apparently been waving like a flag, and folded it over the other one in her lap. "They're plain, I know."

As much as she loved to shop until she dropped, she'd never gotten into manicures. Clear nail polish was about as wild and crazy as she got.

Beneath the bar, his fingers closed around hers. "They're beautiful, subtly elegant just like the rest of you."

He lifted her right hand to his mouth and pressed a kiss

to the palm. Becky drew in a breath, the feel of Max's lips sending ripples of heat running through her. Talk about romantic! She'd always had a thing for men's hands, but she'd never thought of her own as an erogenous zone. Boy, had she been wrong!

Above them on the wall-mounted flat-screen TV, the Times Square countdown to the new year began. "Ten, nine, eight…"

The bartender sidled up and slid two glasses of complimentary champagne and noise makers toward them.

"…Seven, six, five, four…"

Becky turned to Max. Gaze going to his sexy mouth, she acknowledged that her New Year's Eve curse had been broken in a big, big way.

"Three, two, one…Happy New Year!"

Becky couldn't say who was the first to reach out, but the next thing she knew she and Max were locked in each other's arms, mouths crushed together and tongues twining, his fingers threading through her hair.

The blare of a noise blower had them pulling apart. The bartender drew the paper horn from his smirking lips. "It's last call. We're closing early due to renovations. Can I get you anything else?"

Stroking his thumb over the sensitive spot inside Becky's thumb, blood-warmed like the rest of her, Max glanced at her half-finished drink. "Would you like anything else?"

Feeling heat pooling into her panties, Becky shook her head. "Nothing more for me, thanks." At least there was nothing more she wanted from the bar. She hadn't finished her second Flirtini or touched her free champagne. If she was going to have sex with Max, she wanted to remember it.

He turned back to the bartender. "Just the check, thanks."

She pulled her hand away to reach for her purse. New Year's Eve or not, she didn't want him to think she was the type of woman who hooked up with men for free drinks.

Max's hand settled atop hers. "You're my guest." Before she could protest, he leaned over and brushed his mouth over hers, a soft, sweet caress that stole her words and her breath. Pulling back, he smiled over at her. "I'm old school when it comes to who pays."

Becky ran her tongue along her bottom lip, savoring the faint, buttery taste of the Scotch he'd drunk. "Old school is okay…if you're sure."

"Oh, I'm sure," he said, and Becky didn't think he was talking about the bill.

The check came. Max added the gratuity and signed the slip. The tip must have been generous even by Manhattan standards because when the bartender looked up, he was smiling for the first time that night.

"Appreciate it. You have a good night." He glanced to Becky and then Max. "Feel free to hang out as long as you want." He backed away and disappeared through a side door that probably led to a stockroom or outside exit.

Max smiled over at Becky. "Do you realize we've been talking for more than three hours?"

She hadn't realized that, but then, ever since Max had sat down beside her, she hadn't been aware of anything beyond him, including the time. "Three hours might as well be three minutes when I'm with you. I don't want the night to end."

God, had she really just said that? For a split second she thought Angelina had taken control of her voice, but no, not only the voice but the sentiment came from her, albeit a brazen side of her nature she'd never dared reveal beyond her books.

His blue eyes melting into her brown ones, he admitted, "I don't want it to, either. Maybe it doesn't have to. I know we just met, but I very much want to make love to you. Would that be okay?"

Taking her cue from the ever-seductive, ultra-self-confident Angelina, she leaned in, close enough that a tendril of her hair brushed his cheek. "I think that would be better than okay. I think that would be pretty great, in fact."

He smiled, the corners of his eyes crinkling in that sexy way she was coming to love. "Good, that's settled then." He dropped his gaze and traced the edge of her dress's deep V neckline with a single finger. "That's a really nice dress, by the way."

Beneath her bra, her breasts felt heavy and hypersensitive. "I'm, uh…glad you like it."

His voice dropped to a sexy soft whisper. "Oh, I like it all right. I like it a lot." Below the bar, his other hand settled on her knee and then slid slowly up, stopping at her thigh. His eyes widened and his smile warmed. "Are you wearing…garters?"

"Uh-huh." She'd packed the wicked underwear along with the dress without really knowing why. Basking in the glow of Max's warm-eyed admiration, she was so very glad she had.

"Thought so." His fingers played with the lacey strip, circling and then sliding beneath, sending hot chills racing along her spine—and a wet warmth soaking into her thong panties.

The main house lights dimmed, shrouding them in semidarkness. Becky opened her legs wider and leaned into Max's heat. If someone were to walk in from the lounge, his back would shield her from obvious view. Still, being touched in such an intimate way in such a public place was just the sort of wickedly erotic scenario she wouldn't think twice about writing for Angelina but would never have imagined in a million years for herself.

Max pushed back from the bar and stood. Voice husky, he laid warm hands on her waist. "Let me take you someplace, okay?"

Becky couldn't manage more than a mute nod. She had no more need for words, written or spoken. She didn't bother to ask where they were going. So long as she was with Max, he could have shot them both to the moon for all she cared.

When he lifted her, it seemed the most natural thing in the world to wrap her arms around his neck—and her legs around his waist. He carried her through the empty lounge and over to the baby grand concealed behind the decorative metal screen. Kicking the bench aside, he sat her down atop the piano's cool, glossy hood.

"Beautiful, so beautiful." For a handful of moments, he stood looking at her. Then he stepped between her parted legs and bent his head to brush kisses over the bruise on the outside of her knee.

Bracing herself on her palms, Becky forgot about her sore bottom and her former adherence to the Three-Date Rule. Instead she leaned back and let the heat of the man and the moment wash over her like a warm, sexy wave.

Max's hands were on her thighs, pushing her dress up and out of the way. He lifted his head and looked up at her with reverent eyes. "God, you're drenched."

"I know." She reached a hand to his handsome face, her fingertips trailing his gold-dusted jaw.

He grimaced. "I guess I should have shaved."

Tenderness welled up inside her. She shook her head, savoring the slightly sandpapery feel of him. "You're perfect. I wouldn't change a thing."

And he *was* perfect. More than perfect, he was a dream come true. Earlier that day on the street he'd shown her how kind he was, how caring. They'd been strangers then. They were scarcely more than strangers now, and yet in the past few hours she'd felt closer to him, more connected, than she had to her ex after months of dating.

And then there was the whole chemistry thing, which there was no point in fighting, had she been so inclined. Everything about him, absolutely everything, she found endlessly appealing, mind-numbingly sexy. Even his New England accent and the way he had of pronouncing certain words, truncating certain syllables and doing funny things with his *r*'s, brought her close to coming.

He turned his face to the side and captured the inside of her wrist in a kiss. "You're the one who's perfect. You're just like I imagined you in my fantasy only even more beautiful."

It was true. Her sexy mouth was bee-stung from his kisses, her smooth cheeks pink from the brush of his beard, and her shapely legs were spread wide, hips lifting as if begging for the touch of his hand.

"You fantasized about me?" She lifted her head to look at him, brown eyes melting over him like liquid caramel.

He nodded. "I did."

His sexy Cinderella must be packing some kind of fairy-dust mojo because he couldn't remember ever being so completely turned-on by a woman, God help him, not even his wife. Until now he'd thought raw animal lust was reserved for men like his character, Drake, not writers with archeology degrees and bifocal reading glasses, but whatever "it" was, this woman, Rose, definitely brought it out in him.

He bent and kissed the inside of each smooth thigh, then pushed the slender strip of lace panty aside and spread her between his fingers. Dewy wetness coated her nether lips, her rose-petal-pink clitoris standing out from its hood as if begging for his tongue's attention. A younger man might have taken those signs as a green light to unzip his pants and dive in. He doubted she would complain let alone ask him to stop. He hadn't exaggerated when he'd said she was drenched. More than drenched, she was dripping, more than ready to take him as deeply as he could go. But there was something to be said for the thrill of anticipation and the richer reward of pleasure prolonged. Though he knew next to nothing about her, he knew she deserved to be savored like a fine wine or better yet, a single malt Scotch, the subtle flavors of butter and oak not something you swilled but rather sat with awhile, rolling on your tongue, teasing out the subtle flavors.

He sank a finger all the way inside her. Crooking it gently, he knew the moment when he found the supersensitive spot.

Thighs quivering, Rose moaned and slid urgent fingers into his hair. She bucked her hips and tossed back her head of shiny curls and grabbed for his wrist, pressing him closer.

Harder and hotter and thicker than he'd ever been before, he edged his gaze upward, drinking in the stark beauty of her flushed face. "Easy, baby, I'll get you there."

Keeping his finger inside her, he slid his free arm beneath her hips and lifted her to his mouth. He nuzzled the nest of crisp curls, the scent of rosemary mint soap mingling with her own tangy musk. Moving lower, he stroked his tongue along her slit, and her cream spurted into his mouth.

She bucked beneath him, her voice coming out as a raspy moan. "Oh, God, oh, Max, I'm so close. Please don't stop."

"I'm not stopping, sweetheart. I could do this all night. You taste…amazing."

Writer though he was, he was at a loss for words beyond that. She did taste amazing, musky and salty and absolutely, indescribably delicious. He couldn't imagine ever getting enough of laving and licking and suckling her. It was only his mounting sense of urgency that prompted him to hurry. Though he'd yet to unzip his jeans, he knew his balls were drawn up tight and aching, his cock harder and heavier than he could ever remember it being. Like standing on the edge of a demolition site waiting for the hard-wired building to implode, it was only a matter of time. He circled her clit with the point of his tongue, a slow, thorough sweep, and seconds later she came apart in his arms.

Drinking in her orgasm, Max looked up into her wild eyes and moist mouth and felt a trickle of come slide down the side of his cock. "I need to get us out of here and up to my room. You'll come back with me, won't you?" he asked, not sure what he'd do if she were to change her mind now.

Lifting herself up on her elbows, she swallowed hard and nodded. "Yes, Max, I'll come with you. I can't think of anywhere I'd rather be."

5

Inside his room Drake watched the beautiful Brit lift one red high-heeled foot and kick aside the dress at her feet. Covered only in black garters, silk stockings and the silky curtain of her hair, she strode toward him, green eyes holding his in the semidarkness. Since his wife's death the year before, he hadn't been able to bring himself to make love to another woman, but that was about to change.

She drew up an arm's length away from him, a deliberate tease. "Tell me how much you want me. Before we go any further. I want to hear every naughty bit."

Drake was in no mood for games. He closed the gap between them, his arms going roughly about her, his fingers sinking into her tender white flesh.

He slid one callused palm downward over her taut belly and squeezed the plump Mound of Venus between her slender thighs. "Open for me, love, and I'll make both our days."

12:15 a.m. (give or take)

THEY RODE the elevator up to Max's rooftop suite. Becky was in his arms before the double doors closed.

He lifted his face from her hair and looked down. "Thank you for coming upstairs with me. I'm not sure what I would have done if you'd said no." The obvious desire in his blue eyes was a more potent aphrodisiac than any mood- or mind-altering substance hotel guests in the sixties and seventies might have used.

Head tucked beneath his chin, she slid her hands under his jacket, savoring the sensation of shirt-covered muscles rippling beneath her fingertips. "Thank you for asking."

She wasn't sure what she would have done if he hadn't asked. Invited him back to her own small room, she suspected. She'd never propositioned a man in her life, but this was her day for firsts. Certainly she couldn't imagine parting ways in the bar downstairs. The episode at the piano was a prelude, not an ending. As amazing as those moments had been, they had only whetted her appetite for more—more of him.

Never before had she felt so sexy, so completely and thoroughly desired. Knowing how much Max wanted her, seeing and feeling the proof of it in the hot glances he sent her way and the hardness crowning his thighs was an incredible turn-on. Even though she'd climaxed mere moments ago, she was already pulsing with a sweet liquid ache, an ache she knew he could more than satisfy. But more than him giving a repeat performance of the interlude downstairs, it was her eagerness to give back that had her counting ascending hotel floors with the bated breath enthusiasm of a New Year's countdown only in reverse.

Max's thoughts were apparently tracking hers. Glancing up at the lit display above their heads, he blew out a heavy breath. "Suddenly a rooftop suite doesn't seem like the good idea it did when I booked the reservation over the phone."

She smiled into the heat of his strong neck, drunk on the smell and taste of his skin, loving the way his lean, hard body fitted hers. Remembering the amazing feeling of his lips and tongue pleasuring her, the incredible turn-on of looking down and seeing his blond head buried between her thighs, and the erotically wicked feel of doing all those things atop a piano in a public place sent more warm moisture jetting. Though she was sure his suite would be many times larger and many times nicer than her small third-floor room, Becky wished they'd stopped off there instead. She didn't need a fancy backdrop to set the mood for making love. She was already in the mood and then some. All she really wanted was Max naked and inside her.

Another tortured few seconds passed and then the elevator doors opened. Becky stepped out first, her shoe's narrow high heel catching on the metal groove and sending her flying.

Max caught her elbow, saving her from falling on her face. She sent him a sideways look of apology. "Believe it or not, I'm not usually this klutzy."

He held her steady while she slipped her foot back in the shoe. "C'mon, Cinderella, we've already made it past midnight. You haven't turned into a pumpkin yet, and I don't think I can stand to stop and hunt for any more left-behind shoes."

They hurried down the hall, Max leading the way. When they came to his suite, he shoved the key card into the slot and pulled on the handle, cursing beneath his breath when the door didn't immediately open. He succeeded on the third try, and they stumbled inside.

Max fell back against the closed door, bringing her against his chest. "God, you feel so good against me."

He hooked his hand to her nape, and she tilted her face up to receive his kiss. Even wearing her Cinderella slippers, she had to stand on her toes to reach him, but it was worth it—more than worth it. His lips were warm and moist, his tongue flavored with the rich Scotch he'd drunk, as well as some other earthier flavor. It took her a handful of seconds to realize the earthiness she tasted was herself, her essence. She shouldn't be surprised. She had come in his mouth. Like making love atop a piano, that was another first for her. Thinking how gentle and generous he'd been with her, how natural it had felt to open her legs and accept his intimate kisses, to, for once, turn off her brain and live fully and completely in her body rather than vicariously through her fictional characters, she tore her mouth away and kissed his closed eyelids, the corners of his sexy mouth, and the cleft of his square chin. She kissed his lightly lined forehead, his dark blond eyebrows, and the tip of his slightly-too-long nose. She kissed the hollow of his throat, the corded muscle that ran alongside and the sculpted V of his breastbone. She kissed him because she couldn't stop kissing him, because in the small sensory sphere to which her world had been reduced, not to kiss him was unimaginable.

Remembering how impatient Elliot had been to get to the main event, she stopped and said, "I'm sorry. All this kissing, is it too much? Am I…bothering you?"

Max groaned and slid his hand into the back of her hair. "Are you crazy? I love the way you kiss me. I'm drunk on it, but I really need to get you—us—into the bedroom."

They backed across the living room, passing an ornately carved fireplace mantel and several pieces of framed artwork, shedding clothes along the way—Max's jacket,

Becky's coat, the dress she suddenly couldn't wait to get out of and no longer had to.

By the time they reached the bedroom, Becky was stripped down to her black bra and panties, lace garters and silky hose. Shirt hanging open, Max sat her down on the side of the bed, a king-size four poster, and went down on his knees.

He slipped off first her right shoe and then her left. "You have such little feet." He unsnapped her garters and rolled off her stockings, pausing to press savoring kisses along her inner thighs.

Becky glanced down. "My older sister used to say I had funny-looking feet. The second toe is longer than the big toe, see." She lifted a foot to show him. "Maybe that's why I like shoes so much. It's a great way to cover up the flaws."

"I say they're beautiful." As if bent on proving it, he took her foot between his hands and carried it to his mouth. He laid a tingling trail of kisses on her arch and ankle, and then sucked her big toe into his mouth.

Oh, my God. Just as he'd made love to her hands earlier, he was making love to her foot now. And amazingly it didn't tickle. In fact, it felt really, really good.

Hands on her upper arms, he ran his hungry gaze over her as though he couldn't get enough of looking at her. "You really do look just like you did in my fantasy."

"You actually fantasized about me?" When he'd first said so downstairs, she'd assumed he was exaggerating or just being nice.

He nodded. "After you left me standing on the street, I couldn't get you out of my head. On the walk back to the hotel, I kept imagining you wearing the red shoes and nothing else. Well, I imagined your peach panties, too." The corners of his mouth lifted in that oh so sexy smile.

"I fantasized about you, too."

The smile reached his eyes, bringing out that sexy crinkling about the corners. "You did?"

"Uh-huh. When I got back to my room, I took a really long shower."

He cocked a sandy-blond brow. "A shower, huh? A cold shower?"

She shook her head. "A really hot one. Steaming, almost scalding, in fact."

Intense blue eyes bored into hers. "What did your fantasy...involve?"

"Well, first, this..." She slid her hands inside his shirt. Feeling his firm, flushed flesh beneath her fingertips, she slid the garment over his powerful shoulders and off.

Becky sucked in her breath. She'd known even before unhooking the first shirt button out in the living room he would be strong and lean and fit, but not even her writer's imagination could have prepared her for the purely perfect beauty of Max's bare chest, the sculpted planes dusted with golden hair and flexing with muscle. She ducked her head and drew one flat, brownish-pink nipple into her mouth.

Max groaned and sank hard fingers into her hair. "God, woman, what are you doing to me?"

Outside of her books, Becky had never before been so bold. Looking up, she couldn't help smiling, a very Angelina-like smile, she was sure. "I was showing you my fantasy. If you stand up, I'll show you the rest." He hesitated and then rose to his feet. Looking up, she snagged his hungry gaze along with the tab of his zipper. "I imagined taking you as far down my mouth and my throat as you'd go. Would it be all right if I acted on that part of the fantasy, too?"

Gaze riveted on her mouth, he swallowed hard and nodded. "Believe it or not, that was part of my fantasy, too."

"Good, because it's a big part of mine. A *huge* part you might even say." She carefully rolled the zipper down over his erection.

He wasn't wearing briefs, and the backs of her fingers trailed down his bare skin. She slipped a hand inside, drawing him out. Becky sucked in her breath. She'd known he was very hard and she'd guessed by the bulge in his jeans he would also be large—make that *very* large—but she couldn't have known how perfectly shaped he would be, how beautifully formed.

"When I asked you up here, I figured I'd be doing most of the seducing."

She tilted her face to look up at him and ran the tip of her tongue along her lips. "That's not a complaint, I hope."

He let out a ragged laugh. "Not hardly."

"Good." She bent her head and lapped at the creamy bead of moisture crowning the tip. "Hmm, you do taste good, delicious in fact. Mind if I have some more?"

Eyes stark with need, he answered with a sharp shake of his head. "I don't know how much more I can take, how much longer I'll last…"

"Let's find out." She angled her face to his groin and guided him into her mouth, slowly sliding her lips over the silken length of him, savoring inch upon precious inch. "Hmm, so good," she murmured, and then relaxed her throat and drew him deeper still.

"God, I love the way you smell," he said. His hands stayed buried in her hair, fingers threading through her curls, gently pulling her head down. "What's that perfume you're wearing?"

She pulled back and stroked her hand over his balls. "I don't wear perfume. It must be my bath gel."

"Whatever it is, I'm drowning in it. I could buy it by the case."

"We can go back to my room later and take a shower with it if you like."

Smiling, he shook his head. "Now that I have you behind closed doors doing…that, I can't imagine letting you back out anytime soon."

So he meant for her to stay the night or what remained of it. When they'd left the bar, it had been just after midnight. Though she was in no danger of turning into a pumpkin— she had both slippers in close proximity—there were only so many hours left before morning, not nearly enough time to do all the things she was fantasizing about in her mind.

Anchoring her hands to his waist, she pushed the jeans down his narrow hips and then the rest of the way off. Max stepped out of the pants, sweeping them aside with an impatient foot. She slid her gaze over his body, wanting to appreciate him properly before they spiraled further out of control. He was a beautiful man, broad shouldered and narrow hipped with a washboard stomach and a tight ass that made her want to bite into it like an apple. He was muscled in all the places a man ought to be, but not too much, like someone who used his body in a very physical, very real way rather than just pumping iron at the gym.

"I'm sorry, Rose, I can't wait anymore. I need to be inside you." Hands on her shoulders, he gently pushed her back on the bed.

Becky hesitated for the first time since he'd walked up to her at the bar. "I brought condoms with me. They're in my purse on the table in the other room."

Max nodded. "I'll be right back."

Becky took advantage of the time alone to pull back the covers and slip beneath. Max returned a moment later and handed her the purse. Sitting up against the headboard, she opened it and took out the three packets.

The mattress dipped as he joined her on the bed. Holding her gaze, he went up on his knees. "You do the honors."

Becky ripped open one of the gold foil squares and took the disc of latex out, anticipation making her clumsy. She rolled the condom over him, loving how long and thick he was, how beautifully big and hard. Too bad she hadn't considered buying a larger size. Max definitely qualified as *extra* large. He stretched the standard-size prophylactic to its limit.

Finishing, she looked up at him and asked, "Does that, um…hurt you?"

"It's a little tight," he admitted, "but in the next couple of seconds, it's going to feel really good, and I'm not going to care."

He eased her onto her back and straddled her hips. Fitting himself to her, he said, "I'm a lot bigger than you are. You'll have to tell me if I hurt you."

The remark tugged at her heartstrings. Stranger or not, he really was the most tender man. "You won't hurt me."

Looking up into his warm blue eyes, Becky found herself wishing she'd told him her real name if only so she could have the pleasure of hearing him call it out when he came inside her. Though she'd lectured herself ad nauseam over the past year about trusting too much too soon, she knew in this case it was all right. Max really wouldn't hurt her.

He entered her very slowly, very gently but neither of them had counted on how wet she would be, how ready to take him all the way. He glided inside, burying himself to the root, filling and stretching her to her limit. She anchored her hands to his hard shoulders and wrapped her legs around his waist as she had downstairs, loving the way he moved his hips in slow circles and full-on thrusts, reveling in the delicious feeling of having him fully inside her.

He reached down between them and found her clitoris with the pad of his thumb. "I'm sorry, baby, but I can't wait anymore."

Drowning in his eyes, in the throbbing heat his hand was raising, Becky wrapped her arms about his damp neck, pulling him closer. "Don't wait. I don't want you to wait."

Max pulled out and thrust hard and deep. He let out a hoarse cry and came inside her.

2:30 a.m.

BECKY LAY on her back, her legs spread open and knees bent. Max knelt in the space between, resting back on his heels. They'd made love a second time since coming upstairs, a quick, feverish coupling that had left them sweaty and satisfied and lying in a twist of damp sheets. Now that the initial sexual tension between them had been sated, she was ready for a more leisurely ride.

Even fully, gloriously erect, Max didn't seem to be in any hurry, either. He had one finger buried inside her and was patiently working in a second, the milking motion of his hand sending sticky warmth sliding down her thighs.

She lifted her head from the pillow. Never before had a lover treated her with such thorough care. Feeling almost guilty and wholly decadent, she said, "You don't have to keep doing that. I mean, you must be getting tired or bored or…"

"Bored?" He looked at her and smiled. "I could play with you this way for hours. In fact, I just may." He moved the thumb of his other hand over her clitoris. Becky moaned. "Right on your clit, is that where you like it, or do you like it lower, more…here?" He slid his thumb down to her slit. "I want to know how to touch you. It's *important*," he added, as though the fate of the free world rested on her getting off.

Becky hesitated. She'd never before had a lover so eager to please her in every way. "Lower feels nice, too, but it feels…well, it feels *really* good higher."

"I thought so." Pulling out of her, he bent and licked the hood of her clitoris, raising her turn-on to a whole new level of heat. Suddenly she came apart, the spasm striking deeper than she'd ever before experienced.

The last flutter of contraction was still rolling through when Max turned her over onto her stomach. She scrambled to her knees and spread her legs, wanting to share the last ebb of pleasure with him, her hunky blue-eyed stranger, not exactly a stranger anymore. Even though the connection they shared wasn't strong enough to survive the morning light, he was the first lover she'd ever had who'd made it possible for her to fully let go.

He went still behind her. "Baby, your back. You should have told me." Pulling out of her, he pressed a light kiss to her bruised buttocks.

Becky shivered, his lips in that spot raising all sorts of erotic thoughts. Until he'd mentioned it, she'd forgotten all about being banged up. If anything, she'd never felt more whole in her life. "I'm okay—better than okay. Just don't stop. Please."

He entered her again in one smooth thrust. She arched back to meet him, capturing him inside her, deliberately flexing her inner muscles in a way calculated to drive him over the edge.

Max's breath was a balmy breeze against her damp nape. "God, you're so tight. I love the way you fit around me."

"You feel pretty amazing yourself." She bit her lip, absorbing the blunt pressure and the delicious edgy thrill of going down on her hands and knees for him.

Reaching down between them, just above the place where they were joined, he stroked her clitoris.

Palms braced on the mattress, Becky bit her lip. "Oh, God, I'm going to come again." She'd assumed she was through with orgasms for the night.

Max's voice was a warm whisper in her ear. "Go ahead and give in. If you fall, I'll be right there to catch you."

Becky grabbed the edge of the pillow and focused on free-falling into the building climax. She had no doubt Max would make good on his promise. Her sexy Prince Charming had come to her aid two times already, in front of the hotel that afternoon and then stepping out of the elevator tonight. After all that rescuing, what would a third time matter?

Max would be there to catch her—but only until morning's first light.

3:30 a.m.

MAX ROLLED onto his side and reached for her. "Show me how you like to be touched—how you touch yourself when you're alone."

Half asleep, Becky had been having—or was it living?—the most deliciously wicked dream. Pulled from the thrall of it, she lifted her head from the pillow. "What do you mean?"

He kissed her shoulder and thinking of where those lips had recently been, she felt a shiver shoot through her. "You know what I mean." He wrapped strong fingers around her right wrist and drew her hand down to her pubis. Setting it there, he turned his head and gently bit the lobe of her ear. "Touch yourself for me."

Becky hesitated, feeling shy for the first time that night. Silly, since they'd been making love almost nonstop. It wasn't as if she was a prude. After the things she'd done with him already, what he was asking wasn't even all that risqué. Even if it was, just thinking about it was an incredible turn-on. And yet the thought of masturbating in front of him had her feeling vulnerable and naked in a new, not entirely good way. Go figure.

He looked down on her and brushed back the damp curls from her face. "Don't tell me you're going shy on me now." He picked up her hand and drifted it over her pubis. "Touch yourself for me. I want to watch you. In case you have any doubts, I'm going to love watching you. Just thinking about watching you is making me hard all over again."

Even feeling shy, the sexy demand was too tempting to pass on. She felt herself going wet all over again. Her skin had the hot, prickly feeling she normally associated with the early stage of sunburn, the telltale tenderness that told you you'd overindulged in the sun worshipping but, tough luck, it was too late to cover up now. The hot look in Max's eyes when he talked dirty to her, the sight of his broad, damp chest hovering over her, the sense that he really was going to get off on watching her helped her find her courage—and her sense of adventure.

"I've never done that before." He tossed her a skeptical look, and she clarified, "I mean, not in front of another person."

Bringing herself to orgasm shouldn't take long. She'd touched herself so many times over the past sexless year she'd jokingly suggested to Sharon she was thinking of giving classes on the subject. Five minutes when she woke up in the morning was all the time it usually took. Afterward she got up, brushed her teeth, and jumped into the shower. An orgasm might not qualify as a breakfast of champions, but it definitely took the edge off her frustration so she could focus on getting her daily pages written. But could she really masturbate in front of Max? She supposed there was only one way to find out.

Still sensitized from her recent climax courtesy of Max's very talented tongue, she slid her hand between her spread thighs and found the nub of her clitoris with her middle finger. Closing her eyes, she started the slow circular sweep she knew would bring her to a quick, golden peak. At this point, she usually reached into her mental stockpile of fantasies for one of the classic erotic scenarios guaranteed to get her off—a desert sheik, a British nobleman in period dress, a navy SEAL or FBI agent or international spy. But this time her fantasy was flesh-and-blood and right there in bed beside her, stealing the scene—and her heart, if she let him.

"Does it feel good, sweetheart?" Max's sexy whisper floated above her.

Eyes closed, she nodded, focused on the musk and heat of him surrounding her. "You know it does."

"I want to hear you say it."

"It feels good. Actually it feels great."

Performing for him was proving to be a major turn-on for her, too. Alone, she'd never gotten this wet this fast. She spread her legs wider and lifted her hips to match the increasing rhythm of her damp hand.

"Look at me. Open your eyes and look at me." Max's breath blew across the side of her damp throat, raising gooseflesh in the midst of all that heat.

She obeyed, opening her eyes and looking at him. Brown eyes met blue ones—and suddenly Becky was in over her head, drowning in deep waters.

"Tell me again how good it feels."

Becky shivered and bit the inside of her lip. The tingling was rapidly building to a full-blown ache, the first delicious spasm promising a deeply satisfying release only a breath or two away.

"Look at me." Braced above her, Max lifted one hand from the mattress and laid it along her face. "Open your eyes and look at me and jump off that cliff. I'll be there to catch you. Trust me."

Trust me. The last lover she'd trusted had done the equivalent of taking a razor and slashing her heart into bloody strips. But this was no time for cynical thinking. This was no time for thinking at all. Becky opened her eyes and looked up into Max's face, his lean jaw set tight.

She circled her finger one final time—and hurled herself over the cliff edge and into the deep blue ocean of her lover's eyes.

4:45 a.m.

LYING ON HER SIDE with her head resting on Max's shoulder, Becky traced the musculature of his chest with a single finger. "Would you believe the shoes made me do it?"

He shook his head and laughed. "Rose, right now I'd believe anything you told me."

Becky bit her lip, once again wishing she'd been honest with him about her name at least. Even though they'd be parting ways in a few hours, it would be nice in years to come to look back and think of him as a friend.

Steering the subject into safer waters, she teased, "Are you sure you're a travel writer?"

His smile dimmed. "What makes you ask that?"

She slid her palm over the queue of damp golden hair leading down his flat belly to the erection standing out from his thighs. Technically, it was morning already, but dawn was at least another hour away, and in the interim that beautiful thick cock was meant to be touched and tasted and worshipped.

"I don't know. I could almost imagine you wrote about sex for a living." She wrapped her hand around his shaft and lightly squeezed, loving how he let her fondle and play with him, pleased at how effortless it was to turn him on.

He smiled over at her. "If I do, it's only as a hobby." He ran a single finger down the side of her neck, drawing her shiver. "Are you cold? Do you want the sheet?"

"No, thanks." She shook her head, never warmer in her life. Making love to Max was a bounty for all five senses, including visual. She didn't want to cover up any part of him, particularly the part stiffening in her hand.

Settling a hand atop her thigh, he sucked in a breath. "God, I can't believe I just met you today. I feel so comfortable, as if I've known you for years."

"I know. I feel the same way." It was true. She'd never felt this relaxed with a man and at the same time so excited. She glanced over to the torn condom packets lying atop the nightstand and then back at Max. "We're officially out of condoms. Unless you have a hidden stash, we can't— what I mean is, I'm not on any kind of birth control. Sorry."

"I'm the one who's sorry." For the first time that night, Max looked less than sure of himself. "I didn't come on this trip expecting to meet anyone."

Even though what they were sharing was a one-night stand, it had turned out to be the most special night of her adult life, not to mention a truly memorable New Year's Eve. She didn't want him to think she went around picking up strange men in bars, either.

"Believe it or not, I bought those condoms a year ago. I've been carrying them around ever since. As they say, hope springs eternal."

She could tell from the expression on his face that he wasn't sure whether or not to believe her. "I can't imagine a beautiful, intelligent woman like you lacking for partners."

The unexpected compliment took Becky off guard. She clamped her mouth closed before she was tempted to deny the compliment or, worse yet, ask for confirmation. Angelina wouldn't ever turn down male admiration or second-guess it. The Brit's confidence in herself as a woman, as well as a spy, was a pivotal part of her charac-ter. Maybe it was time Becky scripted some of her fictional creation's self-assurance into her real life.

He looked over at her and confessed, "Before tonight, I hadn't had sex in almost two years."

It was Becky's turn to be skeptical. With his face lost to the shadows, she couldn't read him, and she supposed it didn't really matter. Stranger sex was, by definition, a one-time thing. In a few more hours, they'd go their separate ways and never see each other again. There would be no do-over and no repeat performance.

Earlier in the evening, the thought of seeing him for one night and then never again had provided a sexual and psychological thrill. Now, thinking of how little time they had left, she felt more than a little sad. Stranger sex or not, this night was the best of her adult life.

Why was it the good things in life always seemed to go by so quickly?

6

Angelina peeled herself from the Aussie's broad, damp chest and reached for the sheet. She'd just had the best bloody shag of her life and the brilliant part was he didn't have a clue as to who she was. Anonymity was proving to be a potent aphrodisiac, for her at least. Thinking how good he smelled, recalling how amazing he'd tasted, she leaned over and ran her lips along the corded sinew at the side of his throat, sampling the salt on his skin.

He pulled her atop him so that she straddled his narrow hips, his cock pressing into her lower belly. "Angie, you're one hell of a woman."

Angelina froze. Feeling like an acrobat whose safety net had just been taken away in the middle of a high-wire act, she stared down into her lover's blue, bedroom eyes. "How the hell do you know my name?"

BECKY OPENED her eyes the next morning to a new year and a new day. She felt like a fairy-tale princess waking from a dream—a red-hot sexy dream. Rolling onto her side, she reached for her gloriously naked Prince Charming, but the mattress beside her was empty and cold.

"Max?" She opened her eyes.

Wrapping the sheet around her, she sat up in bed. Fully awake now, she spotted the sheet of hotel stationery and single red rose on the pillow beside her.

A rose for a rose…
    Thanks for an unforgettable New Year's night.
Max.

She picked up the flower. He must have snagged it from one of the lounge tables last night or early that morning. Inhaling its fragrance, she felt her throat tighten and her eyes water. This New Year's Eve would always stand out in her mind as the sexiest, most romantic night of her life. Now that it was over, she felt like Cinderella the day *after* the ball.

She read Max's note again, searching for clues much as Angelina might decipher an encrypted piece of code, torn between gratitude that he'd bothered to leave a note at all and hurt that his goodbye was so very brief. But then, he was a travel writer, not a poet, and they'd had a one-night stand, not a love affair. What had she expected, a Shakespearean sonnet in iambic pentameter?

Sliding the silky petals down her cheek, snippets of scenes from the previous evening ran through her mind like highlights from a movie trailer. What a beautiful night, what a beautiful man, what a beautiful…*memory*. If only it might have been more than that.

But it wasn't. They'd had a one-night stand, end of story. Max was a thrilling and tender lover, the *perfect* lover, but none of that meant he had feelings for her beyond lust. What they'd shared was a moment, not a future. Despite his claim that he hadn't had sex for almost two years, for a hot-looking man who traveled for a living such encounters must be commonplace.

Holding the sheet around her, she shuffled out into the living room, the suite echoing with an empty stillness. She checked the alcove for luggage that might indicate he hadn't left quite yet, but it was empty, too, as she'd known it would be. In the bathroom, droplets of water still clung to the glass shower stall, suggesting he hadn't left all that long ago. She picked up a corner of the damp towel hanging on the bar and inhaled his musky soapy scent, the same scent clinging to her body.

Tears stung her eyes. How was it possible to miss someone you hadn't known even twenty-four hours?

Surveying her watery eyes in the mirror, Becky told herself this weepiness had to stop. It was time to start acting her age, or at least to start *living* her life like a grown-up woman, feet firmly planted in the present, not the past, even if the past was just a few hours old. She had to pull herself together and call Pat with her answer. But for sanity's sake, before she did anything else, she needed to wash off Max's scent.

The bathroom in her room was a closet compared to this. She surveyed the deep double sink and separate shower and tub and thought, *Why the hell not?* She didn't have her toiletries with her but there were complimentary travel-size bottles of shampoo and conditioner set out on the counter and a dispenser of all-purpose shower gel inside the stall.

She stepped out of the bed sheet and treated herself to a long, hot shower, almost as long as the one she'd taken the previous evening and even more needed. Along with her bruised bottom, she was sore and stiff in several other very private places. By the time she stepped out again, she was feeling better, or at least more like herself. She dried off with one of the fluffy white towels, wrapped another around her wet hair, and slid on the complimentary guest robe which, wouldn't you know it, smelled just like Max.

Max…Maxwell. Who knew, but maybe meeting Max was the universe's idea of delivering on the promise of fresh starts and dazzling opportunities in her houses of career and love in one fell swoop. She couldn't shake the feeling that the similarity in names was some kind of sign.

By the time she finished drying her hair with the blow dryer anchored to the wall, she'd made up her mind. She would coauthor the book with Adam Maxwell. She really had nothing to lose—well, nothing beyond her dignity—and the sooner she and Maxwell got down to figuring out exactly how coauthorship was going to work for them, the better it would be.

Dressed in her outfit from the night before, red shoes and beaded evening bag included, she stepped out into the hall. She felt a little sleazy leaving a hotel room that wasn't hers in rumpled cocktail clothes, but then again, this *was* the Chelsea.

Back in her own room, she plugged her cell into the wall charger and speed-dialed Pat's number. A few rings later, her editor picked up.

"Hey, Pat, it's Becky. I'm checking in as promised. Look, I've thought over the coauthorship deal, and I've decided to accept."

On the other end of the line, Pat hesitated. "That's great, Becky. There are some kinks to work out before we go to contract, but we can chat about that later."

Picking up on Pat's nervousness, Becky wanted to chat about it now. "What kind of kinks?"

"Maxwell blew a fuse when I pitched the coauthorship. I spoke to his agent last night and again this morning, and so far he's not budging."

Feeling as if the floor was caving beneath her feet, Becky held the phone away from her ear. It had never occurred to her Maxwell would reject *her*. Housewife porn comment aside, she'd assumed he must already be on board with the deal, otherwise why would Pat have approached her?

Thinking about that, her shock rapidly turned into full-blown pissed off. "Who the hell does he think he is, anyway? Does he think Drake is too good for Angelina? That tree-trunk-necked primate should count himself lucky that a sexy, sophisticated woman like Angelina would even let him put his ham-handed mitts on her, let alone agree to share her spotlight."

Becky stopped herself, realizing she'd once again spiraled into her alternative universe, an occupational hazard of writing fiction. The problem, or rather the pain-in-the-ass she had to deal with wasn't a fictional character but its real-life creator, Adam Maxwell. "I need Maxwell's phone number."

"You know I can't do that, Becky. Let me keep working this behind the scenes with the agent and our legal department. You go home to D.C. and I'll call you as soon as I know something."

Becky wasn't going home to D.C. or anywhere else, at least not yet. "If Maxwell still refuses the deal, where does that leave me?" Pat's answer was dead silence, which told Becky all she needed to know. Still, she had to hear her say it. "Unemployed, right?"

Pat sighed into Becky's ear. "I'm afraid so. What I told

you at lunch the other day hasn't changed. I can't offer you another solo contract right now."

Becky shot up from the side of the bed. "In that case, give me a fighting chance. Give me his number, his cell number, not his home. I swear to you I won't give it out to anyone."

Pat heaved a sigh. "I hope not, because if you do, I could lose my job. If he finds out, I still could."

Becky was already reaching for a pen and the hotel message pad. "He won't. You have no idea how charming I can be—or how persuasive."

In life sometimes it was easier to ask for forgiveness than permission—and Becky suspected this would turn out to be one of those times.

AS SOON as Becky jotted down Maxwell's number, she ended the call to Pat and programmed it into her cell. But first—even though he couldn't see her over the phone, she knew she'd feel on firmer footing if she wasn't wearing last night's rumpled clothes. She took off her dress and shoes and changed into jeans and a soft-pink angora cowl-neck sweater before packing up her things.

Sitting down on the side of the bed, she took a deep breath, highlighted his number from her address book, and hit the green send button. It rang a few times and then his voice mail kicked in, inviting her to leave a message. Oh, she'd leave a message all right.

Remembering her promise to Pat to be charming and persuasive, she left a pleasant to-the-point message and then went out of the hotel in search of coffee. Two skinny lattes and five messages later, she was steaming mad, as well as running out of time and caffeine tolerance. She glanced at her watch. Checking out would leave her barely enough time to catch a cab to Penn Station and make the eleven o'clock train to D.C.

She hesitated, asking herself how she would write the scene if it was for Angelina rather than herself. Angelina wouldn't stand by and let herself be brushed off, no matter how big a name Maxwell was in the publishing industry or anywhere else. No way would her intrepid creation give up that easily, or at all.

Becky flipped open her laptop. Balancing the computer on her lap, she logged online. A quick Internet search brought up Maxwell's Web site at *www.drakesadventures.com.* Not so surprisingly, there was no publicity photo of the reclusive author. There was a short bio, though. She skimmed the sparse few lines.

Bestselling author Adam Maxwell writes from his home surrounded by the serene backdrop of New Hampshire's White Mountains region. Like his fictional alter ego, Drake Dundee, Maxwell is an ardent traveler and outdoor enthusiast. He has traveled to more than thirty countries and four continents, experiences that lend an astonishing authenticity to his Drake's Adventures series. Look for his next Drake's Adventure novel in brick-and-mortar and online bookstores this fall.

More than thirty countries—hadn't Max said almost the same when they'd been sitting downstairs at the Serena? It was a further sign that taking the coauthorship was the right decision for her. Now all she had to do was get Maxwell to agree.

The bio's mention of the New Hampshire White Mountains was the equivalent of striking pay dirt. Another search yielded a list of the forty or so towns comprising the region. A little more digging via the Web sites of several local newspapers narrowed it down to the tiny town of Hadley. She couldn't get an address listing but no matter. In a small, rural town, a Big Famous Author like Adam Maxwell couldn't possibly fly under the radar screen.

It was time to reach inside herself for the moxy, balls and persistence her editor had touted as star author qualities at lunch yesterday. She zipped the laptop back in its case.

Adam Maxwell, you have no idea who you're dealing with.

MAX STEPPED inside the foyer to his house. Though he was glad to be done with the drive, he still braced himself before entering all that emptiness. Fortunately his golden retriever, Scout, greeted him at the door, tail wagging. Pushing eleven, the dog was getting white around the muzzle but then, so was he.

"Good boy. I missed you, too. That pet sitter treat you okay? Yeah, I know. There's no substitute for the real thing, huh?"

Parking his luggage inside the door, he bent down to pet the dog. As he did, something—Rebecca St. Claire's paperback romance—fell out of his coat pocket onto the floor. Damn, he'd meant to leave it behind for the hotel maid but had been distracted by a certain brown-eyed, brown-haired, shoe-loving temptress in his bed.

He picked up the book and tossed it onto the marble-topped foyer table next to his stacked mail, thinking his housekeeper might want to read it. He wasn't going to and by now there shouldn't be any need. Harry had had plenty of time to work his behind-the-scenes magic and find a way to break the contract, though the drive home from New York had been ominously quiet. Not only had Harry not called but no one else had, either. Taking out his cell, he saw the reason for the unusual stretch of silence. He'd been so busy that morning coming up with corny notes and pilfered roses he'd forgotten to turn his phone back on.

He turned it on now. With any luck, there'd be a message waiting from Harry to confirm the good news about the broken contract. Despite the agent's hemming and hawing, he was an ace deal maker—and Max reasoned that the flip side of that was he must also be an ace deal *breaker*.

Seven messages waited. Unlike his alter ego, Drake, Max wasn't a fan of surprises. He thumbed through the roster of recent calls. There was only one Manhattan number on the list, and it was Pat's, not Harry's. There was a message from his mother, no big surprise there, and five more messages, the latter all made from the same unfamiliar number, a 202 Washington, D.C., exchange. That was weird. Offhand he didn't think he knew anyone in D.C., except for his pretty Cinderella, and like a dolt, he hadn't written his number on the note he'd left behind.

He punched in the security code and put the phone on speaker, letting the new messages play through. "Max, it's Pat. Look, Rebecca St. Claire just called to accept the co-authorship. I know you're still not crazy about the idea, but I'm asking you one last time to reconsider. You've been with us a long time, Max. Keeping the lawyers out of this is to everybody's benefit. Call me or better yet, have Harry call me. *Ciao*."

If Pat thought the mention of lawyers would bring him

to heel, she apparently didn't know him all that well. He saved the message and moved on.

"Mr. Maxwell, this is Becky Stone calling. Rebecca St. Claire, I suppose I should say. I wanted to let you know I've accepted the coauthorship deal our publisher offered. I'd like to set up a time for us to chat about next steps. I know it's a holiday but please call me back at this number. I look forward to hearing from you and, er…to working with you. Thanks—and Happy New Year."

By the time message four rolled around, she sounded a lot less breezy. "Hello, Mr. Maxwell. It's Rebecca St. Claire again. Per my previous message, please call me to discuss the book—our book."

By the fifth and final message, she was obviously pissed off and taking no pains to hide it. "Maxwell, this is Rebecca St. Claire—*again.* I appreciate that you're busy, and obviously screening your calls, but really, your time is no more valuable than anyone else's. Surely you can find five minutes, and the basic courtesy, to call me back— today!"

Jesus, what a pest. Max deleted her messages and clicked off the cell. More than pissed off, she sounded really desperate. Desperate or not, there was no way he was going to saddle himself with a writing partner. If she was pissed off at him, let her join the club.

But something more than simple annoyance tugged at him. Her slightly husky voice sounded familiar, as though it belonged to someone he'd talked to not all that long ago. Had they met at some publishing event? New York was a big place, so he supposed it was possible. With the exception of her last message when she'd turned kind of shrill, her voice didn't fit with his mental picture of a romance-novel writer. He hadn't bothered to see if her publicity photo was at the back of her book, but he'd always thought of romance writers as plump grand dames with blue hair, feather boas and a brace of snow-white poodles. Rebecca St. Claire sounded a lot closer to thirty than sixty. Not that it mattered.

Max walked into the dining room and over to the marble-top bar. He poured a splash of Macallan vintage thirty-year-old single malt Scotch into a Baccarat crystal tumbler and took a slow, satisfying sip, rolling the liquor on his tongue. Drink in hand, he moved to the bay window. It was too dark to see much of anything, but by tomorrow morning the window would open out to snow-covered mountains, a pine forest and, if it was as clear as it was supposed to be, a canopy of dazzling blue sky. He and Elaina had built the simple Craftsman-style house with just that view in mind.

The thought of Elaina prompted a twinge of guilt. This New Year's Day was the one-year anniversary of her death. It wasn't that he felt guilty for having sex with another woman, at least not exactly. He was only human, after all. Some men in his position would have remarried by now. If he felt guilty about anything it was that he'd gone nearly twenty-four hours without once stopping to pay tribute to her memory or find some ritual to mark her passage. A mental-health professional would likely view that as progress, a sign he was moving on, but he wasn't so sure. What he'd had with Elaina had been wonderful, a special gift. He didn't ever want to forget her.

And yet he knew if he were to walk into the Serena Lounge and see Rose sitting there, he wouldn't hesitate to do the same thing all over again. The whole encounter had the feeling of something that was fated, a meant-to-be. To run into her (literally!) in midtown was one thing, but then to find her a few hours later in his hotel was a pretty incredible coincidence. In a city the size of New York, what were the odds of that?

Once they got to his suite, he'd expected to feel awkward, maybe even a little shy, but he hadn't felt either of those things. Rose was a complete stranger and yet sex with her had felt so unbelievably good, so natural and right, it was as if they'd been lovers in another life. He and Elaina had had a good marriage in every way, but sex had been more tender than adventurous. If he were honest with himself, he'd admit his night with his sexy Cinderella was the hands-down best sex of his life.

She'd said she hadn't had sex in a while, either, and as many times as he told himself he was a sucker to believe her, he did. Not because she'd seemed awkward or unsure—she hadn't seemed either. She was good in bed, pretty damned amazing as a matter of fact. It was more the sense he got from her, a vibe she put out that he couldn't quantify but felt all the same. Their bar hookup aside, she didn't strike him as the sort of woman who slept around.

Celibacy for a woman who looked like she did had to be a choice on some level. She was altogether too sexy and too pretty and too smart to go without a lover for long. It was obvious she liked touching and being touched, kissing and being kissed far too much to be satisfied with taking care of her sexual needs exclusively on her own. Even between lovemaking, she'd kept some part of her connected to him at all times, massaging his neck, sliding gentle fingers up and down his arm, lightly scratching her nails over his back. There was one explanation, a theory really, he kept coming back to. The last man she'd been with must have hurt her badly, badly enough for her to swear off lovers for a whole year.

That he'd been the one whose kiss had brought her back to sexy life felt like an incredible honor. It really was too bad he hadn't gotten her phone number or left her his. But then if she'd wanted him to call her, she would have found some subtle way to let him know. Women were good about that sort of stuff. It was probably for the best. The cardinal code of casual sex was you didn't try to turn your one-night stand into a relationship. What happened in Manhattan would stay in Manhattan, end of story—*theirs* at least.

And yet, were she to materialize miraculously on his doorstep, he knew he'd toss caution to the wind along with just about any rule he'd ever lived by. Just remembering her—how soft her rosemary-and-mint-scented skin had felt on his fingertips, the throaty little noises she'd made when he pleased her, the salty flavor of the sweet spot between her thighs—he felt himself growing thick and hard.

In a week, or at least a few weeks, the memory should start to fade. By next New Year's she'd be a vague recollection that brought about an occasional smile but nothing more. That thought filled him with a sad sense of regret. It might not be manly to admit it, but he wasn't cut out for casual sex. He wanted a lover he could hold afterward, not one who expected him to get up and leave.

One thing was for sure. Be it weeks, months or years, he'd never again think of roses without thinking of her.

IT WAS dark outside by the time Becky drove up the pine-lined drive leading to Maxwell's residence. If it hadn't been for catching the number on the streetside mailbox, she would have missed the turn altogether. But then again, Maxwell was some kind of hermit, albeit a hermit with very vocal opinions about what kinds of books he wanted to write and, more to the point, who he *didn't* want to write them with.

After leaving the hotel, she'd taken a train from Penn Station, only instead of going home to D.C. she'd headed northeast. The five-hour-plus trip was pretty grueling, but it had also provided her with hours of uninterrupted writing time. Her previous night with Max must have gotten her creative juices flowing, as well—before reaching Boston, she'd banged out almost ten pages of Angelina's next adventure while sitting in the café car sipping really bad coffee and picking at an even worse packaged pastry snack. She had no idea how or even if the scenes she wrote would fit into her and Maxwell's joint novel, but there'd been no ignoring the words—or the spark—burning inside her. Whatever else he was—a modern-day Prince Charming, an amazing lay or just a really sweet guy, Max was one hell of a muse.

There'd been one layover in Boston. Getting off the train to stretch, she'd walked into the station bookstore and walked out with Adam Maxwell's latest Drake's Adventures book. By the time she reached her Manchester destination, the nearest stop to Hadley, she'd read several chapters, enough to get a flavor for his style. Becky doubted she was in any danger of becoming an action-adventure fan, but he definitely had a bestselling author's sense of timing and flair. His distinctive voice rang out from the printed pages, pages she caught herself turning pretty rapidly to see what happened next.

She'd picked up a rental car and driven the rest of the way. It turned out Maxwell didn't live in Hadley but rather fifteen miles north. To her knowledge, the town, if you could call it that, didn't have a name. Aside from a two-pump gas station, a truck-stop diner and an apple-cider stand, there didn't seem to be much there.

The drive dead-ended into a gravel lot. She parked and climbed out, muscles stiff from the other day's fall, all the sitting she'd logged in and, well, the previous night of vigorous sex. Her rental car wasn't the only thing running low on gas. She seriously hoped that after they got past the initial clash of wills (his and hers) and star author egos (his), Maxwell would offer to put her up in a guestroom for the night. The one ramshackle motel she'd passed on the way might as well have been the Bates Motel.

Becky looked up the slope to the house. The outdoor lights illuminated a stucco exterior in the Craftsman style, the building's long, low profile suggesting its owner would have more than one bedroom to spare. She wasn't sure what she'd been expecting, but it definitely wasn't this. To someone who rented a one-bedroom apartment, it looked huge, more mansion than house. Action-adventure novels, at least bestselling ones, must have a bigger market than she'd thought.

She left her luggage in the trunk and hiked up the snow-packed pavers, her high-heeled boots slipping in the slush. Reaching the pinnacle, she thought of how far she'd come in just twenty-four hours. She couldn't make fresh starts and dazzling opportunities materialize at will, but at least she was taking positive charge of her life. The very resourceful, very Angelina-like way she'd gone about getting Maxwell's address stood out as a particular point of pride. By some miracle, the diner was open today, and once she'd made it into "town," she'd bought herself yet another coffee and settled in to chat up her fellow customers. As she'd expected, having a bestselling author in their midst amounted to bragging rights for the entire town. Even better, Maxwell was a local boy, a native son. Inside a half hour, she was on her way again, the directions to his house on a paper napkin lying on the front passenger seat. It had been pretty simple.

Now came the hard part: convincing him to team with her.

Becky rang the doorbell and stood back to wait. Damn, it really was cold in New England. Stamping her feet to bring back the feeling, she ran through her rehearsed speech in her mind, a paraphrased version of Pat's lunch-time pep talk. The more she thought about it, the more she suspected Maxwell's last book must not have sold all that well, either. Why else would their publisher pressure him to team with another author? If only she'd thought to get her hands on his Bookscan numbers before she'd left New York, she'd have some solid ammo to hit him with if their conversation started heading south.

Speaking of heading south, she couldn't wait to get her butt back to D.C. It was cold there, too, in January but not *this* cold. Assuming Maxwell relented, she hoped the bulk of their collaboration could be accomplished by trading files over the Internet.

She punched the bell again and squinted, trying to see through the door's glass panel. Somewhere inside the house, a dog barked. She laid her ear against the door to see if she could hear anyone coming. *Get a move on, Maxwell. I'm freezing out here—*

The door opened and Becky almost fell inside. Stepping back, she looked up—and felt her breath freeze along with her body. Max stood framed in the timbered doorway, a golden retriever flanking his side. Wearing a pullover sweater and a pair of stone-washed jeans, he looked very different than he had a few hours before, or maybe it was just the look of a man in his element, in this case, his home.

Meeting his shocked eyes, which must have mirrored her own, Becky felt she wasn't drowning so much as reeling. Her sexy travel-writer lover was the bestselling action-adventure novelist she'd spent the past several hours cursing. The one-night stand she'd planned on never seeing again was standing there in front of her. And if things worked out the way Pat wanted, she'd be seeing a lot more of him.

The retriever chose that moment to go into watchdog mode, barking and snarling like a Cujo wannabe. Snapping out of his zombielike daze, Max reached down and grabbed hold of the animal's collar.

"Scout, heel. *Heel.*" The dog went down on his haunches with a whine. Straightening, Max looked her over, blue eyes bulging. "Rose, what are you doing here?"

Becky swallowed hard. Now that the first shock was wearing off, she was beginning to grasp just how bad her showing up on his doorstep was going to look. Deciding to go for broke, she said, "My name's not really Rose. It's Becky—Rebecca, actually. Rebecca St. Claire."

Pupils huge, he fell back a step. "You're the romance writer Pat wants me to team with?"

Eyeing the doorway, she calculated there was just enough space to squeeze past him. "Yep, I'm her, the one and only." Not about to miss out on the opportunity, dazzling or otherwise, to salvage her career, Becky shouldered her way inside.

"Crikey, you're a bloody spy?" Drake stared at Angelina, feeling as though he was seeing her for the first time. The beautiful brunette had played him like a fiddle, and he'd been too caught up in shagging her to see her for the scheming seductress she was.

Propped against the banked pillows of his hotel-room bed, Angelina folded her arms across her chest, the low-riding bedsheet showing off the high slopes of her breasts, creamy as alabaster. "To be perfectly accurate, I'm an international espionage agent in the employ of Scotland Yard specifically and the British government generally."

Drake paused in pacing the room to glare at her. "Like I said, a spy?"

Angelina nodded. "Basically, yes. You must be something of a spy yourself, otherwise how did you know my first name?"

"Easy. I bribed the bartender to have a look at your passport."

"Clever," she allowed. "Look, Drake, here's the thing. I need a guide to see me to Toro Toro."

"Toro Toro is the deep bush, beyond the black stump as we say. What business do you have there?"

Angelina blew out a breath. As much as she detested being patronized, she did really require the Aussie's help. "I have reason to believe some stolen rocket plans are being concealed in the caves there until they can be passed on to an enemy government. The dossier I have on you from Scotland Yard indicates you're the man for the job. What do you say?

Hands on his hips, Drake broke into a broad grin. "In that case, Angie, I'll lead the way."

"Is YOUR DOG friendly?" Rose, or rather Rebecca, bent down and stuck out her gloved hand for the golden to sniff. "He seems friendly now that I'm inside."

Blind in one eye, half-deaf and arthritic to boot, Scout was no real threat to anyone. In his present mood, Max felt far more likely to bite than his dog.

He slammed the front door closed and wheeled around to face her. "I don't know what your game is Rose, Rebecca, whatever the hell you're calling yourself today, but you have one hell of a nerve."

Cheeks pink and eyes glittering, she withdrew her hand and lifted outraged brown eyes to his face. "I don't have a *game,* as you call it. When you didn't return any of my calls, my *five* calls, I tracked you down on the Net. All I wanted was the chance to talk to you one-on-one. You probably won't believe me but until you opened that door, I had no idea who you were."

She was right. He didn't believe her. The amazing set of coincidences that had brought them together in New York twice in the same day hadn't been coincidences at all. She'd staked him out, set him up and then seduced him, the whole time letting him think it was all his idea. All that astrological bullshit was just another aspect of her act. What remained to be found out was whether or not Pat and Harry had put her up to it. Come to think of it, he had run into her a block from his agent's office.

Whether she'd acted solo or as part of a trio of publishing plotters didn't matter all that much to him, at least not right now. Tomorrow it would probably matter a lot but right now what mattered most—and hit him hardest—was the bloodless way she'd used him. The previous beautiful night had been just one big dirty lie.

Rather than get into the sordid details, he demanded, "Is that how you deal with unreturned phone messages—you just show up on people's doorsteps?"

She pulled off her knitted hat and shook out her brown curls. "Of course not. But in this case, you didn't really leave me much choice. Think about it. If the other night had been about buttering you up, I would have let my name slip when we got back to your room, wouldn't I?" Hat in hand, she glared at him as though he were the one in the wrong.

Max wasn't sure what to think. He raked a hand through his hair, struggling to make sense of it all. If she was telling him the truth, then life really was stranger than fiction— a lot stranger.

"Well, now that you are here, I'll tell you what I told Pat and my agent, as well. I'm a solo act. Always have been and always will be. A solo act—and by the way, I don't take kindly to stalkers."

Or users, he almost added but something in her face, a look in her eyes, held him back. Maybe it was the closet romantic in him but despite all the evidence to the contrary, he still wanted—needed—to believe that something about the previous night had been pure and real and good.

She unfolded her arms and shoved her hands in her coat pocket instead. "I'm not a stalker or a groupie, either. Until a few hours ago, I'd never even read one of your books." She paused and bit her bottom lip as though just realizing what she'd let slip. She was right about one thing. She really wasn't much good at buttering him up. "I'm a writer just like you are. I may not be at bestseller level yet, but I'm getting there."

Bingo. She might not realize it, but she'd just made his argument for him. "Great. In that case, you go write your books and I'll write mine."

She hesitated. "Unfortunately that's not an option for me at the moment."

Reading between the lines, he gathered her last book had tanked. He was sorry about that, but it was happening to a lot of authors these days. But her bad break wasn't his problem. Getting her out of his house was.

"Look, it's nothing personal. I just don't work with partners. I don't believe in them. It's not my process. Besides, the books you write are very…different from mine."

The latter was his best shot at diplomacy, never his strength. Under the circumstances he wondered why he was bothering with it at all.

"By different, you mean pornographic?" One dark eyebrow edged upward, framing the skeptical brown eye beneath.

"I didn't say that." He had, but not to her, at least not that he remembered.

"Actually you did—in your interview with the *New*

Yorker you referred to romance novelists as 'hacks' and romance novels as 'housewife porn.'"

Talk about a "gotcha" moment. The out-of-context quote had come back to haunt him more times than he cared to consider, generating mailbags of angry letters to his publisher from outraged romance writers and readers who'd also seen fit to bombard his e-mail inbox. What could he say? Elaina had been gone just a few months when his publicist at the time had pushed him to give the interview. He'd been struggling to keep it together, and he was the first to admit his judgment hadn't been the best. Looking back, it was no big surprise he'd said a great many things he regretted, most of which had wound up in print. Since then he'd made it a rule to steer clear of the media, earning himself the label of recluse.

"Look, it's late and I don't know about you, but I've had a long travel day and so far no supper. You can stay the night but first thing in the morning I expect you to get in your car and drive yourself back to wherever it is you came from."

He was within his rights to open the door and insist she leave now, but sending a lone woman—and such a small woman, at that—out into unfamiliar territory in the cold and dark on a holiday when most businesses were closed went against the grain. He had seven bedrooms spread across the house's two wings. It wasn't going to kill him to let her have one of those rooms for the night. His elderly cleaning lady would be thrilled. Changing the guest sheets when she came later in the week would give her something to do.

"I just came from New York obviously, but I live in Washington, the city, not the state. I told you last night, remember?"

Her reference to his previous night's pickup had his face

going warm. "You also told me you were a consultant and your name was Rose."

For the first time since she'd barged inside, she looked less than sure of herself. Twisting the hat in her hands, she said, "I *was* a consultant until a few months ago. And Rose is my mother's name." Her expression firmed and she lifted her gaze to his face. "What about you? You said you were a travel writer."

He hesitated, suddenly finding himself in the hot seat. How the hell had she managed that? "When I first got out of college I freelanced for Fodor."

It occurred to him she still had on her heavy outerwear. He reminded himself she was a guest in his home, albeit an uninvited one. "Here, let me take your coat."

Rose—*Rebecca* hesitated. "Thanks." She peeled off her gloves and stuffed them into her coat pockets, and he caught her hands shaking. So she was flustered, too. That he wasn't the only one had him feeling somewhat better.

He stepped behind her. Sliding the coat off her slender shoulders, he tried ignoring the familiar fragrance of rosemary and mint drifting from her hair, but it was no use. Her scent still turned him on, along with everything else about her.

Going to hang the coat in the closet, he asked, "I'm assuming you have some luggage, an overnight bag, with you?"

She paused and then admitted, "My suitcase is in the car trunk."

He closed the closet door and turned back to her. "I'll bring it in after dinner."

Startled brown eyes lifted to his. "Dinner?"

He nodded, tamping down the uncertain, fluttery feeling

she brought out in him before it might take hold. "I was just starting to cook."

She folded slender arms over her breasts. "But—but we're in the middle of a conversation...an argument actually."

"It'll keep." He signaled to Scout lying inside the door and turned to go.

The dog rose on stiff legs and followed his master through the open archway. Becky couldn't believe he apparently meant to continue on with his evening as though she'd never interrupted it.

Trailing after him, she said, "I'm not interested in having dinner until we settle this."

He didn't bother turning around. "In that case, you can keep me company while I eat."

As if on cue, her stomach rumbled, making a liar of her yet again.

Maxwell obviously heard it, too. Turning back to look at her over one broad shoulder, he smiled the sort of smug male smile that made her itch to slap it off his face—the same handsome face she hadn't been able to get enough of kissing and stroking and gazing just that morning. What a difference *less* than a day could make.

He skirted the large living room and headed down a side hallway, his old dog hobbling after him. Becky hurried to keep up, not wanting to lose him in the sprawling, super-size house. She followed him through a maze of rooms into a large timber-framed kitchen. Standing in the doorway, she felt as though she was about to enter a Williams Sonoma catalogue. The cabinetry and appliances and cookware were all top-of-the-line. A bank of tall cherry cabinets hung along one wall above and below a marble-topped counter.

Backless stools lined one side of a center cooking island with an electric cooking range and a second prep sink.

A sunken family room sloped off to the side, three steps down from the kitchen. Shaker-style furniture was arranged around a dressed-stone fireplace flanked by built-in bookshelves. Like most writers, herself included, Maxwell had a ton of books, and, in addition to those on the jam-packed shelving, there were more piles scattered about. A flannel-covered pet bed occupied one corner. The room wasn't messy by any means, but it did have a cozy, lived-in look. Becky could imagine winter nights sitting snug before the fire toasting marshmallows or sipping wine or, better yet, making love on the comfortable-looking couch.

Whoa, wait a minute. Max had started out as her sexy stranger and become, through a bizarre twist of fate, her prospective writing partner. If pursuing a romantic relationship with a one-night stand pushed the boundaries of modern-day relationship rules, certainly pursuing one with a one-night-stand-turned-colleague qualified as going over the edge.

Standing behind the island, he beckoned for her to enter. "Don't just stand there. Come in." His voice, though not angry anymore, carried a definite edge.

She walked up to the backless stools. She still didn't think he'd believed her when she'd said she'd only just found out who he was. Why he seemed hell-bent on thinking the worst of her, that she'd slept with him because of the book contract, mystified and insulted her. It also really hurt. Strangers or not, they'd shared a beautiful night together, the sexiest, most romantic of her life. Now like snow driven through by one too many cars, the memory was soiled.

"I was about to open a bottle of wine." He turned away to open a cupboard door, offering her a bird's-eye view of his broad shoulders and beautiful back. "Is red okay?" he asked.

Remembering how she'd kissed and stroked and clung to those shoulders, she swallowed hard, heat hitting her face—and pooling between her thighs. "Sure, whatever you're having."

Turning around, he handed her a full wineglass—and a folded chef's apron.

"What's this for?"

He looked at her as though she were an idiot. "To protect your clothes while we're cooking."

"We?" She slid the apron back across the counter at him. "I don't cook."

"Everybody cooks." He slid the garment back at her.

She shook her head hard. "Not me. I barely microwave."

"In that case, consider this your golden opportunity to learn. Make that your *dazzling* opportunity."

If he'd said the latter with anything approaching a smile, Becky would have gladly taken it as a joke and responded in kind. But with his eyes looking out at her frozen hard as ice chips and his sexy mouth drawn into a flat line, she knew he wasn't teasing. He was mocking her.

It had her digging in her heels. "I don't want a cooking lesson. I want a book deal and if the only way to get it is to work with you, then so be it."

Over the top of his wineglass, he shot her a frown. "Flattery really isn't your forte, is it?"

He was behaving like an arrogant ass, but then again she *was* standing in his kitchen, which happened to be in his house, which happened to be in the nexus of Nowhereville.

Driving in, she hadn't seen a streetlight or a road sign for the last ten miles. She was damned lucky he was letting her spend the night because she seriously doubted she'd have found her way back to town in the dark.

"I didn't mean it that way."

Acting as though she hadn't mentioned the book, he set down his glass. "Cooking isn't all about the end result, you know. It can't be rushed or at least it shouldn't be. It's a process like writing or dancing or…"

He broke off and turned away, ostensibly to stir the pot, but she was pretty sure she knew what he'd meant to say. Cooking was like making love.

"We're having venison stew, by the way, a departure from the traditional New Year's dinner but the market was closed. It's going to be a while though. If you're not interested in helping, then at least have a seat."

Following his gaze to the stools, Becky hesitated. The last time they'd sat on stools they'd ended up making love atop a piano and then for hours afterward in his room. She wondered if he was making that connection, too, or if the previous amazing night was so run-of-the-mill for him that the memory was fuzzy already. He'd said he hadn't had sex in almost two years, but then he'd also said he was a travel writer. That she'd also fudged some facts and, okay, *lied* about her name suddenly seemed peripheral to the point. Once again she'd put her trust in a man and once again she'd found herself on the receiving end of a nasty surprise.

He opened the double doors of the brushed-metal refrigerator and brought out a wedge of cheese and an apple. Carving off a bite-size sliver of each, he put the two together. "You may say you're not hungry but you look like you're about to fall off that stool—and if my memory serves me, you've done enough falling for one week. Here, eat." Leaning over the counter, he held the snack to her mouth.

For whatever reason, he was testing her or teasing her or maybe both. Becky hesitated and then opened for him, letting him slide the food between her lips. She couldn't miss how he stared as she swallowed. Not so very long ago she'd taken *him* in her mouth, as well as let him sample any number of her body parts in return. After sharing that kind of intimacy, it was stupid to be shy now, but she couldn't help it. Things had changed. They were strangers still, but they were no longer anonymous—or equal. Max might not know it yet but he held her fragile career, her future, in the palm of his hand.

He flicked his thumb over the corner of her mouth. "You had a crumb just…just *there*."

He took his hand away, but Becky felt the residual tingle of his touch down to her toes. "Thank you, I think."

"You're welcome, I think." The heated gaze he sent her told her he knew exactly what his nearness was doing to her. Moreover, he was savoring every uncomfortable minute of it.

She set her wineglass down with a bang. "I know what you're up to, and it's not going to work."

He placed the lid on the stewpot. "In that case, care to fill me in? What exactly am I up to?"

Becky snorted. "You think I can't resist you, that between the cheese course and the dessert course you'll send me running to the hills or at least the interstate rather than risk falling into bed with you, but you're wrong. Last night was a freak occurrence for me. I'm not normally like that."

He lifted a brow and looked at her. "Like what?"

"Like…*that.* I usually have a lot more self-control." That was an understatement. For the past year she'd lived like a nun. "What I'm trying to say is, I don't sleep around." She eyed him, weighing how much more to say. "Hooking up with a stranger, someone I've just met, I've never done that before."

"Are you saying I'm your first one-night stand?"

"Yes." Embarrassed, she dropped her gaze to the cheese he'd left out. Adam Maxwell might be a sexist pig, a prima donna author, and the closest to a nemesis she'd ever come to having, but suddenly it felt really important that he didn't think she was promiscuous.

"Believe it or not, you're mine, too. Now that we've settled that much, I'd better pay attention to the main course. If I burn it, we're going to be eating a lot more cheese."

He lifted the lid and peered into the pot. Whether the stew needed checking or whether it served as a convenient excuse to cut off the uncomfortable conversation, Becky couldn't say. She hadn't been exaggerating when she'd said she barely microwaved.

He turned back to her. "You strike me as someone who needs a job."

Heat stung her cheeks as though she were the one standing over the stove. He must have got his hands on her sell-through numbers for the last book or maybe their mutual editor had told him about canceling her contract. Talking out of school about her to another author didn't sound like something Pat would do, but having recently done some pretty out-of-character stuff herself, how could she know for certain?

She was on the verge of demanding what he'd meant

by that when he added, "Since you don't cook, you can set the table. Bowls are in that cabinet over there. Silverware's in the top drawer to your right, and the dining room's through that door."

Feeling foolish for jumping to conclusions—now which one of them was determined to think the worst?—she slid off the stool and opened the drawer he'd indicated. Neatly stacked cloth napkins, no doubt one-hundred-percent Egyptian cotton, lay folded inside, as well. Thinking of her mismatched plates and the disposable paper napkins in her tiny kitchen at home, she couldn't help being impressed.

Napkins and cutlery in hand, she walked over to the stove. "It smells good."

He looked up from shaking a canister of dried rosemary over the pot and shrugged. "I hope so. We'll see."

Becky hesitated. This was a lot harder than she thought. "About last night, I know you probably still don't believe me, or maybe you don't even care at this point, but for what it's worth, I really didn't set you up."

His blue eyes brushed over her face, and for the first time since she'd arrived, she saw a flicker of the previous day's warmth. "I believe you. I don't know why, but I do."

TWO GLASSES of wine and one very full stomach later, Becky laid her cutlery down with a satisfied sigh. "You really can cook."

He glanced at her bowl. Aside from the china pattern, it was scraped clean. "For someone who wasn't hungry, you didn't do too badly."

"I guess I was hungrier than I thought. I didn't really get breakfast."

Actually she'd had breakfast, in a manner of speaking—she'd had Max. Around sunrise she'd woken up horny as hell, slipped beneath the sheet and gone down on him. He'd been sound asleep when she'd slid her wet lips over him, tight as a vise. Ravenous, she'd licked and laved and sucked him, milking him until he'd come in her mouth. She'd never known a man could be so incredibly delicious. Even now that she knew who and what he was, her mouth watered at the memory—and at the thought of doing it all over again—which was most definitely *not* going to happen.

"More wine?" He picked up the almost-empty bottle.

"No, thanks." She shook her head, which felt wobbly and heavy all at once. She'd only gotten a few hours sleep the night before and now the two glasses of wine, okay, two and a half, were hitting her bloodstream hard. She was way more relaxed than she should be, and they still hadn't settled their business.

"You should know that when it comes to the book, I'm not taking no for an answer, at least not until you hear me out."

"Are you always this bull-headed?"

She could have pointed out that stubbornness went both ways. Instead, sensing some concession on his part, she said, "Only when I'm right. I read your last book on the trip up here, and I think I've come up with a concept that might mesh our strengths."

"In that case, pitch me." He leaned back in his seat as though settling in to be entertained, perhaps even amused. "Let me have it."

Oh, Becky wanted to let him have it all right. The hubris of the man was almost beyond belief. He acted as though she was some newbie writer and he was the agent or editor interviewing her to see if she had the right stuff.

"I'm a multipublished author who has won several fiction awards. I shouldn't have to pitch you. We should be able to discuss this like colleagues. You know, back-and-forth, brainstorm."

"Suit yourself." He shrugged and reached for his wine-glass. "I'm a late sleeper, so you'll have to let yourself out in the morning. Just watch that the dog doesn't slip out past you. Scout is old but wily. Can you find your way back to the interstate or do you need me to give you a map?"

Becky threw her hands up in the air. "Okay, okay, you win. I'm thinking a sort of *Sleepless in Seattle* setup where we have Angelina and Drake connecting emotionally but not necessarily physically—not until later in the book. To make it really clean and to give the protagonists equal weight, we can alternate chapters in each character's point of view, showing them in their element, powerful and yet missing that special something only the other can provide. Interleaving the story arcs will be the biggest challenge, but it's doable." Out of breath and out of ideas, she lapsed into silence.

He folded his arms and stared back at her. "Is that all you have?"

Becky felt her shoulders falling forward in defeat. He wasn't going for it. There was nothing more she could do or say to change his mind. Because of his bestselling track record, disappointing sales on one book wasn't going to break him as it was her.

Dejected and angry all at once, she shook her head. What the hell, she had nothing more to lose at this point. "No, as a matter of fact it's not. The truth is I need this coauthorship. I *really* need it. You might even say my career is riding on it." Suddenly holding back, for pride's sake or anything else, was no longer an option. "You know this business better than I. Midlist authors like me are only as good as our last book. Mine didn't sell so well and unless I can bring my numbers up fast, I may be a research consultant again for real. I know I've drunk too much wine, and I probably wouldn't be telling you this if I hadn't, but what I'm telling you isn't coming from the bottom of a glass. It's coming from the bottom of my heart."

She stopped for breath, looking away so he wouldn't see the tears spilling from her eyes. A year ago when she'd run into Elliot and his new girlfriend, she'd managed to hold back from crying until she'd reached her apartment. Showing weakness in public, or in this case in front of a semistranger, wasn't any more like her than having sex with him the night before had been. That horoscope had really played with her head—along with the sadness and desperation that went with starting out another year still single and alone.

Max clearing his throat had her brushing her hand across her eyes. Dropping her hand, she turned back to face him.

He pushed back from the table and stood. "We can call Pat and set up a schedule in the morning. For now, let's get you to bed." His eyes and voice held traces of the tenderness she recalled so vividly from the night before.

Sniffing, Becky couldn't believe she'd heard him correctly. Without thinking, she reached out to him, fingers slipping over his forearm. "Wait a minute, what are you saying? Are you…you'll do it?"

He hesitated, and then admitted, "Your pitch needs some fine-tuning, but it's good. Better than good—I think it has bestseller potential. I'm willing to give working together a shot, a one-week trial period. If we can manage to mesh our writing styles and our characters, you'll stay here until we get through the rough draft at least. I don't know about you but for me that means about two months. Afterward, we can handle the revisions by e-mail, but for the actual writing, I'm going to need you here."

He paused and Becky realized he was waiting for her to answer. "O-okay. I—I can do that." She wasn't sure how, but she'd figure out the details tomorrow.

Looking down on her, the momentary softness in his face solidified. "But if it doesn't work out, you'll pack your bags and leave by the end of the week *after* you join me in telling our mutual editor that we tried but the collaboration was a no-go. Do we have a deal, Ms. St. Claire?"

Becky wondered what had made him change his mind, her pitch or her crying or both, but she wasn't about to risk looking a gift horse in the mouth by asking. For the moment, at least, her career was saved.

She held out her hand and his big, broad one closed around it, sending warmth surging through her. Doing her best to shake it off, she looked up into his blue eyes and said, "Yes, Mr. Maxwell. We have a deal."

8

"How many times do I have to say I did not lie to you before," Angelina demanded. "I merely omitted the bit about my being a spy. The rest of what I told you is straight on."

Standing on the opposite side of their shared shanty, Drake shrugged. "Omitting, lying, they're flip sides of the same coin. But in the interest of saving the free world, what do you say we set aside our differences and move forward with our mission?"

Angelina arched one black brow and stared at him. Even knowing she'd set him up, he still wanted her. "*My* mission, don't you mean? You're only the hired help."

"The hired help? You need me to get you to those caves, you said so yourself." Drake shook his head. "Like it or not, love, we're in this together."

ONCE BECKY fell into bed in one of her host's many guest rooms, she'd been too excited to go to sleep right away despite being tipsy and exhausted. Still, she woke up the next morning at her usual seven o'clock. She lay in bed staring at the ceiling, ear cocked for some sound that Max might be stirring. Other than hearing what had to be the clicking of Scout's doggie toenails on the uncarpeted hallway floor, the house was silent.

She tried closing her eyes and slipping back to sleep but it was no use. Her body might be tired and stiff and her brain fried, but she was also wired, thoughts racing, anxieties on the upswing as she asked herself just what teaming with Max might mean as far as daily life went. He obviously had no further interest in sleeping with her. The bedroom he'd given her was on the opposite side of the house from his, and when he'd delivered her suitcase to her room a few minutes after getting her settled, he hadn't lingered, though she'd half hoped he might. Instead he'd spoken to her through the closed door and had left her luggage in the hallway outside.

Now that they were colleagues, his standoffishness ought to come as a huge relief—it *was* a huge relief—and yet she wasn't sure how she was going to handle spending the next weeks alone with him. He might not be attracted to her anymore, but unfortunately she was far from being able to say the same. Last night at dinner she'd caught herself stealing glances at his broad-backed hands, his strong forearms and his supersexy mouth. Even though he'd spent most of the tension-packed evening scowling at her, she'd still wanted to kiss him. Who was she fooling? She'd wanted to do a lot more than just kiss.

Another kink yet to be worked out was how she was going to manage her situation back home. Assuming the partnership worked out, she'd be gone two months. There were bills to be paid and plants to be watered, but most importantly there was her cat to be cared for. She'd boarded Daisy Bud at the vet before leaving town, but that wasn't a long-term situation. It wasn't good for a pet to be caged for weeks on end, especially one as catered-to as hers. Boarding over the long haul was also expensive. It was a lot to ask, but maybe after the trial week was up, Sharon could drive into D.C., pick up Daisy Bud, and take her back to Fredericksburg until Becky got back. Because of her rottie-mix, Minnie the demon dog, she'd have to close Daisy off in her spare bedroom, not ideal but still better than a prolonged stay at the vet's.

Becky slipped out from beneath the Shaker quilt and padded across the hooked rug to where her cell phone was charging. Amazed she'd had enough functioning brain cells the night before to remember to plug the thing in, she disconnected the phone and carried it back to the bed.

Shivering, she sat on the side, pulling the quilt over her bare legs. God, it was cold here. The New England winter weather was one of many things she'd have to get used to in the coming weeks.

Sharon answered on the third ring. "Hey, Becks, I didn't expect to hear from you so soon. How did things go in the Big Apple? How many pairs of shoes did you come back with this time?" Despite Sharon's chirpy tone, her voice sounded husky as though Becky had woken her. It was a weekday and her friend would usually be getting ready to go to work. Maybe she had a cold.

"Listen, Shar, it's a long story, but my editor wants me to coauthor a book with this other author, Adam Maxwell, and, well, let's just say I don't have a choice. I'm calling from his house in New Hampshire."

"You're staying with him at his house?" Husky tone or not, there was no missing Sharon's surprise.

"Yeah, but it's not what you're thinking." Actually it had

been exactly what her friend was thinking, only not anymore. "It's looking like I'm going to have to hunker down here for the next month at least, maybe two, while we bang out the draft." *Bang*—a Freudian slip if there ever was one. "I know it's a huge favor to ask but is there any way you could drive into D.C. this weekend and pick up Daisy Bud from the vet's and take her back to Fredericksburg with you?"

There was a long pause, and Becky chewed on her bottom lip. Thinking she might have pushed the bounds of their friendship, she started backpedaling. "Listen, don't worry about it. It's a lot to ask, and I'll figure something else out. The vet can probably recommend a pet sitter or…" She broke off when she realized Sharon was crying. "Sharon, sweetie, are you okay?"

"Not…really. Minnie…died yesterday."

"On New Year's?"

Sharon sniffled. "Uh-huh."

"Oh, no, I'm so sorry."

"I found her when I came downstairs. A heart attack in her sleep, the vet thinks. I couldn't bring myself to sign off on an autopsy to know for sure. She was getting up there, I guess, but, oh, Becky, the house is so empty without her."

Having lost her beloved cat, Gabby, a few years before, Becky could more than understand. "I know, I know. It's terrible. The worst…"

In between Sharon's snuffling, more bad news spilled out. "I called in to work a while ago to say my dog had died and I was too upset to make it in. My boss gave me shit about it and, well, to make a long story short, I quit."

"You quit?"

"It's been coming for a while, and to tell you the truth I think I need a change of scene. This detective guy I've been seeing, well, that's not going so good, either. My rental is up in a month, and I'm seriously considering relocating. The only good thing about this dump was I could have a dog, and now I really feel like I need the vibe of a big city for a while. What would you think about me apartment-sitting for you? I could forward your mail and water the plants and take care of the cat while I job-hunt and figure stuff out."

Becky hesitated but only for a fraction of a moment. "That's a great idea."

If the deal with Maxwell fell through, she'd be back to D.C. in one week rather than two months. Even if that were the case, though, she didn't mind Sharon bunking in with her. The company would probably do her good. Who knew, they might make it a permanent thing. At that point, she'd need a roommate to make the monthly rent.

They spent the next few minutes working out details, and she gave her friend Max's address. Becky clicked off on the call, pulled on her sweatpants, and padded into the room's private bathroom to brush her teeth and comb her hair. The conversation with Sharon had certainly put her current "problems" into perspective. She might not be thrilled at the prospect of coauthoring the book with Maxwell—Max— but in the big scheme of things it wasn't a tragedy. As far as their romantic interlude went, nothing had really changed there, either. It had started out as a one-night stand and that was exactly what it had turned out to be. That might not be the romantic ending she would have written for her character, but for her real-life self it was definitely for the best. At this point, she really needed to focus all her energy on salvaging her career. She couldn't afford a distraction.

Thinking of the six feet plus of blond, blue-eyed *distraction* with his butt apparently still planted in bed, she glanced at herself in the mirror and shook her head. Workout clothes and jeans were pretty much her writing uniform, but before there'd been no hunky writing partner to see her. Their sexual association might be over, but that didn't mean she wanted to walk around looking like crap in front of him. As soon as Sharon settled in, Becky would ask her to courier a few essential items from the apartment. She'd also ask Max where the closest shopping mall was and try to carve out the time to do some basic shopping, emphasis on basic. Now that she was in a place where people had to wear snow boots three-quarters of the year, she doubted she'd run across any Jimmys or Manolos to tempt her.

She tiptoed downstairs in search of coffee. At home she was used to bopping down the two city blocks to her local Starbucks whenever she pleased. The little treks were a big part of her self-reward system, but she knew from driving in the other day that there were no Starbucks or shops of any kind for miles.

After several wrong turns, she found her way to the kitchen. Sighting the coffeemaker on the marble-topped counter, her spirits brightened. Apparently Max drank coffee, too, but then of course he must. When they'd first met, he'd asked her to have coffee with him. What a long time ago that seemed.

The top bank of cherry cabinets presented a daunting prospect, hung too high for her to reach. Feeling like an interloper, she reminded herself she was searching out coffee and coffee accoutrements, not family secrets or hidden jewels. She dragged over a stool and climbed up to open the first cabinet door. Voilà, she found the cone filters on the lower shelf and brought out the box.

"I see you're making yourself at home."

Becky started. She dropped the box, scattering filters to the four corners of the slate-tiled floor.

"Easy. No more falling, remember?" Max was beside her in a minute, laying steadying hands on her waist. "If you're this jumpy without caffeine, maybe you should consider switching to decaf." Without asking, he lifted her down.

"Not on your life." Glad to have the floor beneath her feet, but shaky from the brief but intimate contact, she darted a quick glance at him. She'd never seen him in the morning, at least not with clothes on, in this case a belted blue terrycloth bathrobe that had seen better days. With his short hair mussed and sticking up at the back, he seemed almost boyish, certainly more approachable than he had the night before at dinner—and even sexier.

She caught him staring and realized he must be checking her out, too. Self-conscious, she glanced down at the drawstring of her baggy pink sweatpants. "I know it isn't exactly Victoria's Secret but what can I say, it's comfortable."

He smiled, the corners of his very blue eyes crinkling in that sexy, endearing way. "No, that's not what I thought. It's…" He glanced down at her feet. "I guess I'm not used to seeing you without high heels."

Becky followed his gaze downward, feeling really dumpy, not to mention really short. She'd put on a pair of gym socks to buffer the cold coming up from the floor. "As much as I love my Manolos and Jimmy's, even I don't sleep in them—or wear them to breakfast in the house."

He moved to the refrigerator and opened the double doors. "Speaking of breakfast, what would you like?"

Staring at his sexy profile, Becky could come up with a whole menu of things she'd like—all of them X-rated. "I don't eat breakfast, but thanks. Coffee's fine for me... and maybe some juice if you have it."

Setting a carton of eggs and a stick of butter on the counter, he shook his head and clucked his tongue—the same tongue that had made her feel amazing things just forty-eight hours ago. "Haven't you heard breakfast is the most important meal of the day?"

Needing to put some distance between them, she walked around to the other side of the counter. "It depends on whose day you mean. Mine seems to unfold just fine without it. Personally I think the whole breakfast-as-the-most-important-meal movement is hype put out by the dairy industry."

He shook his head at her though she couldn't tell if he was annoyed or just amused. "You're full of theories, aren't you? Sit—I'll make the coffee. How do you take it?"

Elbows on the counter, she leaned in to watch him. Colleague or not, she found everything about him completely sexy, from the way he moved around in his kitchen, so confident and sure, to the way he gestured with his strong hands.

"Strong with plenty of cream, please, half-and-half, if you have it."

He seemed surprised. "No sugar?"

Becky couldn't resist. "I'm already sweet enough."

Looking up from scooping coffee into the cone filter, it was Max's turn to smile. "In that case, Miss Sweet Enough, take a load off. How do pancakes sound?"

She dragged out a stool and sat. "Like you're on a mission to make me fat."

Grinning, he turned away to the stove, sliced off a pat of butter from the stick and dropped it into the frying pan. Over the sizzle, he said, "I can't imagine you ever being fat. What are you, a size two?"

Becky was a size two petite actually, but the golden retriever ambling into the room saved her from saying so. Being born Angelina tall and curvy hadn't been in the cards—or genes—for her.

"Here, Scout." Max stopped what he was doing to pour dried kibble in the dog's bowl. "That's a good boy." Reaching down, he patted the animal's side. Looking back at Becky, he said, "He used to run with me when he was younger, but he's too old for that now. He has trouble with his hips."

She'd guessed as much from the dog's stiff movements and slow stride. "I'm sorry to hear that. Did you say you run?"

Straightening, he nodded and returned to making breakfast. "Yeah, only in the winter, that means the treadmill. I have a gym downstairs." She'd wondered how he stayed in such great shape. "You're welcome to use it while you're here."

"Thanks, maybe I will." If he kept feeding her as he had the previous night and promised to this morning, she'd better hit the gym, otherwise she wouldn't be a size two for much longer.

He poured coffee into two mugs, adding cream to hers. Watching him, she saw that he drank his black with a heaping spoonful of sugar. She'd licked and sucked and tasted nearly every part of him, but until now she'd had no idea how he took his coffee—how crazy was that?

Sipping her coffee, she offered, "I run, too." Her apartment building backed up to Rock Creek Park. Running through the park and then cutting through the National Zoo was a major benefit of her northwest Washington location. "I'm pretty much good to go until December. Once the really cold weather hits, I hibernate in aerobics class until the spring thaw."

Scout finished his food and headed for the family room, stopping by Becky for a petting. Watching her stroke Scout's ears, Max couldn't help remembering how good those soft, small hands had felt stroking his back and the rest of him. She had the gentlest touch of any woman he'd ever known. Thinking of the magic those tapered fingers and clean scrubbed nails had wrought, heat spread over his groin.

Whisking the lumps from the pancake batter, he cleared his throat. "It looks like you two have made up since last night."

Looking up from the dog's head in her lap, Becky nodded. "I'm a huge animal lover, in case you can't tell. I have a cat, Daisy Bud. She's a tiger-striped tabby. I found her as a kitten in the alley behind my apartment building, or she found me."

Wearing an oversized T-shirt, baggy sweatpants and with her pretty maple-colored curls tousled about her face, she looked soft and approachable, more like a teenager than a grown woman. Even with bed head and pillow face, she struck him as alluringly perfect and completely adorable. If there was a flaw, he'd so far failed to find it—and he was pretty sure he'd explored every square inch of her in New York. Picturing the tight, lithe and very womanly body lying beneath the shapeless clothes, he felt himself hardening.

It promised to be a long couple of months.

Once he'd gotten her settled in her room the night

before, he'd known he wouldn't be able to go to sleep right away, if at all. Instead he'd cleaned up the kitchen, made a fire and then settled in to read her book. By the end of the first chapter, he'd found himself really getting into the story. Although he still couldn't say he was a romance fiction fan—make that mystery erotica, whatever the hell that was—he had to admit she was a damned good writer.

He'd cracked open the book expecting purple prose and cardboard characters. Instead, Becky's writing was crisp and clean and stylish, her characters well-fleshed out even if he did find her protagonist, Angelina, less than sympathetic. Like him, she kept to a basic twenty-chapter structure, each chapter ending on a cliffhanger that propelled the plot forward. Who knew but this collaboration of theirs just might work out. Who could have predicted that his sexy one-night stand would be sitting in his kitchen in her stocking feet, about to eat pancakes and petting his dog? Real life really was stranger than fiction.

He carried the bowl of batter over to the stove and dropped large spoon-size globs onto the hot skillet. It had been a long time since he'd had someone other than his dog to talk to in the morning, let alone make breakfast for. He really should do a better job of keeping up the conversation.

Over the hiss of batter meeting scalding-hot butter, he called out, "I've had Scout since he was a puppy. We...I got him from a breed rescue group. Apparently his hind legs were too short and his eyes too wide-set to show him. He's been a great companion, though. Now that he's pushing eleven, the hip dysplasia is really starting to kick in. I'm not sure how much longer I can keep him going, but while he's still feeling pretty good, I don't mind making my vet a rich man."

He and Elaina had gone to look at the dogs together. Like Becky's cat, Scout had picked them, not the other way around. Max remembered watching the puppy trot up to Elaina without being called and settle onto her lap. It had been a happy day. Thinking of Scout's gray-muzzled head resting in Becky's lap a moment ago, Max felt a funny tightening in his throat.

The night before at dinner, he hadn't been prepared for the gut-wrenching feeling her tears had stirred in him. There was no denying he had a soft spot for the woman. Once she'd admitted her book contract had fallen through, turning her away was no longer an option. What the hell, maybe Harry was right. Maybe Drake could use a little softening and a lot of sex—and maybe he wasn't the only one.

Whoa, Max. She's your writing buddy, not your fuck buddy.

"I called my friend, Sharon, this morning to arrange cat care and she told me her dog just passed away. She's pretty broken up about it." Her big brown eyes were suspiciously bright.

"I'm sorry to hear that. I know from having Scout and other dogs before him that you get really attached."

He glanced at Becky and it occurred to him he was the one in danger of getting attached. Assuming they could figure out a way to work together, she still wasn't staying beyond the two months it took to finish the draft. If the collaboration was a bust, she'd be leaving in a week. And from everything she'd said since he'd met her, she wasn't looking for a relationship. Even if she had been, it was never a good idea to mix professional and personal affairs. Someone always ended up getting hurt and in this case neither of them could afford to let the work suffer. The book had to come first and it had to be good. Better than good, it had to be a blockbuster for both their sakes. They couldn't afford to walk around like hormone-blitzed teenagers.

"Max?" Becky's voice called him back to the moment. Wrinkling her nose, she asked, "Is something maybe... burning?"

Max looked at the skillet and the blackened pancakes within. Damn, he'd zoned out and burned breakfast. That was a first—and a warning sign.

He carried the pan over to the trash can and upended it, the blackened circles sliding off his nonstick skillet. Other than feeling foolish, ruining breakfast was no big deal. He'd make another batch. There was plenty of batter.

Burned pancakes were no big deal. Getting burned by Becky, now that would be a real problem.

BECKY might not cook, but she was a crackerjack dishwasher and she insisted on doing the cleaning up. After polishing off the pancakes—she had been hungrier than she'd realized—she hopped down from the stool and started washing dishes and wiping down counters. Stealing glances at Max sitting at the breakfast bar reading the paper, she was struck by how natural it felt to hang out with him in his kitchen. She and Elliot had never shared such a cozy morning. He hadn't been a breakfast person, either and they'd eaten their other meals out. Looking back, his visits had been so brief and last-minute that they'd never really spent much time just hanging out. She and Max had done more talking in the past forty-eight hours than she and Elliot had in their entire six months of seeing each other. That was certainly a depressing statement.

They parted ways to shower and dress. Thirty minutes later, they met up in Max's office, one of the rooms at the back of the house. Stepping inside, Becky was struck by how quiet it was. Her northwest D.C. apartment looked out onto Connecticut Avenue, a busy thoroughfare. Writing without the backdrop of car alarms, ambulance sirens and honking horns was going to take some getting used to.

Max was already at his computer when she entered. Looking over his shoulder, he said, "I'm e-mailing Pat the details of our deal so she can put together the joint contract."

Becky nodded. "I'd like to look it over before you send it."

"Of course." He turned back to the monitor.

She hoped she hadn't offended him. She didn't think she had. He'd been in the business longer than she. Publishing contracts were legally binding documents, just like signing on the dotted line to purchase a car or a house, and she wanted to make sure he hadn't missed any of the points they'd discussed over breakfast. The provision that either party could break the contract and walk away at any time without being sued was key.

Until he finished, though, there was nothing for her to do. Restless, she roamed the room, focusing on getting her bearings—the location of office supplies, the flatbed scanner, the fax. Compared to the bare-bones setup she had at home—a laptop and flat-screen monitor—Max's office seemed opulent and a little daunting, if kind of dark.

She rounded his desk and pushed aside the curtains to let in the light—and caught her breath. The French doors opened out onto a panorama of snow-covered mountains and clear sky. A pond, obviously frozen, lay about a quarter mile from the house. Other than a gazebo and an ironwork bench, there were no structures, no houses and certainly no skyscrapers in sight.

Sensing eyes on her back, she turned around to find Max standing by the desk, an unreadable expression on his face. "What do you think?" He'd put on a soft blue pullover and stone-washed jeans. The sweater brought out the vibrant blue of his eyes, making them seem bluer still.

Becky felt as though she was on the brink of drowning yet again. To get her bearings, she turned away to look outside. "It's beautiful. I can see why you love it here. The view must be even more amazing come spring."

He joined her at the window, his hip accidentally brushing against hers—at least she assumed it was by accident. "Every season has its unique beauty, but autumn is the best. The mountains are an incredible panoply of color. I could show you photographs I've taken though no camera lens can quite capture what we see with the naked eye."

The innocent reference to *naked* had her thoughts swirling back to their time together in New York. She caught herself holding her breath and wondered why she was still so skittish around him—and so incredibly turned-on. The stranger sex mojo should be wearing off by now if not burned out altogether. Instead, the attraction felt stronger and hotter than ever.

"I'd love to see them sometime." Uncomfortable with him standing so close, she dropped the curtains and stepped away. She had started over to the computer to read over the e-mail when she spotted the leather-framed photograph on his desk.

Becky stopped in her tracks. A man didn't keep a woman's picture lying out in plain view on his desk unless he had strong feelings for her. She was sure Elliot hadn't bothered to set out even a snapshot of her.

Her and Max's amazing night was less than forty-eight hours old, the memory still fresh and achingly tender. She knew she should move on, but she couldn't resist picking up the picture for a closer look. "Your girlfriend's very striking. She reminds me of my heroine, Angelina."

It was true. The tall Mediterranean-looking woman in the picture would have made a good stand-in for Becky's British-born but half-Italian heroine. The biggest difference was that her waist-length black hair looked wavy instead of straight.

Max came up behind her, and Becky felt the heat of him penetrating all the way through her clothes. "Elaina was Greek-American. And she wasn't my girlfriend, she was my wife."

"Was?"

He hesitated and then nodded. "She died last year on New Year's Day." He reached around to take the picture from her.

So that explained his claim of having gone almost two years without sex. It also shed light on why he'd killed off Drake's wife, Isabel, in a previous book. The one she'd read had described her as a tall, dark-haired, dark-eyed cryptologist who'd died helping her bounty-hunting husband on a mission. Isabel must have been based on Elaina.

Surrendering the photo, Becky lifted her gaze to his face. "I'm so sorry."

Setting the frame down, he avoided her eyes. "She was sick for a long time—cancer. Toward the end, the pain got pretty bad."

"Is that why you checked out of the publishing scene and went underground, to take care of her?"

She'd meant it as a compliment, but Max didn't seem to be taking it so. His sexy mouth flat-lined and the light left his eyes, leaving them as vacant-looking as the windows of an emptied-out house on moving day. "I didn't go *underground* as that damned reporter insisted on writing. I didn't go anywhere at all. I stayed right here in this house, the house we built together, and Elaina and I did our thing. It wasn't like I'm some saint or martyr. I did exactly what I'd wanted to do since the day I met her, and that was to be with her. Her being sick just meant we had to figure out a new way to do that and still be us."

Becky looked at him, emotion thickening her throat. Adam Maxwell wasn't just sexy and charming and talented and successful. He was all of those things in abundance, but, even more, he was loyal and decent, trustworthy and true, a one-in-a-million good guy, the kind her friend, Sharon, would call a "keeper."

"Watching someone you love that much die must be so hard. I can't imagine how hard that must be."

"It was hard. It *is* hard. That year was the hardest one of my life, but it was also one of our best. We did a lot of crying but we did a lot of laughing, too—and remembering all the good times we were lucky enough to have shared. We spent just about every waking moment together and nothing got in the way of that, absolutely nothing, not even the book I was working on. I set my laptop up in our bedroom, and I wrote when I could and when it finally got too hard, when she needed me too much, I shut the damn thing down and forgot about it for months."

He'd sacrificed his career and put his life on hold for his wife and the best part was he hadn't done it grudgingly but gladly. To be loved like that, to be wanted like that— Becky couldn't even imagine it. It was horrible to admit, but she was almost envious of a dead woman.

Elliot had the hots for her in the beginning, but whatever he'd felt for her obviously hadn't run very deep. Love and passion, was it really possible to have both with one person outside the pages of a romance novel?

"I'm sorry," she said again and left it at that because really, what more was there to say?

She thought back to the interview he'd given the *New Yorker*. The issue would have come out around the time Max lost his wife or shortly afterward. He must have been raw with grief, devastated, perhaps even angry with the world. By the time she'd come to the housewife-porn quote, Becky had been too pissed off to read the rest. Until now, it had never occurred to her to give him the benefit of the doubt. She suspected there was a lesson in that.

He gestured to the computer. "Have a look at that e-mail I drafted. If it seems okay to you, then go ahead and hit Send. If not, we can talk about any changes you want when I get back." He turned and started toward the door.

Thinking of the beautiful, barren landscape at her back, Becky wondered where he meant to go. There must not be another house for miles.

She followed him to the door. "If you want some company or—"

His adamant headshake cut her off. "I'm going into town for supplies. I'm not sure when I'll be back."

He was obviously upset, and it was all her fault. If only she'd tamped down her writer's curiosity and let the picture pass without comment. Mentally kicking herself, she said, "Max, I'm so—"

He turned and left the room before she could get the word *sorry* out.

9

Shouldering his weapon, Drake looked over at Angelina. Kneeling on the cabin's dirt-packed floor, the beautiful Brit was still arming up. "Crikey, Angie, get a move on. We haven't got all bloody day."

Angelina looked up at him through glaring green eyes. "I always clean my gun and triple-check my taser before going out on a mission. It's my ritual."

Drake yanked off his broad-brimmed hat and scoured the sweat from his forehead before it rolled into his eyes. The blooming woman would be the death of him, and they hadn't yet cleared the cabin. "Is that so? Next you'll be telling me you knock your heels together three times, too."

"As a matter of fact, I do."

MAX AWOKE the next morning late but in a better frame of mind. As much as it had hurt him to talk about Elaina, now that he had, he felt as if something had been released inside him. He showered and dressed and came downstairs humming "New York State of Mind." The half-filled coffeepot confirmed Becky had come down already.

When he walked into his office, coffee mug in hand, he found her at his computer. "Good morning."

She finished typing her current sentence and looked up. "Good morning. I hope you don't mind me helping myself to your computer. My laptop screen is pretty small."

"Not a problem." He sat his coffee down and came to stand beside her, relieved she showed no signs of being pissed off at him for cutting out on what was supposed to have been their first day of work. Last night at dinner she'd been mighty quiet, but then so had he. Looking over her shoulder, he said, "On a roll, huh?"

She nodded, gaze drifting back to the screen. "I'm working on bio sketches for our main characters, including the antagonists. I'm almost finished with Angelina's. I figure you can get started on Drake's."

Max had lived with Drake through three books, longer if you counted the time the Aussie adventurer had first burst into his consciousness. He didn't need a "bio sketch," whatever the hell that was. He knew his character inside and out.

Hoping to avoid the topic of writing exercises, he said, "I finished your book last night."

That obviously got her attention. She swiveled away from the screen and looked up at him. "Dare I ask what you thought?"

"I liked it," he said without hesitation. "I didn't expect to but I did. I thought the Falco character was a little over the top but otherwise the story sailed right along."

"Over the top? How do you mean?" She turned to face him.

"Well, if Angelina is such a crackerjack spy, why would she fall for a guy like that? I mean, it's not like there weren't plenty of signs that he was not only a double agent but also a player."

Becky bit her bottom lip as though the remark struck

some kind of personal cord. "It happens. Smart, nice women fall for jerks all the time. Haven't you ever heard the saying that love is blind?"

He snorted. "In that case, Angelina needs a pair of night-vision goggles."

Becky rolled her eyes. "And this from the man who writes about a middle-aged Australian bounty hunter who's apparently filthy rich yet can't commit to building anything more substantial than a one-room shanty on his own property."

Middle-aged! Max felt his good mood slipping. "Drake doesn't need to flaunt his wealth. It's the land he loves, not material possessions."

And so began their first day of collaboration. It was clear working together wasn't going to be the cakewalk Pat and Harry had pitched it to be. Even agreeing on a writing schedule turned into a major negotiation. Sitting down to block out the book later that day, they quickly learned they had very different ways of working. Max was a fly-by-the-seat-of-his-pants writer who liked to start with a general idea and flesh it out as he went along. Becky was a meticulous plotter who lived and died by her outline. She blocked out each chapter scene-by-scene through to the end before she could even think of writing the book. Surprises made her crazy, while for Max the surprise, the adventure, was half the fun.

They also had completely opposite internal clocks. Max admitted that anything before ten was way too early for him. Working alone, he didn't usually get down to writing until after dinner. Once the story got cooking, though, he'd sometimes write straight through to dawn. That wasn't going to cut it for Becky. A morning person, she did her best work before midafternoon, preferably with an hour's exercise break at lunch. Unless she was on a roll or a deadline crunch, by the time dinnertime came around she was ready to shut down her computer for the night.

Even more challenging than meshing conflicting work habits and schedules was comingling the storylines from their previous books. It was a lot like sending your characters on a blind date with nowhere to go.

With the tension mounting on both sides, Max suggested they move to the family room where it would be easier to relax. He went into the kitchen to put on a fresh pot of coffee. When he came out again, a mug in either hand, Becky was settled onto the couch, Scout sprawled over her feet, a notepad in her lap.

The cozy domestic scene tugged at his heart. He couldn't help noticing how good she looked there in his family room, how right. He carried the coffee over to the low pine table. Setting the mugs down, he hesitated, eyeing the empty plaid cushion beside her. Too close for comfort, he decided—his, at any rate.

He glanced again at his new partner, head bent over the pad and writing meticulous notes in her neat, precise handwriting. Today's ensemble was a soft pink sweater and jeans—and gym socks. For whatever reason, the latter struck him as really cute.

The whole character-sketch exercise, on the other hand, struck him as a pure pain in the ass. Writing wasn't an "exercise" you practiced. It was something you just did. When he was in that magical state known as The Zone, the words gushed out of him like a mountain stream, sometimes rushing out faster than he could type. On those occasions, he put aside whatever else he was doing and just went with it. Still, this character-sketch thing was apparently part of Becky's process and judging from what he'd read so far of her book, it obviously worked for her.

Trying to get into the spirit of the thing, he settled into the nearby leather chair and asked, "By the way, how old is Angelina supposed to be?"

Pen stalling, Becky glanced up. "Excuse me?"

He was pretty sure she'd heard him, but he repeated himself anyway. "I asked how old she is."

She snapped up her chin. "What difference does it make?"

He held up his hands in the air. "Hey, you're the one who insisted on doing character sketches. I'm just trying to get a better feel for who she is."

"She's...thirtysomething."

"You haven't given her a definite age?" From a few feet away, he studied her, wondering why age seemed to be such a tender topic with her. She couldn't be much past thirty and these days thirty was the new twenty, or so the media claimed.

"No, as a matter of fact, I haven't. Why, is that some kind of writing faux pas? I mean, it's not like she's going to settle down and have Drake's baby."

He shrugged, wondering if perhaps he'd hit a nerve. Could it be her snappishness over all matters age-related had to do with her own biological clock ticking? Testing the waters, he said, "You never know, she might. If she's still in her thirties, it could happen. Women in their thirties have babies all the time."

Fuming brown eyes bored into him. "You make it sound so simple, so cut-and-dried, but it isn't. Did you know that once a woman hits the age of thirty-five, her chances of getting pregnant go down by fifty percent? And that after thirty-five, her fertility declines by a steady ten percent each year?"

Max hadn't known that, but then he hadn't made an in-depth study of the subject as she obviously had. In the first half of their marriage, he and Elaina had been too busy with their careers and traveling and generally enjoying each other to think about adding kids to the mix. Like so many people, they'd figured they had time, maybe not all the time in the world but definitely a lot more than they'd got. They'd just started seriously talking about starting a family when she'd been diagnosed.

"Don't tell that to Susan Sarandon," he quipped. A fan, he knew the popular film actress had given birth twice in her midforties.

He could see he'd been wrong to make the joke. Becky stabbed her index finger into the air, but he thought her eyes looked glittery, as if she was holding back tears. "Be that as it may, if you think I'm going to stand by and let Drake knock up my heroine and then leave her high and dry while he rides off into the sunset for his next adventure, think again, mister. Anyway, the point is moot."

"How's that?"

"If you must know, Angelina is on the pill."

"You've given her a birth-control method but not an age?"

He felt a tickle at the corners of his mouth and struggled not to laugh. He was coming to see she took her character a lot more seriously than he did his, yet another difference between them.

"She's very...active." A tinge of pink swept into her cheeks.

"Active, huh?" Wondering just what kind of book

he'd signed up to cowrite, he asked, "You mean she sleeps around?"

She scowled. "If I said a male character was active, you'd say he was a stud, but if Angelina does the same, she's a slut. That's really fair—*not*."

"I didn't call Angelina a slut, you did. And by the way, who are we really talking about here?"

Becky hesitated. Watching her nibble her bottom lip constantly reminded him of all the amazing things she'd used that full, sexy mouth to do to his body. Try as he might, and he had to admit so far he hadn't tried all that hard, he found himself semiaroused more often than not. The steamy scenes kept flashing through his mind like a triple-X-rated movie trailer. Seeing her every day—and every night—for the next two months wasn't going to help with that, either. The sexual chemistry that drew them together like magnets back in Manhattan hadn't gone away just because they'd become writing partners. Sitting across the room from her rather than beside her on the sofa, a deliberate choice, he could still feel the pull of her sensuality across the empty space.

Setting down her coffee mug, she said, "Angelina, of course."

Max wasn't so sure. "Look, for whatever it's worth, I really don't think you slept with me to get the book deal." Catching her skeptical stare, he added, "Okay, I did at first but you have to admit that was a pretty amazing set of coincidences that brought us together."

"That was a weird day," she admitted. "I'd just come from lunch with my editor—*our* editor—and she dropped the bomb on me about my book sales and then pitched teaming with you and, well, the bad news really threw me."

Hearing that the prospect of teaming with him counted as bad news on a par with a bombed book wasn't exactly flattering, but he held back from saying so. If this collaboration was going to have a hope of working, he needed to get into not only her head but the head of her character.

"Sounds serious."

She nodded. "I felt pretty low. After Pat left for her next meeting, I ordered a martini and then went on a thousand-dollar shoe binge at Saks."

"One pair of shoes cost you a grand!"

Growing up in a well-off family, he'd never wanted for anything, but frugality was one of the core values his parents had imparted. Dropping a grand on a pair of shoes wouldn't enter his mind. No wonder she'd been so upset when one went missing—and been so over the moon when he'd found it and brought it back to her. But considering the part those sexy red shoes had played in bringing them together, they were worth every penny.

"Two, actually, at least before tax. I got a second pair of pumps."

Max hesitated. The ice had been broken. There was an opening, if he dared take it. "Since it seems to be confession time, when I first saw you on my doorstep, I thought I must be dreaming or hallucinating. I'd just spent an entire day kicking myself for not waking you up before I left that morning and getting your phone number, not to mention your last name." He stopped, realizing he'd said a lot more than he'd meant to.

She lifted her wide brown eyes to his face. "You wanted to see me again?"

There was no going back now. He nodded. "I probably

shouldn't admit it, but yes, I did." He almost said "do," but caught himself in time.

Her gaze slid away. She fiddled with her pen. "I probably shouldn't admit this, either, but when I woke up in your room and found your note and the rose—that was really sweet of you, by the way—I wished I'd told you my name, my *real* name, so…so we could keep in touch. But I guess it really doesn't matter at this point." She lifted her slender shoulders in a shrug and the casualness of the gesture coupled with her matter-of-fact tone really got under his skin. "What we had in New York was a fling, a one-time deal. It's not like we have to worry about it happening again."

"Right, a one-time deal." Max sipped his coffee, just poured from the freshly made pot. He remembered stirring in his usual shovelful of sugar and yet the brew that had tasted so satisfyingly sweet moments ago suddenly tasted really bitter. "Now that we've squared real life away, do you think we can wrap up this character-sketch bull—business and get down to some actual writing?"

"Not quite. We're not finished. Actually we've barely started." She reached for the notepad.

Annoyed—okay, hurt—by her casual dismissal of their New York night, Max said, "I already know Drake through and through, and as for Angelina it's pretty obvious she's you in a black wig."

Becky's eyes flew open. "That is so untrue. If anything, we're almost polar opposites."

"Opposites, huh? If you believe that, then you not only write fiction, you must also live it."

She glared at him. "What's that supposed to mean?"

"You obviously love to shop. She always dresses in

couture clothing right down to the designer shoes. You're in great physical shape and she's always running or rappeling or hanging out of something. She obviously enjoys sex and you…" He hesitated, sensing he was about to step over a line and asking himself whether or not he cared. "Well, if my recent memory serves me, you're very good in bed."

She shot him a piercing look, confirming the line had been crossed. "Is that all?"

"Not quite. She has your eyes, not the color obviously but the shape. Yours turn up at the corners just like hers do."

"They do?" Her shy gaze met his and Max could almost see the current of awareness pulsing between them.

"Yes, they do." Pressing his advantage, he said, "The one thing of yours she doesn't have is your heart."

She hesitated. "Having a heart can land you in all kinds of trouble."

Some jerk must have hurt her badly. Probing for whatever reason—curiosity, concern or some mingling of the two, he said, "Well, she seems to take the whole British sangfroid thing to the extreme. When it comes down to it, she's pretty bloodless."

Her smile vanished and her eyes turned wintry. "Just because she's not always dissolving into a puddle of tears and standing by waiting for a man to rescue her doesn't make her bloodless. Next you'll be saying she's a bitch."

"Well, now that you mentioned it, she doesn't seem to care much about anyone other than herself."

"And I suppose Drake is a font of empathy?"

Max felt himself bristling. He tried to give her positive feedback and she responded by attacking him. "He's not supposed to be. He's a man."

"That's—that's sexism."

"That's reality. Look, all I'm saying is Angelina isn't every man's walking wet dream. Some of us like our women softer, warmer, more…"

"More what?"

"More like you."

The real-life Angelinas of the world were a dime a dozen. Women like Becky were rare as the prize opal he'd sent Drake out in search of in his second book.

"Like me? But Angelina always knows just what to do and say. She always has the perfect comeback line."

He lifted a brow and looked at her. "You don't do so badly yourself."

"She doesn't take shit from anyone."

He shook his head, amazed at how adept she was at selling herself short. "And this from the woman who left five messages on my cell and then tracked me down hundreds of miles on New Year's Day to show up at my door with luggage and a laptop."

"And she's a crack markswoman, a sharpshooter."

"Not a skill most of us have a need for in our daily lives."

"And she has this perfectly straight, perfectly shiny waist-length black hair. I can put her in a tropical rainforest or in a London fog, it doesn't matter. Her hair never frizzes."

"I've never been a fan of straight black hair. Reminds me too much of Cher. You have beautiful hair. I know women who'd kill to have curls like yours. And it's also very shiny and silky. I noticed it the other night."

The intensity of his gaze holding hers sent a warm shiver shooting through Becky. Self-conscious, she reached up and tucked a curl behind her ear. The heat hitting her face told her she must be blushing. After the no-holds-barred sex they'd shared in New York—the urgent, seeking hands, the warm, wet mouths and the sultry promises they'd whispered to each other in the dark—it was nothing short of ridiculous to be embarrassed over an innocuous compliment and yet...

Shifting in her seat, she said, "If this collaboration of ours is going to have a chance of working, we probably shouldn't keep bringing up New York."

"Who's talking about New York? I meant last night at dinner." He broke into a very broad, very wicked grin. "You must have sex on the brain, Becka. An occupational hazard of being a romance writer, I guess."

"What did you call me?"

"A romance writer."

"No, I mean before that. What name did you call me?"

"Becka. It suits you. Becky sounds like a little girl's name and Rebecca is too stiff, too formal. Becka suits you."

She folded her arms across her chest, alarmed by her heart's sudden fluttering. He'd come up with a special name for her. Nobody ever had before unless you counted Becky, but she'd pretty much given that name to herself. Like many middle children, she'd grown up feeling lost in the pack.

Becky cleared her throat. "Getting back to Angelina, she's tall. She could look you in the eye."

He lifted his shoulders in a shrug, reminding her of how amazing it had felt to anchor her hands to that solid shelf of flesh and bone. "You're plenty tall enough and besides, I didn't mind bending." He opened his mouth but stopped short of saying more. Suddenly he was all stiff-lipped New Englander and guarded gaze. "All I'm saying is don't you sell yourself short. You're beautiful and smart and talented."

"You think I'm talented?" Coming from bestselling author Adam Maxwell that constituted high praise indeed.

He nodded. "You're a damn good writer and you'd be a success in any genre you chose to write."

This time the compliment touched her. "Thank you."

"You're welcome." He took a sip of his coffee. Setting the mug back down, he said, "Now answer me this. If Angelina's so great, then why doesn't she have a significant other—until Drake, I mean?"

"That's the beauty of her—she doesn't need a man to validate her life. She comes and goes as she pleases, she answers to no one."

Suddenly it occurred to Becky that not only didn't Angelina have a steady boyfriend, the supersleuth didn't have so much as a pet or a potted plant waiting for her at home, either. Scratch that—she didn't have a home. Becky, on the other hand, had a lovely apartment, assuming she could still afford the rent, her precious Daisy Bud to greet her at the door every time she came back home, and people like Sharon and her family, all of whom loved and cared about her a lot. Angelina's "life" might be packed with adventure but there was nothing substantive in it, nothing more. It was just possible Max might have a point.

And yet who was he to criticize her? It was childish of her, she was a grown-up author with a book to get out after all, and yet with the sexual tension between them spiking by the hour if not the minute, she badly wanted to wipe that smug smile from his face. If she couldn't take him to bed, the very least she could do was take him down a peg—or two.

Taking a sip of her coffee, she asked, "What about our buff bounty hunter, Drake?"

Max supposed turnabout was fair play, but that didn't mean he had to like it. "What about him?"

"He's obviously you."

After yesterday, she expected him to rocket up from his seat and announce he needed a walk. Instead, he didn't seem fazed. "He's a composite of people I've met over a decade of travel."

It was her turn to express skepticism. "Oh, right. And I suppose it's pure coincidence you both just happen to be six foot three, blond and, er…built. You both have traveled all over the world. Thirty countries, didn't you say? You both have degrees in archeology." *You both lost your wife.* "Except for his Australian accent, you might as well be twins."

Max hesitated. Until now, he'd forgotten how much about himself he'd shared with her in New York. So much for anonymous sex; he'd apparently bored her with his life story straight out of the gate, right down to the deeply personal fact that until she'd come along he hadn't had sex in almost two years. Looking back, it seemed crazy to reveal that much about yourself to a stranger, even a stranger you were planning on sleeping with, but Becky then had been so very easy to talk to. He wished they could get past the crazy chemistry, and whatever else had them at each other's throats, and recapture some of that ease now.

Searching for a new subject, something unexpectedly nice struck him. "By the way, do you realize you just referred to Drake as *our* character?"

Becky hadn't. "I did, didn't I? Do you mind?"

He hesitated and she wondered if he might be mulling

over intellectual property rights and potential future lawsuits. Instead he smiled. "No, I don't mind. Actually it's kind of nice."

Yes, Becky silently agreed, *it kind of was.*

10

Fingers slipping on the splintered wood, Angelina looked up the collapsed mine shaft into the sliver of sunlight. Mere minutes ago she'd stood on solid earth. One misstep onto Falco's booby trap had sent her hurtling underground.

Drake's face appeared in the pinpoint of light. "Hold on, Angie. I'm coming."

A moment later, a thick climber's rope dropped down the hole, the tail swinging just above her. She grabbed hold, releasing her grip on the collapsing wall just as the last of the rotted boards and crumbled earth gave way. Gripping the hemp, she braced her feet on the tunnel wall and climbed as Drake pulled her to the top. As soon as she was within reach, he shoved a large hand through the hole and wrapped his strong fingers about her wrist.

Angelina had never been so happy to be captured in all her life. Feet once more on solid ground, she let go of the rope and wrapped her arms around Drake's muscle-corded neck, burying her face in the salty hollow of his broad shoulder. "Easy, love," he said, stroking the tangles from her damp face. "I've got you safe now." He swiped the smudge of dirt from her cheek with his callused thumb.

Embarrassed by her moment of weakness, she stepped back from his embrace. Brushing dirt from her legs she looked up and said, "Thank you, I think."

Blue eyes, meltingly tender, smiled down into hers. "You're welcome, I think."

BECKY WOULDN'T have believed it those first rocky few days, but by the second week, she and Max had settled into a schedule, a complicated set of compromises that got easier as the days passed. Bit by bit and day by day the written pages were piling up.

Now that they'd started getting into a groove, she found she was enjoying having another writer to bounce ideas off. She was also just plain enjoying spending time with Max. Not Max her nameless midtown Prince Charming, or her sexy one-night stand or even the bestselling author, but rather Max the man who liked dogs and cooking and long walks in the snow.

She couldn't imagine anyone who less fit the stereotype of a spoiled star author. He obviously had money, and yet he was the most down-to-earth man she'd ever met. Other than the sixtysomething housekeeper who came in once a week to change the bed linens and vacuum and dust, he didn't have servants. He didn't even have a secretary. He chopped his own wood and cooked their meals and drove into town to buy plumbing supplies from the hardware store to fix the leaking faucet in her guest bathroom. Becky couldn't help admiring his hands-on approach to living. Drake's Code wasn't a set of stupid macho rules he'd made up for his fictional character but a set of ethics Max lived by.

Except for the sexual tension that never seemed to go away between them, their arrangement was working out even better than Becky had supposed. Other than missing her cat and her friends, especially Sharon, she didn't feel all that homesick. D.C. had never really felt like home to her, and she had no desire to move back to Maryland where her parents and siblings still lived. Visiting her big, boisterous family always left her feeling like a fish out of water, whereas with Max she not only felt at home but comfortable in her own skin.

That afternoon they sat side by side at the computer, Becky manning the keyboard. The chapter they were working on was a love scene written from Angelina's viewpoint. Though Becky had written steamy scenes aplenty in the past, she'd never done so with a writing partner. That her collaborator happened to be a man she'd recently slept with, a man to whom she was still madly attracted, made the whole scenario that much more awkward. With the tension between her and Max mounting by the moment, no wonder the words on paper weren't working.

She drummed her nails atop the keyboard caddy, wishing there was some chocolate nearby. "Drake lifting Angelina's hair away from her neck and running his mouth alongside of her neck just doesn't work for me."

"Why not?" Max asked. He sounded grouchy but then again they had been working crazy hours. "It's an erogenous zone for most women, isn't it?"

Becky trained her gaze on the computer screen, hoping her warm face didn't translate into a vividly visible blush. Her own neck was a particularly sensitive area as Max well knew. Back in New York, he'd kissed and licked and nibbled her throat to their mutual hearts' content. At times such as this, she had to force herself to remember it was Angelina and Drake they were discussing.

"Well, er…I'm not saying it doesn't feel good to her. Of course it feels good—better than good. My point is it's not in her character to stand there passively while he puts the moves on her. She's more proactive than that."

"Okay, I'm wide open here. Let's walk through it step-by-step the way we did the action scenes."

Despite his matter-of-fact tone, Becky hesitated. "Are you sure that's a good idea?"

He shrugged but his gaze was anything but casual. "I'm game if you are. What would Angelina do if a man, Drake, was kissing her neck like…like this?" He angled his head and found the ultrasensitive spot just under Becky's ear with his mouth.

Gooseflesh broke out all over her. She sucked in her breath. "She'd uh…" Damn, but it was just about impossible to think rationally, to think at all, with Max doing… well, *that.* "She'd touch him back, definitely."

He slid his lips down the side of her throat, pressing open-mouthed kisses along the way. "Now we're getting somewhere. How would she touch him…or should I say where?"

He lifted his head, dark blue gaze holding hers, daring her to look away, his fingers toying with the sensitive area of her clavicle exposed by her sweater, raising a thrumming ache inside her pressed-together thighs.

Becky swallowed hard. Though she'd been sipping from a bottle of water throughout the day, she suddenly felt as though cobwebs had sprouted inside her mouth and throat. "Angelina is very straightforward about what she wants, and in this case, she wants Drake. Even though she knows she shouldn't, that it's not in the best interest of the mission to continue sleeping with her partner, she can't seem to stop thinking about him."

Max's hand slid to her shoulder. "That's her motivation but what would she do?" He leaned closer, drawing her toward him, his warm breath striking the side of her face. "Where would she touch him? How would she touch him? She must know he's waiting for her to give him some sign, any sign, that it's okay to break their no-lovers rule."

Rules of any sort suddenly seemed very far away to Becky. Pounding heat pooled inside her panties, her breasts felt heavy and hypersensitive, and her racing heart felt as though it might break through the wall of her chest at any time. Out of the corner of her eye, she caught a flicker of motion from outside the window. Turning to look, she saw it was snowing.

She swung her head back to Max and like an idiot announced, "It's snowing."

Scowling, he dropped his hand and drew back. "It's New Hampshire. That happens a lot here."

"But this looks like a really good snow, a Christmas snow. Let's take a walk."

One dark blond eyebrow edged upward. "I thought you hated cold weather?"

"Just a short walk. The fresh air will do us both good."

Becky couldn't speak for Max but for herself, her next activity was going to be either a cold walk or a cold shower. Either way, she needed to get her temperature back down and her perspective back in line before she did something really stupid, like begging him to go to bed with her.

"Okay. But just remember that tonight when we have to stay up finishing this scene, that this time you were the one who called break, not me."

He pushed back his chair and stood. The position put her on eye-level with his waist and for a fleeting few seconds she imagined herself reaching out to cup him, slowly rolling down his pants fly, and then drawing him into her mouth. Remembering how amazing he'd tasted, how she hadn't been able to get enough, she felt her face flush even hotter—and the pulse between her legs strike even deeper—more evidence of just how much she needed that walk.

"Let's go then." He reached down a hand to help her up.

Reminded of their meeting in New York when he'd picked her up off the sidewalk—and peeked at her under-wear—Becky let him lift her up, glad he couldn't possibly guess how wet the crotch of her panties must be by now.

He ran his gaze over her, his blue eyes looking as hot as she felt. "We need to bundle you up. That low-necked sweater needs a scarf at least." He glanced down to her feet. "And those fancy boots of yours aren't going to cut it, either."

She followed his gaze down to her high heeled Manolos. "They're the only ones I have."

He hesitated, a funny look rolling over his face, and she wondered if he might be considering bagging the walk and getting back to work after all. The thought brought about a bizarre sense of letdown. "I might have something that'll work." He turned and started out into the hallway.

Becky hesitated and then followed him out. As much as she needed to escape the close confines of the house, no way could she wear Max's boots. His feet were huge compared to hers. If she tried, she'd only end up falling, something she'd done way too much since meeting him.

She found him buried head and shoulders inside the coat closet. He backed out and turned to her, holding out a dusty pair of knee-high black snow boots. "These might work."

Becky glanced down at the shoes. Clunky and without a gram of style, they were too small to be his. Reaching out to take them, she almost said so when it hit her. Shit, they must have belonged to his wife.

Avoiding her eyes, he picked up the second boot and dusted it off. "Your feet are a lot smaller than hers were—you're a lot smaller period—but I figure you can stuff some cotton or tissues in the toes if you need to. It's a walk, not a run. I'll hold your hand if you want. I promise I won't let you fall." He lifted his face and looked up at her, and the raw vulnerability in his blue eyes had her forgetting all about how much she hated the cold.

"These are good. I can work with these." She took the boots from him, hugging them against her chest. "Give me a couple minutes to pile on those layers, and I'll meet you back down here, okay?"

"Okay."

She started toward the stairs. At the bottom, she turned back. "Max."

He lifted his bowed head to look at her. "Yeah?"

"I won't let you fall, either."

THEY WALKED side-by-side, theirs the first footprints in the otherwise pristine snow. Scout pranced ahead, more puppy than old dog. The fast-falling flakes were so big and soft-looking Becky could almost imagine the white sky above was one big exploded feather pillow. What had started as a quick way to bring about a short-term sexual cool-down had turned into more, much more. Looking ahead to snow-covered mountains and sparkling ice-crystal-covered trees, Becky felt as if she and Max were the only two people in a magical winter world.

She turned to Max. Reaching out, she squeezed his gloved hand. "Thank you."

He tucked her arm in his and looked over at her, his eyes intensely blue amidst all the winter white. "For what?"

"For—I don't know, taking a walk with me. This is really nice. It's beautiful out here."

He fixed solemn eyes on her face. "There really aren't words to do justice to a New England snow, not even for a writer. You have to see for yourself. And I can tell you really get it. Not everyone does, but you do."

More than the perfect snow or the dramatic mountain backdrop, it was sharing this with Max, the feel of his big hand holding hers, the echo of his boots crunching a twin trail next to hers that made the moment so very special. Even if she was walking in another woman's shoes—literally— she knew in her heart this walk counted among the most special of her life, one of those precious picture-perfect moments when the magic washes over you, and you feel connected to something greater and grander than yourself.

She smiled, her face frozen but the rest of her body toasty warm beneath the layers. "I may rethink always sending Angelina to tropical climates."

Fireside evenings, steaming mugs of hot chocolate or warm apple cider, even walks in the snow—certain life-style aspects of the New England climate were not without their charm. Or maybe it was just that she liked sharing those things with Max. It was a startling and disconcert-ing discovery and one she set aside to consider later— much later.

Their walk, and Becky's reprieve, ended far too soon. Even though her toes felt frozen solid inside the too-big boots, she was sorry to see the house come back into view.

Thinking of the still-to-be written love scene and the very real, very unresolved sexual tension mounting between her and her sexy writing partner, she hated to think about going back in.

They trudged up the gravel drive to the front porch. Protected by the hipped roof, they stood at the door shaking off snow. Standing on tiptoe, Becky finished dusting the flakes from Max's broad shoulders.

He glanced back at her. "Am I done?"

"Yes." Settling back on her soles, Becky felt as though she was the one who was done—done for.

For two weeks now, she'd fought her desire for Max as they'd shared intimate dinners and cozy fireside chats and one-on-one work sessions that lasted late into the night. Ironically it had taken a bracing winter walk to push her over the brink, to make her see that whatever there was between them, it wasn't going to burn out or fade away on its own. Much like Drake and Angelina, the outcome was predetermined, even scripted. She wanted Max even more than she had in New York. Fighting her feelings in the name of professionalism wasn't getting her anywhere. If anything, self-denial was wreaking havoc with her concentration, blocking her creativity and generally muddling her mind.

Max turned around. His gaze dropped to hers. This time she didn't look away as she had earlier in his office. Instead, she reached for her Angelina-like bravery and met his eyes steadily. Remembering his mention of Drake needing some sign, she stood on her toes and rested her hands on his shoulders and brushed her mouth over his, a silent offering.

His arms went around her, anchoring her to his chest. "Christ, Becka, what are you doing to me?"

Mouth hovering over his, she said, "I'm not sure. I just really need you to kiss me. You can consider this a sign if you want to."

He let out a groan. "Oh, I want to all right, I more than want to."

His mouth covered hers, and he slid his gloved hands into her hair, knocking off her knitted hat and pulling her even harder against him. She opened for him and he deepened the kiss, his tongue teasing the sensitive seam on the roof of her mouth before joining with hers.

He stopped to run his leather-sheathed thumb over her bottom lip, drawing a shiver that had nothing to do with the cold air. "Don't be sorry. I'm not."

To show how very not-sorry she was, she pressed closer, rubbing her breasts against him through the layers, finding a warmed patch of exposed skin on his neck with her lips and tongue, losing herself in the wonder of him, drowning not only in his eyes but in all of him. It was like being back at the Serena Lounge when they'd first come together like magnets, without conscious thought, words or even real names. Only, despite cold noses and bundled clothing, this was even better because it wasn't a stranger she was kissing. It was Max.

Breathless, Becky broke off the kiss and settled her flat-soled feet back onto the porch planks, second-guessing herself. She always felt so much taller, stronger and braver—so much more Angelina-like—wearing her heels.

"Max, this is crazy. What are we doing? What *is* this?"

He shook his head, his blue eyes melting her with their warmth and tenderness. "Damned if I know. If you figure it out, be sure and tell me. On second thought, don't, not now anyway. For now, let's just go with it. It worked pretty well back in New York."

"That was different. We didn't know each other then, not even our names."

He lifted one dark blond eyebrow and stared at her, looking sexier than any man had a right to look. "Are you saying only strangers can have good sex?"

She shook her head. "No, of course not, but coauthoring a book together changes everything. We're writing partners. Adding a sexual component to the mix is adding yet another unknown. We don't know how it will affect the work. It might be disastrous."

"It might be pretty damned wonderful, too. We'll never know unless we give it a shot." He slid his gloved hand beneath her chin, lifting her face to his. "Come to bed with me, Becka. Come to bed with me and let me make love to you."

In the midst of feeling more turned-on than ever before in her life, Becky felt purely, powerfully afraid, and not only because of the potential impact sex might have on their writing. Before, in New York, they'd been strangers. Beyond the pleasure of the moment, a one-night stand wasn't supposed to mean anything. If she made love to Max now, though, it would mean something, to her at least. For his part, it was obvious he was still crazy about his dead wife. Regardless, if she slept with him again, leaving at the end of the two months wouldn't just be hard—it would be brutal. It had taken her a full year to get over Elliot, and he was no Max. Could she really risk pain on that par again?

Max's seductive whisper interrupted her agonizing debate. "Come to bed with me, Becka. Before we write any more lovemaking scenes for Drake and Angelina, we need to create some for you and I."

MAX SAT on the side of his maple four-poster bed, Becky standing in the space between his thighs, his hands resting on her slender hips, hers anchored to his shoulders. They'd scripted nearly the same posture for Drake and Angelina's first time together in the outback hotel room, only Becky's petite, tightly packaged body was a thousand times sexier than Max could imagine her fictional heroine's ever being.

He reached up and started on the row of dainty pearl buttons fronting her angora sweater. Unlike Angelina, who frequently sported unisex designer biker gear, Becky was all woman right down to the pretty, feminine things she wore. Even her winter sweaters were soft and warm and delicate.

"So beautiful…"

He slid the sweater off her slender shoulders and reached for the zipper of her jeans. A glimpse of peach-colored silk greeted him, bringing him back to their first meeting on the New York sidewalk, the image of her spread white thighs burned into his brain for all time.

He felt a trickle of come slide down his penis and swallowed hard, determined to hold back for as long as he possibly could. "I need to get these damned jeans off you."

Feeling as though he was unwrapping a week-old Christmas present just discovered beneath the tree, he tugged her jeans down over her tight little behind and shapely legs. Becky stepped out of the pants and then lifted one slender foot to slide the pile aside.

She turned back to him and Max caught his breath. She was even prettier than he remembered, and he remembered her as being very pretty indeed. Wearing only her silky peach-colored bra and panties, she reminded him of a pocket-size Venus, all soft curls, warm brown eyes and alabaster skin.

Before Becky, petite women weren't what he'd thought

of as his type. Elaina had been built much like Becky's fictional heroine, almost six feet tall and, before she'd gotten sick, generously curved. In comparison, Becky was tiny, and yet her body was perfectly proportioned, tight and toned; her breasts small but lovely, the areolas dusky pink, the nipples pronounced and, if his memory served him, ultrasensitive.

Determined to take his time, he reached up and traced the outline of her bra with a single finger, drawing a shiver. He buried his face in her cleavage and inhaled her rosemary-mint fragrance in one intoxicating breath. "God, I'd almost forgotten how good you smell, how beautiful you are."

She skimmed her soft fingers over his jaw. "You make me feel beautiful. You have ever since I met you."

He lifted his head and met her shining eyes and knew she was remembering their sexy night in New York, as he was. That night was many things in his mind, one of them a hell of a lot to live up to. His hands, warm a minute ago though they'd only just come inside, suddenly chilled to ice.

Becky must have noticed because she reached down and took his hand between her two tiny ones. "We don't have to do this, you know. If you're having second thoughts, if you don't want me—"

He cut her off with a shake of his head. "Not want you? Are you crazy? I can't stop wanting you—and don't act like that comes as some kind of big surprise, either."

Since she'd pushed her way inside his front door and back into his life, he hadn't been able to concentrate on much beyond wanting her. Coauthoring the sexy book day in and day out without being able to touch her was nothing short of torture. If he had to write one more bedroom scene for their fictional protagonists while being denied the very real pleasure of Becky's body, he'd implode.

And yet he was nervous, which at first didn't make sense. They'd had sex before, in New York, not once but several times. Between the dim lights and the drinks and the overall anonymity, the experience hadn't felt entirely real, which had made it easier for him to give himself up to the sexy, surreal moment. This time was different. This time he knew her name, the way her mind worked, and something of her heart. She wasn't a stranger anymore or an empty fantasy, either. His sexy Cinderella had become much more to him than a one-night stand and going to bed with her was going to mean something.

As if reading his mind, she said, "Things were a lot simpler when we were strangers."

"Simpler doesn't always mean better."

Rather than say more and risk breaking the mood, he unhooked the clasp at the front of her bra. Her breasts swung free, her dusky-rose-colored nipples already hard for him, which was only fair. God knew he was hard for her. He bent his head and drew one firm bud into his mouth, loving the trusting way she leaned in to him, how readily she peaked against his tongue.

She let out a low moan, one hand leaving his shoulder to slide into his hair. "Oh, God, Max, you're torturing me but don't stop. Not yet, anyway."

"Don't worry, baby. Stopping isn't anywhere on my mind. I'm just getting started." To prove it, he bent and tongued her other breast while his thumb played with the nipple that was already warm and wet and hard from the ministrations of his mouth.

Becky gasped and ran frantic fingers through his hair. "God, Max, it feels so good. *You* feel so good."

He looked up at her. "Not as good as you feel. Sometimes I catch myself staring at you and remembering how wet and tight you felt around me, and I think I'm going to explode."

"I know," she said, her pretty face flushing. "Writing those love scenes, there were times I could hardly keep myself from mounting you there in the office." She bit her lip. "I can hardly wait to take you inside me now."

They'd been stupid, stubborn fools to waste these past weeks. Determined not to waste a moment more, he slid two fingers between her parted thighs and stroked her slit through the moist silk, then bent his head and laved kisses over her mound. Inhaling her musk and heat, remembering the salty taste of her, his mouth watered and his swelling cock thrummed.

He angled his face to look up at her and slid his fingers inside her panties. "You're going to have to, for a while at least."

She was very wet and very warm, almost scalding. His digits glided inside her, her tight channel closing around him like a fist.

She gasped and ground her hips into his hand, her curls streaming over her pretty face. "Oh, God, that feels so good, so amazing."

"It's supposed to."

Buried deep inside her, he worked his fingers scissors-style, slowly at first and then increasing the tempo. Becky rocked against him, her hips matching his rhythm, her other hand cuffing the back of his neck and urging his greedy mouth to make love to her breasts.

Like a bowstring drawn tight to the point of breaking,

suddenly she snapped back, her body going rigid. "Oh, Max!" She shuddered, her release rolling through her, her tender inner flesh quivering against his cream-coated fingers.

She pulled back to look at him from beneath heavy lids. "That was so good. I can't tell you how good."

He tucked a silky brown curl behind her ear. "You don't have to tell me, baby. This isn't a scene we're writing. It's real life. And the best part is I'm nowhere near finished with you."

"You're not?" Her mocha eyes scoured his face.

"Not by a long shot. Think of this as a really fancy banquet, and we're still on the appetizer course."

Laying his hands on her slender waist, he stood and swung her around, changing places to seat her on the side of the bed. She was such a little thing, so small and light. He'd noticed that the night in New York when he'd lifted her and carried her over to the piano. Sometimes it was hard to fathom that such a tiny woman could have such force of will, such unyieldingly opinions, but over the past weeks he'd come to appreciate that about her, too.

"Oh, Max." She rested her forearms on the mattress, slipped off her panties and opened her legs for him.

Standing over her, he took a moment to appreciate the view. She was drenched, her labia rosy-pink and glistening, wetness leaking from her slit from where she'd come moments before.

He shucked off his sweater and the T-shirt beneath and then dragged over a pillow and slid it beneath her head. "You can watch me if you like. I want you to watch me." The thought of her watching while he tongued her brought on a sharp tug of desire.

Holding her gaze, he went down on his knees on the

side of the bed. He buried his head in the sweet spot between her slender white thighs and lapped the cream from her labia, then used his fingers to spread it over her clit.

Becky moaned. She lifted her head from the mattress. "Max, please, don't make me wait any longer." She sat up, then reached for his jeans' zipper and rolled it down.

He wasn't wearing briefs and his swollen cock sprang free, harder and thicker than he'd ever known it to be. When she took him in her hand, he knew he couldn't wait any longer. He reached over to pull open the night table's bottom drawer and brought out the box of condoms, one of several "supplies" he'd picked up on his last trip into town. At the time, he hadn't been sure he'd get the opportunity to break the seal on the box, but he was very glad he would.

He rolled on the prophylactic and positioned himself over her slit, sliding the sheathed tip up and down, a slow, salacious tease. She moaned, "Please," and arched up to meet him, her hands anchoring her to his hips, her nails grazing him in her eagerness.

Max didn't mind. "What do you want, baby?"

She shifted her head on the pillow and looked up at him with feral eyes. "You know what I want."

"Say it, then." His voice came out as a hoarse command.

She hesitated. "I want you…I want you inside me. I can't wait. I don't want to wait. Oh, please…"

Max didn't need to be asked again. He entered her in one smooth, clean thrust, burying himself to the root. Becky cinched her strong runner's legs around his waist and the pressure of her straining to meet him almost pushed him over the edge.

Almost. Keeping his distance, keeping his control, he

pulled out of her and entered her again, slightly harder this time. She wriggled on her bottom and begged for more, and he got a dark pleasure in going still and making her wait, making them both wait, until they were so crazy for it they wouldn't be able to get enough.

"Please, Max." Her seeking hands slipped from his hips to his backside, her soft fingers kneading his buttocks and then trailing the seam between.

He arched back and hooked her slender ankles over his shoulders, increasing the angle, the pressure, the pleasure that was almost pain. "Is this what you want, sweetheart?"

"Oh, God, yes, yes!"

He pulled out of her and sank hard fingers deeply inside her, searching out the spot he knew would drive her wild. Her sudden soft shriek told him he'd found it. Moisture slid over his fingers and rolled to the inside of his wrist. Taking away his hand, he sank his cock into her once more, her inner flesh so searing he felt sure it would melt the condom.

"Oh, God, Max!"

He knew the instant the orgasm hit her, her inner muscles milking him like a small, silk-gloved fist. Max couldn't take it anymore. He reared back and drove into her, hard and fast, full and deep, her spasms shooting them both over the edge and beyond.

"Becka!"

"YOU HAVE some crazy ideas, you know that?" Max said sometime later. They were lying in bed, and Becky had just whispered her next salacious suggestion into his ear.

It was dark outside and, book deadline or not, they'd been too lazy to get up and switch on a light. She couldn't make out his face in the shadows beyond the whites of his eyes and the gleam of his grin, but the husky timbre of his voice assured her that in this case *crazy* constituted a good thing—a *very* good thing.

She stroked a hand down the side of his lean jaw and wished to God she didn't want him quite so much. Never before had she lost such complete control of her body in bed. Could her heart be far behind? "You bring it out in me. No one ever has before."

As much as she'd steeled herself to be like Angelina and have sex like a man, with no thought for the future, no emotional investment beyond the moment, putting that plan into play was proving to be a lot harder than she'd expected. The more time she spent with Max, the more she found herself feeling.

And yet the wound from Elliot's betrayal was still more scab than fully healed scar. When she entered her next real relationship with a man, she wanted to do so as a whole, healthy, totally together person. She just wasn't there yet and, until she was, "friends with benefits" was about all she could handle. On second thought, better make that "colleagues" with benefits.

Determined to switch her busy brain back off and savor the moment as Angelina would, she turned her head to the side and laid her cheek against his broad breastbone, the taut skin at once very warm and amazingly smooth. "You're six foot three and I'm five foot one. That's more than a full foot's difference and yet we fit together, don't we?" From the photograph, his wife had looked to be a tall woman, close to Max's height.

He lifted his head from the pillow and looked down at her. "I hadn't thought much about it, but you're right. We do fit. I'd say we fit damn near perfectly. We're good together. Not just this but…well, everything."

Uh-oh. Becky held back from answering. She knew Max liked her, certainly he lusted after her, but friendship and sexual attraction didn't add up to love. And how could he love her or anyone else when he was so obviously still passionately in love with his dead wife? Not only did he keep Elaina's photograph out on his desk but he kept her snow boots in his hall closet. Who knew how many other mementos were lying about? Even if she were in the market for a committed relationship, she didn't want to settle for being somebody's rebound. She'd already spent one afternoon walking in Elaina's shoes. She didn't want a future living in the dead woman's shadow.

Her dark thoughts must have found their way to her face because he lifted his head from the pillow and asked, "Becky, what is it? What's wrong?"

So much for shutting down my mind and living in the moment. She studied the sheet in her hand, avoiding meeting his eyes. "I just don't want either of us to get too used to this, that's all."

The mattress shifted as Max sat up in bed. "So what are you saying?"

She edged her eyes up to his. Why the hell did being a grown-up have to be so hard? "Whatever this is, whatever we are right now, it's a plot twist, and a wonderful one, but the basic outline stays the same."

"Casual lovers like we were in New York, you mean? No strings, no…feelings."

Holding on to the sheet, she sat up and looked over at him. With his hair mussed and the sheet riding his waist, he looked rumpled and sexy and yes, good enough to eat.

The only thing spoiling the picture was the wounded look in his eyes.

Hating that she'd hurt his feelings, or at least his pride, she reached out and laid her hand on his bicep. "Just be my lover, Max, that's all I ask. That way when the book's finished we can go back to our lives without any hard feelings on either side. No strings, regrets and above all, no sappy goodbyes, okay?"

Glancing down at her hand banding his bicep, Max almost laughed aloud at the irony of his situation. It was shaping up to look as if Becky really wasn't that different from her character after all. Had he really survived the past year of hell and come back to life only to fall for the female equivalent of a player?

Hiding his disappointment, he reached down and covered her hand with his. "If that's the way you want it, Miss St. Claire, then once again we have a deal."

11

Angelina sat cross-legged before the campfire, naked beneath the heavy quilt. Staring into the purple and orange flames, she felt dreamy and sated and altogether unlike herself. After her near miss at the mine shaft, she and Drake had come back and made camp for the night—and love for hours. Her typical post-coital reaction after such a vigorous sexual session was to mount her motorcycle and ride off into the sunset. Instead she didn't want to move so much as a muscle.

Drake came up beside her and handed her the bottle of whiskey. "Here, love, have a drink of this. It'll warm you."

She smiled up at him. "You've already done that but thanks." Taking the bottle, she sensed something was amiss. "What is it?"

He ran a hand through his short blond hair. "Scotland Yard just rang on the mobile. The two weeks we had to track down Falco and the plans for building the next-generation missile system have been winnowed to one."

MAX AND Becky sat side-by-side on the family-room floor, toes stuck out toward the dancing flames of the fire, the printout of the first ten chapters of their book stacked on the floor between them. Red pen in hand, Becky had decided to give her eyes a rest and make the markups on the hard copy. Max sat next to her, head bent over the portable computer resting on his lap, typing out the next chapter draft. They were both trying hard to be good and work—just not quite hard enough.

Max set the laptop aside on the floor and turned to her. "Hungry?"

She nodded. "Always."

He'd left a pot of lamb stew simmering on the stove, the delicious aroma floating down to tickle Becky's nostrils, a far cry from the frozen dinners she was used to eating back home. Since she'd shown up on Max's doorstep, he'd spoiled her with his dinners and his back-rub breaks and yes, his lovemaking. She was going to miss all of it once she went back home but mostly she was going to miss him. Her boyfriends before Elliot had, for the most part, been nice enough guys but there'd either been a sexual spark with little in common, or a lot in common with next to no spark. With Max, there was an abundance of both. It was really too bad she'd met him sooner rather than later. Once she was ready for a real relationship, she couldn't imagine finding a man to match him.

Reaching over, he took her chin between his thumb and finger and turned her face toward him. "Me, too, though not for stew."

He traced the outline of her bottom lip with the pad of his thumb, making her shiver. Running it along the seam of her lips, he teased them apart.

Torn between needing to be good and wanting to be bad, she shook her head, feeling as if a tiny devil was perched on her one shoulder and an equally tiny angel on the other. "You're determined to distract me, aren't you?"

"Uh-huh." He slid the edge of his thumb inside. "How am I doing, by the way?"

"Pretty good." Better than good. The devil was definitely winning the upper hand.

"Just pretty good?"

"Okay, very good. But you should stop."

Blue eyes brushed over her face. "It doesn't feel good?"

She started to answer, and he seized the chance to slide the tip of his thumb inside her mouth and then out. "Because—because we're supposed to be working."

He smiled his warm smile, gaze riveted on her mouth. "In that case, think of it as research."

"Research, huh?" Giving up, she set the papers aside and reached for him, her hands sliding atop his shoulders, loving the strong, solid feel of him beneath her fingertips. "I usually rely on Internet search engines and books for that."

He grinned. "See, that's another area where we differ. Me, I'm into experiential learning. You might even say I'm a hands-on kind of guy."

He leaned in and kissed her. His warm tongue tasted spicy from the mulled cider they'd drunk earlier. He slid it between her lips as he had his thumb. "Sorry." Pulling back, he looked anything but. "There I go kissing you again, but how can I help it? You're very kissable."

"I am, am I?" She met his teasing smile with one of her own.

"Uh-huh. And you taste amazing." The wicked look in his eye hinted he wasn't only talking about her mouth.

A moment later he confirmed that by sliding a hand between them and palming her through her jeans. Becky sucked in her breath. At this point, the angel was out of the picture—completely.

"Three guesses where I'm thinking of kissing you next." His hand's slow, kneading strokes seared through the denim, bringing moisture pooling into her panties.

"Is it lower than my mouth?"

"Uh-huh."

"My breasts, then?" she asked, warming to the game.

He lifted his other hand and cupped her with a slight squeeze. "You do have beautiful breasts. I want to kiss them, too, but in this case I'm thinking even lower."

"Lower?"

His fingers went to the zipper of her jeans. Holding her gaze, he tugged the zipper down. "I want to kiss you there, right there. In fact, I could lick and tongue you all night, starting right now."

She leaned back against the side of the sofa, opening her legs. "We don't have all night. We have a book to write, remember?"

"I remember. But you know what they say about all work and no play." He slid two fingers inside her open jeans and slid them along her damp, lace-covered crotch.

Becky's breath hitched. She tilted back her head, a hairbreadth from coming. "Let me guess. It makes Becky a dull girl?"

"Uh-huh. And it makes Max a very frustrated boy."

The office phone rang like a siren. Looking at each other, they shared a collective groan. Max rolled to his knees, resting back on his heels. "I should pick up. Not too many people have that number. It must be important." He glanced at the manuscript she'd set aside. "Keep working so we can play when I get back."

"Sounds like a deal," she said though she seriously doubted she could focus now.

Watching his sexy, jeans-clad butt walking away, she held in a sigh. Distractions aside, in another few weeks the book would be done and there would be no real reason for her to stay on. Having a built-in relationship expiration date rendered every second of every minute they spent together infinitely precious. Instead of wondering where their relationship was headed and fretting over the future as she always had before, she could let down her guard and live in the moment.

Sexually she'd never been able to let go like this before, not even with Elliot. Her ex had kept her on such an emotional roller coaster straight from the start that it hadn't been easy to relax with him in or out of bed. Lately she'd caught herself thinking that what Max and she shared might be the real deal, not just a fling. But then, blurring the line between fantasy and reality was an occupational hazard of fiction writing that had cost her big-time. She'd spent months deluding herself into believing Elliot loved her back, not to mention dealing with the financial fallout of having quit her job. Max seemed as different from her ex as day was from night, but having made such a huge mistake in judgment once—and not all that long ago—how could she trust herself to know for sure?

Max's return brought her out of her musing. "That was Pat. She says they need the book a month earlier."

Still struggling with her dilemma, Becky took a moment

to absorb the news. Once she did, the jolt hit hard. "That's crazy, maybe even impossible."

Max heaved a sigh. "Not impossible, but I agree, crazy."

"Why the rush?"

"She found out through the publishing grapevine that a project being touted as the next big action-adventure blockbuster book is coming out around the same time as ours. Even though the mystery and erotica components set our story somewhat apart, she doesn't want us to have to face that kind of stiff competition for the lists. If we can get this in by the end of next week, we might have a decent shot at beating them to the shelves—and the top ten."

"She really thinks our book has bestseller potential?"

"She knows it does, and so do I. Don't you?"

Becky hesitated. Like any other writer, she'd had her share of bestseller fantasies but before now, she'd been content simply to be able to support herself with her writing. Since teaming with Max, she'd found herself reaching for the stars on a daily basis. It was scary to build up her hopes that high, but it was exciting, too—an adventure.

"What did you tell her?"

She was almost afraid to hear his answer. Of course they'd do their utmost to make the new deadline. With so much riding on this project, what choice did they have? Still, if he'd signed them up for what promised to be two weeks of hell, two weeks of too much coffee and too little sleep, without talking to her first, she was going to be really, really pissed.

"I told her I'd talk it over with you, and we'd get back to her in the morning."

We. She liked the sound of that. "Thank you."

He sent her a questioning look. "For what?"

Smiling, she held his gaze for a long moment. "For being my partner."

MAX SAT at the computer, putting the final spit and polish on chapter fifteen of the novel's twenty chapters. They were down to the wire, with just another few days to go, but fortunately the manuscript was close to complete. There was the one fight scene yet to rework with a secondary character added in, but overall the manuscript was in good shape. He calculated they were another day from finishing. If they kept the momentum up, they might even wrap things up later that night. If so, not only would they have met the Deadline from Hell but beaten it by a day.

Even in its current form, the book was the best thing he'd ever written. He knew the cause, of course. Becky. The chemistry between them was coming out in their two main characters in a major way. The sex scenes between Drake and Angelina sizzled, but so did the rest of the manuscript. Reading over the working draft, he found himself agreeing with Pat. The book had movie deal written all over it. The downside was that the sooner they finished, the sooner Becky would be leaving. It was crazy but these last few days he'd caught himself coming up with distractions to draw the writing out.

Max ran a hand through his hair. It felt slightly greasy but then he hadn't showered since the morning of the day before. His legs were stiff and the small of his back pounded as if someone was hitting it with a hammer. He thought of the all-nighters he'd pulled back in college and grad school and then those a few years back when he'd sat up with Elaina and shook his head. If he'd gone looking for a custom-made reminder he wasn't a kid anymore, this was it.

"Okay, let me try this out on you. What do you think about Angelina…"

He stopped when she didn't immediately answer. By now he knew she wasn't shy about jumping in. It wasn't like her not to have an opinion, especially where her fictional creation was concerned.

"Becka?" He turned to look at her over his shoulder.

She was asleep. Curled up on her side on his leather office couch, her delicate hands tucked beneath her head, she looked serene and lovely and innocent, the throw blanket slipping off her shoulder. This was his golden opportunity to shape the book without consultation or compromise, and yet at some point over the past few weeks he'd gotten used to doing both. It wasn't that he didn't trust his talent or his writer's instincts—he did. The thing was, he'd grown comfortable working as part of a team. More than comfortable, he'd grown to like it—a lot.

He crossed the room and went down on one knee beside the couch. Laying a light hand on her shoulder, he said, "Hey, sleepyhead, rise-and-shine time. We have a book to get out."

She cracked open an eye and looked up at him. "I guess I fell asleep, huh?"

"Yeah I guess so, and I need to pick that plotting brain of yours. Our characters are trapped in that collapsed mine shaft and time and air are running out. There's a crawl space at the top. The air will last longer if there's only one of them there."

She pulled herself up on her forearms, caramel-colored curls streaming her face. "Okay, give me a sec to wake up, and then I'm on it."

"You got it." He kissed the tip of her nose.

Feeling as stiff-legged as Scout, he got up and crossed over to the computer. Once she got up from the couch, he might trade places with her. He could use a power nap himself. In the interim, he reached for the remote and switched on the TV. One of the drawbacks of a tight deadline was that complete immersion in the work meant cutting oneself off from the outside world. He hadn't read a newspaper or watched television in days. For all he knew, North Korea could have conquered the world.

He found a cable news program in progress and stopped surfing. Hoping to gather the highlights, he settled back in his desk chair to watch. The anchor was asking his guest, a good-looking gray-haired man in a dark suit, to weigh in on the issue du jour, something to do with subway safety in the context of the latest terrorism threat. The camera panned over to the guest commentator for a close-up. The guy's lean, youngish face, deep-set dark eyes and broad shoulders filled the TV's flat screen. Max couldn't think of his name, but he'd seen him from time to time on similar programs as a consultant or special guest. Whoever he was, he was an authority in his field—some kind of counterterrorism work. For whatever reason, he'd always struck Max as a little too sure of himself, a little too smooth.

Staring straight at the camera, he addressed the host. "As I was saying to Katie Couric over coffee just the other day, since 9/11 the Feds and law enforcement have made enormous strides in ensuring that transportation security is tighter, and the public is safer than ever before. That's *ever*, Doug. But in a free society such as ours, there's always going to be some level of threat…"

Jesus, what a name dropper. Max would bet anything that off camera he was a first-class prick. He picked up the remote to switch channels but before he could, Becky shoved the quilt aside and marched across the room.

She punched the off button on the set and swung around to face him, eyes glittering in her very flushed face. "Is it possible to have some peace and quiet to work in around here or is that asking too much?"

Max looked over at her, wondering what her problem was. Ordinarily she preferred writing with the television or music playing in the background. "You must have woken up on the wrong side of the couch. What was that about?"

She shook her head, gaze sliding away. "I'm just worried about finishing on time, that's all. Sorry."

He got up to stand beside her. Touching her arm, he realized she was shaking. "Why is it I don't think that is all?"

She shrugged and fixed her gaze on the computer behind him. And suddenly it struck him. Gray hair. Lean face. Dark, deep-set eyes. All-black wardrobe. Explosives expert.

He shot his gaze to her face. "That guy on the TV is Falco, isn't he?"

Her eyes flashed open. She bit her bottom lip. "Don't be ridiculous. Falco is a composite character. I'm a fiction writer. I make up stuff all the time. That's what we do, remember?"

"Sorry, Becka, but I'm not buying." He shook his head, wishing he could get himself to the studio in New York where the program was being broadcast from in time to plow his fist into the cocky bastard's face. "Ever since I first met you, I've had a gut sense that some jerk must have burned you pretty badly and then reading your last book confirmed it. Angelina is obsessed with Falco."

"She is not." She shook her head, though she still

couldn't look at him. "You're letting your imagination run away with you."

Max hesitated. They should be having this conversation with both of them fully awake and fully functioning, not buzzing on caffeine and adrenaline and the effects of sleep deprivation. And yet, who knew when he'd get another shot? Right now she was still sticking to her plan to leave in another week. This might be his one chance—make that his dazzling opportunity—to break through to her. Once he did, maybe he could change her mind about leaving. It was worth a try. Whoever this former G-man jerk was, it was obvious he'd hurt her badly. To react so strongly, she must still have feelings for him.

Pushing jealousy to the back of his mind for now, he said, "Come on, Becka, let it out. You'll feel a hell of a lot better afterward. Trust me, I know."

She looked at him, the raw misery in her eyes tugging at his heart. "I don't know what you're talking about. There's nothing to let out."

He blew out a breath. She was a tough nut to crack, that was for damned sure. "Lying to me is bad enough but lying to yourself is a whole lot worse."

"I'm not lying to anybody."

"In that case, look me in the eye." When she still wouldn't, he grabbed hold of her shoulders. He brought his face down and rested his forehead against hers, willing her to see how much she meant to him, how much he…loved her.

Christ, he loved her, he really did. When they'd first met, he'd lusted after her and in the course of the past weeks of writing he'd grown to like her a lot, so much so that he'd admitted he wanted her in his life and not just as a writing partner. But love, well, that was a hell of a big deal. After Elaina, he hadn't been able to imagine himself ever loving another woman again. Loving somebody made you vulnerable, it made you raw. Practically speaking, loving a woman still so obviously hung up on her ex wasn't the brightest of moves and yet here he stood with his heart on his sleeve, head-over-heels smitten. Over the past weeks, his sexy Cinderella had gotten under his skin—and penetrated straight to his heart.

Pulling back to look down at her, he prayed he wouldn't do or say anything to wreck his already slender chances. "I love you, Becka. I don't know what that jerk did to make you this way, but I'm going to find a way to break down that goddamned wall you've built up around yourself if it's the last thing I do."

She lifted haunted eyes to his face. "I can't let myself love you or anybody right now. I'm sorry but I just can't. Somebody did hurt me, really badly, and I can't risk letting that happen again. I want to believe that you're different, that we're different, but I just don't know how to tell for sure."

Max pulled her closer, willing her to melt into him. "This is the real thing. I know it. I can *feel* it. All you have to do is let go and let yourself love me back. Let go, Becka. I'll be here to catch you, I promise."

Holding her flush against his chest, he could feel the tension in every rigid muscle. To hell with the book. If need be, he'd set aside the day and make love to her until she not only saw how much he loved her but felt it, too.

Mouth pressed to her ear, he said, "I'm not going to hurt you, Becka, and I'm not going to walk away, no matter how hard you push me. Let me love you, Becka. Give me a shot at least. If I screw up, at least it's my screwup and not payback for some other guy's mistakes."

"I'm sorry, I can't." She shoved against his chest with both hands.

He dropped his arms to his sides. "Becka, wait."

Shaking her head, she backed away toward the door. Reaching it, she turned and tore out of the room. It took all Max's force of will not to go after her. In the back of his mind, he remembered an old saying, a favorite of Elaina's.

If you love something set it free. If it comes back, it's yours. If it doesn't, it never was.

Standing in the middle of the study, he asked himself how something as beautiful and basic to human nature as loving someone could be so complicated, so hard.

RENTAL-CAR keys in hand, Becky got as far as the gravel lot before the episode in the study sank in. She swung around to look back up at the house—Max's house. Over the past weeks it had become more of a home to her than she'd ever had before, and not because she liked big, sprawling rooms with timbered ceilings and pine paneling.

Max loved her. He'd said so, not only with his mouth but with his beautiful blue eyes—tender, earnest, loving. Max loved her. And, she saw with thunderbolt clarity, she loved him back. Loving him wasn't something she had to work on. It wasn't something she had to try harder to do. She loved him, she just did, and every error in judgment she'd ever made in the past, Elliot included, paled in comparison to the blazing brilliance of that beautifully simple fact. Her sexy Prince Charming from midtown hadn't just captured her heart. He'd made her trust in love again, and beyond that, in herself.

Retracing her steps up the path, she wondered what he must think of her—emotional basket case, high-maintenance lay or psycho girlfriend? Given the way she'd run for the hills, she wouldn't blame him if he told her to just forget it. There was only one way to find out.

Inside the house, she didn't bother with hanging up her coat. Walking into the study, she stopped in the doorway, one foot inside, the other still in the hallway, a fitting metaphor for how she'd approached their relationship until now.

Max sat on the side of the sofa. He looked up, his eyes holding a silent question.

Hands shoved in her coat pockets, Becky hesitated. She'd never been good with talking about her emotions and since the Elliot episode she'd bottled up her feelings even tighter. But looking into the twin pools of Max's weary blue eyes, she told herself that this time, with this man, it was okay—safe—to let go and fall in.

"I love you, too."

His eyes widened and then brightened. "Wow, you romance writers don't waste time with lead-ins or segues, do you?" He got up and started toward her.

Becky reached out a hand to hold him off. "Before you say anything more, you need to know what you're getting into."

He halted in midstep, expression turning wary. "All right. It's not going to change a damned thing, at least not on my end, but go on."

She bowed her head, unsure of where to begin, or even how. "His name is Elliot Marsh."

Becky stopped to swallow back the lump building in her throat. This was hard, so hard, but not because she was still in love with Elliot. She wasn't, she knew now. But looking into Max's face and seeing the honest love shining forth from his clear blue eyes, it hurt to think she'd once been willing, make that *desperate* enough, to settle for so very much less.

Clearing her throat, she continued, "I met him through a friend at the consulting firm in D.C. where I worked. He's a media consultant for a major television network now, but he used to work for the Feds. He comes into Washington once or twice a month, or at least he used to. There was a spark between us and he was, well, very complimentary." Now that she'd taken the lid off her personal Pandora's Box, she couldn't seem to stop the bottled-up feelings from spilling out. "We had this amazing weekend—well, more like an amazing thirty-six hours—and I thought, 'This is it, what I've been searching for all my adult life, romance like I'd dreamed about ever since I read my first Gothic novel in middle school.'"

He kept his distance, but his gaze held hers. "He played you, led you on." It wasn't a question.

She hesitated. "Looking back, it was more like *I* led me on."

Wow, another revelation. Until now, she'd chalked the episode up to poor judgment. Now she saw that her need to feel loved, to feel special rather than lost in the crowd, had been a big part of it, too.

"There were plenty of signs from the beginning. I just didn't want to see them. He asked me to move out to L.A. with him and said I should start thinking about what kind of engagement ring I wanted and whether to get married on the east coast or the west. I even let him talk me into quitting my consulting job. He said if I wanted to make it as a writer, I had to really focus on my craft. He certainly acted like he was willing to support us both."

He stood and crossed the carpet toward her. "What happened?"

"He dumped me. No Dear Jane e-mail or phone call or any explanation. One day he just showed up in D.C. at what had been our favorite restaurant with a twentysomething blonde on his arm. I guess he decided it was time to trade up."

"Not up but down." He took a step toward her and reached for her hands. "You're a knockout, Becka. Any man with half a brain would be proud to be with you. I know I am. You're also funny and smart and talented and kind. Anyone who can't see that must have blinders on— and that includes you. As for Elliot, I don't know what his problem was. Personally, I've always had a thing for grown-up women. I'm just weird that way." He lifted her chin with the edge of his hand.

"I like that you're weird that way. I more than like it. I meant what I said. I really love you, Max."

Now that she'd put herself out there and said it, *really* said it, the sense of relief was enormous. Tears filled her eyes and spilled over to trickle down her cheeks.

Gaze tender, Max swiped the pad of his thumb over the wetness. "After Elaina died, I thought I could never love someone again."

"And now?"

He didn't hesitate. "Elaina will always hold a very special place in my memory and my heart, but my time with her is in the past. My present and my future are with you."

Becky felt as though she'd stepped inside a romance novel or better yet, a fairy tale, only the love in Max's eyes when he looked into hers was one-hundred-percent real. She launched herself into his arms, wrapping hers about him as tightly as she could. "Oh, Max, I've loved you ever since I fell head over heels for you on that sidewalk in midtown—even before you rescued my shoe. I just didn't trust myself to believe it before. I was so afraid of messing up again and getting hurt."

"What about now?"

She lifted her head from his chest and looked up at him. Her gaze met his and she steeled herself to take that age-old leap of faith, trusting that he would be waiting on the other side to catch her. "It's taken me a while to get there, but I can finally trust myself to know a good thing, and a good man, when I see him—and I'm looking at him right now."

"In that case, Cinderella, shut up and kiss me."

Max leaned in and covered her mouth with his. His lips, soft and gentle, brushed over hers, his tongue sliding between her parted lips to touch hers. Though they'd kissed countless times before, somehow this felt like the very first.

Holding her face between his hands, he ended the kiss. Smiling down at her, he asked, "You know what I want to do right now?"

Feeling breathless and light-headed as any storybook princess kissed awake by her Prince Charming after a centuries-long sleep, Becky shook her head. "I could probably guess, but tell me."

His smile broadened into a grin. "I want to take you upstairs and take your clothes off piece by piece and make love to you as slowly and as sweetly as either of us can stand. How does that sound to you?"

"Like a sexy fairy tale come true." She glanced over to the computer, their current chapter filling the monitor. "But can we spare the time? We did leave Drake and Angelina in kind of a bind."

"Let them figure it out for themselves. They need to learn to be more independent, anyway." Taking her face between his hands, he leaned in. "Right now, I'm all about the muse."

12

Drake swung one leg over the side of the camp bed. He had one foot on the dirt-packed floor when Angelina called him back. "Lie here and be still with me."

They'd been on a near death march for days now, stopping only long enough to snatch a few hours of sleep before dawn broke again. The success of their mission depended on their reaching Toro Toro in the next twenty-four hours, recovering the stolen plans, and getting the hell out of there.

Thinking he must have misheard her, Drake looked over his shoulder and asked, "Come again?"

Angelina swallowed hard, the ripple traveling along the elegant column of her bare throat. "We can carry on with the business of conquering evil and reclaiming the stolen missile plans and saving the free world in another moment or so. For now, though, just lie here and be still with me."

FACING EACH OTHER in Max's bed, Max carried Becky's hand to his mouth and pressed a kiss to the sensitive spot inside her wrist, smiling when she shivered. She had more erogenous zones than any woman he'd ever known—and he didn't think he'd ever get tired of hunting for more.

But unfortunately they had a book to finish. With regret, he reached to pull the covers down and get up. "We should probably get back to our characters. Time's running out for them and us."

Throwing a shapely leg possessively over him to keep him there, she slid her hand slowly down his chest to his stomach and then beneath the sheet. "I think you should stay right here and make love to me again. I vote for that." She wrapped her small hand about his shaft and slid it slowly up and down.

Throbbing against her palm, Max blew out a breath, about a minute away from losing his willpower and his work ethic. "Unfortunately, we have a manuscript to finish." With regret, he eased her hand away. Looking down at his erection tenting the sheet, he said, "We'll save this for later. Think of it as our motivation to churn out those final chapters. You get some rest. I'll come wake you up when it's your shift."

She slid a hand to the side of his jaw. Brushing her mouth over his, she said, "Write fast, Max. Write really fast."

SHRUGGING into his shirt, Max opened the door and stepped out into the hallway. Given the breakneck schedule they'd been on, he couldn't resist letting Becky sleep for a few more hours. Since the call from Pat, they'd been working crazy hours and earlier he'd seen her pressing a hand to her lower back as though it hurt. Back pain was an occupational hazard of writing. She needed the sleep more than he did. While she rested, he'd get to work on the scenes they'd agreed in advance he would take the first crack at writing. By the time she got up, he'd be able to turn them over to her for editing and catch some shut-eye himself. Once they'd gotten into tag-team mode, the writing had gone a lot faster. He'd been so sure when it came to his work that he was a solo act, but writing was turning out to be a pretty good metaphor for life overall.

It was easier to get through with a partner.

Before Becky, he always thought the next woman in his life, assuming there was one, would be a facsimile of Elaina. Another tall, big-boned girl with soulful dark eyes and a messy mane of dark hair. Becky was petite, blond, and about as all-American as they came. Elaina had favored oversized sweaters, no-nonsense jeans, and sensible shoes. Becky was into couture clothing and designer footwear. Elaina's temperament had been placid as a midsummer sky. Becky's was more like that summer sky once it had split with the first thunderbolt of an unexpected storm. Elaina had accepted him for who he was.

Becky challenged him to become all the things he'd yet to be.

THEY FINISHED the manuscript around noon the next day. Seated at the keyboard, Max hesitated, the cursor hovering above the send button that, once struck, would catapult their manuscript into cyberspace and land it in Pat's e-mail in-box in a matter of moments.

He turned to his pretty coauthor. Even running on empty, she was a sight for sore—*really* sore—eyes. "You should do the honors."

Becky stood behind him, hands clenching the computer chair, a lump in her throat. Funny how she was experiencing none of the adrenaline rush that always came with completing a manuscript. If anything she felt oddly reluctant to let the book go, a first for her. Though Max had said he loved her, and she loved him, she wasn't yet sure what that meant. They were two very different people who'd carved out distinct lives for themselves. How those lives would mesh once the book collaboration was out of the picture remained to be seen.

She stepped back from the computer, willing herself to shake the negative thoughts from her head. If nothing else, the past few weeks of fresh starts and dazzling opportunities should have taught her to trust in the universe—and herself.

"No, thanks. You go ahead."

Max twisted his head around to look back at her over the shelf of one muscular shoulder. "You're sure?"

After making love earlier, he'd collapsed on the office couch for some much-needed sleep. The side of his face still bore creases from the imprint of the couch pillow and the back of his hair stood up in a cowlick worthy of Dennis the Menace. Becky thought he looked amazing.

Becky nodded. "Yes, I'm sure."

Max clicked Send. Seconds later Drake and Angelina and Falco and all the rest were hurtling into cyberspace. Exchanging first high fives and then congratulatory kisses, their creators went back to bed.

BECKY WAS still sleeping the next morning when Pat called to say she'd read the book in one four-hour marathon sitting and had loved it. There'd be a few minor editorial changes coming, mostly fluff stuff, but otherwise it was as pristinely perfect a manuscript draft as she'd ever seen. In fact, she'd already passed it to the bigwigs upstairs and the in-house buzz was building at breakneck pace. It seemed the powers that be were willing to front list the book, which meant putting major promo dollars behind it.

The second call came an hour later from Harry on the home line. Max ran to answer it, hoping to intercept the phone before it woke Becky. Harry might be an A-list agent, but he couldn't seem to hire a decent receptionist to save his life. Whoever he sat out front always managed to mix Max's office and home numbers up.

Busy picking up several days' worth of collected clutter, he switched the call to speakerphone. "Hey, Harry, what's up?"

"I have great news, Maxie. I just got a call from my coagent out in L.A. I sent him a copy of your manuscript." Harry's voice was jubilant.

"You mean Rebecca's and mine," Max corrected.

"Whatever. I can't say much, we're at a very preliminary stage of the negotiation, but you should know that a major Hollywood production company is considering optioning it for a motion picture film. We're talking bigscreen, Max, and that means big bucks."

This was just the break Becky's career needed. More thrilled for her than himself, Max answered, "That's fabulous. Becky's sleeping right now, but this definitely merits a wake-up call."

"Not so fast. For the moment, let sleeping dogs—or in this case, coauthors—lie. If the deal goes through, and it will, the producers want you to write the screenplay solo."

Max hesitated. Dialogue was more Becky's strength than his. "I'm a novelist, not a screenplay writer."

"So you'll learn. They'll assign you a cowriter behind the scenes to show you the ropes."

"What about Becky?"

"Do not fret, my friend. Rebecca St. Claire is history. We couldn't do anything about the coauthorship on the novel, that's a done deal, but you have my personal guarantee you will never have to coauthor anything, including the Drake and Angelina screenplay, with that woman ever again."

Max snatched up the receiver. "Are you saying you've found a way to cut Becky out of the screenplay deal?"

Harry hesitated. "She will be compensated for creative translation of her character to film, of course, but that's the tip of the iceberg, a small piece of the pie. You won't have to worry about her ever again. You don't have to thank me, Maxie, it's the least I can do."

Max held the phone away from his ear, feeling sick inside. The very last thing he'd wanted his agent to do was cut out Becky.

"Why am I not hearing champagne corks popping, huh? I thought you would be pleased."

"I'll have to call you back. In the meantime, you should know that unless the screenplay deal is revised to include Becky as coauthor, there is no deal. Got it?"

"But Maxie—"

Max hung up. A month ago Harry's news would have shot him clear over the moon but not so now. He would refuse, of course. In the interim, he didn't want Becky to find out. She'd really pushed the envelope on her writing these past weeks, not to mention taught him a thing or two. She felt deservedly good about the book they'd sent in, and he didn't want anything to wreck that for her. He'd fix things behind the scenes so that when the screenplay deal came around, she'd be a full partner. A Hollywood screenplay would open up a world of new contacts for them both.

Another coauthorship would, of course, require they continue to spend time together. So far, neither of them had broached the sticky subject of when Becky was leaving—

or when she might be coming back. He wasn't really interested in living in D.C. but he remembered her mentioning her family was in Maryland. He didn't yet know how important it was for her to stay near her relatives and friends. On the positive side, she no longer had her consulting career tying her to the area, but she still wasn't crazy about cold weather or the countryside. Who knew? Maybe they'd split the difference and get an apartment in Manhattan? He could hold on to his house in New Hampshire as a weekend and holiday retreat. The dog would miss running off leash outside but then again the old guy didn't move so fast or so far anymore. Becky had a cat, and Max wasn't thrilled about that but he wasn't allergic. Somehow they'd all learn to adjust.

Max stopped himself when he realized he was picking out honeymoon locations and naming their two point five children. Before he planned any further, he should probably consult his sexy partner. The new year had brought a bounty of fresh starts and dazzling opportunities, not just for Becky but for them both. It was like coming downstairs on Christmas morning as a kid and having so many presents under the tree to unwrap you didn't know where to start. Having too many wonderful choices was the sort of "problem" Max was happy to have.

BECKY HUNG UP the phone in her bedroom, Max's betrayal ringing in her ears. After hearing him say "Are you saying you've found a way to cut Becky out of the screenplay deal?" she'd quietly replaced the cordless in its cradle. She didn't need to hear any more to know that Max had sold her out.

A few weeks ago, she wouldn't have been all that shocked. He was the bestselling author, after all, and as an up-and-comer she'd heard the horror stories. It wasn't unheard of for a big-name author to steal work from someone lesser known.

But that was before they'd made love and it had meant something, before she'd poured her heart out to him about her failed relationship and stupid mistakes, before he'd wiped away her tears and kissed her lips and told her how much he loved her. If she hadn't just heard him say the damning words with her own ears, she never would have believed it.

Hearing footsteps coming up the stairs, she snatched up a book and moved away from the phone to the rocking chair by the window. He entered her darkened bedroom a few minutes later. "I'm sorry if that phone call woke you up."

Closing the book she was pretending to read, she said, "That's okay. I was awake anyway. Who was it?" Out of the corner of her eye, she kept close watch on his face.

"No one really."

"No one?"

She turned to look at him, her heart turning over at the slick ease with which he lied to her just like…Elliot. Her former lover, she felt sure, wouldn't hesitate to steal someone's glory. It seemed that once again her judgment had failed her. Though they looked and behaved very differently, both men were cut from the same cloth.

He shrugged, but she didn't miss how he couldn't look her in the eye. "You know telemarketers. There's no getting off the phone with them. It's probably just better to hang up."

"Yeah, I guess so."

"I'm going to drive into town for groceries. We're down

to our last egg and Scout's kibble bag is scraping bottom. You want to come? Lunch at the truck stop, all the blue plate specials you can eat on me. Surely you can't resist an offer like that." Max winked at her, and Becky felt as though an invisible razor were slashing at her heart.

"No, thanks. I think I'll hang out here and take a bath."

He stopped in his tracks and turned around. "You okay?"

"Sure, why?"

"You don't seem like yourself."

Look who was talking. "I guess these late nights are finally catching up with me."

He crossed the room to her, stopping behind her chair. "Okay, you rest up. I'll be back in a couple of hours and then we'll celebrate—really celebrate—okay?" He leaned in to kiss her, but she turned away at the last minute. His lips met her cheek instead.

Pulling back, he looked down on her and asked again, "You sure you're okay?"

"Positive."

This was worse than her restaurant run-in with Elliot. She'd realized now she'd only been infatuated with him. She'd fallen in love with Max. And once again she'd placed her trust—and her heart—in the hands of the wrong man. Would she never learn?

The crunch of Max's car tires on the gravel drive had her adrenaline kicking in. She jumped out of the chair and rushed to the window in time to see him back out of the drive, leaving her own snow-covered car behind. Thank God she'd held on to her rental, otherwise she'd be stuck. Heart thudding, she turned her attention to packing. Fortunately she didn't have much beyond the outfits she'd brought for her overnight New York stay and the few essentials she'd picked up over the past month, an extra pair of jeans and some toiletry products. The fancy shoes from Saks, including her Cinderella slippers, took up most of the space in her suitcase. Picking out one of the pair, she zipped up her suitcase and headed downstairs to Max's study.

He'd left his notepad by the computer. Tears welling, she bent over to write her farewell note.

Max,
Congratulations on the screenplay deal. Just so you know, you don't have to bother getting your agent to work any behind-the-scenes deals to cut me out. I'm cutting myself out. I never want to work with you again. I never want to see you again—period.
 If the shoe fits…
Becky

Becky backed out of the room, leaving the note and the high-heeled red slipper on Max's chair.

13

Angelina strapped on her helmet and zipped the front of her Belstaff jacket before mounting her bike—a 1974 Ducati Imola 750 she'd picked up the day before. The vintage bike was her reward for another mission accomplished. It hadn't been easy but she and Drake had reclaimed the rocket plans and gotten out of Toro Toro amidst heavy enemy fire and copious explosions. The papers now resided in a vault in an undisclosed and highly secure government location.

She swung her leg over the side of the bike and revved the engine. It roared to life and seconds later she was zipping through the winding Venetian streets, long black hair lashing the arid Italian air like a dragon's tail. Only, instead of contemplating her next erotic encounter and mystery-solving adventure, she found herself wondering about Drake. Where was he? Did he ever think of her?

Was he…happy?

Wrong, wrong, wrong!

Becky stared at her laptop screen through bleary eyes. She'd rewritten the first fifty pages of her new book so many times over the past month, she felt as if she'd come full circle. No matter which version of the manuscript she picked up, the prose was the pits. Falling in love had softened Angelina so that she'd lost her edge. Instead of planning her next solo adventure, she was preoccupied with missing Drake. It was pathetic.

Exhausted as she was, Becky had to get out of the apartment, if only for a little while. Maybe a jolt of caffeine would help. "I'm out of here," she said to no one in particular.

"Well, if you're going to mope, then good riddance."

She swung around to find Angelina perched on the edge of her kitchen counter, long legs tucked beneath her. Wearing an oversized cashmere sweater with Diesel Super Slim stretch jeans, she was her usual fashion-forward self down to her Manolo leopard-print pumps. Still, something seemed different…missing.

"Who's moping? I was just going out for a walk." Even though she had one foot out the door, she slipped back into her computer chair. They hadn't had a creator-character heart-to-heart in a very long time. Judging from her muse's pout, Becky had been neglecting her, among other things. "How have you been, by the way?"

Angelina put on her game face and smiled. "I'm brilliant, absolutely brilliant. Where are you sending me on my next adventure, by the way?"

"Honestly I have no idea," Becky answered.

The pisser was she really didn't. She was burned out on planning exotic adventures for fictional characters. "Any place in particular you'd like to go?"

Angelina let out a sigh. "I'm bored to death of Italy, France and England, and the Greek Isles have been done to death. I used to have a fancy for Malta but…I don't bloody care, Rebecca. You decide."

Uh-oh. Angelina not having an opinion was a huge red flag that something must be really wrong. Becky gave her creation the once-over, struck by how much Angelina had altered in one month. Her upswept eyes looked more muddy than jade, there were dark, puffy circles beneath, and her waist-length hair lacked its usual luster. Becky recognized this as the face of a woman who'd come out on the wrong side of love.

"If you'll pardon my saying so, you don't look so good. You're missing Drake, aren't you?"

Angelina snapped up her head, but this once her curtain of hair failed to fall back perfectly around her shoulders. "Don't be absurd, Rebecca. You're the one who's pining, not me."

"Is that so? There's no point in trying to pull the wool over my eyes. I created you, remember?" If you couldn't have a frank talk with your own fictional creation, what was the world coming to?

The corners of Angelina's sensuous mouth dipped down. "Why did you do it, Rebecca?"

"Why did I do what?"

"Ruin everything by giving me a soul." Angelina tossed Becky an exasperated look. "Bugger! Things were good for us before Drake and Max came on the scene. We were free to come and go as we pleased, we could shop until we dropped, come in at any hour of the day or night, sleep with anyone we fancied—well, *I* could, at least. But no, you had to tinker with perfection. You had to open Pandora's bloody Box and introduce soul mates into our lives, and now look what we've come to."

Becky hesitated. "Do you really think Max and Drake are our soul mates?"

Angelina lifted one perfectly-plucked eyebrow and regarded her. "You ought to know the answer to that, Rebecca. After all, you wrote the book."

I WROTE the book, I wrote the book, I wrote…

The butting against the top of her head brought Becky out of the dream. It took several seconds before she realized she must have fallen asleep at her computer. She lifted her head from her folded arms and looked straight into Daisy Bud's amber-colored eyes. From her perch atop Becky's computer cart, the cat leaned in and nuzzled her neck.

Becky reached out and scratched the cute little white spot beneath Daisy's chin. "Sometimes I wish you could talk—people talk, I mean. The whole spaying incident aside, I bet you'd be a pretty damn good relationship advisor. You always manage to get exactly what you want out of me while giving back so much more."

Back in D.C. and with Sharon gone home to Fredericksburg, Becky ought to be a lean mean *writing* machine. Instead she'd found it really hard to focus. She couldn't seem to get Max out of her mind. The other day, she'd had the radio on when the DJ had played Billy Joel's "New York State of Mind." She'd thrown it into the nearest wall and cried for a solid hour.

From a career standpoint, though, everything seemed to be working out for the best. Thrilled with the coauthored book, Pat had offered her a contract for a spin-off series on far better terms than anything she'd had previously. Provided she could meet the demanding deadline

schedule—and without Max in her life, what else did she
have to do but write?—Becky would be a guaranteed bestseller in her own right. She wouldn't need Adam Maxwell
any more than he apparently needed her.

The problem was she'd liked having a partner, or rather,
having Max for a partner. Working on the next Angelina
book without him and his character was turning out to be
hell on wheels. No matter how hard she tried coming up
with a new love interest for her heroine, she simply
couldn't create one who was Drake's equal. No matter
whether the hero in her book was blond or dark haired or
blue eyed or brown, in her mind's eye he was always Drake
in disguise—and that meant he was *always* Max.

Padding into the kitchen, she poured kibble into Daisy's
bowl and considered fueling up, too, starting with coffee.
Her Starbucks fix was obviously overdue.

She went into her bedroom, changed into better clothes
and tidied her hair. Still thinking about the dream, she
stuck twenty dollars and her key in her jeans pocket and
headed out into the hallway. In the past she'd used
Angelina as a means to experience life at arm's length
without having to dive in and really live it. She'd let her
creation have all the adventures, all the fun that she was
too chicken to go after. Maybe it was high time she cast
herself as the leading lady, the heroine, of her very real life.

One of the first things she'd done after coming back
from New Hampshire was to dig out her Christmas wish
list: Become bestselling author. Take trip to Ireland. Go on
motorcycle ride. Go to animal shelter and find feline friend
for cat. Save up down payment for house. Meet man of
dreams and fall in love…"

She supposed she could cross the last one off her list.

She'd met and fallen in love with Max. Too bad she'd forgotten to stipulate that he be trustworthy. She couldn't do much about that, but she had made some progress on the other items on her list. The other day she'd set up a meeting with a travel agent to book a trip to Ireland for June. She'd started saving in earnest, including putting herself on a shoe diet. Not that she regretted splurging on her red satin "Cinderella slippers" for even a minute. The shoe she'd kept resided in its Saks box at the back of her closet. She wondered what Max had done with the one she'd left behind. Thrown it out, she supposed. The thought not only depressed her, it made her heart hurt.

Becky took the hall elevator down to the lobby and exited through the double glass doors of the main entrance. The first person she saw when she stepped outside was the college kid who delivered her Thai food on Friday nights. Since she'd seen him last, he'd toned down his dyed ink-black hair to a more natural nut-brown and pared his body piercing ensemble to a single safety pin stuck through his left eyebrow. Goth-style aside, he'd always struck her as a decent, hardworking kid. He stood on the apartment pull-up next to a parked motorcycle talking to a pretty blonde. They each wore thick, black leather biker jackets and had helmets tucked beneath one arm. Judging from the silly smile on his face, he liked this girl a lot. Becky bet she could slip by without him even seeing her.

She started walking when the glimmer of sunlight striking chrome stopped her in her tracks. *Go on motorcycle ride.* The hulking Harley seemed like her modern-day equivalent of a knight in shining armor's white horse.

Becky had never been on a motorcycle in her life, not the vintage Italian one Angelina favored or the kid's

Harley. Like her knowledge of foreign countries, the little she knew about bikes came from the Internet or books, not firsthand experience. Maybe, just maybe, it was time to change that.

Chalking up her courage, she turned back and walked up to the edge of the sidewalk. The couple stopped talking and stared at her as though she was a creature newly landed from outer space, which was about how she felt—odd, out of step, and yes, old.

"You probably don't remember me, but I live here in apartment 812." She jerked a hand to indicate the highrise behind her. "You deliver my Thai food."

The kid pulled his gaze away from his girlfriend. "Sure I remember you—shrimp pad thai and a side of tod mun."

God, I am so predictable. Her delivery order struck her as a metaphor for everything wrong with her life.

"Yeah, right, that's me." She really ought to move on, but she couldn't, not yet anyway. "Is that bike yours?"

As conversation starters went, hers was pretty poor. Obviously the bike belonged to him. Why else would he be standing next to it wearing full gear? Duh!

"Yeah, I just bought it. I've been saving for a couple of years now."

So that's where her five-dollar tips had gone. Well, at least he'd had a goal and the determination to make it happen. Good for him.

She looked from the kid to the bike and back at him, her heartbeat kicked up to a rapid fire pace. "I know this may come off as a weird request, but what would you say to giving me a ride on the back of your bike?"

His eyes widened. "Seriously?"

She answered with a jerky nod. "Seriously." She'd apparently already lost her mind, but she hoped he'd say yes before she lost her nerve, too.

He exchanged glances with the girl and then turned back to Becky, expression sheepish. "I don't know. We're supposed to catch the matinee of *Lawrence of Arabia* at the Uptown."

The girlfriend chimed in with, "The actual one with Peter O'Toole—back when he was really hot," she added.

In the midst of her nervousness, Becky felt the corners of her mouth kick up. As far as she knew, there'd been no remake of the classic 1962 epic film. Impressive, though, that they even knew who Peter O'Toole was, let alone were setting aside a Saturday to hang out at a refurbished Art Deco movie theater. She was liking these kids more by the minute.

Remembering the twenty she'd stuck in her pocket to pay for coffee, she said, "What would you say to twenty bucks for one ride around the block?"

The boy's eyes popped. "Are you serious?"

"Totally."

He looked over at his girlfriend and asked, "Mind?"

She shrugged her narrow shoulders. "It's no big deal. We can always catch the last show."

He swung his head back to Becky. "You're on."

He introduced himself as Nathan and the blonde as Lisa. Lisa let her borrow her helmet and gave her a few pointers about balancing on the bike. "When he turns the corner, lean in, don't jerk back. He won't go fast but you should borrow my jacket, too, just in case. You never know what kind of shit—I mean stuff—will fly up from the road."

Heart racing, Becky slid her arms through the sun-warmed leather and strapped the helmet onto her head. Stepping back, she divided her gaze between them and asked, "How do I look?"

It was a stupid question with an obvious answer. Thinking back to when she'd been their age, she remembered how anyone over thirty had qualified as, if not exactly ancient, certainly solidly middle-aged. So much for thirty being the new twenty....

Nathan surprised her by giving her a thumbs-up. "You look really good, Miss Stone."

"Hot," his girlfriend added, and Becky suddenly felt a warm, confident feeling override her nervousness.

"In that case, let's rock 'n' roll." She mounted the bike behind him, swinging her leg over the seat in one fluid motion that would have done even Angelina proud.

"Hold on tight, Miss Stone."

She wrapped her arms around the kid's slender waist and leaned ever so slightly in. He revved the engine and they took off, Springsteen's "Born to Run" rocking inside Becky's head.

A HALF HOUR later, Becky walked back inside her apartment with windblown hair and chapped cheeks. The motorcycle ride around the block had been so exhilarating she'd cajoled Nathan into taking her around a second time. She doubted she was in danger of becoming a biker babe anytime soon—glancing into the bathroom mirror, she decided the whole helmet-head scenario was probably a deal buster—but daring to try something she'd always secretly wanted to do felt like a step in the right direction. Even if it was only a baby step, it was a step forward all the same.

She was pulling her hair back into a ponytail when the phone rang. Ordinarily she screened her daytime calls so as not to break her train of thought when she was writing, but she hadn't gotten back to work yet. Still buzzing from her recent adventure, she hoped the caller was Sharon. Her friend had decided to stay in Fredericksburg for the time being, a development Becky suspected had to do with an upswing in her romance with a certain sexy detective.

Instead of Sharon on the phone it was Pat. Becky felt her glow fading. She hadn't spoken to Pat since she'd overheard the phone conversation between Max and his agent. Ordinarily her editor preferred communicating any editorial changes by e-mail unless there was something substantive to discuss.

"Becky, it's Pat. I have some fabulous news for you."

Well, at least this time a phone call really did mean something positive. Relaxing, Becky said, "That's great. What is it?" She held her breath, half hoping Pat's "fabulous news" had something to do with Max.

Indeed it did. "I just got the call from Harry Goldblatt. His coagent out in L.A., the one who handles film rights, called to say that Spielberg picked up a three-year option on your and Max's book. We're not talking a TV movie of the week but a major motion picture. The news is all very hush-hush for now, though, so don't tell anyone, not even your mother. We want to make the announcement at the book launch party."

Having overheard Max on the phone with his agent, the news didn't come as a complete surprise. Still, Becky felt overwhelmed. "Back up and tell me what book launch party?"

"It's two weeks from today. Publicity's booked the Rainbow Room at Rockefeller Center. Everything's going to be first-class all the way. Everyone who's anyone in publishing will be there, including the media."

Becky hesitated. "That sounds great but I…I don't think I can make it."

"Why the hell not?"

She seized on the one excuse every editor should respect. "I have a deadline, remember?"

"Consider yourself granted a week's extension—two weeks if you need it."

"My, er…pet sitter is going to be out of town. I don't have anyone I can trust to take care of Daisy Bud."

That wasn't exactly true. Daisy would be fine at the boarding kennel at the vet's as long as the stay didn't extend beyond a few days. But hard-bitten New York editor that she was, Pat was also a huge animal lover. She had a pair of standard poodles, a cockatoo and a tank of tropical fish all crammed into her midtown west one-bedroom.

"So board her or ask a neighbor to look in on her. We're talking one day away, two days tops. She'll be okay."

Back to the proverbial wall, she fished, "I guess Max will be there?"

Pathetic, Becky, really bad. Pat worked for a publishing house, not a dating service. Manuscripts were her business, not matching lonely hearts.

"Now we're getting down to it."

She'd wondered how much Pat knew about her and Max's personal relationship, and her editor's tone alone answered that question. She must know everything more or less.

"What has he said to you? I mean it, Pat, I want to know."

"To me, he hasn't said a word. Other than e-mail, I haven't spoken to him in a month. He's apparently back in hermit mode, though Harry's sworn on a stack of Bibles that he'll be there for the party."

Max. How could she possibly face him, let alone face him in front of a roomful of members of the publishing elite, reviewers and camera-popping paparazzi? Even after a month apart, the memory of the very Elliot-like way he'd betrayed her still really hurt.

Pat wasn't taking no for an answer. She spent the next few minutes doing her usual sales job, citing all the good publicity Becky going to the party would bring and finally making it clear Becky didn't have a choice—again.

"Cheer up, kid. This is your big break. The kind of break most writers only ever dream about. You've worked too long and too hard to blow it now because some macho male writer made you cry."

As much as she hated to admit it, Pat was right. She was acting like an infant. If anyone should feel embarrassed about showing his face, it was Max, not her. She hadn't done anything wrong. She had no reason to hide.

And yet, when she clicked off the cordless and replaced it in the phone cradle, the irony of her situation hit her like a pie in the face. Her big break had finally come around— and wouldn't you know it, the only thing she felt breaking was her heart.

14

"Mind you don't move so much as a muscle, Falco, or I'll blow your bloody head off."

With her nemesis caught in her rifle's crosshairs, Angelina found herself missing Drake, not only his weapon backing her up but his warm blue eyes and sexy smile. Even when you were an internationally sought-after sleuth turned secret government agent, life worked better with a partner.

Hands in the air, Falco advanced, more than six feet of trained-killer male sheathed in a black Ducati leather jacket and matching chaps. It had been almost a year since she'd lured him back to her hotel room, seduced him and tied him up, all to get him to give up the whereabouts of the stolen missile plans. Now that she and Drake had recovered them, she was free to act on her own behalf. Encountering him out of the blue in a pub in London's Haymarket theater district was a dazzling opportunity she didn't mean to waste.

Smile cocky, Falco dropped his hands and edged menacingly closer. "Angelina, love, you're bluffing—again. You wouldn't harm me, not after that amazing night we spent in Chelsea."

"Is that so?" Angelina pulled back on the trigger—
and blew the bastard to kingdom come.

BECKY CAUGHT an early train from Washington's Union
Station to New York on the morning of the party. Once
there, she treated herself to a nice lunch, a strictly necessary pilgrimage to Saks for a kick-ass dress and finally a
soothing massage in the hotel day spa.

The Chelsea was booked when she called to make her
reservation, which was probably for the best. As much as
she loved the place, she wasn't sure she was ready to go
back just yet. Besides, Max was probably staying there in
his usual suite. It was hard enough knowing she'd be
seeing him later that night. Bumping into him in the lobby
or, worse still, the lounge, didn't feel like something she
wanted to sign up for just now.

Instead she booked a single room in the Hilton on
Avenue of the Americas. Though she generally didn't like
big hotels, she couldn't fault the location. The hotel was
within easy walking distance of Rockefeller Center where
that night's book launch gala would be held.

She had a few hours to kill before she needed to get
ready and as badly as she wanted a pre-event glass of wine
to calm her nerves, she also wanted a walk. It was spring
and springtime in New York wasn't to be missed. And yet
when she stepped out the front of her hotel, she couldn't
bring herself to start down Avenue of the Americas where
she'd literally run into Max. She thought his agent had an
office somewhere close by. Either way, she didn't think she
could handle any more "coincidental" meetings. So far her
horoscope predictions from January had both come true.
She had indeed gotten more than her share of "fresh starts"

and "dazzling opportunities." What she hadn't gotten was a happy ending, at least not when it came to love.

So she headed around the corner and cut down to Seventh Avenue on the outskirts of the Theater District. Rosie O'Grady's was a steak and seafood house in the tradition of the venerable turn-of-the-century New York saloons. On weekdays the street-level bar was a popular watering hole, drawing patrons from the after-work office crowd, as well as tourists from the nearby hotels. If she were lucky maybe she could snag a table to herself and get not only a glass of wine but a snack, too.

She walked inside and bypassed the hostess stand for the bar—and found herself staring straight ahead at the tall silver-haired man who'd once broken her heart. Elliot. What the hell was he doing in an Irish bar in midtown Manhattan? Sure, he came to New York from time to time, but the trendier bars in the Village or Alphabet City were more his style. Hoping he hadn't seen her, or that if he had he would stick to treating her as though she was invisible, she whipped around and headed for the door.

"Becky. Becky Stone!"

The slightly husky voice she remembered all too well stopped her in her tracks. Bracing herself to face him, Becky turned around.

He left his buddies at the bar and sauntered over to her. "Becky, I thought that was you. You look…you look amazing."

He slid his gaze slowly over her, taking in every detail, missing nothing. If she had any thoughts his remark might be empty flattery, the open admiration in his deep-set dark eyes confirmed it. She must look pretty damn good—make that *amazing*.

The last time she'd been alone with him, he'd left her wrapped in a bath towel, a sex flush and a cocoon of false hope. But then the universe had a funny way of seeing that loose ends were tied up, or so it suddenly seemed. She'd imagined this moment so many times, prayed for it even, and now that it had materialized, instead of facing him weak-kneed and stammering, she was able to lift her chin and meet his gaze head-on.

"Thanks, Elliot. You look good, too."

Tall, broad-shouldered and prematurely gray, he was more or less his same handsome self. Staring up at him, all macho self-confidence and cool, practiced smile, she realized he didn't have nearly the effect on her he'd once had. Instead she found herself studying him with a critical eye. The bridge of his nose was wide, really wide. Funny how she'd never noticed before. It was such a prominent feature. And the lines on his forehead were more deeply chiseled than she remembered, or maybe they'd always been that deep and she'd overlooked them until now. And how was it possible that she could have missed the cruel curve to his mouth or the soulless vacancy to his deep-set brown eyes? A year ago that tall, broad-shouldered body had driven her crazy, but now he struck her as too thin, borderline gaunt. And she remembered that he waxed his chest. When they'd been together, she'd written off the practice as an L.A. thing, but now it struck her as really vain.

"I was just having a drink with some friends from the studio." He gestured over his shoulder to the handful of men who, like him, wore designer dark suits and silk ties. Turning back to her, he said, "Why don't you join us? I'll introduce you to some people."

Amazing how he hadn't bothered to speak to her the last time he'd seen her in public but now that they'd met again by chance and he happened to be dateless he seemed to have all the time in the world.

She shook her head. "I can't. I have to get ready for an event—a launch party for my new book, actually."

Rather than congratulate her or ask what she was working on these days, he said, "That's too bad. We could have had dinner and relived old times."

Even at the height of her hormone haze, she'd recognized he had a supersized ego, but now she sensed his behavior bordered on narcissism. Still, she couldn't really regret the six months she'd spent under his spell. Yes, he'd hurt her, deeply and profoundly, deliberately and cruelly, but looking at him now she suddenly understood that his hurting her was part of the gift. It had freed her to love someone else, the *right* someone else. Because of him, she'd been free to love Max.

Max. Finding herself face-to-face with Elliot brought the contrast between the two men into even sharper relief. Whereas Elliot was all about himself, Max was more interested in hearing about other people. Unlike so many writers at his level, he rarely if ever let his ego get in the way of the work. He was so low-key about publicity, he'd gotten a reputation in the publishing world as a hermit, whereas Elliot loved the camera entirely too much.

The more she thought of it, the harder it was to believe Max had betrayed her. Thinking back to the phone conversation she'd overheard, she tried telling herself she was only making excuses for a man's bad behavior once again but something just didn't...well, it just didn't *feel* right. Now that she'd started trusting her intuition again, she couldn't dismiss the sense of unease. Even with the damning dialogue echoing in her ears, running off had been a big mistake. Until she confronted him, she'd never have closure. Fortunately, tonight's book launch party would provide her with the chance to get to the heart of the matter once and for all. It was time for Cinderella to stand tall and dig in her heels rather than run away.

Elliot's lowered voice pulled her back to the present. "I feel really badly about how things ended between us." Leaning closer, he confided, "I must have written you a dozen e-mails I never sent."

Uh-huh. Sure you did. She must have honed her judgment over the past year because her ex struck her as transparent as glass. Were she to meet him as a stranger again, she didn't think she'd be so easily taken in.

She shrugged, sensing a huge weight had been lifted from her shoulders. "Don't worry about it, Elliot. Looking back, I figure you did me a favor."

He'd never made her happy, not really, and now he'd lost the power to make her miserable ever again. Looking up at him with eyes wide open, she saw him for what he was, just another player with a fake smile and a smooth pickup line—and a hollow heart.

If she hadn't seen him with the twentysomething in D.C., she might still be on the hook waiting for him to call, making plans she knew in her heart he wouldn't keep, darting gazes around a party wondering if he hadn't found someone younger or prettier or both to sneak off with. That was no way to live. It wasn't living at all. Remembering how much of her energy that relationship had drained, she could appreciate her time with Max. With Max, she'd always felt energized and upbeat and good about herself on all levels.

His tense look relaxed, and he flashed his signature smile, the one she'd once found so irresistibly sexy but which now struck her as smarmy. "I'm coming into D.C. later this month. Maybe we could get together for dinner or…something."

Becky wasn't even tempted. "Thanks, Elliot, but no thanks. You take care of yourself, though." She reached out and patted his arm as though he were a puppy.

Leaving him staring after her, she turned and walked out of the restaurant, a spring in her step. The smile breaking over her face barely waited for her to clear the threshold. Grinning from ear to ear, or at least that's what it felt like, she walked back up Seventh toward her hotel. She did indeed have a publishing party to attend—and unfinished business with Max to settle once and for all.

FEELING LIKE a reluctant Cinderella, Becky stepped off the elevator to the Rainbow Room later that night, her new hair and evening gown props to set the scene and cover her nervousness. She'd chosen the floor-length chocolate taffeta halter dress with care and, she realized, Max in mind. Looking into the Saks dressing-room mirror earlier that day, she'd thought the rich shade worked well with her hair and eyes. Usually she shied away from wearing long dresses, feeling that they made her look even shorter, but in this case the straight skirt with its flared hem flattered her petite figure by giving her a longer, leaner line while the deep V-neckline and knotted front made the most of her small breasts. And of course, she had on a killer pair of satin-covered Manolos and carried a beaded Kate Spade evening bag to set the whole thing off.

She surrendered her wrap to the girl working coat check and then followed piano music down the corridor to the event room. The pianist wouldn't be Max this time, but regardless she hoped he wouldn't play "New York State of Mind."

Located on the sixty-fifth floor of 30 Rockefeller Plaza, the landmark restaurant and nightclub had been the premier venue for posh Manhattan social functions since the 1930s. But it wasn't the crystal-cut Art Deco chandelier crowning the high ceiling, the revolving dance floor or the spectacular multicolored lighting engineered to produce a rainbow effect that had Becky catching her breath. It was the view. Floor-to-ceiling windows provided a peerless panorama of the Manhattan skyline. A quick look around was all it took for her to spot several landmarks—the distinctive spire of the Met Life building, the Empire State building, the large green patch that was Central Park—and Max.

Backlit by the setting sun, he stood beside one of several easels bearing a poster-size blowup of their book cover, looking more like a model for *GQ* magazine than an author, even a bestselling one. His black tuxedo fit his broad shoulders and tall, lean body as though it was painted on, and he'd let his dark gold hair grow to brush the back of his collar.

The telltale flicker of his brow confirmed she'd caught his eye, too. His gaze met hers and Becky found herself drowning once more in that deep blue soulful sea. There was no looking away, no moving out of his field of vision. Suddenly it was as if they were the only two people in the room, the world, and she realized she wouldn't have it any other way.

He shifted his attention back to his conversation companion, a pretty twentysomething redhead in a tulle-skirted black cocktail dress that Becky recognized as a Vera Wang, and her heart dropped to the floor like Universal Studio's Tower of Terror amusement park ride.

God, I am such a fool. On second thought, better make that twice a fool.

Running into Elliot that afternoon had shown her how many times stronger her feelings were for Max. Elliot hadn't broken her heart so much as bruised her pride. Seeing him from the perspective of more than a year apart, she realized she hadn't loved him any more than he'd loved her. Sure, she'd been infatuated with him, but never once in the short time she'd spent with him had she felt so much as a flicker of the flaming passion and soul-deep connection she'd known with Max.

But you could only hold on for so long. She ventured another glance across the room to Max, yet another relationship she needed to release if she wanted to move forward with her life.

Pat hailed her from halfway across the room. "Becky, there you are." Wearing a beaded, black, long-sleeved top and skirt, the older woman sallied up beside her and opened her arms for a hug. "I was beginning to wonder if maybe you weren't coming."

Becky returned the greeting, relieved she wouldn't have to walk in alone after all. Stepping back, she shot her editor a wink. "What? And ignore a direct order from my commander-in-chief?"

For the first time in their five-year association, Becky saw the older woman blush. "Well, it wasn't an order, not exactly. More like a strongly worded suggestion."

"So said Mussolini." Becky accepted a glass of champagne from one of the circulating servers. "At any rate, I'm here now. And by the way, I absolutely love the cover. The folks in the art department went all-out again."

"Everyone got the word from on high that this project

was to be first-class all the way." Pat hesitated, biting her bottom lip. "Max was pleased, as well."

"Was he?" One eye on her coauthor, Becky couldn't resist asking, "Who is the red-haired woman he's talking to?"

Pat glanced their way. "That's Lydia Evans, the in-house publicist assigned to this project. She planned this fabulous event, and she'll be working closely with you and Max on the post-launch promo."

So the redhead wasn't Max's date. That was a weight off her mind but hearing Pat speak of her and Max as though they were partners still brought a stab of pain. She didn't want to be just his writing partner or for that matter, his casual lover for one night or one month. She wanted him for keeps. And yet knowing how he'd sold her out, how could she possibly trust him with her heart?

"I see. Well, she's done a great job."

Pat swept a satisfied look over the packed room. "We're counting on tonight to really build the industry buzz. Once the book hits the shelves, there are several publicity spikes planned, including a national book tour."

Becky choked on the sip of champagne she'd just taken. "You're sending me and Max on tour together?"

As if taking her gratitude for granted, Pat beamed. "It was supposed to be a surprise, but, well, I hate surprises, especially when it means I'm the one who has to hold back the secret. Yes, there's a month-long tour in the works but don't thank me. Thank Lydia. She set the whole thing up. Ten major U.S. cities with book signings and cable television and radio spots and well...why don't I just introduce you and let her go over it all?"

Becky panicked. Meeting Lydia meant coming face-to-face with Max, and for that she needed to work up her courage. "That's okay. They're obviously in the middle of a conversation. I'll meet her later."

Pat took hold of her by the elbow. "Don't be silly. Any conversation they're having might as well include you. It'll save Lydia from having to repeat all the plans to you later."

Becky started to protest but Pat was already steering her through the packed room toward Max. For someone who claimed she was allergic to working out, the older woman's grip was like iron.

She didn't let go until she delivered Becky to them. "Sorry to interrupt, kids, but look who I found."

Max shifted his gaze from the publicist to Becky. "Who, indeed."

Praying her voice would hold steady, she said, "Hi, Max."

He nodded. "Becky."

Their eyes met, melded. Memories flooded her—the scent of his skin, which always reminded her of the beach, the warmth of his hand shaping her hip as though he were smoothing away her every care in the world, the deep, low groan he gave just before he came.

Though it had only been a month since she'd seen him last, she found herself marking slight but noticeable changes. He certainly didn't look like a man gloating over cutting his partner out of a major contract deal. He looked thinner than she remembered. It wasn't a dramatic difference, but she suspected he'd dropped a good five to seven pounds. For a fleeting moment, she dared hope the weight loss meant he was missing her, but that was crazy. Even if he did miss her, a pretty big if, men didn't pine the way women did. She, on the other hand, had dropped a dress size, a fact discovered when she'd been trying on evening gowns in the dressing room of Saks earlier that day. That first week back in D.C., she'd barely been able to choke down a frozen entrée.

Becky held out her hand, alarmed to see it shaking ever so slightly. "Lydia, it's very nice to meet you. You've done a wonderful job with the event. Everything is lovely." She gestured toward the ice sculptures meant to represent Drake and Angelina, the cloth-covered food stations, the waitstaff butlering champagne and canapés.

"Thank you, Miss Stone. I am so incredibly thrilled to be working on this project. My mom is a huge fan of yours. She must own every one of your paperback Regencies, even the out-of-print copies."

Catching the flicker of amusement in Max's eyes, the first warmth she'd felt from him since she walked up, Becky bit her lip. "That's…very flattering."

Small talk, mostly centered on the upcoming events, made the circle. A tuxedo-clad server stopped by with a tray of champagne glasses and even though she suspected alcohol was the last thing she needed at the moment, Becky exchanged her half-empty glass for a fresh one.

Pat laid a light hand on Lydia's arm. "If you'll excuse us, there are some people I'd like Lydia to meet."

"Of course," Max said, and even though Becky knew she had no claim on him, never had and never would, she couldn't help feeling gratified that he didn't seem to give the redhead so much as a goodbye glance.

Left alone with Becky for the moment, Max raked his gaze over her. "Good dress."

His frank appreciation had her blushing from scalp to collarbone, but for the sake of her pride, she wouldn't allow herself to look down or away—not even to follow his eyes, which seemed to be devouring her.

"Thank you."

"You're welcome." His gaze came back to her face. He sent her a long, lingering look. "When you first walked in, it took me a moment to recognize you—and once I did, you took my breath away. You cut your hair."

"Just this afternoon." Self-conscious, she reached back and touched the back, which came just below her nape. "I'm still getting used to it."

The stylist had cut it in graduated layers, leaving the front longer to frame her face. Walking back to the hotel after running into Elliot, she'd realized that not only was she over him but she had been for some time. Since she'd met Max, she'd thought of Elliot rarely, if at all. Such a momentous epiphany deserved some sort of celebration, or at least an outward sign to commemorate the change.

"You look beautiful, but then you always do." Before she could step away, he touched the side of his hand to her cheek.

The caress was Becky's undoing. "Don't." She backed up a step, nearly knocking into an older gentleman she recognized as a book reviewer for *Publishers Weekly*. "Pardon me." Turning back to Max, she shook her head, tears welling. "Damn you, Max. I thought I could do this, but I can't." She turned to go.

Strong fingers banded her wrist, the warm hold she remembered all too well anchoring her in place. "Becka, don't. Don't disappear on me, not again, not before we've had a chance to talk."

Having him call her by the special name he'd given her was nearly her undoing. She felt the press of tears at the backs of her eyes and a telltale lump lodging in her throat.

This wasn't fair, this wasn't right. How could he stand there staring at her with wounded eyes as though she were hurting him when he was the one who'd done all the hurting?

She wrenched away. "I didn't disappear. I left you a note, remember?"

He snorted but his expression was pained. "A short note saying I'd sold you out, I couldn't be trusted and you never wanted to see me again? You call that closure?"

"Well, you can't be trusted—can you?"

"There's only one way to find out. Let's get the hell out of here." He took hold of her hand again, lacing his fingers through hers, and this time she didn't think he'd be letting go so easily.

Before she could answer, a pale-faced young man stepped forward and introduced himself as a photographer with the *New York Times*. "I want to get a photo of the two of you for the book section. Can you stand by the cover poster?" Lifting the camera dangling from the strap around his neck, he gestured them over to the blowup on the easel.

The dreaded publicity photo op had reared its ugly head. It seemed there was no escaping. Could this evening get any harder? Becky had no choice but to take her place at Max's side and smile for the camera.

The photographer took several shots, promised them each copies and then faded into the crowd. Max swung around to Becky. "We need to talk, but first I'm getting you the hell out of here."

Plate piled high with canapés, Pat pounced on them. "Did I hear you say you were leaving?"

Max answered for them both. "Yes."

"But you're coming back, right? I mean, you're just stepping out for a cigarette or…or something."

Max shot their editor a bland look belied by the fire in his eyes. "I quit smoking years ago."

It was Becky's turn to speak up. "I'm afraid we're calling it a night. At least I am."

Pat divided her horrified gaze between them. "But you can't leave. You just got here. You're the guests of honor!"

Becky spoke up, "And it's been a lovely party. Please tell Lydia again how much we appreciate all the trouble she's gone to. We'll be in touch."

His palm pressed to the small of her back, Max steered Becky through the crowd toward the exit. Several guests stepped into their path to offer congratulations but beyond an obligatory smile and a handshake, Max kept them on course. Out in the hallway, he tipped the attendant to retrieve Becky's wrap, slipped it around her shoulders and headed for the bank of exit elevators.

The elevator opened at once, no common occurrence in a building that boasted sixty-seven stories. Max let go of her hand and stepped back. "After you."

She hesitated and then stepped inside. Max walked on behind her. The elevator doors closed, cutting them off from the world beyond. Fixing her gaze on the display above their heads, she watched the numbers fall, reminded of that magical night at the Chelsea when they'd stood arm in arm in the hotel elevator, impatient to reach Max's rooftop suite so they could continue making love.

Turning to Max, Becky swallowed hard. "You'd better talk fast. We just passed thirty-two."

Yanking his bowtie loose, he said, "Sounds like a lucky number to me." He reached across her to the control panel and hit the emergency button. The elevator jolted to a stop.

Unable to believe what she'd just seen, Becky whirled

on him. "Have you lost your mind? The security guards will think terrorists have taken over the building."

He shrugged. "If spending the night in a police lockup is the only way I can get you to listen to me, then I'll make the sacrifice."

She shook her head, suddenly weary of everything that should be easy turning out to be so very hard. "If you're not crazy, then you must be drunk."

His clear-eyed gaze met hers, and she saw he wasn't intoxicated, just determined. "I'm not drunk. I only had one Scotch, half of which I just left behind. As for the crazy part, you bet I'm crazy—crazy about you."

She fisted her hands on her hips, dug in her high heels, and glared up at him. "Were you so crazy about me when you sold me out for the script-writing deal? Don't bother denying it. I heard you talking on the phone to your agent."

Max stared at her for a long moment, and then he tossed back his head and laughed.

"What's so funny?"

Swiping the back of his hand across watery eyes, he shook his head. "Didn't your mother ever warn you that people who eavesdrop never hear any good?"

Leave it to a man to put you on the defensive when he was the one in the wrong. "I wasn't eavesdropping. The phone rang right beside my bed and I reached for it. I wasn't sure you were even in the house until I heard your voice on the line. It was dumb luck that I heard you congratulating your agent on cutting me out of the screenplay deal."

"Too bad you didn't stick around to hear the rest of it."

"The rest of what?" A sinking sensation that had nothing to do with the elevator ride hit her full force.

"The part where I told him that unless the deal was rewritten to include you as coauthor, there was no deal."

Becky shook her head, which spun as though she'd downed a whole bottle of champagne instead of a few measly sips. "Is that the truth?"

Max moved closer. "The whole truth and nothing but."

As much as she ached to throw herself against him, to lock lips with him and feel his strong arms wrap around her, she held her ground and kept her distance. The physical chemistry they shared was nothing short of amazing, but this was too important an issue to be swept aside because of surging hormones. She needed more from a partner and more from herself than great sex alone. She also needed mutual trust and understanding and respect— and above all, true love.

For once in her life, this once, she wasn't willing to settle.

She took a small backward step, eyes looking up into his. "How can I be sure you're not just telling me what you think I want to hear? When I asked who'd called, you lied and told me it was a telemarketer."

"I was trying to protect you. I didn't want your feelings to get hurt or for you to start doubting your talent." Max laid his hands atop her shoulders. "That was wrong of me, I see that now, but what I said about the screenplay stands. I'll call Harry in the morning and have him send you a copy of the contract so you can read it for yourself. You'll be getting one anyway. For the deal to go through, two signatures are required—yours and mine."

"W-why would you do that?"

He shook his head, his gaze melting. "Drake really misses Angelina."

"He does?"

"Uh-huh. He's been living on microwave dinners and self-pity for a solid month now, and it's getting really old. What about you?"

"Angelina's miserable, too. She hasn't cleaned her revolver in a month and the last time she dropped in, her shoes were looking really scuffed."

"That does sound serious. Do you think there's any chance of those two ever getting back together?"

"I think there might be if…"

"If?" His eyes pierced hers.

"If Angelina thought Drake really loved her, I think she'd come around pretty quickly."

"He does love her, Becka. He loves her with his whole heart. In fact, she's the only woman in the world for him." Smile gentle, Max lifted her chin with the edge of his hand. "I've come to a similar conclusion myself."

"You have?" She felt a tear splash her cheek, a happy one this time, and didn't bother to wipe it away.

"Uh-huh." He caught the tear on the pad of his thumb. "Both my writing and my life work a lot better with a partner—as long as she's you."

Just a month ago that declaration would have been more than enough—she would have made it be enough—but a lot had changed in the past four weeks and most of the changes had happened inside her. She felt as though she'd climbed to the top of the mountain, faced down every demon she'd ever had and then climbed down again, stronger and more clear-eyed than she ever would have believed she could be. She didn't want to be Max's casual lover or his writing partner or some contemporary combination of the two. She wanted to be his partner in every way—his lover, his colleague, his best friend and, yes, his wife.

"Are you through?"

"Not hardly." He swallowed hard. "I thought that after losing Elaina, nothing, absolutely nothing, would have the power to scare me ever again, but I was wrong. Living without you this past month has been scary as hell for me. I miss you, Becka. I more than miss you—I love you and the thought of living the rest of my life without you in it scares the hell out of me. Say you'll marry me, Becka, and I promise I'll spend the rest of my life coming up with new adventures and new ways to make you happy."

"I don't need new adventures. All I want is a fresh start and the dazzling opportunity to be happy—with you."

"In that case, we'd better get to work. The clock on the screenplay is ticking, and I'm going to need some serious inspiration, in the form of you naked in my bed. I have that suite at the Chelsea through the weekend. You remember it, don't you?" He slanted her a sexy half smile.

Happy tears welling, Becky nodded. "But I'm not sure I can wait to get there. We just might have to make do with the backseat of a taxi—or perhaps a stalled elevator."

Max's arms went around her. "I like the way you think, Miss St. Claire." He pulled her against him and angled his face to hers.

"Just try to keep up, Mr. Maxwell." Locking her arms about his neck, Becky leaned into his kiss, feeling as though she'd finally come home.

Reaching for her gown's side zipper, Max whispered into her ear, "Think of this as the first chapter of the first book in a brand-new series."

Drowning in his deep blue gaze, she asked, "Will it be erotic romance, mystery or action-adventure?"

Max rolled down her zipper and slid a warm hand inside her gown. "Knowing us, I'd say all of the above."

Epilogue

SEATED ACROSS from one another at the linen-draped table, Angelina and Drake clinked champagne glasses. "Good thing we finally got that lot together, eh, Angie?"

Angelina nodded. "Your idea to stage that book launch party was bloody brilliant. It really saved the day—and the plot—from sinking. Without it, I don't know how we would have budged Becky out of D.C. or Max out of New Hampshire. They're both so bloody stubborn." She held out her glass. "Is there any more champers?"

He pulled the bottle of Cristal from the ice bucket and topped off both their glasses. "And no more brilliant than your notion of bringing the Elliot bloke on stage as a secondary character in the final chapters. Seeing him in that New York pub really sharpened the story arc, not to mention opened Becky's eyes to how much Max meant to her."

"Quite." Feeling a kindred spirit with her creator, Angelina smiled back. The dark passion she'd felt for Falco paled in comparison to the rich kaleidoscope of love, partnership and, yes, lust she shared with Drake, her unlikely leading man. The diamond-in-the-rough Aussie adventurer had stolen her heart—no small feat given that until recently she'd existed without one.

He captured her hand and pressed a kiss into her palm. "I venture to say our two creators are going to live happily ever after."

New soul aside, Angelina shook her head, her curtain of glossy black hair falling back into perfect place around her bare shoulders. "*Happily ever after* is the closing line for fairy tales, not mystery-erotica novels."

He lifted a dark blond eyebrow. "You mean *action-adventure* mystery-erotica novels, don't you?"

Rather than argue, she let out a sigh. He really was the most impossible fictional male creation—impossible to resist, that was. "The best a novel in any genre can manage is to end hopefully. These days a happy ending is never guaranteed."

"Is that so?" He took the champagne glass from her and reached for her hand. "There are bloody few guarantees in fiction or in life," he admitted, pressing her palm to the left side of his chest where his own newly issued heart announced his love for her with every fierce beat. "But when it comes to love, we can pledge to do our very best to love our partners with all our hearts and minds and bodies have to give. Surely we can manage that much at least?"

Smiling into Drake's earnest eyes, Angelina nodded. "Yes, love, that much we can manage—and perhaps a good deal more."

* * * * *

KIDNAPPED!

BY
JO LEIGH

Dear Reader,

This is so politically incorrect it's embarrassing to admit: I've had kidnap fantasies since I was about twelve. I saw a movie back then where a young woman was kidnapped and it set my imagination on fire. I don't remember the name of the movie, or much else about it, just that there was something about being stolen, being taken away from all I knew that intrigued and excited me.

So it was with great anticipation and a little evil glee that I set about writing Michael and Tate's story. In so many ways this book is the essence of fantasies that have been with me for years. But it was only as I finished the book that I realised in all my dreams, in all my late-night visions, the outcome was always, always...*love*.

Come and visit me at www.joleigh.com.

Sweet dreams,

Jo Leigh

JO LEIGH

has written more than thirty books since 1994. She's a triple RITA® Award finalist, most recently receiving a nomination from the Romance Writers of America for her Blaze® novel, *Relentless*. She also teaches writing in workshops across the country.

Jo lives in Utah with her wonderful husband and their cute puppy, Jessie. You can chat with her at her website, www.joleigh.com, and don't forget to check out her daily blog!

To LWW.
Because he's better than the fantasy.

1

IT WAS TUESDAY AT one-fifteen in the afternoon, and with the precision of a Swiss watch Tate Baxter's therapist leaned back in her chair, closed her notebook, smiled, then said, "Is there anything else you'd like to tell me?"

Tate's response was just as mechanical. "No, Dr. Bay. Nothing to report."

"Well, I have something I'd like to show you."

Tate lifted her head. One-fifteen was the end of the session. Dr. Bay never went over. Never. "Oh?"

The doctor flipped her notebook over and pulled out a newspaper article. "Take a look at this," she said.

Tate took the paper, torn between reading the article and watching Dr. Bay. The therapist, whom Tate had been seeing for almost two years, was clearly excited. That hardly ever happened. In fact, it never had. Not like this. Dr. Bay was a behaviorist, always setting up new challenges and goals for Tate to accomplish between sessions. The outcome never elicited anything but a favorable reaction, no matter the performance. Even when Tate had surpassed her own expectations, the doctor had always been reserved. But now Dr. Bay's eyes were wide with anticipation and her pale cheeks looked flushed.

Tate glanced down and the headline sent her own pulse racing. *Kidnapping For Hire.* She looked back at Dr. Bay.

"It's all right, Tate. Please, read it."

After a moment of hesitation, Tate started reading.

It begins with a list of your wildest fears. For a few thousand dollars Jerry Brody's personalized kidnapping service will make them come true. Your kidnappers might stuff you into a duffel bag or blindfold you and take you to a faraway cabin. In the dark you might see an alien's mask or a man in a filthy suit stinking like a garbage Dumpster. No two abductions are staged the same way. Your custom kidnapping could stop at a code word or go on for days. Brody and his team might snatch you when you're on the subway or showering in your apartment. After the "event," which some clients compare to meditation, you may feel relief, exhilaration or a newfound sense of personal power.

Tate had to stop. She'd come a long way since she'd first told Dr. Bay about her kidnap phobia and she hadn't had a full-blown panic attack in months. But this? This was—

"Breathe, Tate," Dr. Bay said. "Remember what we've practiced."

Closing her eyes, she went to her safe space. After several deep breaths, she focused on each part of her body from her toes to the top of her head.

"You're safe. You're in my office and no one's going to hurt you. Picture the glade."

Tate followed Dr. Bay's instructions. By the time she'd finished the awareness exercise she had regained her equilibrium. Her eyes opened to the security of the familiar—and the disappointment that she was still, after so much work, at the mercy of her fears.

"Do you want to talk about this now?" Dr. Bay asked, gesturing at the paper still in Tate's hand.

"You want me to hire this man? To let him take me?"

"I want you to think about it. I've been researching this approach for a long time now and I've spoken to a number of colleagues who have used similar techniques. There are reliable case studies where the subjects have been transformed. But remember, it's simply an idea. You're doing very well following the course we're on, and I realize this is unconventional."

Tate winced at the understatement. She could barely imagine what her father would say about this "unconventional" approach.

"When you go home tonight, I'd like you to do some work in your journal. Not about your reaction to the article but about what your life might be like if you could overcome this fear. Okay?"

Tate nodded. "I'll try."

"That's all anyone can ask. For what it's worth, you did a great job of calming down. It didn't take long at all."

Tate glanced at her watch. It was a quarter to two. Not bad, considering. It hadn't been that long ago that even the suggestion of something like this would have put her in a panic for days.

She put the article on the side table and grabbed her purse. "I'll see you next week."

"Don't forget to meditate."

She never did. And it had helped. She went out more frequently these days, and the nightmares weren't plaguing her nearly as often. Three cheers for the safe place. If only it could exist somewhere outside of her head.

As she was leaving, she nodded at Stephanie, Dr. Bay's receptionist. There were two people in the waiting room, both of whom appeared perfectly normal. She imagined they thought the same thing about her.

There was no one in the elevator as she stepped in, and she took a moment to push her hair back behind her shoulders, to daub the corners of her mouth, preparing herself for the streets of Manhattan.

Not that she would be on the streets—unless one counted being driven in one of her father's black limousines. The tinted windows hid her from view, making her feel as if the city was one giant store display.

The elevator slowed at the fourth floor. She inched back as a man entered. He was tall and silver-haired, wearing a tailored black pin-striped suit. His shoes looked equally expensive, and when he smiled she could see his veneered teeth had cost him a pretty penny. Not surprising, given the address. Dr. Bay's office overlooked Park Avenue. Her clients all understood, even before the first session, that if they had to ask about the fee, they couldn't afford it.

The man turned to stare at the elevator doors as they

rode the rest of the way to the lobby. Only, the doors were reflective and he clearly had no qualms about giving her a very thorough once-over.

She counted the seconds until they reached the lobby, and when the doors slid slowly open she placed her hand strategically so the elevator couldn't be fetched, waiting until the man was halfway across the lobby before she stepped out.

What would her life be like if she stopped being afraid? She had no idea. It was too foreign a concept.

Despite her improvement, her life was about fear, and it had been forever. At twenty-four, she'd resigned herself to living inside the bubble her father had created for her, going from limo to apartment to business appointments that had all been prescreened and determined safe.

She knew beyond any doubt that anyone looking at her life would believe it was perfect. Why wouldn't they? She had more money than anyone truly should, she'd been given her father's fast metabolism and her mother's striking blue eyes. Her education was exemplary, and if she decided she didn't want to do anything but shop for the rest of her life, she had the means to do just that.

She knew that her agoraphobic tendencies appeared to many as conceit and arrogance. The fact that she was so terrified of being kidnapped that her world had shrunk to a stultifying routine meant nothing. There were real problems out there; she just had an active imagination and a constant state of terror that kept her from enjoying the gifts she'd been given.

She walked outside the building to the busy street,

her gaze fixed on the limo parked just a few feet away. Michael, her driver, opened the back door for her. To those hurrying past he seemed like any other limo driver. Black suit, white shirt, humble demeanor. But behind his dark glasses he was scanning the area with laser intensity and the reason his jacket wasn't buttoned was so that he could, if necessary, get to his weapon in a heartbeat. He drove her, but that was his secondary job.

She passed him closely as she got into the back of the car and marveled again at his face. He wasn't classically handsome. Too many sharp edges and flaws. But his looks had grown on her since he'd come on board six months ago. She hadn't really thought about him that way in the beginning. There were lots of people in her life whose job it was to keep her safe. Some of them were also dear friends—like Elizabeth, her assistant—but most weren't. Her father didn't like her getting too comfortable with the staff, and she'd fallen into the terrible habit of seeing them as employees, not people.

Michael had turned into something else altogether. Not a friend, not really. They never did anything except drive. But they talked. About everything.

She'd learned he liked reading the Russians—Tolstoy, Dostoyevsky, Turgenev. But he also liked the graphic novels of Frank Miller. She liked to tease him about his comic books, but she'd secretly ordered a few Miller novels online, and they were…well, interesting.

He shut the door, then walked around to the driver's side and settled himself inside. She could see his sunglasses in the rearview mirror and wished, as always, that he would take them off.

"Where to?"

"Home."

"No stops?"

"Not today."

He smiled at her, and she settled herself back on the cool leather seat.

She'd also learned that he didn't have a girlfriend. Which was a lot more interesting than his taste in books.

MICHAEL PULLED INTO the mess that was traffic in midtown Manhattan, heading toward Tate's Carnegie Hill penthouse. Something out of the ordinary had happened in the session today. He'd seen that the moment she'd stepped out of the building. He'd wait and see if she wanted to talk or if she would call her friend Sara. He liked it when she spoke to Sara. Tate never hid anything from her closest friend, and for the last few months she hadn't whispered into the phone when she talked. It was her way of telling him about her life without seeming to bare it all.

His gaze shifted from the road to the mirror, where he was met by a pair of cornflower-blue eyes. He knew she was smiling and he smiled back, although he shouldn't. When Tate was this flirtatious it meant that she was running from something unpleasant. He'd been right about her session.

"So how's the doctor doing?"

Tate shifted so all he could see of her was her right temple. "Fine."

"Wonder what she talks about when she sees *her* shrink?"

"Probably about how whacked-out her patients are."

"I don't know. She seems pretty professional to me."

"You met her once. For about five seconds."

He grinned. "Yeah, but she was professional for the whole five seconds."

Her eyes were back in focus. Smiling. "Sometimes she comes up with some weird ideas."

"For example?" A cab slipped in front of him, forcing him to slam on the brakes. Hitting the horn was tempting but futile, not to mention illegal.

"Nothing," she said, her voice softer, flatter.

He didn't push. The call to Sara would clear things up. The whole phone ploy was actually pretty smart. It didn't completely break down the barriers between them, but overhearing her chats gave him tremendous insight, which helped him do his job. Besides, she was pretty funny.

Hell, if he had to work as someone's trained pony, he was glad it was Tate. She might be rich as Croesus, but she didn't act like most of the trust-fund babies he'd met. He'd wondered, often, whether she'd be so nice if she didn't live every moment in fear. Poor kid. He wished that shrink would move it along. Let Tate really live while she was still young.

"Did Elizabeth tell you about tomorrow?"

Michael nodded. "She gave me the schedule for the week."

"Good. Okay, well...."

He glanced in the mirror, but she wasn't looking at him. The phone call should be coming right up.

He saw an opening for the damn boat of a limo and

he took it, daring the Yellow cab next to him to inter-
fere. By the time he'd gone a half block Tate had the
slim cell phone to her ear.

"Hey, it's me."

He wished he could hear both sides of the conversation, but at least he was privy to Tate's voice.

"I don't know, Sara. I think Dr. Bay's gone over the
edge this time. She gave me this article. It's about this
nutcase artist-cum-therapist here in New York. He
kidnaps people for money."

Michael's hands gripped the steering wheel as he
struggled not to turn the limo around, using a sidewalk
café as a new traffic lane, and go right back to Dr.
Bay's office.

"You have? When did you hear about this?"

What in hell was Bay thinking? Maybe she'd had
one too many Xanax this morning.

"She thinks that maybe if I go through the experience when I know it's safe, I'll finally get past it. Trial
by fire, I suppose."

Shit, Tate needed a new psychologist—and she
needed one now. He could just imagine what her father
would say to this crazy business. William would have
a heart attack on the spot, but not before he'd had Dr.
Bay's license revoked.

When Michael had signed up for the job, he'd had
a lot of questions, like why this young woman
needed a level of security that would make the president feel safe. William had told him that kidnapping
was a danger and that he would go to any lengths to
protect Tate.

Michael had agreed that someone with her wealth

was a target, but guards 24-7? Ex-CIA case officers as a cook and a secretary?

Then he'd heard bits and pieces about the basis for the paranoia. At fifteen, Tate and her cousin had been kidnapped. Tate had escaped out a small bathroom window, but her cousin had been murdered. Tate had done her best to find the kidnapper's hideout, but she'd been so traumatized she hadn't been much help. Then, five years after that, when Tate was in college, there had been another attempt. A couple of local idiots had taken her at gunpoint from her car, demanding two million dollars. Luckily the kidnappers had been inept fools, and the FBI had found them within hours, but the experience had scarred Tate deeply, and her father had become determined that she'd never be vulnerable again. As his fortune had grown, so had his security measures.

"I hyperventilated," Tate said with a self-deprecating laugh. "But seriously, Sara, I promised her I'd give it some thought."

He finally reached Carnegie Hill and turned the limo toward the entrance to her building, easing up on the gas so he wouldn't miss out on the end of the call.

"I can't see it, either," Tate said. "But she asked me something just before I left. She asked what my life would be like if I wasn't afraid. I had no answer for her."

Michael was all for Tate getting over her fear of being kidnapped, but throwing her into the fire was ridiculous. There had to be another way.

"We're here. I'll call you later. We'll talk some more, but don't worry. I'm not saying yes."

He pulled the car into the driveway that would take

them to the underground garage. There was a spot near the elevator that was reserved for the limo, which made things easier. But he'd ride up to Tate's place with her, make sure she got inside safely.

The garage itself was extraordinarily well lit. Not just now but day and night. That was courtesy of William Baxter, who spared no expense in keeping his only daughter safe. Elizabeth would be upstairs doing typical assistant things while maintaining her sharp-shooter status and carrying a concealed but legal 9 mm Glock. Everyone who worked with Tate had a similar skill set: good at the normal stuff that helped Tate get through her days, great at the stuff that would scare the bejesus out of the most hardened criminals, if they only knew.

Hell, right now three men would be observing every inch of the penthouse via the most sophisticated cameras in the world. If Tate so much as tripped, there would be at least three trained security personnel to pick her up within sixty seconds.

He parked the limo, then got out to open the back door. Tate gave him a look before she tucked her purse under her arm and climbed out. It had amazed him when he'd first started this gig that she could maneuver herself out of the backseat with such grace. Then he'd realized she'd been doing it her whole life. This was the kind of car that had taken her to school. To the movies. It wasn't just for prom night or a funeral. It was part and parcel of her daily existence.

She headed toward the elevator and pressed the button. There was another example of how she wasn't like so many other overprivileged women: she pressed her own buttons. She made her own phone calls. She did her best to keep up with the lives of those on her staff, although the ex-agent types tended to be on the private side.

The elevator had one of those shiny doors that could double as a mirror, but he kept his gaze lowered. Tate, who was attractive and always kept herself looking sharp, didn't like being watched. Which was fine. It wasn't his job to look at her. He had to keep her safe, which meant looking at everything that surrounded her. Even this elevator. It was checked first thing every morning for bugs, for explosive devices, for anything that could possibly harm its inhabitants.

There wasn't even a long way up—five floors. Since she owned the whole penthouse, it made security easier up there. All told, there were twelve guys who worked for him, and they rotated duty so that none of them ever got too comfortable. Some of the team had been with Tate for years, but Michael had recruited his four top men. It hadn't taken long for all of them to become a unit he could be proud of.

The elevator door opened, and Tate glanced his way before she stepped into the hallway.

He joined her, checking the small area for anything hinky. She had her key out, and he watched as she unlocked both deadbolts. She had such delicate hands. Long, graceful. Her nails were on the short side and they were polished some creamy color that was just a little darker than her skin. No rings, no jewelry at all except for the small diamond-stud earrings. She wasn't a flashy kind of woman. In fact, she did everything she could to blend in. But there was something she couldn't hide—or change: she was a class act. Everything about her said she had money, background, education. She was different, exceptional. Anyone who passed her in the street would know it.

"Thank you," she said.

"You'll be in for the rest of the night?"

"I will."

"All right, then. I'll wait until I hear the deadbolts click in."

She smiled and her pale cheeks filled with a blush. He knew she wanted to ask him in. That her flirting wasn't just about avoidance. She toyed with the idea of having an affair with him, and it made him feel good that she did. Of course, there was no way it could happen. Even if it wasn't completely unethical and dangerous for him to be with Tate, there was no way. She was American royalty and he was a bodyguard. More than one universe apart.

He took two steps back. That was all she needed to decide that today wasn't the day to be bold. She went inside and closed the door. True to his word, he waited until both locks clicked into place. Then he got out his two-way radio and made sure the man on duty had her safe and sound.

By the time he was halfway down to the garage he'd already decided he was going to find out everything he could about this joker who kidnapped people for money.

2

MICHAEL STRAIGHTENED his tie as he waited for Tate to come to the door. They were going to her father's place, which never made for an easy day. William was a powerful man who'd made millions—actually, billions—in construction and real estate. He and his brother Joseph had started small, but they'd been smart and ruthless and they'd gotten some prime government contracts that had taken them from their roots in Missouri to penthouses in half the major cities in the world. Although they'd been more successful than anyone could have imagined, there were costs involved, including a daughter and heir so terrified of being kidnapped that she barely lived a life.

Michael knew there was a real threat and that measures had to be taken, but there was also a need for balance. At least some room for Tate to breathe. Unfortunately there wasn't much an outsider could do. Especially not someone as low on the totem pole as a bodyguard.

He heard the locks slide open one after the other. The door swung open to reveal Tate dressed in a pair of beige pants, a pale yellow silky blouse and enough makeup to tell him that she'd had another crappy night.

"Michael. I'm running later than I should. Come in while I finish gathering my things."

He stepped inside a foyer as large as his apartment. He'd grown accustomed to the world of the rich, although it never ceased to make him wonder who the hell was in command of the planet.

It wasn't easy to like the very rich, either, although Tate was pretty decent. She never actually meant to make people feel like poor slobs. It just happened.

She went toward the kitchen, and Michael took the opportunity to do a surprise inspection. He moved his right hand in a specific signal, one that would easily be missed if his people weren't on the ball, watching his every move on the cameras set discreetly around the penthouse. Two minutes would be all the time he needed. If E.J. wasn't here by then, he'd be looking for a new job.

He made it in one minute and forty-two seconds. E. J. Packer was young, twenty-four, but he'd been an excellent sniper in the Delta Force when he'd been badly scarred in a shoot-out with Syrian terrorists. He hadn't lost any of his ability, but he was distinct now, recognizable for the angry red mess that was the left half of his face. Michael didn't give a shit about that. He wanted a crack team that not only knew what to do at the party but understood that no matter where they worked—or for whom—it was a military operation and there was no excuse, ever, for slacking off.

He nodded at E.J. "That was close."

"I'll do better next time, sir."

"I know you will. Carry on."

E.J.'s shoulders moved just enough to let Michael know he hadn't let go of the trappings of being a soldier.

Didn't matter as long as he did the job. As long as he didn't make Tate feel like a bug under a microscope.

The young man disappeared, melting away as silently as he'd entered. Michael thought about going into the kitchen, talking to Pilar, Tate's personal chef. But he just walked the perimeter of the foyer, checking out the artwork.

This place had always felt more like a museum than a home. Marble floors, antiques of inestimable worth, paintings he recognized because they were master-pieces. He took in a deep breath to combat the tight-ening of his throat. It wasn't that he resented her for having the money. Okay, so he resented it a little. But what really pissed him off is that this was what his life had come to. Babysitting.

"Michael?"

He turned at Tate's voice.

"Would you like some coffee? I'm going to be another ten minutes or so. I've already warned Father."

"Sure, that'd be great." He waited until Tate disap-peared back into the hallway, then he went into the kitchen.

Pilar was there pouring him the promised cup of coffee. He wasn't one for fancy java or any of that flavored crap, but he had to admit the coffee in Tate's kitchen was some of the best he'd ever had. He wasn't sure what it was and he'd never asked. No chance he'd ever get those beans for his coffeemaker.

"How are you, Michael?"

Pilar was born in Brazil and moved to the U.S. when she went to college at eighteen. Her accent made her seem exotic and sophisticated. Or maybe that was just Pilar. She had trained at the CIA—the Culinary Institute of America—which was one of the reasons she was working as Tate's chef, but she'd also trained at the other CIA, and that was why she had a chef's coat with a custom pocket that held her Sig Sauer.

"I'm fine," he said, taking the too-delicate cup from her hand. "How's the new kid working out?"

She smiled at him, and he tried to remember if he'd ever seen her without her deep crimson lipstick expertly applied to her generous mouth.

"Don't you think of anything but business?"

"No."

She laughed. "No wonder you have no love life."

"How do you know?"

"Michael, my dear, if you can resist me, then you can resist anyone."

He held back his own grin. "How do you know I'm not gay? Living the wild life with my lumberjack boyfriend?"

Her laughter actually echoed in the kitchen. It was ridiculously large, like something out of Windsor Castle, all for one woman whose only guests were business associates, all of them involved with the Baxter Foundation, a charitable organization funded by Baxter, run by Tate.

"Believe me, I'd know if you were gay," Pilar said. She picked up her own cup and took a sip, leaving no trace of her lipstick on the rim. "It's a shame you don't let yourself relax, though. It isn't healthy."

"I relax."

"I don't even think you know the definition of the word."

"What word?"

Michael turned to see Tate standing at the hallway door. "Are you ready?"

"Not really, and we're not late. I just got off the phone with a very obstinate woman at the MacArthur Foundation and I need to calm down."

"So you're getting coffee?" he asked as she handed Pilar another cup.

"Yes. I am."

"Okay by me."

She took the full cup back but didn't drink. Instead she focused her attention on him. Her expression became pensive and she opened her mouth, but then a blush stole over her cheeks and she turned to Pilar. Two sips and five quiet minutes later they were in the elevator, on the way down to the limo. Tate looked at her shoes the whole time.

SHE STARED OUT HER tinted window, watching New York pass by, chewing once again on the idea Dr. Bay had fed her last week. It was easy to make excuses for her fears, which were, in fact, legitimate. She could be kidnapped, held for ransom, murdered. Such things had occurred, could occur again. It made sense to be wary, to keep her guard up.

On the other hand, her guard was up so high she couldn't see the world behind it. Yes, it could all go to hell tomorrow. But it hadn't gone to hell yesterday or the day before or many years before that. She'd put all her eggs in the fear basket, and wouldn't she feel like the biggest idiot on earth if she went on to live to a ripe old age, completely safe and having missed the whole thing.

She sighed as she gazed at the back of Michael's head. His dark hair was wavy and thick and she wondered if the messy-chic was on purpose or just truculence. Somehow she doubted Michael owned mousse or gave a damn about how he looked—which, in her opinion, was incredibly juicy even on his bad days. It helped that he kept himself in battle-ready shape. He even walked as if daring anyone to try anything funny.

How had she let her fear of being kidnapped morph into a fear of everything? College had started out so well. She'd finally been able to put Lisa's death behind her, at least enough to get by, and then—whoosh!—it all had vanished on that one awful day when Ian Stark and Bruce Halliday had kidnapped her.

After that everything had gone to hell. Her relationship with Graydon, never great to begin with, had soured until she'd had to get out. She'd started spending more and more time in her apartment, only leaving to go to class or one of her self-defense classes, which, instead of making her feel more in control, had brought her terror into sharper relief.

She had given in to the panic attacks, the nightmares—and they'd taken over. And now look at her. She hadn't even been able to ask Michael a simple question. She saw him almost every day. They talked and talked, and yet when it came to something as foolish, as personal, as the origins of the scar on his chin, she became tongue-tied and shy as a kitten. It wasn't as if she wanted to ask him if he preferred boxers to briefs. The scar was right there for anyone to see.

Pathetic.

HE STOOD AGAINST THE wall in the executive dining room along with the two ex-Secret Service agents who protected William Baxter. One, Jim, was William's driver, and the other, Peter, was his executive secretary. But mostly they were there to make sure no one got too close. Paranoia hadn't hurt just Tate but her father, too.

Michael despised this part of his job. It would be different if he'd been protecting a president or prime minister, someone who was doing something for the good of the people, not just an industrialist's daughter. He'd tried to justify his position, given that Tate ran the Baxter Foundation and that they did help people with their dollars, but that had grown as stale as the sandwich he'd been offered in the staff kitchen.

He shifted his gaze to William. The man was sixty-four but he looked a hell of a lot older. He could afford the best of everything, including plastic surgery for that turkey neck of his, but he preferred to spend his money on things that others would covet. This building, his home, his airplane. His daughter. It was hard for Michael to keep his composure when he was with William and Tate. The man treated her like a child. Like an invalid child. And she let him.

He shifted his position so that he wouldn't get stiff. In all his years in the military he should have grown accustomed to standing, to waiting. He still hated it. He'd rather face a dozen armed men than do nothing but stand and watch.

Tate laughed, which was a damn rare, good thing. He wondered if she knew that she was pretty. That her long neck, her skin, the way her eyes lit up when she was captivated made her incredibly appealing. He didn't think she thought of herself that way at all. She dressed in the camouflage of a woman who doesn't want to be noticed. Beige, cream, taupe, khaki. Pale colors that blended with her pale skin.

His thoughts jumped to the information he'd downloaded about the kidnap artist. Jerry Brody was his name. Michael had read everything he'd been able to find. The guy sounded like a first-class jerk, full of himself and how he was exploring the "human condition." Michael didn't understand how anyone could be fooled by his shtick. Yes, he had a degree in psychology, but come on. According to the papers, he'd kidnapped dozens of people, stolen them from their homes, their cars, from movie theaters. He'd tied them up, blindfolded them, taken them to a small, barren room and kept them isolated. Feeding and communication were used as weapons to make the experience more realistic.

That Tate's shrink proposed this idea was unbelievable. Where had William found this quack? The woman should lose her license over a stunt like this.

Michael had to make sure Tate wasn't going to agree to it. That was all. If it came down to it, he'd talk to William. No way the old man would put up with this crap.

Tate laughed again. It was good to see her so relaxed, but Jesus. They were at the top of the Baxter Building in the middle of Manhattan, on the sixtieth floor, in the executive dining room. Every table but one was empty. None of the managers or supervisors or whoever normally used this place were allowed in when Tate came to lunch. In addition to Michael and the two Secret Service men, there were also men stationed at the door, in the kitchen and at the elevator.

Her whole goddamn life was one big maximum-security prison.

TATE SETTLED AGAINST the black leather seat of her limo, avoiding Michael's gaze as he shut the door. She had to blink away sudden tears, swallow a lump in her throat.

The lunch had been fine. Her father was in good spirits, the food superb, the conversation productive. All had been right with the world...until she'd looked at Michael and caught the pity in his eyes.

It was only then that she'd seen the empty tables all around them, heard the echo of cutlery on china. Shame had hit her with a wicked gut punch, and she hadn't been able to touch her sorbet.

He hadn't said a word to her, not in the elevator nor in the garage. He'd treated her with respect, as always. He'd even given her one of his rare smiles as he'd opened the limo door. But his look of pity lingered in her mind's eye.

Pathetic. There wasn't an area of her life that was free from the effects of her own personal monster. Her father only wanted her to be safe and happy, but she didn't feel, either. She liked administering the trust, but there again she did almost everything from her home office. Her world had shrunk to a pinpoint. If it wasn't for Sara... How had this happened?

"Tate?"

"Yes?"

"Home?"

"Yes, thank you, Michael."

"No shopping to do?"

"Not today, no."

"Okay."

His voice sounded normal. No reprimand in his tone at all. And in that heartbeat she made her decision. She would do it. Be kidnapped. She would call Dr. Bay first thing tomorrow and she'd start the process.

Her hands shook at the enormity of the decision. Which just made her more determined. This was her life, and as of this moment she was taking control.

3

MICHAEL SAT AT HIS kitchen table, a cold beer half-finished, newspaper and magazine articles spread in front of him. All of them seemed to cover the same territory about Jerry Brody and his lunacy. Unfortunately none of the articles gave him enough information about Brody's clients to lead him to an actual ID. Michael had put in calls to every one of the reporters, but only two had phoned back, neither one willing to name those who had used Brody's service.

He'd even left a message with Brody himself, his intention to pose as a would-be client, which would give him a lot of information, and he'd also ask for personal referrals.

He just hoped that all this work was for nothing. He didn't imagine Tate would be foolish enough to walk into a nightmare scenario like this, but he had to plan as if it were a go. What he couldn't decide was whether he should tell William about this or just go see Dr. Bay himself.

He stretched his head to the right, then the left, trying to work out some of the tension in his neck and shoulders. What he needed to do was get his ass to the gym. He hadn't been in three days, and that was unacceptable. Besides keeping him in fighting shape, his brutal workouts were his best defense against stress and depression.

He didn't belong in New York, at least not like this. He should be in Iraq or Afghanistan, doing what he'd been trained to do. Not babysitting.

He took another swig of beer. Of all the useless things in his life, wishing he could change his situation was the stupidest. He'd left the military of his own free will—but not because he'd wanted to. He still felt the decision was the right one, even if it did mean he'd have to live this life.

Needing the distraction, he went back to reading the last of the articles about Brody. It was as useless as the rest. He turned the page anyway. Maybe—

A knock at his door made him jump, but he relaxed just as quickly. Only one person came to his apartment these days. One person Michael didn't want to see.

Yep, it was Charlie. The real reason Michael was a glorified babysitter.

His brother knocked again, louder this time.

Michael went back to the table and gathered his work into a file. That he put into the small safe in a cabinet in the living room. Only then did he let his brother in.

"What the hell?" Charlie said as he crossed the living room to the kitchen. "Were you in the crapper?"

"You ever heard of calling first?"

Charlie opened the fridge and took one of Michael's Heinekens. He looked like shit, but that wasn't unusual. Charlie was the only member of his family still living, and that was some kind of miracle because the way he played so fast and loose with drugs, booze and the horses, he should have been dead years ago. Nothing worked in Charlie's life, never had. Ever since Michael could remember, Charlie had been the screw-up. Part of that was probably due to their mother's death when Charlie was only five, but that excuse could only go so far.

Their old man had tried his best to get Charlie some help, but there wasn't a rehab center on the East Coast Charlie hadn't ditched.

Michael supposed he loved his brother on some level, but that level was buried beneath a steaming pile of resentment. The old man had made him swear to take care of Charlie. Michael didn't have the guts to go against a deathbed wish, although it probably would have been better for both of them.

Michael would still be in military intelligence, and Charlie…

"Mikey, listen. I know I promised I wouldn't ask for no more money, but I'm in a hell of a spot."

Michael fetched his own beer and sat down in his leather club chair. He might as well be comfortable for the argument that was about to start the moment he said, "I told you, Charlie, the bank of Michael is closed."

Charlie sat down on the couch, his beefy hand holding on to his beer so tightly Michael wouldn't have been surprised if it shattered. He really did look like shit. He'd been about thirty pounds overweight for years now, but at least when he was younger he'd been solid. Now there was a look of undercooked dough about him. It didn't help that he was wearing a filthy

T-shirt and jeans that hadn't seen the inside of a washing machine in God knows how long.

"Mikey, you don't understand. I'm in a real mess. I had me this sure thing. You remember that trainer I told you about? The guy with the limp and the broken tooth? He swore, Mikey, swore to God himself that the race was fixed, that he'd done the fixing himself."

"I'm not bailing you out again. We already discussed that. You gave me your word."

"And I meant it. If I hadn't heard the words from that trainer guy for myself, I never would have—"

"Charlie, stop it. I don't care why."

His brother, two years his junior and as different from Michael as day was from night, gave him a look of such hatred it made him sick to his stomach. He'd bailed Charlie out too many times to count, and this was what he got? One no, and Charlie looked as if he could kill him as soon as pass him the salt.

"It's Ed Martini, Mike. You know his reputation. He's gonna kill me."

"He isn't. What good are you gonna do him dead?"

Charlie shook his head, a drop of sweat flying off the end of his long, dirty hair. "He said he was gonna make an example of me. You know what that means? He's gonna kill me, but he's gonna hurt me—bad— before it's over. That dude, Jazz, who works for him? I swear to God, he's a psycho. He loves to hurt people, Mikey. I swear to God."

Michael figured about ten percent of whatever Charlie said was true. The problem was, which part? "I'll pay for you to go back to rehab. And if you stick it out, I'll help you get a job and a place to stay after."

Charlie got up so fast his beer shot out of the bottle, soaking Michael's shirt. "I'm not gonna live long enough to go to goddamn rehab. Don't you listen? They're gonna kill me!"

Michael swore under his breath as he got up. "Just shut up, Charlie. Sit down and shut up. I gotta go change my shirt."

Charlie seemed surprised, as if he hadn't noticed what he'd done, but at least he sat.

Michael went into his bedroom and got another shirt from the dresser. As he changed, he debated giving Charlie the money. It wasn't as if he was rolling in it, but he could spare some. He shouldn't. He'd told his brother in no uncertain terms that he was finished. Yet how could he live with himself if Martini really did kill him?

He tossed the wet shirt in the bathroom hamper, then went back to the living room. Only Charlie wasn't there.

Michael went to the door and looked down the hallway. Charlie was already on the stairs; Michael heard the heavy clump of his brother's boots.

He shut the door, locked the deadbolts and debated getting another beer. It was after ten, though, and he wanted to get up at five to make it to the gym.

In his tiny living room he wiped the trail of beer off the floor, then turned out the lights. He'd more than likely get a call from Charlie tomorrow. And if he was lucky, he'd hear from Jerry Brody, too.

"IF YOU DON'T WANT to do this, we'll stop right here."

Tate tried to squeeze her hands into submission, but the shaking wouldn't stop. "No, I want to. I just…"

"I understand. But remember, you'll have your safe word. You can use it anytime, and the moment you say it, everything stops and you're returned safely to your home. No exceptions."

"So they won't cover my mouth."

"Absolutely not."

Tate believed Dr. Bay and didn't believe her at the same time. Jerry Brody sat across from her at the conference table, while Dr. Bay sat next to her. He didn't look like a performance artist or a therapist. He reminded her, in fact, of the doorman at Sara's apartment building. Round in the middle, shallow in the chest, his balding head his most striking feature.

They'd been in the meeting for half an hour, and Brody had explained that he wasn't in the business of hurting people. He would accommodate Tate's wishes to the best of his ability and he would oversee her adventure himself.

The first time he'd called it an adventure, she'd given him a look that should have seared off his eyebrows. After that, he'd approached her more carefully. Still, she wasn't sure he understood the depth of her phobia.

"I'd like to add that to the contract, Mr. Brody," Dr. Bay said. "No covering of her mouth at any time."

Brody nodded. "That's fine. You realize she won't know when we're going to take her? It's a natural reaction to scream or call out. I don't want any of my people being arrested."

"Please don't talk about me as if I'm not here," Tate said. "As for being arrested, it won't happen if you do your planning adequately. Which reminds me—

we'll have to make sure that Michael knows the plan. If you surprise him, he'll do a lot more than arrest you."

"Michael?"

"Her driver and bodyguard." Dr. Bay put her hand on Tate's. "Don't worry. If we decide to go ahead, we'll bring him into the loop."

"He's not going to like it."

"I don't doubt it."

"Maybe there's a way we can send him on vacation or something," Tate said. She could feel her cheeks fill with the heat of embarrassment, which was something of a surprise. It occurred to her that she didn't want Michael in the loop or to even know this fake kidnapping was being discussed. She knew he'd have serious objections, but worse than that, he'd think she was a fool.

But he wasn't afraid of his own shadow.

"I'm sure," Dr. Bay said, "that once he realizes you'll be completely safe, he won't have any objections. Perhaps he can take a meeting with you, Mr. Brody, and you two can go over his concerns."

Brody might be a self-proclaimed artistic genius, but he wasn't much of an actor. He clearly wanted his show to be run his way, with no interference.

"Let's continue," Tate said. "I'll decide about Michael later."

Dr. Bay smiled. "That's a good idea." She turned to Brody. "Let's discuss constraints."

"I typically use rope and handcuffs. Since she—" He stopped, turned his head a half inch so he was looking at Tate. "Since you'll only be with us for a few hours, the constraints won't be too extreme. And I'll be there every step of the way to make sure nothing goes wrong."

"It won't do me any good to have you go so easy I don't get any part of the experience. I believe the purpose is to make sure I survive, right?"

"I don't think that will be a problem," Dr. Bay said. "You'll feel as if it's real."

Tate blushed again. She got the message loud and clear: her phobia was so severe Brody wouldn't have to do much in the way of convincing her. "Fine. Let's move on."

"You're insane."

"Thank you," Tate said as she handed Sara her plate. Pilar had made a sinful lasagna, which happened to be Tate's favorite dish, but the casserole was large enough to feed an army.

"I'm serious. Personally I think your precious Dr. Bay has a screw loose. This has to be one of the dumbest things I can think of."

Tate took her own plate, which had a small square of lasagna and a spinach salad, and her glass of wine and followed Sara as she made her way up to the solarium on the roof. It was their favorite place to eat, to talk. In her little area of New York the buildings weren't skyscrapers; the view was of Central Park, and her rooftop garden was the highest thing around.

Sara got herself comfy, and Tate thought her friend had never looked better. Sara had been her downstairs neighbor since second grade, when they'd both lived in a brownstone on East Forty-fourth Street. They'd stayed close all these years.

She had always thought of herself as chubby, even though Tate had told her that size ten wasn't in the least fat and that she was beautiful. It was the company she kept that made her feel big. Sara worked as an editor for *Vanity Fair* magazine, and most of the women she knew were bulimic and looked as if they'd been starved.

This year, though, something had changed. Sara had finally decided that she'd just focus on being healthy— tonight's lasagna notwithstanding—and she'd been working out with a private trainer for months.

"You look fabulous."

Sara had just put a large forkful of pasta in her mouth, and at Tate's compliment she nearly choked. When she finally got her breath back, she shook her head. "No way you're changing the subject."

"I wasn't trying to change anything. I just think you look—"

"Fabulous. Right. Now here's my question—have you or haven't you invited Michael inside after work?"

Tate felt the instant rise of heat in her cheeks. "Not yet."

"Not yet." Sara put her fork down and somehow managed to look stern and motherly despite the fact that she was Tate's age and her hair was a mass of wild blond curls. "You can't even ask Hotty McSwoon into your home, let alone into your bed, and you're going to get kidnapped? By strangers? With rope and hand-cuffs? You don't see a problem with this?"

"I know. It sounds crazy. But the whole reason I haven't invited Michael in is because I'm scared. Of everything. Or haven't you noticed?"

"Of course I know you're scared, but let's look at the progression here. First kidnap, then sex?"

"Yes. And I don't know that he'd even want to have sex."

Sara laughed. "Oh, please. The way you two look at each other in that limo? I'm surprised you both don't come at every stoplight."

"Sara!"

"It's true and you know it."

Tate got busy with her lasagna, wishing now she'd taken a much bigger piece. Just thinking about Michael was enough to get her all hot and bothered, and even though Sara was her closest friend, she didn't like to feel like this except in the privacy of her own bedroom.

"Tate, what's going on in that head of yours?"

"Nothing."

"Talk to me, girl. This is a huge decision."

"I know. I'm just so tired of being me. If I could have an exorcism, I would. But I don't think it's a devil that makes me so scared. I've set up my whole life to be safe, but the cost is huge. I would love to go to the gym with you. I'd love to go back to Italy. I can travel anywhere in the world, but all I see is this place." She felt tears burn her eyes, and dammit, she didn't want to cry. "I really think this kidnapping thing will change me. I have to take the chance."

"What does Michael think?"

"He agrees with you. That it's insane. But I have to go with my gut on this. I've made sure that I can stop things in a minute if I need to. I hope I don't have to. I want to be a real person, not a shadow." She pushed her plate away, suddenly not hungry. "I need you to support me, Sara. Please. I need all the good karma I can get."

Sara reached over and put her hand on Tate's. "I'll support you no matter what, okay? Think it through. Make sure this isn't going to make things worse."

"It can't get much worse."

Sara sighed. She looked around the solarium, at all the plants and flowers, the miniature fruit trees and the tall grasses by the fountain. "I want you to be happy. For what it's worth, I think Michael's a really great guy, and you could do a lot worse than getting back in the game with him. But let him in on the kidnap plan. Let him make sure nothing goes haywire."

"No. He can't be there or it won't be real."

"It's not going to be real."

"You know what I mean."

Sara sighed. "Yeah, I do."

Tate grinned. "Can you stick around for a movie?"

"Sure I can. But only if I get to pick."

"We're not going to watch *Notting Hill* again."

"Spoilsport."

"Deal with it."

Sara lifted her glass of wine. "To stubborn women."

Tate raised her own glass. "Amen."

SHE DIDN'T THINK about the kidnapping or Michael until after Sara left. Tate had gone to her bedroom where she'd washed and gotten into her sleep shirt, then climbed into her bed. She wished she had a cat or a puppy, something to sleep with her. Her father was terribly allergic, so she'd never had her own pet, but this was her house, and if he didn't like it, he didn't have to visit.

The moment she closed her eyes she knew it wasn't a pet she wanted sharing her bed. She wanted Michael.

He really was an exceptional man. She knew he wasn't thrilled with his life, that he wished he was back doing his 007 thing, but when they were together, him in the front seat, her in the back, there was a connection between them. Even Sara had noticed.

Of course, there was no real future with Michael, but that was all right. Sara had hit the nail on the head—Michael would be ideal as her first after so, so long. He'd be gentle and caring....

A fling. That's all she wanted. Really.

4

As he stood leaning against the limo, waiting for Tate to finish her shopping, Michael thought once more about going to William. It had been a week since Tate had told him she'd agreed to the kidnapping. In that time Michael had met with Brody, talked with three of his past "victims" and gone over the plan about fifty times. He still thought it was a ridiculous and dangerous game, but Tate had made up her mind.

There was still time to go to William, who would put a stop to this nonsense, but Tate was adamant that her father be kept out of the loop. When he'd suggested that he come along for the stunt, Tate had nearly wept insisting that he stay the hell away.

Wasn't going to happen, of course. Although Brody had said he'd give no warning before the actual snatch, Michael was going to see him tomorrow to persuade him that it was in Brody's best interest to take him along. Tate wouldn't know, and that was fine, but there was no way he was going to let her get taken to some unknown location for an indeterminate period of time without him watching every goddamn second. He could just see himself trying to explain to William how Tate had been hurt—or worse—while he'd been watching basketball on ESPN.

Of course, if Brody continued to object, Michael had a plan B. He always had a plan B.

He checked his watch and figured he'd give Tate another five minutes. She was in the Prada store having a fitting. He still couldn't figure that damn store out. There was practically nothing on display. It was all hidden in some way that clearly appealed to women.

He'd waited out enough fittings to know he couldn't rush her, but he also didn't like her to be out of his sight. Of course, Elizabeth was with her, and he trusted her. Even better, Tate trusted her. A former CIA case officer, Elizabeth knew her way around a weapon.

His cell phone rang. It was George, one of his tech guys who worked on the alarm system at Tate's. They were replacing some of the equipment, and Michael had asked for regular updates. As in all things concerning Tate, he wanted the hard-core work to be done when she was sleeping or out of the penthouse. She tended to get nervous when she caught glimpses of what it really took to keep her safe.

"What's going on?"

"It's all good, boss. We have the equipment in and we've just finished the test run. We'll be all cleaned up in ten."

"What did you think of the test?"

"It's everything they promised."

"Good, I—" He saw Tate come out of the shop carrying two large bags. Just as she reached the center of the sidewalk, she stopped and handed the bags to

Elizabeth, then she looked inside her purse. "George, she's coming. I'll talk—"

A movement caught his attention, someone in a hooded coat right behind her. A second later the man shoved Elizabeth into a passing group of students. Michael tossed the phone and got out his weapon as he ran. A white van drove up onto the sidewalk, the side door wide-open. The hooded man shoved Tate inside and the van took off.

He lifted his weapon to shoot out a tire, but civilians crowded in front of him and he lost the shot. Brody had covered the license plate with mud, and there was nothing else identifying about the van as it turned the corner out of his view.

He raced back to the limo, cursing Dr. Bay fifty ways to Sunday. If it was the last thing he did, he was going to find Jerry Brody and break his neck.

He picked up the cell phone he'd dropped. It still worked, and as he pulled out of the shopping mall valet parking lot, he hit *2.

"Elizabeth here."

"I'm going after her," he said, "but I'm dropping off the limo and taking my own vehicle. Got that?"

"Yes, sir. I'm sorry—"

"Just make sure Daddy doesn't get inquisitive. If all goes well, I'll have her back by nightfall."

"Yes, sir."

He clicked off the phone, tossed it on the seat and pulled out another electronic device, the one the size and shape of a BlackBerry. It was actually a GPS—a global positioning system—with only one target. The moment he saw the light on the map he relaxed. He'd find her and bring her home. There would be plenty of time to kill Brody afterward.

For now, he concentrated on not killing any pedestrians or getting arrested as he broke a great many laws. He had to get out of this limo if he wanted to have the least bit of stealth. He'd taken his motorcycle to work this morning, which was a good thing. He could move quickly and get into tight spots with that baby, and there weren't many cars on the road that could catch him.

Michael figured the van was registered to Brody and that it was heading toward Long Island, where Brody lived. But he wasn't a hundred percent sure and he wasn't going to take any chances.

Tate knew about the GPS tracker—at least the one in her wristwatch. She didn't know about the one in her purse. But that was fine. She didn't need to know everything. Besides, if she hadn't actually passed out from fear, she'd be too busy with her panic attacks to think about global positioning systems.

SHE WAS IN A VAN and there was a bag over her head. Tate could barely feel her hands or her feet, but she could feel the bag being sucked into her mouth as she struggled for breath. The air was foul, sick, and her heart pounded hard in her chest.

"Stop," she said, only it was a croak, not really a word. "Stop." It was only a tiny bit better. They wouldn't hear her. He'd promised to stop if she asked him to, but he had to hear her.

"Stop!"

That was louder, that was more of a scream, but the

van kept going, kept rocking, and no one touched her or listened. She tried to kick out, to make them listen, but her legs were tied together and she could hardly move.

"Stop! Stop!" She used all her strength to thrash, to get their attention. And her heart—it was filling her chest and squeezing her lungs so she couldn't breathe.

"Stop, stop, stop, stop!"

No one answered. She was alone and she was going to die in the back of this van. There was no air, no escape. It was over and there was so much she hadn't done.

The blackness came from the inside out. It was welcome.

HE MADE IT TO THE garage in Tate's building, then jumped out of the vehicle and climbed onto his rebuilt Suzuki GSX. He docked his GPS just above the speed-ometer and squealed out of the garage, heading toward Long Island. He wasn't exactly sure where Brody lived, but he thought it might be Little Neck.

Didn't matter. He was following the purse. Brody had no reason to scan Tate for a GPS, so he had no need to get rid of her purse. Even if the pervert wanted to take her clothes, they'd still be in the van.

Trouble was, it was Friday and it was four-thirty, and the expressway was a parking lot. He could get around the cars all right, but there was a great chance he could be popped in the process. The last thing he needed now was to have to explain this to the highway patrol.

He inched the bike forward and thought again about Brody. The man wasn't exactly living on his perfor-mance art, despite charging an arm and a leg for his kidnappings. Michael knew Tate had already given him ten grand—half the fee. But Brody himself lived off his wife's income. She was some big cosmetic surgeon who Botoxed politicos and movie stars. She was why he could afford to play with his art.

As he put his leg down once again to wait for traffic to move, he watched the blip on the GPS moving steadily forward on the same expressway, only about ten miles ahead.

Screw it. He'd explain to the police if he had to. In the meantime, he was gonna find Tate.

Swerving the bike into the fire lane, he gunned it. He tried to keep an eye out for cops, but between looking at the signal and trying not to be killed by motorists, he had his hands full.

There was a car stuck in his way a few miles in, so he went back into traffic. Despite the laws against it in New York, he did the bob and weave, skating past SUVs and Toyotas with a couple of inches to spare.

He couldn't understand how the van was making such good time, but as the minutes ticked by and the GPS kept purring, he closed the distance.

Just as he thought he might get a visual, he heard the dreaded sound of a police siren.

Glancing back, he saw the NYHP coming up the fire lane.

Michael slowed down and found himself a nice place to idle right in front of a grocery truck. Traffic moved at about five miles an hour, and he just stayed put, preparing his explanation.

The blip on the GPS went farther away with each painstaking inch, and so did the siren. Finally he saw the lights in his side mirror. Even the cops weren't going very fast. When they reached his side, they didn't stop, and he let out a held breath. They were after something else, an accident probably, but with them so close he didn't dare pull any stunts.

He tried to be patient. He wasn't successful.

TATE WOKE, STILL IN the darkness of the rocking vehicle. She had no moisture at all in her throat and she felt as if she would choke to death. She tried to cry out again, to tell them they had it wrong, but she couldn't.

Her tears felt hot on her cheeks as her heart pumped beyond its endurance. She thought of her father, how furious he would be at her for getting herself into this mess. How he would have to live with the fact that her death was her own fault.

She thought of Michael and how all this could have been prevented if she hadn't been so vain. He would have stopped this, he would have saved her.

She'd wasted so much of her life, only to end up throwing her life away on a stunt. On this idiotic game.

What she didn't understand is why they weren't following the agreement. Brody had signed the contract. Didn't he realize he'd be in trouble once they discovered he'd ignored the rules?

She gasped again, licked a tear off her lip. She would give anything, any amount of money, if only they would let her go. She'd never do anything this stupid again. She'd be good, she'd pray every night, she'd—

The truck turned, causing her to roll to her right,

then stabilize again. Maybe they were close to wherever they were taking her. They'd have to listen then, wouldn't they?

But she probably wasn't going to make it. Not when she couldn't catch her breath. Not when her chest was about to explode. It was over. Her life was ending. What a pathetic waste.

IT HAD BEEN AN accident, a big one. Two SUVs, one overturned, a fire truck, an ambulance and several patrol cars. Michael had no choice but to wait until he'd passed the worst of it before he could even get to a decent speed.

The van was already past it all. It had turned off the expressway onto the surface streets of Port Washington. He knew the area, but not well.

By the time he got to the right exit he saw the van heading toward Sands Point. According to Michael's research, neither Brody nor the wife were Sands Point rich. Hell, he knew of one estate that was for sale there right now—price tag of twenty-eight million. That was William Baxter territory, and it didn't sit right.

The traffic wasn't all that great even now that he was off the LIE. Too many commuters coming in from the city, trying to make it to their nice Long Island homes. The blip on the GPS had stalled. He lifted the unit from the cradle and pressed a couple of buttons. Seacoast Lane. That was on the very edge of Sands Point.

He'd driven Tate to Sands Point once about four months ago, to a literary luncheon given by an author who lived there. Susan somebody. Tate and he had talked about the village. She'd told him that there were no stores of any kind in Sands Point. Only homes and gardens and an animal shelter. The residents—who included the CEO of a large pharmaceutical company, a former governor of New York and the family that owned the estate that many believe was the inspiration for "East Egg" in Fitzgerald's *Gatsby*—were all rich enough that they could live in this garden suburb where the gates and the security guards kept out all but the anointed.

None of that colorful history helped him now. He drove past well-tended yards and kids toting back-packs filled to the limit. Even the frequent suburban stops didn't slow him down as much as the express-way traffic, and soon he was in Port Washington, the town that supported the wealthy lives of those who lived in Sands Point.

It was all so peaceful out here. No honking horns, hardly any pedestrians on the main street. Only twenty-five miles from Manhattan, it felt like another world.

As he approached the gated community, Michael turned his attention to his GPS screen. The blip had stayed right there at Seacoast. He pressed another button, moving in on the target.

Not a second later he was looking at an aerial view of 200 Seacoast. It was a huge estate with only one big semicircular road in and out. The house looked large enough to supply a battalion, and the grounds were ex-pansive. It had to be at least twenty acres. The estate was also surrounded on three sides by Long Island Sound.

Michael put all his concentration now on getting to

Seacoast. First he had to get past the guards, but that was ridiculously simple. He followed another motorcycle—one with a teenager driving—gave the guard a wave and that was that. Then he found the estate, and it was just as impressive as the GPS had indicated.

Ditching his bike was simple in the vast acres of old trees. The last thing he wanted was for Brody to get wind of this rescue and pull some other stupid stunt. By the time he was finished, no one would find his bike.

He had his gun just in case he needed to get pushy. And he had his GPS, but now he used his old-school skills to lead him to his target. He had no idea what kind of security there was and he didn't relish setting off any alarms.

It was still light out, this being the middle of March, so he'd have to be damn careful. He hoped Tate was holding up all right. He also didn't think Sands Point had a psychiatric hospital.

TATE WOKE TO DARKNESS. She lay on a mattress, her right handcuffed to something behind and above her head. Every part of her body ached as she shifted her position.

She tried to think. She'd been in the store with Elizabeth. Karen had been doing a hem. And she'd bought two shirts for her father. It was blank after that.

This was it, of course. The kidnapping. She could feel the familiar symptoms of a panic attack coming over her like a wave. Her accelerated heartbeat, her constricted throat, the narrowing of her vision as she felt as if she was going to die.

"Please," she said, but her voice broke and turned into a sob. "Please, stop this."

She wept and struggled for breath as her stomach churned. It felt as if she was on the water, rolling with the waves, but that couldn't be.

All she wanted was to go home. She'd been crazy to think this was a good idea. It was her worst nightmare come to life. "Please," she said again, this time louder, but no one answered.

He hadn't covered her eyes though he'd said he was going to use a blindfold. But it didn't matter because she couldn't see anything but dark and she couldn't hear anything but her own silent scream. Her body spasmed and she barely felt the pain in her wrist. Everything was too closed, too tight, and she couldn't breathe. If she could just get outside, stop this pounding in her chest…. She would die, and then Michael would never know. He would only remember her being so stupid. *God, please, make it stop. Please, please. Can't breathe.* She was going to throw up, she knew it. She would die like this, in this small room, and she hadn't lived at all.

A light burned her eyes and she struggled more, desperate to get out, get free. Someone was over her, touching her, holding her shoulders.

"Please stop it. Stop. I don't want this. I have to get out, please!"

"Quiet, you damn fool. You're bleeding."

She opened her eyes, adjusted painfully to the light. The man was dark and small and she didn't know him. She'd never seen him before. It wasn't Brody. Brody had promised….

"Stop struggling. You're tearing open your wrist."

But she couldn't. The more he pressed on her shoulders, the more desperate she became. The smell of liquor made her gag, and he stepped back. She opened her mouth, ready to plead, to beg, but she screamed and screamed.

He slapped her hard across the face, and it was as if she'd been doused with cold water. She stopped screaming and for a moment, a horribly vivid moment, she was clear, she was there, in this strange room with the awful man.

"Shut the hell up. You're gonna piss him off—and you don't want to do that."

"Let me go," she whispered, barely recognizing her own voice. "Stop this now. I'll pay you. You won't lose any money, but please let me go."

"You'll pay, all right, but there's no way we're letting you go."

"Where's Brody?"

"Who the fuck's Brody? Just shut up. Be still and it'll be better for you."

"What?"

"If you calm down, I'll put something on your wrist."

"Who are you?"

He smiled, and his teeth were large and his eyes were small. "Don't matter who I am. What matters is who you are."

"You're not Brody."

He shook his head. "You want to bleed to death, that's okay with me, only he don't want his bed all filled with blood, see?"

"Who is he? Where am I?"

"Listen to me. Just give me your father's phone number, okay? That's all you have to do. Then everything'll be just fine."

"What?"

"The phone number. There's nothing else you need to worry about. Just give us the number."

"Why?"

"Look, just give it up. You're a pretty lady. You don't want to get hurt now, do ya?"

"Oh, my God. You're not Brody. This isn't the plan. You've kidnapped me. You're going to kill me."

"Now who said anything about killing you? We just need the number."

She'd awakened from her nightmare straight into hell. This was the real thing. She'd been kidnapped. Every bad dream she'd ever had was true and right now, and there was no bargaining, no going to a safe place. She would die and all she could think as she closed her eyes was that she hoped it wouldn't hurt too badly.

She'd never even asked Michael into her home. And now she'd never get the chance.

5

No lights were on inside the house. From where Michael was hiding, behind a band of large elm trees, it appeared that no one was home and that the exterior lights were all connected to a security system.

Getting to the back of the estate was going to be tricky. The last thing he wanted was a police cruiser catching him trespassing. He supposed he could tell the truth—that he was trying to prevent a fake kidnapping—but he doubted the officers would let him continue on his way.

If it had been his place, he knew just where he'd focus his motion sensors and where he'd put the cameras. There was a very narrow window between this estate and the next where motion sensors became a pain in the ass. It wasn't wide enough for an automobile, but it would work for him as long as the fence held out. There was only one way to find out.

He took off, wondering who owned this place. Now that he was here, he couldn't picture Brody living here. The house was ornate, ostentatious. It spoke of old money with its sculptured gardens and heavy drapes behind the closed windows. Brody was modern and eclectic and he would always want to be seen as avant-garde. Unless this was somehow his wife's estate? That didn't fit, either.

He made his way back far enough that he could hear the ocean. The salty scent had been in the air for a while, but the sound of water lapping against a pier or a dock or a boat… He'd been in enough oceans to have some discernment, but he'd never been a SEAL.

Would he have taken her to a boat? Was that all part of his plan? If so, it was goddamn stupid. A woman with a panic disorder and the ocean didn't mix. It was far too easy to picture an ugly death in a boat.

But perhaps there was some other building behind the main house where he had her. He hoped so. It had been too long since she'd been taken. He doubted Tate was handling things well.

Shit, by now her disappearance had to have made a stir. She was Tate Baxter, after all, and the kidnapping had taken place in broad daylight in a very expensive section of Manhattan. William would be going insane and he would want his security chief's head on a platter.

Well, it had been an interesting job while it'd lasted. Once he got Tate back home, he'd resign and he'd distance himself as much as possible from his team. They didn't need to collect unemployment just because he'd been suckered.

The edge of the main house came into view, and behind it he could see the ocean. There was a yacht, at least a 65 footer, moored at the edge of a small pier. Parked right by the dock was a white van with muddy plates. Lights glowed from inside the yacht, and as he ran faster, he could see a man's silhouette.

There was no other building. They had her on the water. But not for long.

"WAKE UP."

Tate fought to stay cool, but the sharp pains in her wrist and on her arms were more insistent than the man. She opened her eyes. There were more lights on, and she could now see him clearly.

He was of some mixed heritage, maybe black, maybe Hispanic. His eyes were almost golden, which didn't make much sense. He looked intent and excited; he was smiling as he shook her, and his teeth were crooked, large. He exhaled garlic in her face, and she tried to move her head, which hurt worse than her wrist.

"She's awake."

Another voice, a man, older, behind him. She didn't want to see him, but she looked anyway. He was nothing like his companion. She was right about his age. He was tan, and while his hair was completely white, his face was unlined except around his eyes. He seemed very tall, although from her position on the bed that could be an illusion. He wore a blue shirt and he had a large silver chain around his neck.

"Who are you?"

"You don't need to know that," he said. "Move back, Jazz."

The small man let her go and got off the bed. Now she could see the tall man more clearly, and he reminded her of the men in her father's club, pampered and false, as if they'd used every trick in the book to stay the hand of time.

"What's your father's phone number, Tate?"

"I won't tell you."

"Yes, you will. The only question is how much Jazz will hurt you until you do."

The panic started again and she felt a scream building in her throat.

"Just tell us. It will be so much easier."

"You'll kill me if I tell you."

"I'll kill you if you don't."

"Go ahead."

"Oh, no. That's not how we play the game." He nodded at Jazz.

The small man smiled wider, his glee apparent at the anticipation of her pain. He reached over her head and took her hand in his. He pulled it, hard, and the scream grew as it felt as if he were tearing her wrist apart.

She kicked and found that her legs were no long tied together. It didn't matter, though. She couldn't reach anything or stop the tearing. All she could do was scream and thrash, her free arm as useless as her legs.

"Give us the number, Tate. This is only the beginning. He'd like nothing more than to ruin that hand of yours forever. He'll cut it through the artery. He will. Then he'll have to stop the bleeding, and the only way he knows to do that is to cauterize it. You know what that is, don't you?"

The image of her flesh burning made her gag, but there was nothing in her stomach. Maybe she should tell them. Then they'd kill her and it would be over. That was better, wasn't it?

The big man sighed loudly. "Again," he said as if he were asking Jazz to change the channel.

Tate closed her eyes as Jazz reached for her hand. The pain took her breath and, with it, her strength. She knew what they wanted from her father, and just like all those years ago, they would win.

"All right," she said, her voice nothing more than a whisper. "Stop. Please."

Jazz let her go, but it didn't help much. The pain shot up her arm and wrapped around her chest. Was it really just today that she'd been picking out shirts at Prada? That she had daydreamed about Michael looking at her with pride?

"Well?"

She wiped the tears from her cheeks with her free hand, wishing for a miracle, knowing none would come. "212…"

MICHAEL MADE IT TO the pier without the police showing up. Nothing mattered now but getting to Tate. It was too easy to imagine her in serious trouble, the kind that didn't clear up with a cup of tea and a good night's sleep.

His gun in his hand, he moved toward the yacht, the *Pretty Kitty,* and tried not to make any noise. If the yacht owner was at all security-conscious, Michael had already set off the alarm. Nothing he could do about that except prepare. He had to remember to ask questions first, which wasn't his usual MO.

Brody might be an ass, but that wasn't against the law in New York. If Michael killed him, it would be bad. On the other hand, if Brody tried anything stupid, a bullet in the kneecap might just show him the error of his ways.

He made it to the stern, jumped over the gunwale and got a peek at the main saloon. It was just as luxurious as he'd supposed, nicer than his apartment. Up three stairs was the wheelhouse, but there was no one there, either. Everyone, it seemed, was behind doors.

He kept moving alongside the boat, keeping as low a profile as possible. There was a porthole just ahead, slightly higher than his crouch. Making sure he kept quieter than the water, he made his way there and looked inside.

Tate wasn't there. Neither was Brody. But he did know the man sitting at the small table, his beefy hand holding on to a beer bottle.

Charlie.

It didn't compute. What the hell was his brother doing on a boat in Sands Point?

Michael stood, not caring at the moment if Charlie saw him. Unfortunately he didn't hear the footsteps on the dock until one second before the butt of the gun smashed into his temple.

WHEN TATE WOKE, HER first thought was that death hurt like a son of a bitch, and that filled her with such anger she cried out. Only then did it occur to her that she hadn't been killed. That her pain meant that she'd passed out again.

Her heart sank as she realized the ordeal wasn't over. That they were waiting to kill her when she was fully conscious and able to experience everything as it happened.

Didn't they get it? She'd given them her father's phone number, and by now he probably knew she'd been kidnapped and was already gathering up the cash he'd need for her ransom. She wondered how much they were asking, but it really didn't matter. Her father would give them his last cent if he thought he could save her.

But he knew, just as she did, that paying the ransom meant nothing. She would never get off this boat alive. It made perfect sense, now that she thought about it, for them to bring her to a boat. All they had to do was weight her down and toss her overboard. She'd never be found.

She shifted on the bed. Not only was the pain in her wrist getting scary but most of her arm was numb. She was thirsty, too. Normally she drank eight glasses of water a day, but today—was it still Friday?—she hadn't. Which was probably good, because it didn't look as though they were going to give her a bathroom break anytime soon.

She used her free hand to pull the small pillow farther down, which seemed to help the pressure on her wrist. Oddly her heart wasn't beating terribly fast, and she was breathing mostly in the normal range. Even her thoughts were coherent. So, what, now that she was certain she was going to die, the panic was gone?

That made her angrier still. What was this all about? She'd been paralyzed by panic for most of her life and *now* she got all Zen about death? Oh, come on.

She wished she could have one more talk with Dr. Bay. First she'd tell her that her kidnapping idea? Not so bright. That her friend Jerry Brody had played them all for the fools they were. Except for Michael.

Michael hadn't liked this from the start. He was the only one who'd told her she was in danger. Of course, he always thought she was in danger. That was simply how he saw it.

But he didn't only see evil. There was a part of him that yearned for peace—that much she knew for sure. The books he loved, the music he listened to…they were all filled with hope. Yes, even some of the Russians made a case for love and kindness.

She remembered the time he'd told her his favorite piece of music. She'd had to weasel it out of him, and it was the only time she'd ever seen him blush. At first he'd insisted that it was "Highway to Hell." But she'd wheedled him into his true confession. His favorite song was "Clair de Lune" by Debussy. It was one of her favorites, too, but when she'd asked him why he was embarrassed, he'd said it was girlie music. That had really made her laugh. Girlie music.

How was it possible she was smiling? On the verge of death, and still the thought of Michael made her smile.

Of course, the real Michael, the 24-7 Michael, probably wasn't close to the man she'd created in her head. Her Michael was, she had to admit, too perfect. The real Michael would never have met her expectations. He couldn't have. So it was probably good for her to die now, before she'd gotten brave enough to pursue him. Before the disillusionment. Right?

She wiped her eyes, then her wet hand on the bedspread. It wouldn't have hurt her feelings if they could have slept together. Just once. He would have still been her dream man, but she'd have had one night of experiencing his body for real. God, how many nights had she gone to sleep imagining what it would be like with him? How it would have felt to have Michael fill her, take her. More than that, kiss her.

She hardly knew kissing. Graydon—the only guy she'd ever had sex with—had stunk at it. He practically swallowed her. No finesse, no joy. She'd hated the taste of him, the way she'd had to wipe her mouth. But she'd always known kissing could be wonderful. How, she wasn't sure. Probably all the books she'd read. All the romantic movies. If that many people seemed to like it so much, there had to be something more to it.

Well, it wouldn't do her any good to think about that now. The best she could do was try and go out with some dignity. And pray that her father would survive the ordeal.

IT DIDN'T MATTER A damn to Ed Martini whether he threw two bodies or three overboard. All he wanted was to get the ransom money and get the hell out of town. At least until Sheila, that skinny bitch, stopped hawkin' him about her goddamn alimony. He'd thought about throwing her overboard, and while the idea made him happy, the police would be all over him in a heartbeat. Sheila'd made sure of that.

So he'd take the five million and go for a holiday. Maybe St. Thomas or even just the Keys. When he felt like it, he'd come back. Give the bitch her money. What would he care if he'd already covered his assets?

Ed looked over at the guy tied in the chair. He didn't recognize him, although something about him seemed familiar. Probably one of Sheila's hired detectives. Bitch.

"What's your problem?"

Ed turned to see Jazz poking Charlie in the shoulder. Charlie looked like he was gonna have a heart attack on the spot.

"What's your problem?" Jazz repeated.

"Nothin'. I'm just wondering when we can go get the ransom, you know?"

Jazz gave him another shot to the arm, but Charlie, he didn't seem to be so worried about the ransom as he was about the guy in the chair.

Ed leaned back in his leather chair, thinking maybe in a few minutes he'd have the cook bring up some dinner. A nice piece of salmon, maybe. "Jazz, get the guy's wallet."

Jazz—the only one in his whole outfit he could trust completely—bent next to the passed-out guy and took his wallet from his back pocket. He opened it up. "Michael Caulfield."

At the sound of his name, the man in question moaned and lifted his head. It fell back to his chest, but he tried again, and this time he succeeded.

"Hey, Charlie," Ed said. "You wanna explain to me why we have a man with your last name come to my boat with a gun in his hand?"

"I—I—"

"I'm the one that told him about Tate."

Ed looked at the brother. Except for the blood seeping down the side of his face, he looked a lot smarter than Charlie. Of course, a potato was smarter than Charlie.

"You did, huh? What exactly did you tell Charlie?"

The brother sniffed, wincing at that small movement. "I told him she was worth millions. That she was planning this fake kidnapping, so nobody would be the wiser if he was the one who took her."

"And you knew this because...?"

"I'm her bodyguard."

Ed smiled. It was just what Charlie had told them. "So, great, you told him. And he told me. You both did good. But now I think you both don't need to stick around."

"Wait a minute," Charlie said, his voice high and scared. "I'm supposed to help with the ransom, ain't I? Isn't that what you said? That I help with the ransom and then we're square? I didn't owe you five million dollars, Ed. I owed you hardly nothing compared to that. Tell him, Jazz."

Jazz moved over to the big leather chair and crouched down beside his boss. "You know, I don't care about the brother, but Charlie, we could still use him."

Ed leaned to his side, keeping his voice as low as Jazz had. "For what?"

"After we kill the others, after we get the money, we make sure the cops start sniffin' at Charlie. And before they catch him, he has an accident. And they don't sniff any further."

This was why Jazz got the big salary. He might look like your junkie cousin, but he was a smart spick. Always thinking. Ed gave him a slight nod, then turned to Charlie. "Relax. I was just kiddin'. Wasn't I, Jazz?"

"Yep, just kiddin'."

"About you, at least. I think you'll agree that your brother has served his purpose."

Charlie looked at his brother, then back at the two men. His eyes were wide, his nose was runny and he looked like he was gonna puke. "We don't have to kill him. He told me all about this deal, you know? We wouldn't even be here if it wasn't for Mikey."

"That's true, Charlie," Ed said, "but the man brought a gun into my home. That's very disrespectful. I'm sure you can see that."

"He didn't mean nothin' by it. I swear to God, Ed, he didn't mean to offend."

Ed sighed. "It's too late for apologies." He looked at his watch. It was almost eight-thirty. No wonder he was so hungry. He turned to his right and picked up the intercom that led to the galley. That's where the cook was. And the pilot, too. "Pauly?"

He waited a few beats, and just when he was going to speak again he heard, "Yes, boss?"

"You got some dinner ready?"

"Ten minutes, boss. You want something special?"

"If you have a nice piece of salmon, that would be good."

"Yes, sir."

"And, Pauly, make enough for…" He looked at Charlie and wished he'd go wash his face. But he'd feed the stupid bastard. Jazz, too. And he had to feed the woman because they might need her between now and when they got the money. "Make enough for four of us, okay?"

"Yes, sir. Right away."

He put the intercom down and nodded toward the small refrigerator in the bar.

Without a word, Jazz fetched him a beer. Opened it for him, put it down on a nice napkin on the little table next to the chair. Then Jazz turned on the TV that was mounted on the wall across from the table. There were four sets so Ed could watch a bunch of different games. He had to know where his money was coming from. That's why it didn't matter where this boat went—he could always be in touch with Ronnie at the office, via satellite. Ronnie, his eldest son, ran the day-to-day.

He took a big drink of the ice-cold brew, then waited for the burp. Once he was comfortable, he turned back to Jazz. "Kill him."

Jazz grinned and got out his gun. It was a .45, a birthday present from his old man.

"I didn't tell him everything," Michael said.

"Don't even try—"

"I didn't tell Charlie about the real money." The brother turned his head and looked at Ed. "The ransom is chicken feed. I know how to get fifty million. Tax-free. No one the wiser."

"Fifty million?" Jazz slapped his head just where he'd hit him before.

The brother hissed, but he didn't pass out.

"Hold on a minute, Jazz. Just what are you trying to tell me, Mr. Caulfield?"

The brother swallowed, blinked, then straightened his back. "The woman is worth ten times that. But the money I'm talking about is in a numbered account in the Cayman Islands. If you kill her now, you get five million. If you get her bank account number, fifty million gets transferred to your account. No questions. No taxes."

"And what do you want from this little deal?"

"You think I want to babysit a spoiled brat for the

rest of my life? I figure two hundred thousand in the Caymans? I'm a king."

Ed leaned forward, his interest definitely piqued. "Mr. Caulfield, I realize you told us this information to save your life. But I must ask—now that you have told us, what do we need you for?"

"I'm the only one who can get you that account number."

"And why would she do that for you?"

The brother smiled. "She's in love with me."

6

TATE TRIED TO FIGURE out how long it had been since they'd gotten her father's phone number. She didn't have her watch and she couldn't remember if she'd left home without it this morning or if they'd taken it from her. It had been dark the first time she'd been conscious, and it was still dark, so that didn't help.

She couldn't see much from where she lay. There was the low ceiling and the little port window. Across from the bed was a dresser and a small vanity table with chair. Everything was bolted down, of course. There were no loose objects anywhere. The lights, she'd seen when they had come on, were recessed. There were no table lamps.

There was also a second door. They'd come in and out of the one kitty-corner from the berth. This one, she had come to believe, led to the head. Which she would really like to use. Soon.

She still couldn't get over how calm she felt. Other, normal people probably wouldn't consider this calm, not with her still-pounding heart and the numbness in her limbs. But given her circumstances? She was doing damn well. She wasn't going to bet the farm that all her panic issues were resolved, but this was okay. This was survivable. Which was irony at its finest.

In between figuring out the second door and trying to hear if someone was coming, unwanted memories came to haunt her. The first kidnapping, not the second. The one that had cost her Lisa.

They'd been taken from Tate's bedroom. Lisa, her best friend and cousin, had spent the night, which was something they did often. The two of them had been held in a basement for two days. Somehow, for reasons that had eluded her and made guilt a part of every single day, she'd escaped. Lisa hadn't.

She froze again, listening hard. Nothing. She heard the lap of the waves against the boat, but even those were soft, barely audible. She heard her own breathing, too. But at least she could hear things over the pounding of her heart, which was an improvement.

She lifted her right leg, making sure to keep her cuffed arm as still as possible. It actually wasn't that bad. She was able to move without screaming or trying to slash her own artery so she'd bleed out.

Then she lifted the left leg. It worked as well as the right.

One of the things she had done in college was work her body. Thank goodness that, in addition to yoga and Pilates to keep herself limber, she'd taken those self-defense classes. She'd learned to shoot and shoot well. She'd done those things to make her feel courageous, and none of them had worked worth a damn.

But as of this afternoon her universe had changed. She wasn't sure if she would remember one thing she'd learned from any of her classes or if she'd just pass out again the moment the door opened, but she was going to move forward under the assumption that in this universe she kicked ass.

The first thing to do was to move her legs, stretch the muscles. It was vital that she had control over every part of her that still worked. One hand, two legs and a brain. With luck, she'd get in at least a few licks before they tossed her into the ocean.

"WHY SHOULD I BELIEVE you?"

Michael wished they'd undo the rope that was cutting him across the chest. Of course, if they did, the first thing he'd have to do was kill his brother.

Goddamn Charlie. He must have gotten into the safe when Michael had gone to his bedroom to change shirts. There was no other explanation, and for that, for this, whatever deal he'd made with his father, deathbed or no, he was through with Charlie. Assuming they both weren't killed in the next five minutes. "You should believe me because you're here. You think Charlie could have put this together?" He laughed and he wasn't the least bit sorry to see the look of hurt in Charlie's eyes.

"Speaking of being here, how did you find us?"

"I got that one covered, boss," Jazz said, holding up Michael's GPS.

"That's great, Jazz. What's he tracking?"

"The woman."

Ed Martini, who Michael deduced the tan gentleman to be, sighed. "What on the woman is he tracking?"

"Oh, crap."

"Want to share, Mr. Caulfield?"

He debated lying, but all they had to do was bring the GPS in proximity to Tate's purse and it was all over. "Her purse. It's wired."

"Jazz, ask Danny to come up, would you? Then have him take Miss Baxter's purse and dump it somewhere in New Jersey."

"Sure thing, boss."

Ed turned back to Michael. "I still don't see how you'd convince her to give you that number. You'd have to kill me and pretty much everyone I knew to convince me."

He looked back at Ed, willing himself not to move, not to do what his training had ingrained in him: escape. "Tate Baxter has been rich her whole life. The kind of rich that alters her perception of money. I think fifty million dollars is one hell of a lot. But when you've got over a hundred billion dollars in assets…"

Jazz whistled. "I knew she was loaded—"

"Look up the Baxter Corporation online," Michael said. "Look William Baxter up in the Forbes 500. He's the third wealthiest man in the United States, and that doesn't include his numbered accounts."

Michael forced himself to relax and to keep his mouth shut. The ball had been lobbed over the net, and he had to see whether they were going to put it in play.

He wished he'd thought of something smarter, something that would get them both off this boat tonight, but it wasn't a terrible plan. Ed Martini was a bookie, one of the biggest on the East Coast. He was a man who liked to play the odds. The potential of a ninety percent profit would appeal to the gambler in him.

What did he have to lose by checking it out? Michael knew Ed wasn't about to forget the five million. No one seemed to be in a huge rush to get it, so they either hadn't called in the ransom yet or they must have given William some time to gather the cash. Michael's whole objective was to buy time.

Eventually the circumstances for victory would come his way. This was the kind of thing he'd trained for all his adult life, and these guys? They knew nothing but the brute fundamentals. He'd win and he'd get Tate out of this in one piece. If they believed him right now.

"Yeah, that's all swell, but the five million, we don't need her for that. And there's no guarantee—"

"She's crazy about him, Ed," Charlie said. "You threaten to hurt Mikey and she'll do anything you want."

Ed barely gave Charlie a glance. "It seems like a lot of trouble."

"Not so much trouble," Michael said, "not fifty million dollars' worth. Completely untraceable."

"But if she signs over the money, she can just as easily blow the whistle."

Michael smiled at Jazz. "I don't see how, unless she can communicate from the other side."

Jazz's thin eyebrows came down as he frowned.

While Michael waited for him to *comprende,* he took a moment to think about a particularly juicy way he would kill the man when the time came.

"Oh. The other side. I get it."

"Once you know the account is legit and you make the transfer, there's no way anyone's going to trace the transaction. Not if you put the money back into the same bank under your name."

Ed chuckled just as the hatch opened at the front of the saloon. A bald guy came up the stairs. He stopped there and pulled a big tray filled with food up from the hold. Then another. Following the second tray there came a man in a white chef's coat.

Michael turned his attention back to the bald guy. He was older than Michael by at least a couple of years, but, shit, he was in great shape. Michael would need to bring a weapon along to kill that one.

Evidently he was Danny. The one who was going to lose the GPS tracker. Jazz made him wait as he went into the berth at the inside of the saloon. He came out again holding the Coach bag. Before he handed it to Danny, he took the cash out of Tate's wallet and her wristwatch.

Michael changed his mind. He would kill Jazz with a dull fish knife instead.

The chef was nothing. A chef. If this was everyone who would be on the boat, he could manage. There was only one guy who truly scared him and that was Jazz. Michael knew the type—he enjoyed his job. The more people he could hurt, the better.

The discussion was over, at least for now. As the chef and baldy set up the table for Ed's dinner, Ed finished his beer, then told Jazz to cut him loose.

"Take him into the cabin and cuff him next to his girlfriend."

Michael didn't show his relief. All he cared about now was making sure Tate was okay.

WILLIAM BAXTER STOOD in his upstairs closet, staring at the shelves of his safe. He'd never given much thought to the heft and weight of five million dollars, but he did so now. He knew, because it was important to know such things, that one million dollars in one hundred dollar bills weighed twenty-two pounds. Therefore, five million dollars would weigh one hundred and ten pounds. He needed a vessel, something he could fit into a public trash Dumpster, something that wouldn't look suspicious to someone passing by, something that would hold one hundred and ten pounds of hundred-dollar bills. It was a serious matter. One, if he got it wrong, that could mean his daughter's death.

His eyes closed as he tried to regain his bearings. He kept remembering the phone call. The electronically altered voice.

Your daughter is ours. Bring five million in unmarked hundreds to the Central Park carousel. At two-thirty this morning put the cash in the Dumpster with the red X. No police. No tracking chip or dye packs. You deliver the money by yourself. One thing goes wrong, Tate is dead.

He had to get a grip on himself. There was nothing he wouldn't do for his daughter, including giving these people his money. If only he could believe that following the instructions to the letter would be enough.

He knew only too well that if a man was capable of kidnapping, he was capable of murder.

It occurred to him that the vessel he was desperately searching for had been so obvious, if he hadn't been this close to tears. He would use an old gym bag. There were a couple downstairs.

But to go downstairs would telegraph that something was wrong. The last thing he needed was for the staff to gossip. Any oblique reference at all could be enough to cause damage.

He would have to call Stafford, his majordomo. Just as he stepped out of the closet, his intercom buzzed. His heart leaped in his chest, but he made it to the phone. "Yes?"

"Sara Lessing returning your call, sir."

"Yes. And, Stafford, please come to my room and bring one of those old gym bags from the storage room. Discreetly."

"Sir."

William pressed the lit phone line. "Sara."

"Hi, Mr. Baxter. Is something wrong?"

"Is Tate with you?"

"Uh, no."

"Would you happen to know where she is?"

"She didn't say anything to me about having plans."

"I see," he said, sitting down before his knees gave out. He hadn't realized how much stock he'd put in the idea that Tate was simply with her friend and this was all a prank.

"Mr. Baxter, have you tried her cell?"

"Yes. I have."

"What about Michael? Or Elizabeth? They'd know."

"Mr. Caulfield is also not available by phone, and Elizabeth suggested Tate was with him."

"Oh. Wait."

"Yes?"

"Okay, nothing's wrong. Not really. Except…well, I wasn't supposed to tell you…."

"Sara, please—"

"Of course. I'm sorry. Tate is participating in this, well, sort of stunt."

"Pardon me?"

As William listened to Tate's best friend outline the lunatic plan, every part of him wanted her words to be true. He hadn't wept since his wife died twenty-two years ago, but he wept now, knowing that the silly plan to fake Tate's kidnapping had gone so horribly wrong.

"Sir?"

"Thank you, Sara. I appreciate your explanation. However…"

"Yes?"

"An hour ago I received a ransom call."

Sara didn't say anything for a long time. "Michael is with her. He'll make sure she's safe. I know he went after her. He was against the whole idea."

"Was he?"

"Oh, God."

"I have to go. Needless to say, if you hear—"

"Of course. And if there's anything—"

"I'll call you." He hung up, and only then did Stafford enter the room, carrying a large black gym bag.

"Is this fine, sir?"

It was perfect. All five million dollars fit inside with just enough room to zip it closed. He had several hours to kill until the drop-off. Plenty of time to imagine the hell Tate was in.

THE DOOR OPENED AND all Tate's bravado vanished. Before she could even see who had opened it, she was hit by a massive panic episode. Heart, lungs, legs, brain…all the things she had counted on were no longer under her control. The fear had her tight and the room dimmed.

"Tate."

She opened her mouth, but his name wouldn't come.

"Tate, look at me."

The side of the bed dipped, and she felt his cool fingers on the side of her face. The tunnel vision, which blocked out so much, softened and let her see who it was. "Michael."

He smiled. He wasn't wearing his sunglasses, either, so she could see his eyes. "You're hurt."

"It's okay. You found me."

"I did."

"Thank you. I was so scared. I was sure… Is my father here?"

His smile sank and the light in his eyes went out. "Oh, Christ, Tate, I'm sorry. I can't take you home. Not yet."

"What?"

"Lover boy here is joining the party."

Tate looked just past Michael. The small man was there, leering at her as if her heartbreak was better than cable.

"I'm sorry. I followed you, but when I got to the boat, they found me."

"It's all right," she said, even though she could hardly understand. It was Michael, and he was supposed to save her.

He leaned down close. "Don't fret," he whispered. "I'll get you out of this. I promise."

"Come on, my dinner's getting cold."

Michael spun away from her and stood up to Jazz. "Get that cuff off her now so I can clean her up. In case you've forgotten, you still need her. Then, when she's clean and there's a bandage on that wrist, you can bring in our dinner."

For a moment it looked as if Jazz was going to shoot Michael, but then he burst out laughing. "Man, you got you some pair."

"Whatever. Just get the cuffs off her."

Her breathing grew more stable as each moment passed. Well, as long as she kept her gaze on Michael. He took her into the head to wash her wrist, but then he must have noticed her discomfort, because he left her there, closing the door behind him.

She trembled so violently it was difficult to do the most fundamental things, but she managed, and then Michael joined her again, washing her wrist as if she might break. Which, when she thought about it, was entirely possible.

"I know that has to sting like hell."

"It's okay. This is the best pain I've had since—"

"I let you down. I'm sorry."

"You couldn't have known. Brody has a great deal to answer for. He's behind this, you know. He might not be here, but he's the only one who knew about the plan, so it follows."

He didn't say anything, but she watched his lips narrow and become pale. Never, though, was his touch anything but gentle.

"Michael?"

"Yes?"

"Did they call my father?"

He turned off the small faucet and got her a towel from a silver bar on the wall near the enclosed shower. With the same care, he dried her. "Don't touch that," he said, nodding at the very red and raw flesh.

He looked in the cabinet above the sink, choosing a bottle of aspirin, then in another cupboard near the door he found a first-aid kit. "Let's go sit. I want you to eat."

"I'm not hungry."

"I don't care. You need to eat. To be strong."

She sighed. "No amount of food is going to help with that."

"Let's do this before our friend Jazz gets too antsy."

She followed him to the bed, where she blushed like a fool as she climbed to the middle of the mattress. This was, for all its horror, a very intimate situation. She'd had her fantasies about Michael, but his actual touch, the scent of his skin, the closeness was something she hardly knew how to handle.

The good part was her awkwardness with Michael kept her from thinking about her own imminent death.

"What's so funny?"

"Nothing. Do I have to put that stuff on?"

He held up the antibiotic ointment. "This? It doesn't hurt at all."

"Promise?"

He nodded. "Promise."

He was true to his word. It didn't hurt. His touch did, but she didn't mind. He'd clearly done this kind of thing before. Probably in the military. When it was a matter of life or death.

She was just about to question him about his medical training when Jazz walked in, gun out and aimed at Michael. Immediately behind him came a very large bald man carrying a tray.

"Where's this supposed to go?" The bald man sounded as if he was from the Bahamas or Jamaica.

Jazz seemed stumped, so Michael took over, setting the tray on the dresser, then setting a napkin in her lap, along with a fork and a dinner plate.

He brought his own over, and when he sat down on the edge of the bed, Jazz said, "Hey."

Michael looked up.

Jazz glanced from Michael's food to the other room.

"Get your plate. You can eat in here and shoot us if we don't pass the salt."

Jazz didn't think that was quite so funny. He walked over to Michael and pressed the barrel of the gun into the center of his forehead. "You wanna be careful there, buddy. There's a big ocean out there and a lot of hungry fish."

"Got it," Michael said. "I apologize."

"That's better."

Despite his anger, he did as Michael had suggested. He ate at the vanity, his gun within easy reach.

She did her best to ignore him as she ate. It was superb salmon. In fact, the whole meal was perfectly prepared, but it was still difficult to swallow.

She kept thinking about her father. About how scared he must be. Each time she started to slide to the bad place, she looked at Michael. It helped so very much.

7

CHARLIE WIPED HIS forehead, wishing like crazy he could get off this stinkin' boat. He needed a fix and he needed it now, but Mikey was in there with that skinny chick, and Ed, he wasn't feeling so generous.

He looked down at his plate, but there was no way he was gonna eat, even if it was all cooked by some fancy chef.

All he wanted was for them to get the ransom. Then he could leave and he wouldn't owe Martini any more money. Nothing. In fact, with his cut, he'd be able to set himself up just fine. Screw Mikey. He should have helped him, that's all. If he had helped, none of this would have happened. Goddamn, he'd promised Pop he'd help. Now they were both in it up to their necks.

"Charlie."

He wiped his forehead again, this time with his napkin instead of his sleeve, then turned to face Ed. Jazz was in the other room with Mike and the skinny chick. So it was just him and Ed. "Yeah, Ed?"

"Charlie, why didn't you tell me about the bank account in the Caymans?"

Shit, shit and more shit. He didn't like answering

questions. Especially when the wrong answer could get him killed. "I didn't know."

"Your brother didn't tell you?"

"He told me about the kidnapping thing, right? About how she was paying somebody to snatch her. And he told me she was worth, you know, a lot of money. And that's what he told me."

"Nothing about the bank account."

Charlie shook his head. "He doesn't always tell me everything. He thinks he so damn smart and that I'm just his loser brother."

"He never mentioned that he was going to follow you?"

"He might have. I don't know. Maybe not."

"Tell me more about him. Has he been her bodyguard for a long time?"

"Hell, no. Only about six months. Since he got out of the Army."

"He was in the military?"

"Yeah. Some big shit. They all kissed his ass."

"Why isn't he still some big shit?"

Charlie felt his cheeks heat. He didn't want to tell this part, but Ed would know if he was lying. "Because of me."

"Really? What happened?"

"I, uh, took some things from one of his Army friend's car one time."

"Things?"

"Some papers about a weapon or something. I'm not even sure what they were. They were just in this locked briefcase, so I figured they must be worth something. I didn't get to sell it, though. They caught me and I did some time. He said he was through with me, but I'm his brother, you know? He promised he'd look after me."

"I see."

"Anyway, I was wondering…what time are we gonna get the ransom? Because I have some, you know, things I gotta do."

"Not for several hours, Charlie. Just finish your dinner, and I'll let you know when we're going to leave."

He nodded, turned back to his plate. But now he was even less hungry. Damn that Mikey. He shoulda helped out his only brother.

FINALLY, JAZZ LEFT. He turned off the light and he locked the door behind him, but they were finally alone.

"I know," Tate said, shaking the cuff against the bar. "It's really uncomfortable."

After dinner, Jazz had cuffed him right next to her. They were lying down with plenty of pillows behind them. He'd even gotten Jazz to cover them with a blanket. But there was no way he was going to be this uncomfortable for the whole night.

"Tell me something, Tate. What is it you like about that Prada store?"

She didn't say anything for a minute, then she giggled. Tate was not the giggling type. It sounded pretty good on her.

"It's not that I like the store so much. I know people there and I like the way their clothes look on me. What are you doing?"

He had gotten his comb out of his left back pocket and was now inching his way up the bed to get in the best position. They'd hooked him up with his right hand, unfortunately, but his left would do.

As soon as he could maneuver properly, he pressed the far edge of the comb down on the pawl. It took him a while to disengage the pawl from the ratchet, but once that was done, the cuff popped open.

"Was that what I think it was?"

He followed the same steps with her handcuff. He left both cuffs hanging from the bar as he moved down and closer to Tate.

"How did you do that?"

"My uncle was Houdini."

"Really?"

"No. I wasn't always a limo driver."

"I know. You were a spy."

"Sort of."

"Why sort of?"

He moved even closer to her and decided he'd better just go for broke. "Lift up." He tapped her on the back of her neck.

She did, and he slipped his arm in back of her, cradling her head.

"I was in military intelligence, which is, yeah, the spy division. We broke into places, stole information, coordinated military operations and the CIA presence."

"Sounds terrifying."

"It could be. But when I say I was well trained, I'm not kidding."

"Why in the world aren't you still there? Doing important things?"

"Taking care of you is important."

"Oh, please. I'm a spoiled rich girl with psychiatric issues. How important can I be?"

"To me?"

She didn't respond except for a little shiver. Good. He didn't want her to be scared. He wanted her to believe that he could get them out of this. If not tonight, then in the near future. He needed her to do whatever he asked of her, no matter what. And for that she needed to be panic-attack-free.

It would all be so much easier if his own brother wasn't sitting in the next room. What killed him was that he'd let Charlie get the better of him again. The first time had cost him his military career. This time it would cost a hell of a lot more. He couldn't even blame his brother. Charlie was Charlie. Nope, this was his own damn fault, and before he got fired, quit, whatever, he was going to make damn sure Ed Martini and Jazz would never bother anyone again. He would make sure that none of the Baxter money was taken and he'd do whatever the hell it took to make sure Tate Baxter went home safely.

"Michael?"

"Yes?"

"Is something wrong?"

"No. No, I'm just angry at myself. I should never have let you go into that store alone."

"I wasn't alone."

"But Elizabeth—"

"Is amazingly capable. She isn't at fault. I won't have her lose her job over this."

He smiled, glad she couldn't see him. "Okay. Elizabeth stays."

"Good."

"Speaking of good, you're doing damn well yourself."

"Not really." She snuggled in closer, and he was glad to have her warmth. "I passed out. Several times."

"Understandable."

"And when I was conscious, I was in full panic mode. I didn't do any of the stuff I was trained to do."

"It's a whole different ball game when it's for keeps."

"I'm just sorry, that's all."

"For what? None of this is your fault."

"I don't know. Maybe all these years of focusing so much energy into my fear of being kidnapped…"

"You did not bring this on."

She sighed, and he felt a small drop of wet on his shoulder.

"Talk to me, Tate. I've heard…"

"That I'd been kidnapped?" she asked. "That we— me and my cousin—were taken from my bedroom?"

He wasn't sure if he should push or just let it go. Maybe talking about it would help, but he was no psychiatrist. Of course, she'd probably told Dr. Bay about this, but Dr. Bay, he now knew, was an ass.

He nodded, squeezed her shoulder.

"Her name was Lisa. She was my best friend. My only friend. Because her father and mine worked together and we were the same age. We did everything together."

"Same age, huh?"

"Yep. Her mother—my aunt Sharon—made sure we stuck close because my mother died when I was two."

"I didn't know you were that young."

"I don't remember much about her. But I remember everything about my childhood with Lisa."

"Tell me about it."

"She had really long hair and I used to love to brush it. I would pretend I was a hairdresser and we'd play every day. I was sure that's what I was going to be when I grew up."

"You? A hairdresser?"

"Why not?"

"I can't picture it."

"Back then, when we were little kids, we weren't really rich. Not like we are now. My father and his brother had gotten some lucrative government contracts, which is basically what made the company, but we were as nouveau as it gets. We were so happy. We traveled, we explored. Lisa and I did everything together. We were as close as sisters."

"What happened?"

"We were fifteen. So that's—"

"Nine years ago."

She nodded and her hair brushed against his neck.

"Since we traveled so much to places like Italy, England, Spain, we'd been taught to be really careful there because of all the kidnappings. Lisa and I barely thought about it, but there was always someone watching out for us. Damn, it was fun. I never felt lonely. We had the same tutors and the same homework. We wore the same clothes. We actually didn't look that much alike, but everyone thought we were twins."

"Sounds great."

"It was."

That little shiver he'd felt just a few moments ago was back, but it meant something completely different now. He'd seen her tremble just before a panic attack. Just before her breathing became labored and her skin turned deathly pale. He'd meant for the conversation to relax her, to help her trust him. Not send her into a tailspin.

"I never had anyone I was real close to when I was a kid," he said. "I was into sports, mostly football, but I kept having to change schools."

"Why?"

"My old man was a drunk. We had to skip on the rent at least once a year."

"Oh, my God."

"Yeah, well. He was the reason I signed up for the Army, so I guess it wasn't so bad."

She turned to look at him. It was so dark in the room he couldn't make out her expression, although he had a good idea what it was. "Wasn't so bad? I can't believe you're so cavalier about it."

"I've lived with it all my life. One adjusts."

"I don't think it's nearly that easy."

"You've adjusted."

"No, I haven't. That's the whole point. I should have adjusted years ago. I should have put my fear in the proper perspective. I mean, come on, what are the odds that—"

He heard her take a swift breath, then laughter. Not giggling this time but the real thing.

"What's so funny?"

Her answer was delayed as she got herself under control. "What are the odds," she said, "that I'd get kidnapped three times?"

He grinned. "I'd say they were pretty good."

"Yep."

He stroked her hair, which was softer than he'd even imagined. "Well, the odds of you getting kidnapped four times have to be astronomical. So once this is over you're home-free."

She laughed again, and he joined her, and it was maybe the best thing that could have happened. Her whole body relaxed. Hell, at this rate, she might actually get some sleep tonight. They both needed to eat, sleep, stretch. He had no idea when opportunity would knock, and they both had to be ready.

He thought about getting up, but then her hand went to his chest and he realized she hadn't finished her story.

"Anyway," she said, her voice softer now, "we were really careful in Europe but not so much back home. It wasn't that no one thought anything could happen to us, but—"

"Home turf. It's hard to stay diligent."

She nodded. "We spent the night at each other's houses all the time. The night they took us we were at my place. It was summer, hot. I wasn't a big fan of the air conditioner, so I had my bedroom window open. It was nice to feel the breeze."

"Sure," he said.

"I remember a hand over my mouth. It smelled like stale cigarettes. We were dragged out the window in the middle of the night. Both of us were blindfolded, gagged and tied up. We were thrown in the back of a truck. We rode for a long time and then we were carried inside, down some stairs. It was a basement, and it smelled like cigarettes and beer.

"It gets fuzzy after that. I only remember a few things. Lisa screaming. Someone taking off my night-gown. Praying. Then I was on a street I didn't recognize and I was wrapped in a white sheet. I was alone."

"You escaped."

"I got out, but I don't know if I had anything to do with it. Someone could have put me there, for all I know."

She wasn't shaking. Her voice was steady. Even her skin felt warm and dry. Had she told the story that many times? Or would she fall apart if he said a wrong word?

"I saw a woman in a window and I went to her door. She called the police."

"Lisa wasn't so lucky."

"No. She wasn't. They found her body three days later in a field that was covered with junk. They hadn't bothered to dress her, they just dumped her like so much trash."

"Tate—"

"It's okay. It's good to remember. To focus on the fact that it isn't over until it's over."

He pulled her close, resting his cheek on her soft hair. "There's nothing fair or good about any of it," he whispered. "I hope the bastards burn for eternity."

"Yeah," she said.

He rubbed her arm with his fingers, a very light, hypnotic touch. They didn't speak, and she didn't weep, but all the same the next hour was about calming down. About coming back to now.

When finally she sighed, he knew he could do what he had to do, even if it meant leaving her. Not for the whole night but for as long as it took him to do some recon. He'd been too busy fixing her wrist to really check out the bathroom. He was sure he would find something in there he could use as a weapon. Then there was the vanity and the dresser. Probably closets, too, although he didn't remember seeing them.

He looked over at the door, and there was still light coming in around the edges. Which meant if he turned on the light in here, it wouldn't be noticed.

"Tate, I have to move. I'm just going into the head. Will you be all right?"

The hand on his chest lifted slowly. "I'll be fine."

"I'm sorry, but I have to do this now. The light's still on in the saloon."

"Ah. That makes sense."

"I won't be long." He climbed out of the bed and went to the door. Even though he knew it was locked, he tried it anyway. Mistakes happened, and sometimes not by him. "Close your eyes," he said. "Light."

As soon as his eyes adjusted, he went to the vanity. This cabin was clearly used to accommodate women. He found a hairbrush, a mirror, makeup, creams, sprays. Nothing particularly helpful.

There were clothes in the dresser—women's, and some of them were mighty skimpy.

The head, however, held his interest. A package of safety razors. Those could come in handy. A long pair of scissors. Some isopropyl alcohol and a book of matches along with a scented candle. He could work with this stuff. He just had to be careful how and when, because Tate was his weakest link. He wouldn't allow them to use her as a bargaining tool, so he'd have to make damn sure if he struck, he'd win.

There was also the question of Charlie. Yes, he

wanted to kill him for his role in all this, but truthfully he wasn't sure he could, so there was another weak link.

If it had been just him, he'd have had no problem with the crew. He could get rid of Jazz in two shakes. The man was a brute, nothing more. But the bald guy, he might be trouble. The chef was no big deal, and Martini was too used to letting others do the dirty work.

But it wasn't just him. Tate's safety overruled everything.

He rearranged some of the equipment in the head, then he leaned out and said, "Just one more sec," before he closed the door with his foot.

After he'd washed, he went back into the cabin. Tate was still in the same position, the blue blanket pulled up above her breasts, her head resting on a mound of pillows. She looked pale and scared, but she hadn't simply been resting, waiting for him to return.

There was a fierceness about her he'd never seen before. Curious. Was it the talk of her little cousin? Or was it the laughter that had brought her a few steps closer to fighting back?

"What's that smile for?" she asked.

He hadn't realized. "You've made a decision."

"Pardon?"

"Nothing. It's not important." He turned off the lights and was once again amazed at the depth of the darkness.

"Are you going to be able to find your way back?"

"Eight steps," he said.

"Now that sounds like something a spy would say."

He got back to the bed and climbed in, shifting until he had her comfortably beside him again. "Those kinds of details make all the difference. Next time you go to the head, count. And when Jazz comes into the room, watch him. Does he go to the right or the left? Is he ready before he turns on the light or does he take a few seconds to adjust?"

Her hand touched his chest again. "Is it always like that for you? Everywhere?"

"Most of the time, yes."

"So how do you relax?"

He chuckled. "Well, there are a couple of ways...."

There was that little shiver again.

"I have a confession."

"Oh?"

"I've been meaning to invite you for dinner."

"Really?" Of course, he'd known about that for months, but he wasn't going to spoil this moment for her.

"I've always enjoyed our talks. I thought it would be nice to spend some time with you off the clock."

"It sounds nice."

"I know. Unfortunately I'm a big chicken. I was afraid you'd—"

"What?"

"I don't know. Just afraid."

"We're here now. And I don't see a clock anywhere."

Her hand moved. Not much and not under his shirt, but it was a start.

He stroked her hair once more and, as he did so, pulled her tighter against him. It wouldn't be easy to kiss her in such a dark place. He could miss by a mile. Unless...

He took her chin in his left hand and held her steady as he lowered his lips onto hers.

8

TATE'S EYES FLUTTERED closed at the whisper of his
lips. She held her breath waiting for him to pry her
mouth open, for the gaping maw that was all she'd
known of kisses. But he barely touched her. Just a
brush, an *almost* that made her quiver. She tried to
remain still, to let him show her what he wanted, but
the way he teased her, nearly touching, made her arch
forward.

Even then, even with him truly kissing her, he was
soft and deliberate. As if he were testing, putting his
proverbial toe in the water.

The metaphor made her smile, and when he smiled
in return, she felt it. Felt his lips curve and his warm
breath mingle with hers.

A moment passed, and he must have decided that
the water was fine because there was no more teasing.
He took her mouth and his tongue slipped inside. In
that instant she realized everything she'd known about
kissing in the past was wrong.

He didn't swallow her whole or do anything that
would spoil the moment. With his arm holding her
head, his fingers still guiding her chin, she felt amazingly, astonishingly safe.

How was it possible to have the worst and best experience of her life happen at the exact same time?

Gathering her courage, she touched his tongue, and that was a sensation beyond thrilling. He let her lead the dance for a moment, then he was in charge once more.

She didn't mind. In fact, all she wanted was to surrender completely, let herself fall into this, into her dream become flesh.

He pulled away, only to return, nipped her bottom lip, then soothed her with the flat of his tongue. Kissing was wonderful. Better even than in her feverish imagination.

He moaned with his passion and hunger, and she laughed, it was so good. She'd made him moan. This sexy, experienced man of the world.

"What's so funny?"

"Nothing."

"Are you okay?"

She sighed. "I'm perfect." Then she kissed him.

He pulled her closer, and now that he had her, he let go of her chin to stroke her hair, to touch her cheek. Just as she pulled back to bare her neck, the door opened, throwing light all over the bed.

Tate jerked away as if she'd been caught doing something nasty.

"Hey, what the hell?" Michael said, leaning forward to block her from the intruder.

"Sorry to break up the party, but— What the—?" Jazz rushed to the side of the bed and held up the empty cuff. "Are you kidding me?"

"They were uncomfortable," Michael said.

"I'll show you uncomfortable." Jazz shoved his gun into the side of Michael's cheek. "Get up. Now."

Without moving, Michael said, "Tate, you just relax, okay? I'll be right back."

"I wouldn't count on it," Jazz said.

Despite the immediacy of the threat, Michael moved off the bed with incredible grace. The moment he stood, Jazz poked him in the ribs with his gun. "Cuff her."

"She's not going anywhere."

"Cuff her or I'll do it."

Michael obeyed, and her hand was once more above her head in a position that simply couldn't be comfortable. That was the least of her problems. Where were they taking Michael? God, what if he didn't come back?

"Please, can you tell me what's going on?" she asked.

"Shut the fuck up—that's what's going on." Jazz made Michael take his cuff off the metal bar, then Jazz cuffed his hands behind his back.

"I'll be back," Michael said. "You just get some rest."

She would have laughed if she'd had any control over her breathing. Or her heartbeat. It was all she could do not to beg Jazz to let him go, and when they left the room, slamming and locking the door behind them, she fell apart.

ED WAS STILL IN HIS big chair, but the dishes were gone. There were navigation charts on the table, two different cell phones, a laptop and a bottle of champagne in a silver ice bucket.

Ed looked up when Michael was pushed in front of his chair. "What was all that?"

"They were out of the cuffs."

Ed's gaze moved to Michael. "Really?"

"It's a handy parlor trick."

"I'll remember that. Do you have the account number?"

"No."

"Why not?"

"It's too soon. I need some time."

"You don't have time."

"Look, it doesn't matter if you have the account number. You can't get the money without Tate. She has to be there in person to sign the papers or the bank won't transfer that amount of money."

Ed just stared at him. He didn't move or frown or anything. "Jazz, uncuff him."

Jazz seemed affronted by the idea, but the keys came out and Michael was soon rubbing his wrists.

"You go back in there and you make sure this lady is going to do everything we need her to do. If she doesn't, we'll kill Charlie. Then her. Then you."

"TATE? CAN YOU HEAR me?"

Tate blinked as she pulled in an inadequate breath.

"I'm back. I said I would be back and I am. Can you look at me, Tate?"

It felt as if she were swimming up from the bottom of the ocean. There was light up there and warmth and safety, but it was so very far away.

"Come on, honey. You can do it. You're all right. Nothing's going to hurt you tonight. I'll be here the whole time and I won't let anything happen to you."

She jerked her hand again. She wasn't sure if she was trying to get loose or if she just needed the pain to jar her out of her nightmare.

"Shit, you're bleeding again. We need to get you to the bathroom so I can change the bandage."

"Michael?"

"I'm right here, Tate."

"They took you and I thought—"

"I know. But I promised—and I don't break my promises."

She focused. He was right next to her. The overhead lights were on, so she could see he wasn't hurt. And he wasn't cuffed. "What did you promise them?"

He sat back. "What?"

"What did you promise them? It's okay. I know you had to tell them something or they would have killed you."

"You're right. I did. I needed to buy us some time."

She could feel the real world become solid around her. The pace of her heart slowed, the tunnel vision expanded. It occurred to her that Michael had become her new safe place.

"I told them you have a numbered account in the Cayman Islands. That I was going to persuade you to give me the account number and that Martini would be able to transfer fifty million of your money into his account."

She thought about what he'd said for a moment. She could see the logic. If they thought they could get that much money, her life became a lot more valuable. "Actually, you're right. I do have a numbered account at the Grand Cayman Bank. But there's no way he can make that transfer. Not if I don't sign the papers in person."

"I was right?"

She nodded. "I'm surprised you're surprised. I figured a spy like you would know all about my finances."

"I don't know anything about them. It's not germane. Well, it wasn't until a few hours ago."

"Is that going to botch the deal? The fact that I have to sign the papers?"

"No. In fact, I think it can work in our favor. I'm pretty sure they're getting the ransom tonight. They're not going to be reckless about it, either. There's no way we're getting off this boat just yet. But if Ed believes you have to sign, then we've got all the way to the island to perfect our escape."

"I don't know about you," she said, "but I'm not that good a swimmer."

"He's going to have to get fuel, supplies. There will be opportunities."

"I don't know…. Remember what Jazz said—there's a big ocean and a lot of hungry fish."

"The man who kidnapped you is Ed Martini. He's one of the biggest bookies in the States. For fifty million dollars he's not going to take any chances. You'll be fine."

"Until I sign the papers."

"It won't come to that."

"I'd like to believe you."

"I came back, didn't I?"

She smiled. "Yes. You did."

"What do you say we get that bandage changed."

WILLIAM CHECKED HIS watch again as he drove slowly along the Sixty-fifth Street traverse. In a few minutes he would be at the carousel, and a few minutes after that he'd put the bag full of money in the red bin.

The drive in itself had been terrifying. He hadn't been behind the wheel in four years, and that had been in England. It meant nothing. To get his daughter back he would have walked here on his hands.

He'd obeyed the kidnapper's instructions to the letter, but after his discussion with Sara, he knew that someone from inside his organization had to be involved. He would deal with the incredible idiocy of the whole concept of fake kidnappings later. For now, he was looking at Michael Caulfield as the most likely traitor.

Sara's conviction that he would never do anything to hurt Tate was simply another nail in his coffin. William had hired Caulfield because he was supposed to be the very best at what he did. But he hadn't paid enough attention to why the man had been discharged. There was the whole unsavory business with the brother.

There was no question that he would get to the bottom of this. There was also no question that whoever had taken his daughter would pay with his life.

He had already passed the dark and shuttered Tavern on the Green. Everything was closed at this hour. However, the carousel was still illuminated. He would have preferred softer lights with some character to them, but these lamps weren't to entrance, they were to scare off the drug users and the teenagers who looked for dark corners to get their thrills.

He had to get close to the red-crossed trash bin. Not because of the instructions but because five million dollars was heavy and he wasn't a strong man. He wished he had followed his doctor's advice about exercise.

None of it would matter if he didn't get his girl back. He'd gone all these years with her safety as his vanguard. No matter where they'd traveled he'd spared no expense. Without Tate, he had nothing.

There it was. The only red-marked trash receptacle near the carousel. Though it was large, he'd have to work at getting the bag inside.

He parked the borrowed Cadillac. Stafford had wanted to drive it himself, but William had to do this alone. At least the Cadillac was easier to maneuver than his limousine. Once outside, he took the key to the trunk and lifted the lid. The gym bag was securely zipped. No casual passerby would think it contained blood money.

He took in a deep breath and hauled the bag up and over the rim of the trunk. Staggering as he walked the few steps to the marked bin, he had to rock his body so the bag would hit the opening.

After a moment to catch his breath, he shoved the bag into the bin until the whole thing fell. And fell.

He looked down, bracing his hands on the edge of the bin. There was no bottom. There was a trash-bin-size hole dug through the cement and the earth beneath. But all William could see was the end of his world.

WITH HER NEW BANDAGE and the comfort in knowing she wouldn't have to be cuffed again at least for the rest of the night, Tate finished up in the bathroom, grateful there were guest toiletries, including a couple of toothbrushes still in their boxes. She wasn't crazy about using the soap on her face, but as she washed she realized just how insane that was.

She was still alive when it could have so easily gone the other way. In fact, not much about this kidnapping had turned out like her fears.

Because of Michael.

She stared into the small mirror above the sink, wincing at the woman who looked back. Her eyes were red and puffy, as were her cheeks. She looked as if she'd been through hell. She had looked like this when he'd kissed her, and now it felt quite suspicious. Had he just been trying to keep her distracted? Calm her down? Probably. Shouldn't she mind a lot more?

Of course, she'd clearly gone quite mad when the truth had penetrated that she'd really been kidnapped. How insane does a person have to be to worry that her new potential boyfriend might not like her skin tone when on the brink of death? If they lived through this, she would definitely need a new therapist.

Well, she couldn't stay in the head all night. It just seemed so odd that he was out there. That they would be sharing a bed.

That sucked her breath right out of her lungs.

They were sharing a bed. It might be her last night on Earth. The math wasn't difficult. She thought of the kisses and how it had felt to finally have a real man want her. Even if it was all an act, she didn't care. As far as last wishes went, this was a good one.

A shudder shook her body as once again reality and delusion smacked into each other. This was so different than anything she'd imagined—and she'd imagined so much. In her nightmares there was no rest, no relief from the terror. There was certainly no kissing and no trust that somehow she'd survive.

A tap on the door sent her heart into overdrive.

"Tate? You okay?"

"I'm fine," she said. "I'll be out in a minute."

He needed to brush his teeth, to get himself ready for bed. Although she'd like to, she couldn't stay here for the rest of the night.

She took one last glance in the mirror—which was not terribly smart, considering—then went into the small bedroom.

Michael stood by the door, an easy smile on his lips. Part of her ease with him was a conditioned response. Michael only took off his sunglasses when they were having their wonderful conversations. The more she connected with his gaze, the calmer she felt.

"You need something?" he asked. "There are some clothes in the drawers. Maybe you could find yourself something more comfortable to wear."

She couldn't. The idea of wearing someone else's things...

"I'll be out in a minute. The door's locked. You'll know if someone's trying to come in."

She looked at the door, then back at Michael. Selfishly she wished he didn't have to go, even for a few minutes. "I'll be fine."

"I know," he said. A moment later he was in the head and she was alone. Only it didn't feel quite so bleak.

She went to the dresser and opened the top drawer. Bikinis. Many of them. All so tiny they made her blush. Second drawer down had cover-ups, but they were mostly transparent. God, what must go on in this boat.

She shook her head at her prudishness. She'd been around a lot of sex in her life, even though she hadn't been the one having it. In her fancy prep school she'd spent many a night wearing headphones so she wouldn't have to hear the grunting coming from the other bed.

In college things had gotten more personal. Graydon had taken her to parties where the drugs and alcohol had flowed like water. Inhibitions were nonexistent, and she'd become inured to the sight of her fellow students going at it like bunnies.

But then she'd retreated to her world of fear, and so much of the outside world had taken on sinister tones. At the very least it had become unfamiliar. More real by far was her fantasy life. It was in bed she truly lived. That's where all her plans were, her dreams. And that's where sleeping with Michael made sense.

She breathed deeply, closed her eyes. Pictured herself as a warrior, complete with combat boots and semiautomatic weapon. A minute of positive self-talk and she got into bed.

If she'd known she was going to be kidnapped, she would have dressed differently. Certainly she wouldn't have worn the linen pants. But this was what she had and she'd cope. By tomorrow… No, she wasn't going to think about tomorrow. Her only decision at the moment was about her shoes.

They were pumps, two-inch heels. Great for shopping at Prada, lousy for self-defense—but better than her bare feet. The idea of sleeping in them was disconcerting.

Nothing to be done about it. She lifted the pillows and pulled back the comforter. The blanket Jazz had brought wasn't terribly warm, and as long as they could be comfortable, she supposed they should be.

Fully dressed, she climbed into the bed and pulled up the covers. She plumped the strange, too-firm pillow beneath her head and closed her eyes.

This was going to be one long uncomfortable night.

She sighed at the absurd thought. What, was she expecting a designer kidnapping?

Well, that made her laugh because, yes, that's exactly what she'd expected. Designed to her exact specifications with three gourmet meals a day and furry handcuffs and a stop to it all at her first whim.

God, she was some piece of work.

"Tate?"

She looked up to find Michael standing by the bed. He was clearly concerned at her outburst, but he'd also caught her contagious laughter, so he was grinning, too.

Which made everything funnier. By a lot.

"Tate," he said, trying hard to keep his cool. "What's going on?"

"I'm a first-class twit," she said, although she doubted he understood her because she really couldn't stop laughing.

"You're a what?"

The way he looked at her, so shocked his eyes had widened and he was actually blushing, let her know he'd misunderstood. She struggled once more to get some decent breaths. "What did you think I said?"

"Nothing that you would ever say."

Then she got it. "I said *twit*."

"Aah. Much better."

That was it. She was crying now. Laughing so hard her stomach ached.

He sat down, grinning and shaking his head.

It was just the kind of scene she'd dreamed of, in her bed, alone, in the dark. Everything about him was perfect. The situation wonderful, like something out of a Nora Ephron romantic comedy. Except for the danger that hovered a whisper away.

Before she could catch her breath, he was next to her under the covers and she was in his arms.

9

SHE TREMBLED IN HIS arms, and all he could think about was going into the saloon and killing everyone on the boat. Maybe that's what he should do—end this thing right now. Of course, he had no idea what kind of weapons were stashed up there. He could take Jazz out, but it was more than a fair bet that Ed had a gun on him, and he wouldn't hesitate to kill everyone in front of him. Martini didn't get to be in his position without a lot of buried bodies.

Despite Michael's fury at his brother, he didn't want Charlie to die. And Charlie would go down first, there wasn't much doubt about that. As terrible as it sounded, he'd be willing to risk it if it meant getting Tate off the boat and to safety.

That was the wild card. In the old days he'd never consider pulling off a job with so many unknowns. That was how people got killed. Before he'd take out a position, be it a hostage takeover of a plane, a bunker or a terrorist cell, he and his men would know everything there was to know about the targets. There were always risks, but his job was to minimize them, not subject this terrified woman to living her last moments in her worst-case scenario.

"It's okay, Tate," he whispered. "I'm here. I won't leave you. I won't let them hurt you."

"I'm sorry," she whispered, her voice muffled against his chest.

"No need to apologize."

She sniffled, then moved her head so her mouth wasn't pressing against him. "I keep thinking I'm fine, that I've got it under control."

"You've been doing great."

"For the record, you were right. The fake kidnapping was a lousy idea."

"Yeah, and this one's not so hot, either."

She sighed, her body shuddering with the exhalation. "I'm really worried about my father."

"He'll be busy trying to find us. Besides, he's a tough old man. He's dealt with dangerous circumstances before."

"That's what's got me so concerned. When my cousin was kidnapped, my uncle Joseph did everything he was supposed to. He didn't call the cops, he got all the money together and took it where they told him to. He followed their instructions to the letter. Once the kidnappers took the cash, they didn't give Lisa back. She was found three days later."

"Shit."

"She was fifteen. They'd hurt her, raped her. Then they killed her. Strangled her to death. Nothing was ever the same again."

"I thought you were—"

"I was. I escaped. I have no memory of it. None. I don't know why I got out and she didn't."

Michael didn't know what to say. No wonder Tate

was so phobic about being taken. She had every reason to be terrified. And because of him there was a damn good chance she was going to die, just as her cousin had.

He had to tell her about Charlie. No matter what, he couldn't let her find out on her own. It wasn't that he didn't relish facing her anger and disappointment; he deserved everything she could dish out. The problem was that she was hanging on by a thread here, and the only reason she hadn't lost it completely was because she trusted him.

Telling her that his own brother had given her over to the ruthless bastards out there was going to be a heavy blow. He had no clue if she'd be able to recover from it.

On the other hand, unless they got off the boat in the next few hours, it would be inevitable that she'd find out. Jazz and Ed—hell, even Charlie—had no reason to keep his secret.

He had no choice. He had to get them off this boat. In order to do that, he needed Tate to sleep. It was already late, and he didn't want to wait until everyone was fresh in the morning. His window of opportunity was in the next couple of hours.

Unfortunately he had no convenient means of helping Tate get some rest. No pills, no booze. He certainly wasn't going to knock her out.

"What's wrong?"

He looked down and met her gaze. "Nothing."

"I felt your whole body tense. What aren't you telling me?"

The urge to confess about Charlie hit him hard, but he held back. "You need to get some rest."

"That's not news. For that matter, so do you."

"You're right. So why don't we both try to sleep?"

Her quiet little laugh made her lips vibrate against his chest. "I have insomnia on good days. You think I'm going to be able to nod off here?"

He brushed the side of her face with his fingers, then lifted her chin so he could see her once more. "There are other ways to forget about what's out there."

She studied him while he took deep breaths. He probably shouldn't do this. It would add insult to injury when she found out about Charlie. But if he did it right, sex should put her right to sleep.

Not that the job would be difficult. He was already getting hard at the thought of touching her. He wanted to make her come so hard she'd pass out. Well, at least fall asleep. The trick would be not coming himself.

He liked to think he could be ready for anything, anytime, anyplace, but even he had to admit that there were certain circumstances… If she'd been a stranger or one of his friends who didn't think twice about hooking up for a night, there'd be no problem. But he liked Tate. He also knew that this wasn't a woman who took making love lightly.

The last thing he wanted to do was mess her up in this area, too. Jesus, he couldn't believe how screwed up this all was. He'd had an outstanding record his entire time in the service. Commendations, promotions. He'd led men into fights with no chance of success, only to come out the other end bloodied but unbowed.

Now he was on the cushiest job he'd had since college,

and it was fucked up beyond all reason. The worst of it was that Tate was the one paying for his mistakes.

"Michael?"

He reached down until he had a grip on her, then drew her up so she shared his pillow. He kissed her, wanting to make this as good as he could. He wanted her to know how he admired her, how beautiful she was and how extraordinary.

He might have had his fair share of terrific women, but Tate…Tate was different. Tate was—

MICHAEL TOOK HER mouth desperately. She came alive inside, kissing him back, clutching at his neck in her need to get closer.

It was like drowning in a riptide, being tugged under by forces so elemental there was simply no fighting back. She didn't want to fight.

Yes, *they* were out there, but in here she was being caressed by large, warm hands. He pulled his arm from underneath her neck so he could get at her buttons, and she reached for his. Inelegant—in fact, clumsy—they managed somehow to take off each other's tops and do some serious French kissing at the same time. It would make an interesting Olympic event, one she'd like to train for.

Her bra was off and she wasn't sure how. All she knew was that she liked the way her breasts felt as they pressed against his chest. Even better was his hand cupping her, brushing her very sensitive nipples before he squeezed her flesh.

Giddy with sensation, she ran her hand down his chest and stomach, amazed at the hardness of him, then down his pants, where she discovered a whole different kind of hardness. He was impressive. Not so big she'd walk funny but large enough she'd fill her diary with exclamation points. He was straining against his pants, hissing as she rubbed him.

Braver still, she found his zipper and managed somehow not to hurt him as she lowered it. Inside was her surprise. Hard, hot, thick, the moment her hand circled his shaft, his cock jumped as if he couldn't contain his eagerness.

"God, Tate," he murmured, his moan as deep as his thrusting tongue.

She loved touching him, but her hold was awkward, so she released him and tackled his belt.

That needed a more deft hand than her own, and being attentive, Michael pitched in. A moment later his pants were halfway off, leaving her feeling quite overdressed.

He caught her in another astonishing kiss, then leaned back. "Get undressed," he said. "I'll be right back."

The bed felt instantly cold as he left her there, and once she realized he was going into the bathroom, she hurriedly wiggled out of her pants and panties. The rush was so she could get out of her really ugly socks. They were made to wear with pants, but to the untrained eye they looked like old-lady stockings. She wanted so badly to be appealing to him, to not spoil it by doing one of a hundred things she'd fretted about in the past. And, no, it didn't matter at all that it was too dark for him to see.

With Graydon, she'd worried about looking fat, about making bodily function sounds even though she knew they were perfectly natural. She'd worried about not being tight enough, about being too tight. She had never quite pleased him, although he wouldn't tell her what it was that made him want to get up after he'd come to watch TV on the couch. He would always fall asleep in the living room, leaving her to wonder.

At least she'd always come. A lot of times she'd had to take care of that for herself, but for an overall selfish man, Graydon had stepped up to the plate his fair share. It still bothered her that they'd stayed together for so long, for all the wrong reasons. Thank goodness he'd found another heiress, someone who matched his family's net worth. They had broken up with a handshake and no regrets. Well, he'd had none. She'd felt as if she'd wasted the only good years she ever had. So soon after college she'd turned recluse, and that had been the end of a traditional sex life for her. But she was quite certain that being alone was far better than being with someone like Graydon. Of course, being with Michael was best of all.

She hoped.

The bed dipped with his return, and she cursed her bad luck for not watching him. She'd like to see him naked, all of him, standing in good light. She'd pictured him so many times; she wondered if she'd gotten any of it right.

He held up a box. "Condoms."

"That makes sense, considering the clothes I found in the drawers."

He got close, his body chilled from his brief foray out. It felt delicious as he pressed up against her. One thing for sure—the trip hadn't dampened his enthusiasm one bit.

"You feel good," he said, his fingers brushing her hair back from her face.

"So do you."

"I've thought about this a lot," he said. "Imagined this a hundred times."

She raised her head, checking his face for lies. "Really?"

"Really."

"I had no idea."

"You weren't meant to. It wouldn't have been appropriate."

She sighed as she settled against him, resting her head on his pillow. "I suppose all bets are off now."

"Yep," he said. "Until I've got you home, this is a whole new ball game. I want you to tell me if anything is uncomfortable or frightening. Aside from the obvious, of course."

"I will."

He touched her chin and made eye contact. "Anything. That means you get to say stop anytime. You can change your mind, and it'll be just fine. Got that?"

She nodded.

"Seriously."

"Michael?"

"Yeah?"

"I appreciate it, but I'm in."

He studied her for a long moment. "Thank God."

She laughed, but his kiss silenced her. Soon his hands were exploring all her private places, touching her with a fascinating mixture of reverence and greed.

Since she'd always been a fan of quid pro quo, she decided to throw caution to the wind and discover

Michael to her heart's content. She wasn't satisfied simply to stroke his cock. She cupped his balls. Delighted at his response, she pinched his delectable ass.

"Hey!"

"Shh," she said before she kissed him again, thrusting her tongue inside him. That quieted him down. Except for his moans, which did strange and wonderful things to her insides.

Nothing she'd felt prepared her, though, for the sensation of his fingers parting her lips, rubbing her all the way up and down, then sliding into her once, twice. Her muscles tightened and her heart beat faster, but there was no panic now. Nothing but excitement and anticipation as his finger found her clit.

He was tender there, the tip of his finger moving in tiny circles, but it still made her eyelids flutter closed, made her abandon his mouth for her own soft, "Oh."

"You like that?" he whispered.

"Mmm," she mumbled, moving her hips to the rhythm of his rubbing.

"You're so wet and hot." He plunged into her again, this time not so gently.

She eased her left leg over his hip, giving him permission to plunder away.

"You're making me crazy."

She smiled. "Me? I'm not the one with the wicked fingers."

"I was going to ask you about that," he said. "I've always imagined you being very, very wicked."

"Me?"

"Oh, yes. Don't forget, I know what you read. What you think is funny. You're not normal, Tate."

"What?"

"I said you're not normal."

"I don't know…." she said. "Should I be insulted?"

"God, no. I love that on the outside you're so prim and together. They all think you're sweet, don't they? They all assume you live so quietly because you're just a good girl who does what she's supposed to."

"I am."

"Yes. But I was there for the discussion of *The Story of O,* remember? I know exactly how you felt about that one scene in *The Big Easy.* You may have been on the phone with Sara, but you were talking to me."

"Oh, God," she said, burying her head in the pillow so he couldn't see her blush. "Was I that obvious?"

"I can't hear you when you mumble into the pillow."

She lifted her head and repeated the question.

"Yes. You were."

She groaned, and this time it wasn't from his busy digits.

"Hey, I liked it."

She shook her head, not wanting to hear his excuses. She knew he was just being polite, and that killed her.

He leaned down so his mouth was close to her ear. "I used to go home and stroke myself to the memory of your voice."

A shiver raced down her spine, and she ended up squeezing his finger quite tightly.

"See? You do like to tease. And you can't tell me you didn't know the effect it had on me. There were all those times when I stood behind the limo door after letting you out. I can't believe you didn't know why."

Looking up once more, she tried to figure out if he was playing her. Was it all just a way to make her forget that she probably wasn't going to live to have sex again? He looked sincere, but that didn't mean a thing. The only real proof she had—if she could call it that—was his very hard dick. Of course, he might be getting off for any number of reasons, only one of them being that he truly wanted her.

"What are you thinking?"

"That this could all be some ploy to distract me."

"It's not. But if it was…?"

She smiled. "Good point. Distract away."

His fingers stilled, his body tensed and the way he looked at her gave her gooseflesh. "Know this, Tate Baxter. I think you're an amazing woman and I'd never do anything to hurt you. Got that?"

She blinked back sudden tears, but he didn't see because he was kissing her again. When he pushed her to her back, she went eagerly, spreading her legs for him. It had been a long time, but she was so ready that when he pushed inside her, she nearly passed out from the pleasure.

While he was in her, fully in her, he somehow lifted her butt and shoved a pillow underneath. So when he moved the next time, he not only filled her perfectly but he rubbed her already engorged clit.

She'd read about this neat little trick but always assumed it was fiction. Boy, was she glad to be wrong.

It was her last coherent thought as Michael proceeded to rock not just her world but all the worlds in the galaxy.

She came like a Roman candle, and he had to kiss her so she wouldn't wake everyone on the East Coast.

Flushed, gasping, eyes closed, she felt him remove the pillow from under her butt, then pull the covers up to her chest. She wasn't sure if his gentle kiss on the forehead was real or a dream or both.

HE GOT OUT OF THE bed and went straight for the bathroom so his moaning wouldn't wake her.

He pulled off the damn rubber, then turned on the cold water, whispering every curse in every language he knew. He'd held off before, but damn, it had never hurt like this. He was getting old, that's all. Old and unable to control himself as well.

It seemed to take forever for his dick to calm the hell down, and even then getting dressed made him swear again. He'd done his job, all right. She'd fallen asleep, as predicted. Now all he had to do was make sure she didn't wake up in the middle of his escape.

He got his comb out of his back pocket. No one ever thought to take the comb. Not only was it good for handcuffs, he could open one hell of a lot of locks with this puppy. It was cheap, too. He'd bought a pack of fifty for five bucks.

He slipped the scissors into his pocket, then turned off the light. He'd get himself into the saloon, praying no one was watching the door. All he'd need was a few seconds of good surveillance and he could go on the offensive.

He stepped out of the head to find Tate still sleeping. Then he turned off the cabin light and made sure there was no bleed of light around the door. It was dark, which was just what he needed.

He quietly made his way to the door, which only took him a minute to unlock. Then he was in the saloon and he closed the door behind him.

Martini wasn't sitting in his big leather chair anymore. Charlie had fallen asleep on the couch, and Jazz had drifted off with his head on the side counter.

He made his way toward Jazz, determined to get his gun before taking him out, just in case. As he reached for the weapon, pain tore through him like lightning. Then black.

10

TATE TOUCHED MICHAEL'S shoulder, really worried now that the hit on the head had done serious damage. He'd been out for hours, and the swelling, despite the damp cloths she'd kept on it, was bad.

Just after he'd been dumped on the bed, the boat had pulled anchor and set out. She had no idea if they were going to the Cayman Islands or simply out to sea to dispose of bodies, but she did know they were traveling fast. When she'd looked out the porthole, she'd seen no land at all in the early-morning light.

If only he'd wake up.

She sat back on the bed watching his chest rise and fall. He'd been so wonderful to her last night. It had changed everything for her about sex, and if this hadn't been the single worst experience of her life, she'd have been in heaven.

More then ever she wanted to survive this. Not just to get over her fears but to see what would happen between her and Michael. Was she the worst person on Earth to be thinking of their future together while he might be seriously hurt? She supposed it was no worse than her prognosis. They'd either die tonight, in the cold depths of the sea, or in about a week, after she'd signed her money away. Or Michael would recover and he'd save her.

She decided right then to focus on option three.

Her father wouldn't have hired him if he wasn't the best, right? And he'd gotten them this far. Okay, so his escape plan last night hadn't gone so well. But, come on, the guy had had no way of knowing what was behind the door. At least he'd tried.

Things would get trickier now, though. Assuming they were heading for the Cayman's, they'd have to get fuel. She wasn't sure how often they'd have to stop, but when they did, there would be a chance.

She looked at his face, at his very dark, long eyelashes. At his lips, perfect for a man. His nose was pretty damn nice, too. Oh, who was she kidding? He was a babe, and even her, with her limited knowledge about men, knew he'd been around the block many, many times. Probably with fabulous women, because, well, come on.

Had he really told her the truth last night?

She shivered remembering his whispered words just before he'd made love to her. God, that was the sexiest thing ever. She sighed, knowing she was behaving like an adolescent.

And why not? She'd stunted her growth, her heart had atrophied—and for what? All that planning, all that fear hadn't helped one damn bit. She'd still been kidnapped. So she could have been having a fabulous life all this time instead of whining about her regrets.

At least she wouldn't regret last night. If she had to go, this was the way to do it. Well, not *this*. This sucked. She needed Michael to be okay. She could face whatever came next if he was beside her. Alone? She'd rather die than be that scared again.

A moan made her freeze, hold her breath. She watched him, afraid to blink, as he moaned again, moved his head. He winced, and that had to be a good sign, right?

"Michael?"

He opened his eyes just a little, then closed them again. "What happened?" His voice sounded thick, dry.

"They hit you."

"With what? A refrigerator?"

"I don't know. They brought you in last night. Well, early this morning, although I'm not sure what time. They dumped you on the bed and told me to tell you that if you tried that again, they wouldn't be so nice."

He tried to lift his head but just winced again. "Yeah, they were real swell."

"It was brave of you to try," she said. "Hold on. I'll cool down the washcloth." She took the small blue towel from behind his head, making him hiss, then hurried to the bathroom. The water was really cold, which was good. She wished she had ice, though.

When she got back to the bed she saw he hadn't moved at all. She tried to be gentle as she applied the cold compress, but she hurt him anyway.

"Is it me or are we moving?"

"We set off sometime around sunrise. I think."

"Right." He put his hand on the back of his head, trying to feel the extent of the damage, but in the end he just held the cloth and slowly sat up. "Jesus."

She reached over beside the bed and brought back

a glass of water and a bottle of aspirin. "I got this ready. I figured—"

He moaned again and took the aspirin bottle from her hand. He brought the cap up to his mouth and snapped the bottle open with his teeth. Then he dumped a bunch of the small white pills in his mouth. At least six.

"Won't that—"

He dropped the open bottle, took the glass and drained it in a few hard gulps.

"That's a lot of aspirin," she said.

"It's a very large headache."

"You need to eat something, then. Your stomach lining will get very irritated."

He looked at her through shuttered eyes. "I appreciate the concern, but my stomach lining is the least of our worries."

"Fine."

He patted her hand. "Don't be hurt. It's good of you to care. But I've taken this many before and I've been okay."

"Still…"

"You're right. I hope they feed us soon. I promise to eat every bite."

She sat back, adjusting some of the pillows so she could look at him comfortably. "How did you get into the other room? I didn't even see you go."

"You were sleeping."

"I gathered."

"I'm pretty good with locks."

"I gathered that, too. But we have no idea how many people there are on board. It would have been pure luck if you'd been successful."

He winced again, and she was pretty sure it wasn't about the pain in his head.

"I'm sorry," he said. "I shouldn't have let things get this far."

"You've done everything you could."

"Not everything."

"What do you mean?"

"Nothing. I'll figure this out. I won't let them hurt you."

She reached over and touched his hand. "I know."

He looked away, and she wished she'd never brought up the subject. "Let me get you some more water."

"It's okay. I'll go."

"No, you're—"

"I want to wash up," he said. "And you should go through those clothes again. I'm pretty sure I saw at least one T-shirt that would fit you."

"I don't know…."

"Try. A shower will make you feel better."

She smiled at him, amazed that even now he was thinking of her. That he could look so good even when he was in so much pain.

Once he'd closed the bathroom door, she went to the dresser and found a couple of men's T-shirts that she thought they could each wear. There was also a bikini that would substitute for underwear. She'd wash her own in the shower, then…

Would she be alive tomorrow to put on her own underpants? Did she want to die wearing someone else's skimpy bikini?

Tears welled at the thought of never seeing her father again. He'd overprotected her, but he'd done it out of love. For all his preoccupation with business, he'd always kept her close. Loved her the best way he knew how.

And, oh, God, never to see Sara again? That hurt as deeply as the thoughts of her father. Sara might not be a blood relative, but in every way that mattered she was a sister. A damn good one, too. They hardly ever fought, but she never hesitated to tell Tate the unvarnished truth.

The ache to see her friend again took her breath away, and she sat down on the edge of the bed. It was probably a good thing Dr. Bay wasn't around. What an idiot. Fake kidnappings. Please. The woman needed major therapy herself.

Tate sniffed, her anger at her therapist distracting her from the pain of her losses. Once again she thanked God for Michael. She'd have lost it without him. She just wished she could do something to make him feel better.

AT LEAST, MICHAEL thought, there was no way he could feel worse. What the hell had happened to him? He was supposed to be a goddamn warrior, a fighter, a champion.

As the water poured down over him in the small shower, he couldn't think of one thing that had gone right in the last two days. Even the good parts made him feel like shit. Tate was going to find out about Charlie. She was. And he had to be the one to tell her. Only…how? Especially now, when he didn't have a plan other than to wait and strike at the next opportunity.

He'd be lucky if she didn't strike him first.

He didn't even know who'd hit him. Or with what. Or how many people were currently on board. Or what direction they were going.

Maybe it was just his turn. Charlie'd been the bad-luck magnet all these years. Maybe now it would come up roses for his brother while Michael went straight down the tubes.

He grabbed the soap and scrubbed up, shaking off his self-pity and thinking about how he was going to tell her. It seemed so naive, from this vantage point, to think his problems could have been solved by sexing her to sleep. Talk about stupid. Talk about thinking with his dick.

He moaned as he fell forward, then groaned when he actually hit his sore head against the fiberglass wall. He should go into that saloon and fight until he couldn't fight anymore. With luck, he'd wipe them all out before he flung himself overboard to be eaten by sharks. Then Tate could radio for help. The end.

She'd still find out Charlie was his brother, but he'd have died bravely trying to save her, so that would prove that he hadn't been…

"Shit." He sighed deeply, closed his eyes and turned the shower to dead cold.

ED MARTINI FINISHED his eggs Benedict while he watched the final race at Santa Anita. He wasn't even thinking about the money he'd just made from the race or the five million stashed in his safe back at the house. He was thinking about fifty million tax-free dollars. The dough wouldn't make a big difference in his life. Hell, he did everything he wanted now. But

he'd know, goddammit, he'd know each and every day
that he had fifty million fucking dollars that Sheila
wouldn't be able to touch. Not even with those god-
awful two-inch fingernails of hers. What the woman
wanted with little palm trees painted in green on her
fingers was beyond him. They looked like crap, but he
supposed they went along with her bleached hair and
her wide-load ass.

The trick would be to let her think he had the
money. She couldn't be sure, because if she was sure,
she'd sic the IRS on him. But she had to think he had
it and he wasn't giving it to her. That would make her
insane. More than any new girlfriend, even one who
was twenty-five. More than any new car. It would kill
Sheila that he had that much cash that she couldn't
spend. The bitch.

"Hey, boss?"

"Yeah, Jazz?"

"I never been to the Cayman Islands. They nice?"

"Yeah."

"Nice women?"

"Oh, yeah."

"How long is it gonna take us to get there?"

"This boat? If we hit good weather? Maybe eight
days."

"Fuck. What are we gonna do for eight days?"

Ed leaned back in his chair. He knew just what he
was gonna do: conduct his business, like usual. Just
'cause he wasn't in town didn't mean he wasn't raking
it in. "Jazz, you just concentrate on keeping your eye
on our happy couple. You caught him last night, but
he still managed to get out of that locked room."

"It won't happen again."

"Be sure it doesn't."

Jazz, who had eaten his bacon and eggs in about ten seconds, then cleaned his gun, lowered his voice. "What about him?" he said, nodding toward Charlie.

"Charlie," Ed said.

The kid stopped eating, nearly choking on his bacon. "Yeah, boss?"

"You finish your breakfast, then take food in to your brother and his girlfriend. You make sure he understands that if he tries anything like he did last night, it won't be good for your health."

Charlie swallowed again. "Okay, sure. He won't do it again. I swear to God. He won't. He promised my old—"

"I don't care. Just make sure he understands."

Charlie nodded unhappily as he pushed his plate away.

THE SHOWER WAS SO small she kept bumping her elbows. Hers at home was quite large, with three different showerheads. It doubled as a steam room, and she could also simulate the patter of a rain-forest squall if she so desired. Here, the water was marginally warm, the soap was blue and smelled like antiseptic. And she didn't trust for a moment that one of those men from the saloon wouldn't burst through the door.

Yes, she still had faith that Michael would stop anything bad from happening, but she'd discovered early on that logic had little to do with irrational fears. Hence the word *irrational*.

She kept washing, wondering what her hair was

going to look like after using that dime-store mousse she'd found. What her skin would feel like after a few days away from her Intensité Volumizing Serum. Oh, well. She'd make do. What choice did she have?

Without even reading the label, she washed her hair, then put conditioner on, and as she rinsed she wished she'd brought the darn razor in with her. Although she wouldn't have been able to shave her legs, not in this small space. So she'd do it after. She could still rinse off in the shower.

She thought about Michael for the hundredth time since she'd climbed in the shower. He'd smelled awfully good after his. But then, he was a man. Oh, was he ever.

She laughed at herself, wondering if she was going to be this moony teen the whole way to the Caymans. It wouldn't matter, she supposed. No one would know. And why shouldn't she do exactly as she pleased?

Most people thought she did, anyway. She knew they didn't dare compare her to Paris Hilton, but there were other trust-fund babies that were around her age. She'd heard them talk about how ridiculous she looked in her old-fashioned limo, how she dressed like Queen Elizabeth. She wasn't completely protected from the gossip and the backbiting.

How many nights had she wept herself to sleep watching those awful newsmagazine shows? She hadn't really wanted to shock the world. Well, mostly. But she had wanted to make some kind of splash, even a little one.

The charities didn't count. Anyone could do her job. Anyone with the right connections. It was easy to give

money away when you had her father's strict guide-
lines to follow.

But she'd never been to a big premiere or an
opening night on Broadway. She'd never been to any
of the clubs or found herself searching for a predawn
breakfast after carousing all night.

She didn't just dress like Queen Elizabeth, she
partied like her, too.

Tate turned abruptly, tired of her pity party. She
turned off the water and stepped out onto the blue
fluffy towel. As she dried off she promised herself
that she wouldn't go to that place again. If she had to
dwell on the past, it would be to remember all those
self-defense classes, her weapons training.

There was no reason she shouldn't stand shoulder
to shoulder with Michael. Fight no matter what.

She grabbed the tiny bikini and put the sucker on. It
was tight. And, jeez, her boobs looked huge. But that was
okay. So was the T-shirt. Also tight but not too horrible.

She'd also dug out a pair of shorts—men's, but they
were a size medium, and if she tied the little waistband
inside, they wouldn't fall down.

Dammit. She'd forgotten to shave. She rubbed her
leg, and it wasn't so bad. Tomorrow, though, for sure.
For now, she put on the mousse and combed her hair.
She debated a moment about using the hair dryer, but
it would probably be better if she let it dry naturally.

Then she looked at the makeup that had been left
in the bathroom. It was no use. She couldn't use some
other woman's makeup. Not for anything. It was as
bad as sharing a toothbrush.

So she washed her panties and her bra, and as she

went to hang them in the shower she heard shouting just outside the bathroom door.

Immediately her heart started pounding as though she was seconds from an attack. When she turned to the door, the tunnel vision started, taking her straight down the road to immobility and failure.

She closed her eyes. Took several deep breaths. She pictured her safe place, but the vision of her waterfall didn't help. The voices—Michael's and another man's—were too loud.

Then she changed her visualization. It wasn't her old green meadow. It was Michael. His face. His eyes. The way he looked at her, then smiled.

She smelled his skin and remembered his taste. Salty, sexy. She brought up the memory of his fingers on her face, and then his fingers weren't near her face. He was leaning over her, and his intentions were incredibly clear.

He wanted her. He wanted *her*.

The vision changed once more, and she was carrying her Sig Sauer. And there was Michael. Tall, handsome as sin. And he had his gun, too. He had her back. And she had his. No one was getting past the two of them.

She went to the bathroom door, and as she swung it open she heard the other one yelling.

"You swore to him, Mikey! You swore to our father that you'd take care of me. You think breaking in to hurt Mr. Martini is keeping me safe? You got to cool it, Mikey, or he's gonna kill all of us, okay?"

Tate's vision narrowed once more. All she could see was the look on Michael's face. Shock, anger. Guilt.

He was in on this. He was in on this. She'd slept with him, and he was in on it.

11

MICHAEL SHOT A LOOK at Charlie that had him scrambling out the door, but his main concern was Tate. She looked unsteady, panicked. Everything he'd hoped to avoid.

He went to the bathroom door and put his arm gently around her waist. It was a testament to how bad off she was that she didn't slap him in the face. "Come on. Let's get you to the bed."

She struggled, but so faintly he figured he'd better get her to lie down before she fell down. Goddamn Charlie. It wasn't enough to fuck up his own life, he had to fuck up Tate's. Good job, asshole.

As he took her to the bed, he reached for her wrist and got a feel for her pulse. Dammit, it was off the charts, a full-blown panic attack, and he wasn't at all sure he could help her.

He turned her around and pressed gently on her shoulders. She sat, her hands limp by her sides, her face pale and lifeless. The only thing animated about her was her breathing. She took great gulps, as if the oxygen was far too weak to sustain her.

He wished he could enjoy her shorts, her tight little T-shirt, but he gave them only a glance as he tried to gauge his next move. He needed her to understand what was going on. He expected no forgiveness at all, but he did think they could work together until this horror show was over. If he could just get her to hear him—to believe him.

He sat down next to her, his shoulder touching hers. She didn't move, but she didn't lean into him either. "Tate, I need you to listen to me. First, this is all my fault. However, it wasn't intentional. My brother has been a pain in my ass for a long, long time. I should have cut it off between us years ago, but…

"Anyway, he came to my place, and when I had to leave the room, he broke into my safe. He saw the information I had on Brody. I wouldn't give him the money to pay off his bookie, so he stole that information and used it as a way of getting out of debt. That's why you're here—because I let Charlie into my apartment. I didn't realize he'd go this far—and I should have."

As he paused he saw her eyes jig over to look at him, but they went back to staring straight ahead a second later. "I know it's hard to believe anyone could be stupid enough to let Charlie in the same borough, let alone his apartment. He's been nothing but trouble from the time he was a kid. He stole, he took drugs, he had no sense about the world. It was always someone else's fault with Charlie, mostly mine.

"My mother had died a long time ago, and my father did his best to keep Charlie out of trouble. He got sick—my dad, I mean—and he made me promise I'd take care of Charlie. I gave him my word, and that's not something I take lightly.

"It was all right because I spent so much time overseas. You know I was in intelligence work, but you don't know why I left the service. It was Charlie, one more time. He stole a briefcase from a fellow officer's car. He was caught and he went to jail, but because of me they didn't charge him with treason. I couldn't stay in the service after that."

He wasn't sure, but he thought she'd leaned a little more his way. Hell, he wasn't even sure if she was listening or, if she was, whether she believed any part of his story. The only concrete change he saw was that she wasn't struggling quite so hard to breathe.

"You feeling a little better? I can get you some water."

She shook her head, and he wondered if she was saying no to the water or to feeling better.

"Is there anything I can do?"

"Why should I believe you?" Her voice was low, a monotone of bleak expectation.

"There's no reason at all. I had planned on telling you about Charlie, but honestly I wasn't sure when. I didn't expect you to have a minute of sympathy for my situation, but I didn't want you to hate me so much that you wouldn't accept my help."

"You made love to me."

"Oh, God. That's what I was most afraid of. I didn't have ulterior motives—no, that's not true. There was a hope that, after, you could get some rest. But the motivation for kissing you, that's been around for a long time. I'm not sorry we did it, only that I wasn't smart enough to know the best way to handle this situation. You've been doing so great. Your attacks have been less frequent and less severe, and if you can keep that up until we're safe, then it'll change your life."

"When did you know?"

"That Charlie was behind this?"

She nodded.

"When I followed you here. When I looked into the saloon I saw him. A few seconds later I was knocked out."

She turned her head to look at him. At least she had a little more color. "The fifty million, heading off for the Caymans…it's too much to believe."

He nodded. "I know some things about Ed Martini. There's a reason we're on this boat. Once he'd gotten the ransom from your father…"

"He'd have killed me."

Michael nodded.

"I imagine he'll kill me after I sign the papers at the bank. The question is, will he kill you?"

"He won't kill either of us. I told him about the bank to stall for time. I had to make the prize big enough, so I told him fifty million. I had to make it far enough away that he'd have to take on fuel and supplies."

"They knocked you out last night when they should have killed you."

"Because they think I'm the only one who can get you to sign the papers."

She shook her head a little, and her eyes welled with tears. "You tell a good story, Michael. But then, that was your job, wasn't it? Telling stories to manipulate people?"

"That's right."

"So how can I know? How can I possibly believe what you've told me?"

"I don't know. I do know that I'm going to resign as soon as I have you back safely."

"I wish I hadn't heard him," she said. "It was so much better."

"You would have found out. It was inevitable. Ironically, I'd planned on telling you right after your shower."

"Michael," she said, whispering, "why does it bother me more that you made love to me than that you had me kidnapped?"

He wiped his face with his hand, wishing like hell he could tell her at least one thing that would convince her that he wasn't lying. "It's because you doubt yourself. How attractive you are. How smart and funny."

"Oh, don't. Don't do that to me. It's hard enough."

"Is there anything I could say that would help?"

"I know that I can't trust anything you've said or will say. I might have a panic disorder, but I've been well trained about con men. I've got that fifty million. And my father, he's got so much more."

Her color was back and her cheeks looked flushed. She wasn't gasping for breath any longer. Her panic had diminished as her anger had grown, which was good. She needed to be angry.

"I imagine you've seen your share of gigolos."

"Some of the best. That's why—"

"Why what?"

"I can't have this conversation." She stood up and took a deep breath. "I can't be in this room with you."

He was the breathless one now. Why had he thought the truth would be enough? It rarely was, and if he were Tate, he wouldn't have bought it, either. He just hadn't realized how much he'd wanted a miracle. "I understand." He looked up at her. "Unfortunately there's nowhere for me to go."

She looked behind her, at the door. "You can go be with your brother."

"Uh, no. Martini already let me know that if I didn't get you to sign the papers, he'd kill Charlie first."

"Why should I care?"

"Because he said he'd kill you second."

SARA WAS GOING TO lose it. They'd heard nothing, absolutely nothing, and William had delivered the ransom hours and hours ago.

She'd paced all six thousand square feet of Tate's place. She'd tried to comfort William, but he was inconsolable. Believed his daughter was dead. Believed Michael had been behind the kidnapping. There were security people all over the place, all his phones had been forwarded to Tate's main line. And they'd heard nothing, not a word.

What concerned her most was William having a heart attack. She'd called his personal physician to be here until this was resolved, and the doctor should be arriving any minute. She went to the fridge again and took out a head of lettuce. It wasn't her usual kind of snack, but it was here and she had to stuff something in her mouth. She broke the lettuce up into chunks and put it in a colander to drain.

"Is there something I can make you?"

Sara jumped at Pilar's voice. "No, thank you. If I have a bite of something decent, I'll never stop. I'm going to chew lettuce."

"I can fix a quick vinaigrette—"

"Thanks, Pilar, but I wasn't kidding. I will never stop."

"I understand. Food is oddly comforting."

"Maybe you can fix something for Mr. Baxter."

"He's refused me several times."

"You know, I think if you put a platter near him with bite-size treats, he'll end up taking one, and that will lead to more."

Pilar nodded. "I'll do that. I've got twenty minutes until I have to take the casserole out for the staff."

Sara sighed as she took the lettuce from under the running water. She let it drip, thinking about how incredible Pilar's casseroles were, and put a chunk of the not-quite salad into her mouth. It tasted about as good as she'd expected.

"Michael didn't do this," Pilar said.

"I know."

"Mr. Baxter doesn't."

"He needs someone to blame. This family has a history with kidnappings."

Pilar went to the fridge and pulled out an array of goodies. She set up on one of the huge counters and started to prepare delectable treats without a glance at a cookbook. Huge fresh figs were sliced down the middle, then stuffed with a wedge of Gorgonzola cheese. Just looking at them made Sara feel way too sorry for herself.

It was the doorbell that saved her, and she hurried out, all thoughts of figs buried beneath her prayers. Unfortunately it was the doctor, not Tate.

The doctor. She made sure he sat with William, and despite the older man's objections, he started an immediate checkup. "William, I'll be back," she said.

"Where are you going?"

"To pay someone a visit."

He looked at her, concerned.

"Don't worry. I'll be fine. It won't take me long. I'll be back before you can blink."

"Please."

She strode toward the elevator, knowing this had to be done and knowing she was the right person to do it.

MICHAEL WAS RIGHT—there was nowhere for him to go. But she needed some time to think without looking at him. The only place was the head. She'd been so positive in there, what, fifteen minutes ago? Maybe she could find something to hang on to in there.

Without a word, she went back to the head and closed the door. It looked smaller, uglier. It didn't matter because Michael wasn't here.

Michael wasn't there, either. Not the Michael she thought she knew. What was she supposed to believe? Everything had come together so easily. They had to have been aware of Elizabeth or they wouldn't have put her out of commission so easily. They'd known exactly where she'd be. How, if Michael hadn't told them?

She sat down on the toilet and willed herself— uselessly, it turned out—not to cry. The tears were heavy and hot, and her chest hurt as if she'd been kicked by a mule.

He'd set her up. There was no other conclusion she could come to, right? He'd been dismissed from the one job he'd loved and been forced to become a baby-sitter. It had to be humiliating. It only made sense to want revenge, and since he couldn't get back at the

Army, he could get even with her. The stupid rich chick who was a perfect mark. She was already crazy, it wouldn't take much to immobilize her. Persuade her that he was on her side. That he would be her salvation. Of course she'd sign over her money if it meant saving her life, but it didn't, did it? She would never be released. He would sneak about the boat, but he wouldn't be successful because that wasn't the plan. All he had to do was have her believe in him. Have her need him again.

The real tragedy? She wanted to. Desperately.

Last night had been incredible. Not just the sex but the fact that she hadn't spent every single second trapped in a panic attack. She'd slept. She hadn't had a nightmare.

It was better than anything she'd ever anticipated, better than she'd been even in imaginary scenarios.

More than that, Michael had been the safest of her safe places. She remembered the feelings that had coursed through her body as she'd pictured him in her mind. He'd been right there with her, but she'd never seen him more clearly than with her eyes closed.

Her heart was beating hard even now, just thinking about it. She'd liked him so much. Those talks in the car—those couldn't have been faked. Wasn't possible. He'd never known what they were going to talk about. He didn't know what books she'd read, what movies she'd seen. So his reactions had been real. Honest.

God, what if he was telling her the truth?

She unrolled some tissue and blew her nose, then got some more and wiped her eyes. She wished she could talk to Sara. Sara would know. Sara would tell her the truth and she'd completely look out for her. Unlike Dr. Bay.

SARA FELT AMAZINGLY calm as she read the new issue of *Vanity Fair*. She'd never get tired of seeing George Clooney as the cover subject. Not ever. She'd seen him in person three times, and he was the single dreamiest man on earth. And, yes, she'd seen Mr. Pitt in person, too. Of course, if forced, she'd also go out with Brad, but her first choice would be George.

The door opened and Sara stood up. She'd had to wait longer than she'd hoped, but it was worth it. Or it would be in another minute.

She approached a well dressed woman. Very well-dressed. Her short, dark bob was perfect and so was her makeup. She lived the life, here on Park Avenue. "Dr. Bay? I'm Tate's friend, Sara."

She nodded. "Has there been any word?"

"No. None."

"Oh, my God."

"I do have one thing to tell you."

"If I can be of any help, of course I will."

"I think you've been about as helpful as you're going to get."

"Pardon me?"

"There is no pardon for you. What kind of moron takes a girl who's been absolutely traumatized by her own kidnapping and the death of her best friend and suggests she stage her own kidnapping? I mean, of all the idiotic, irresponsible—"

"Now you just wait a minute. I don't know who you

think you are, but my suggestions to my patient were completely legitimate and not in the least irresponsible."

"What are you, insane? She's been kidnapped. For real. And it's entirely possible she won't be coming back. Which will only mean one thing—they've killed her. You understand what she went through? Her worst fear in the world, and she had to live through it. She had to know she was going to die." Sara wiped the tears from her face with the heel of her hand. "If Michael wasn't with her…"

"I'm very sorry for what's happened to Tate, but you must know that I bear no responsibility. This was purely a coincidence, a tragic one, but it had nothing to do—"

"Don't you dare. Don't you—" Sara turned, fury so great inside her that she thought she might burst or go crazy or… She pulled back, and when she swung it was with all her weight behind her. The crack was loud and the pain shot up her arm and hurt like the devil. But Dr. Bay, who wasn't responsible, who had nothing to do with anything, had gone flying back into her pristine office with the fresh flowers and the expensive furniture. Her hand was on her cheek and she was crying. Finally.

"You're just lucky it was me who came after you. If it had been Michael, you'd be dead."

HE SAT ON THE BED, waiting. Remembering when he was a kid, when Charlie was really young and his mom was still alive. Charlie hadn't been a screwup then. He'd just been a little kid, like every other little kid, and he'd been Michael's responsibility, even back then. When anything went wrong with Charlie, his mother had given him this real disappointed look.

He still saw that look. Felt it. As fucked up as Charlie was, Michael was still responsible. Even now. With Tate in the bathroom. With Tate believing the worst. Still, the idea of walking into the saloon and shooting Charlie made him sick.

What if it came down to that? To choosing between Tate and Charlie? What then?

His first responsibility was to Tate. That was a fact and nothing would change it. He just didn't like the idea of Charlie dying. Not because the stupid son of a bitch didn't deserve it, but Michael had a deathbed promise hanging over his head, and even though he knew it was superstitious nonsense, it didn't feel that way.

Charlie had crossed the line. If there was a way to save him, then Michael would—as long as it didn't endanger Tate. If not, well, then he'd tell his father he was sorry when he joined him in hell.

Decision made, he went back to waiting. Worrying. Wishing. It wasn't like him. He didn't wish for the impossible. He never had. But when it came to Tate, he did a lot of things he'd never done before.

12

AFTER AN EXCRUCIATING night of no sleep, of remembering what it had been like to make love to him, of reliving the moment of betrayal over and over, Tate finally slept as the sky began to soften into day.

She woke, startled at the sound of the door slamming shut. There was Michael in his borrowed T-shirt and his chauffeur's pants, holding a tray with food and coffee. At the sight, her stomach clenched, and she knew she wouldn't be eating much. Of course, it didn't matter, did it? Nothing did. She would die soon and this torment would be over. That's all she wanted. In fact, maybe there was a way to speed things up. She'd have to think about that.

Michael put the tray on the dresser and turned to her. She wasted no time in slipping out of the bed. She no longer cared about the clean clothes problem or shaving her legs.

"Tate, we need to—"

She slammed the bathroom door closed behind her. By the time she'd washed her face, brushed her teeth and her hair, she'd realized she couldn't go out there. He would end up convincing her that he'd had her best interest at heart. That he wasn't a thief, that he'd made love to her because he'd been attracted, or in love or some other fairy tale.

At least she could sit down. Of course, the john wasn't exactly her idea of a great chair, but it was better than looking at him. Her real shame wasn't that she'd been deceived but, that knowing she'd been deceived, she still wanted him.

That's what made her sick. That's what terrified her.

How could she want so badly to believe him? Why did she have to force herself out of the fantasy where they lived happily ever after? She truly did need a shrink. Not Dr. Bay, of course, but a good shrink.

She laughed as her chin dropped to her chest. Too late for shrinkage now. She wondered if they'd kill her first before they threw her in the water. That's something she'd beg for, if she had to. The thought of drowning...

"Tate?" Michael's voice came from directly outside the door. "Do you want some coffee? I can hand you a cup. You don't have to come out."

"No." She waited, but he didn't respond. She wished there was a peephole. It would have been so much better if she could know where he was.

She stood, whipped off her clothes and got under the shower, not taking the soap or the shampoo; she was there for the water. She'd always had her best ideas in the shower, and now would be a really good time for something brilliant to occur.

She laughed, inhaling water, then choking for a long, long time. Which was when she had the thought. She wasn't sure it was brilliant—in fact, it was probably an excellent example of how she'd lost her mind—but there it was. And there it stayed. All day.

MICHAEL GLANCED OUT the porthole, not surprised to see the red sky of sunset. He hadn't taken a drink or eaten a bite because he really hadn't wanted to bother Tate in the bathroom, but things were getting a bit hairy.

His personal problem wasn't nearly as worrisome as what Tate was going through. He hated that he'd put her in this position, but he couldn't figure out what to say to make things better. He'd told her the truth and he feared that anything else would sever any slight hope that she could believe him. But the truth seemed meager and foolish. Perhaps if he had told her the moment he'd been shoved inside the cabin, she'd have bought it. But he'd been an idiot about that, too.

It was difficult not to put all the blame on Charlie. Granted, Charlie deserved a great deal of it. But then, he did, too. As long as he was able to get an accurate picture of what was real, then he had a chance to save her. If he indulged himself in blaming Charlie, he would lose sight of the objective: keep Tate alive. That was his whole purpose, and he could put nothing ahead of that. His second goal was to keep Tate sane. To help her not be terrified every minute. Right now, that was the more difficult task, but again, if he kept his eye on the prize, he could get—

The head door opened. Tate stood in the doorway, leaning on the jamb, her arms crossed over the boys' T-shirt they'd found in the dresser.

She looked good. Her color was fine. In fact, she seemed a bit flushed. Her chest rose and fell normally. There were no apparent tremors. The only thing that looked off was the puffiness of her eyes, but even that was in the regular range. He wanted to say something, anything, but he held back, afraid that whatever he did say would be wrong and would send her straight back to panic.

"So these are my options," she said, her voice even and considered. "I can do the completely logical, rational thing and not believe one thing you've said. It makes perfect sense that you set me up for this. I mean, who else knew we were going to be at Prada? That Elizabeth wouldn't be able to get to me in that tiny little window of opportunity? It makes sense that you came after me, knowing I had a great deal of money in a secret account. Why else was I taken to a boat? It made getting the money easy and my disposal a snap.

"It also makes sense that you would bring your brother into this. That he'd know someone who had the boat, had the means, had the manpower. Everything points to you. I'm not being melodramatic, either. Any cop on any *Law & Order* would nail your ass before the first commercial."

She straightened, and with arms still crossed, still protective, she took two steps toward him. "Or, against all logic and reason, I can believe you. I can shift my focus to our relationship in the car. How much I enjoyed our long conversations and how much I admired your own logic and reason. I can remember how you made me laugh.

"And I can think about making love with you and how you made me feel. Of course, if I choose to believe you and I find out I was wrong, I will want to die, so that works in your favor. If I'm right, and you're innocent and then you die… Well, you're just not allowed to, okay? Because I am taking a huge, stupid risk here. It makes no sense, and if my father knew, he'd strangle me for my own good."

She walked a little closer to the bed, and when she stood in front of him, telling him in no uncertain terms that she was on his side, she dropped her arms. He looked up at her face. She looked beautiful, with her hair thick and wavy, with no makeup, with no defenses whatsoever.

He stood. "Tate, I can't believe I'm going to say this. Unfortunately I have no choice."

Her face got sad and she bit her lower lip.

"No, it's not like that. Don't fret. But I have to use the toilet." He squeezed her shoulders. "You were in there a really long time."

Desperate now, he dashed the few feet to his objective, kicking the door shut behind him.

Tate stared at the closed door. She smiled despite herself, and a moment later she was laughing, picturing the poor guy crossing his legs as the hours had crawled by. She'd taken advantage of her location a couple of times, but it hadn't occurred to her that he might need to, too.

She sat on the edge of the bed as she laughed, not just at his predicament but at her own willingness to live knee-deep in denial. It was utter nonsense to believe him, and she knew it, but if this was the end, she'd rather go out with the charming liar, thank you. She'd rather have as much sex as was humanly possible. She'd prefer not to have any more panic attacks and to continue to use Michael as her safe place.

Either way, believing him or not, she doubted she

was walking away from this, so what the hell? She'd wasted so much time, so much life, that this seemed the sanest decision she'd made since dumping Graydon.

"So you think that was funny?" Michael had taken her place leaning against the doorjamb. His arms were crossed over his chest, which was too bad. He had a great chest.

"Yes. I think so. Although I do apologize for putting you in that dire circumstance."

He nodded. Kept staring at her.

"Well? Comments? Suggestions?"

His wonderful lips curled up into a great smile. "A couple of comments. No suggestions."

"Go ahead."

"I completely understand not believing a word I said."

"Thanks."

"I thought about laying all my theories on the table, but now that seems irrelevant. This is clearly an act of faith."

"That's true."

"I just want to state what I know about you. These aren't opinions, by the way. They're facts."

"Uh-oh."

His expression grew serious. "Don't jump to conclusions." He came to the bed and sat down next to her. When she looked into his eyes, he looked straight back. "I know you've got strengths that are invisible to you. I know that you haven't been helped to see them by your father or your shrink. I know that Sara's been a damn good friend and that you should listen to her more closely.

"I know that it feels insurmountable, this panic

disorder of yours, but I'm damned impressed by how you've handled yourself since we've been here. By all rights, you should be comatose by now. A drooling mess. But you're not, are you? You've made a very tough decision, and that's not easy for the sanest people out there. You chose life, Tate, and given all the evidence, you shouldn't have."

She turned away from him as the tears threatened to fall. She'd never have guessed he'd use this opportunity to talk about her. To give her the single greatest pep talk of her life. She'd imagined him shoring up his alibi, redirecting her suspicions.

Maybe believing in him wasn't the stupidest decision she'd ever made.

"There's food here, and I know you haven't had any all day."

She sniffed, blinked, then turned to look at the plates. Each one had a sandwich, a few baby carrots and a bag of chips. Suddenly it looked better than a meal at Nobu.

She grabbed one of the plates and tore off the cellophane. Michael laughed and did the same with his plate. For the next ten minutes they did nothing but scarf. He got up once and went to the vanity, where there were two sodas. Even though neither was diet, she took hers eagerly.

The idyll didn't last long.

Michael wiped his mouth with the small paper napkin and put his empty can on the clean plate. "That sucked and was great all at the same time."

She took both plates back to the vanity. "That's also true." As she turned back to him, she was caught completely by surprise by an enormous belch. She felt her cheeks heat as she put her hand to her mouth.

Michael grinned as if he'd just seen Santa.

"I'm glad my humiliation pleases you so much."

"Hey, tit for tat."

"I suppose so," she said. "It's weird not being able to retreat."

"Is that what you want to do?"

"Not right now, but I did about twenty seconds ago."

"You clearly never had a brother."

She shook her head. "I had Lisa. Then Sara. That's it."

"That sounds pretty good to me."

Tate had a rush of anticipation for what the night would hold as she walked back to the bed. She sat next to him and touched his thigh. "There's no Sara in your life?"

"Nope. I had some good friends in the Army. But that's over."

"Are you sure your friends are over? Or are you just embarrassed?"

"I'm sure. *They're* embarrassed, and that doesn't tend to work with us military types. It's easiest for everyone if I stay under the radar."

"I hope you make more friends after this is over. Without Sara…"

"Hey," he said. "Sara."

"You can't have her. She's mine."

"Oh."

"Not that way. Jeez, are all men so predictable?"

"Yes."

She smiled at him and he smiled back. She wasn't

going to waste any more time doubting her decision. After all, she'd chosen life.

"ED? JAZZ?" MICHAEL banged on the door a couple more times, then stepped back as he heard the lock click.

"What are you banging for?"

"I need to speak to Ed."

"He's busy."

"I'm sure he is. But I need to speak to him."

Jazz looked behind him, then sighed. "Wait." He shut and locked the door.

Michael smiled at Tate as he waited, trying to make her see that this meeting was in her best interest, but she didn't look persuaded. All he could do was tell her the truth.

The lock clicked once more and the door opened just a bit.

"Turn around and give me your wrists."

Michael just wanted to talk to Ed, so he made no noises. It was logical that they'd given up on handcuffs with him, but damn, they could have used softer rope.

Jazz tied him up tighter than a turkey, then held his gun on him as he turned. "Don't do anything funny."

"I'm serious as a heart attack," Michael said.

Ed Martini was sitting in his favorite chair. Charlie looked even worse than he had before, and it made Michael wonder if it was strictly withdrawal that had him so torn up.

"What do you want?" Martini asked.

"She needs clothes."

Ed laughed. "I need more hair."

"If you're taking her to the bank, she needs to look

like she's there legitimately. She can't do that in the clothes she has."

Ed looked at Jazz, his smile fading, then back at Michael. "What kind of clothes?"

"She'll make a list. With sizes and designers."

"You knock again, hand the list to Jazz."

"When?"

"Tonight. And don't get any ideas about doing something while we're docked. I've already decided that whenever this boat stops, you're going to be inconvenienced. Or, if you don't stay where I put you, dead."

"Got it."

"Do the list."

Michael turned, then stopped. "I'm going to ask for a couple of things for myself."

"Yeah?"

"Yeah. I don't want to make her regret her feelings about me. So I need to look nice. Smell nice."

"Fine."

"We'd both appreciate some more to eat. And to drink."

Ed sighed. "Want a fucking massage while we're at it?"

Michael turned. "You need her. You need me. We're not asking for anything outrageous."

"Get the hell out of here," Ed said, his cheeks red, his eyebrows lowered.

Jazz shoved him in the back with the barrel of his gun, then made him stand at the doorway to the cabin while he undid the ropes. A second shove, and the door clicked shut.

Michael rubbed his wrists as he moved toward Tate,

who was standing at the porthole, staring out at the dark night.

"Can you see anything?"

"No, not really. But it beats staring at the wallpaper," she said, "or the vanity or the dresser or the bathroom."

He touched the small of her back. "I need you to make a list of clothes and whatever. Don't skimp and be very specific. If you want a certain brand, ask for it. Clothes you'd wear on holiday, knowing you'd be going to your bank."

She leaned back into his hand. "Makeup and hair, too?"

"I'm pretty sure we're going to dock in Miami or the Keys, so the shopping won't be an issue. Say what you need. He doesn't care if he spends twenty grand of the ransom if it means he gets the big prize."

She didn't say anything, but when she turned, she kissed him. Not too long, not too deep. A hint of things to come.

FORTY MINUTES AFTER Jazz came for her very complete and somewhat embarrassing list, there was another knock. Michael sent her to the far side of the room before he opened the door. It was Jazz again, with a tray. Michael took it; Jazz locked up behind him.

Michael put the tray on the bed, and when she registered what Jazz had brought, she looked at Michael with new respect. "Lobster tails and wine?"

"It helps to be the squeaky wheel," he said.

"A tip to file for future use."

"Want to talk or eat?"

She smiled as they crawled up on the bed together. It was odd to eat here, to sit next to Michael, to be a prisoner with such good wine. Everything felt off, but not in the way she'd expected.

Her fear remained, pulsing in her bloodstream, but somehow she still could function. Was this what Dr. Bay had wanted for her? Not the real kidnapping but this functional panic, this total awareness that she could die any moment, which made every nondeath moment something extraordinary?

"Hey," he said.

She realized she'd been looking his way—staring, really—but not seeing him. Quickly she averted her gaze. "Sorry."

"No need. I was just wondering what was going on in there."

"Random thoughts. I really like this wine."

"Those weren't food-review thoughts," he said, then shook his head. "It's fine if you don't want to tell me. None of my business."

"It's okay. I was thinking about my ability to talk. To eat, to smile, to sleep. I'd never have guessed."

"We're pretty adaptable creatures."

"Maybe it wasn't such a horrible idea to be kidnapped. Well, not by these louts but by someone safe."

His expression darkened. "No, it wasn't a good idea. None of this was. There was no way you should have been exposed to the possibility of danger."

"No? The only way to avoid it was to trade my life for safety. You think it was worth it?"

He looked at the dresser. "There had to be another way."

"Michael…" She put her glass down on the tray. "I wanted to ask you out—well, in—for five and a half months. I'm not talking about wanting to seduce you, I'm talking about dinner. A drink. I was frozen. My fear had leached into every single area of my life. From work to friends to dating. I was as much a prisoner in my apartment and that damn limo as I am here."

His gaze had come back to her face, to her eyes. She was glad there were no sunglasses. Just his vivid, open stare. Finally, after a long while, he blinked. Frowned. "You didn't want to seduce me?"

She laughed as she felt her face heat with a blush. He didn't shift his gaze, not even a bit, and every instinct told her to look away. But she was through being scared. At least of Michael.

13

HER FACE CAME ALIVE with her blush. It made her look young, innocent. She was, in fact, both of those things, but in her day-to-day life where she was the administrator of millions of dollars, where she was William Baxter's only daughter—where she was terrified from morning till night—she looked and acted much older, and her innocence hid behind a mask of tension.

She kept wanting to look away, but every time her gaze skittered, she forced herself to stay with him. The moments ticked on, marked by the sounds of their breaths, the motion of the boat. He waited as patiently as possible for Tate to relax, and finally she did.

It was eventually okay to do what he'd wanted to for a long time. He leaned in, slowly so she'd have time to adjust or, if she chose, to stop him. Her eyes stayed open until her breath, fruity with wine, brushed his mouth.

Only then did he close his own eyes as he touched his lips to hers. Again he had to wait, to let her adjust, which wasn't easy. His body urged him to take her, to toss the trays on the floor and do every kind of wicked thing to her. But his body wasn't in control. Not this time.

Tate needed a patient, gentle hand. Not something

he was accustomed to offering, but he'd do his best. He didn't want to spook her. That would be a crying shame for both of them.

It felt odd, this closed-mouth kiss, as if he was standing just outside the candy store. When he couldn't stand it another second, he parted his lips just a bit, then slipped his tongue out for a taste of her.

Mistake.

The rest of him really, really wanted to play. First thing, though—the trays.

As if diving into an icy stream, he pulled away quickly before he could change his mind. Her soft, disappointed moan made his dick, which was already paying attention, strain for more.

He put his tray to the side of the bed, then he practically sprinted out himself. Both trays ended up on the dresser, but then he was faced with another dilemma. Undress? Stay clothed? Undress her?

She was watching him, her blush back, and damn if she didn't lick her lips. Maybe if he took off his shirt. Her gaze shifted up, to the lights above them.

He shook his head at his own stupidity. Of course she'd want the lights out. It was Tate. The moment the room darkened he heard her sigh. A good sign. The sound of clothes shifting, a better one.

IT MADE ED NAUSEOUS to even look at Charlie. He gave Jazz a questioning glance, but Jazz, he was on the phone, making arrangements. Jazz was itching for a promotion, and Ed was running out of excuses to let him go. Jazz and him, they'd been together a long time. The boy was nuts, but he could control himself for Ed.

Jazz had recommended Ricky from his Brooklyn off-track parlor to take his place, but Ricky smelled like pickles all the damn time.

His gaze went back to Charlie. What a fucking loser. He had a shower that worked in his cabin, there were clothes that were clean in that room. So why was he still stinking up the saloon? His hair was stringy and he had gunk on the side of his mouth. It was enough to make a man lose his lunch.

If it wasn't for his usefulness in controlling the brother, he'd toss the bastard over right now.

"We'll be docked by three," Jazz said, folding his little phone and putting it in his pocket. "I've lined up a shopper to put together the stuff for the woman. Pauly's got the food being delivered at five. We'll be ready to take off by ten o'clock, latest."

"Good job. Did you tell Pauly I wanted those limes?"

"Absolutely, boss. He knows how much you like that key lime pie."

"Good. That's the pleasure of traveling without a woman—nobody to nag me about my damn cholesterol. She don't know what my cholesterol is. She just wants to control me, you know?"

"Yeah, I know. That's why I don't hook up for longer than a weekend. So is this Cayman Islands like Aruba?"

"I was only there once. But, yeah, it's like Aruba. Only with more banks. And more businesses. Lot of businesses."

Jazz raised his eyebrows. "They do off-track?"

"I don't know, Jazz. It's something to look into once we get the dough."

Jazz, always on his feet, so much energy, so much

going on in that bizzaro brain. The opposite of Charlie, who couldn't string two sentences together, who thought of nothing but himself, nothing but what he wanted that second. Like a five-year-old, that one. It made Ed wonder which of the brothers was adopted. Had to be one of them.

"Charlie," Jazz said, poking the listing slob on his shoulder. "Go to the cabin, would ya? You're making me lose my appetite."

"Fuck you, Jazz."

Jazz had his weapon out in two seconds. "What's that?"

"Nothing, nothing." He lurched toward the edge of the banquette and stumbled to his feet. "I thought you were someone else."

"Well, get the hell out of here before I throw you overboard."

Ed watched Charlie until he was out of the saloon.

"We have to keep him, boss?" Jazz asked. "I can make the brother behave. I can make the bitch behave. Trust me."

Ed shook his head. "No, I don't think you can. Those two, they've got some strength, okay? We need Charlie. Just until I'm off the boat with the woman. You can stay behind and watch the brothers kill each other."

"That," Jazz said, smiling, "I'd pay a nickel for."

HOW LONG HAD THE dark scared her? It felt as if it had been her whole life. The dark held secrets and bad things, terror and helplessness. Only, she didn't feel scared. Well, not that kind of scared. She was with

Michael and they were going to make love. Finally, at the edge of her life when she wasn't sure about the next sunrise or the next five minutes, she was sure about him.

Her hands found the bottom of her shirt and she pulled it over her head.

The room wasn't pitch-black. In fact, she could see him standing at the foot of the bed. Not his expression, not the small details, but enough. So she was pretty sure he could see her, too. He knew she was undressing and why.

As she moved to undo the clasp of her bra, Michael seemed to snap out of whatever had held him so still, directly into fourth gear. Before she'd gotten the bra off, he was down to his shorts. She couldn't make out the pattern in the dark, which was a blessing.

She tossed her bra to the floor, her blush coming back in spades. But this was her brave life, and she wasn't going to let her shyness stop her. In fact…

She climbed off the bed to stand in front of Michael. It was tempting to tell him to turn on the light—but, no, she wasn't that brave. Not yet. But she did continue to take off her clothes. Every last stitch.

And there they were.

He had the physique of a Greek athlete, which wasn't a shock, considering how serious he was about his workouts. She felt very soft and flabby in comparison. She should have worked harder at her Pilates, that's what.

"You're so beautiful," he whispered.

"Me?"

He laughed softly as he stepped closer. "Yes, you. You're incredibly beautiful. I like seeing you with your guard down. Without those suits you like so much."

"I like them because they blend in. They make me disappear."

"I know." He stepped closer, so close she could feel his body heat. "I like you like this. Naked. Vulnerable."

She did feel vulnerable. Too much so. She started to cover her breasts, but then he touched her. One hand on her waist, cool, broad, and the side of his other hand lifting her chin.

"And so very brave," he said.

She looked into his eyes, cursing the dark now. "I'm working on it."

"You're doing great," he said. Just before he kissed her.

She melted against him. His lips, his tongue, the pressure of his hand on the back of her head…it was all perfect. He made her wet and eager and braver still.

She put her hand on his stomach then, kissed him back as she went lower and lower until she felt the small patch of hair down there. A second later he bumped her wrist. She smiled around his tongue as it happened again. Someone wanted attention. Badly.

He moaned, and that's all the push she needed. She touched his cock. Warm, hard, thick and so very, very anxious. He pulsed in her hand. Strained as she stroked him.

He threw his head back for a second with a long groan, then pulled her to the bed. Before she knew what had happened, she was lying down, her head on the pillow, with Michael at her side, pulling her into his arms, into his kiss.

His leg went between hers, his thigh up to the

junction, where he pressed against her. She had no choice but to move, to ride him as he touched her breast, sucked her tongue. They went on like that for long, languorous moments. A gasp or a moan the only break in the accompaniment of their breathing. It was heaven, but it was also not quite enough.

She squeezed his cock, then let go, afraid she'd gone too far.

Michael sat up so quickly she gasped, and he gripped her shoulders tightly. When his mouth was a scant inch from her own, he said, "I can't stand it. I'm just not that strong."

His kiss was searing, melting her brain and stealing her breath. His body felt hard and hot.

Another man touching her with his fierceness would have made her cry out, struggle to break free, but she wanted Michael's possessiveness. A part of her wanted to see bruises, proof, in whatever tomorrow she was granted.

He moaned and she could taste his desire painted on her tongue. The sound of his rough breathing, all through his flaring nostrils, was like sex itself. Even the pulse of his chest against hers made her think of nothing so sweet as making love but of something far more primal. That's what she wanted from him.

William Baxter's troubled daughter. The one who was always pale and frail and didn't know what to do with her hands.

She knew now.

Trembling, still matching him breath for breath, she touched his skin, rubbed him, kneaded his flesh. There was so little give it disappointed her for a moment, but then she remembered it was Michael, not some soft man. He had muscles, big ones—not that you could see from across the room, but when you got close, when he moved—

He pushed her down to the bed, to the blue-and-white checked bedspread. His knee went between hers once more, but this time it was completely different. This time he didn't ask, he took.

Before her cry had subsided, he pulled her hands up above her head. With his broad left hand he captured both her wrists.

She stared at him as he loomed over her, a willing captive. "What are you doing to me?"

"I don't want you to forget this. If we die tomorrow, you'll remember this in your next life. In all your lifetimes."

He held her gaze as his mouth opened into a silent roar and he plunged inside her.

He filled her completely, but that wasn't why she wept. The tears were from somewhere very deep, something always longed for, and finally, finally…

He kissed her again, and it was brutal until it wasn't. Until he caressed her lips with his own, until there was no space between his breath and hers.

He was as deeply inside her as he could be. Michael was part of her. She would have shared her blood with him, her bones, but she didn't need to because he was right there. *Right there.*

MICHAEL, BURIED IN wet heat, didn't really understand what was happening to him. He'd wanted to make this special for her. He'd wanted to be careful, gentle.

Shit. He hoped he wasn't screwing it up, because there was no way he was gonna stop now.

He'd never been a patient man, not when it came to sex. Most of the time, he was on his way from one danger to another, so he'd mastered the art of the sentimental goodbye. Better to leave them wanting more, right?

But this… Tate was another thing altogether. He'd been with more beautiful women. Certainly tougher women. She was vulnerable in a way that made him vulnerable, too.

He kissed her, wanting the thoughts to stop. She was so responsive. Just listening to her could have made him come. He had to hold back, to not hurt her, but his resolve lasted seconds. And when he did hurt her, she pushed him for more.

They would be gone by tomorrow, heading out across the ocean to the Caymans. His glorious plan hadn't turned out so well. Nothing had. Except this.

He'd never felt more of a failure—and he'd never experienced a triumph like being inside her.

He lifted his head, took in great, deep breaths, pumped into her until his arms shook. And then he reached between them, sliding his right hand down her belly until his fingers found her clit.

He watched her as he shifted his position, thrusting and rubbing her at the same time.

God, it was amazing. There was just enough light. Her eyes weren't closed, but they weren't focused, not on him anyway. Her mouth had opened as she'd arched her neck. It was stunning. He licked the sweat off her temple because he couldn't lick where he wanted.

Her head thrashed, banging against the wall as he kept up an unrelenting pace, but he knew it was going to end soon. He could feel the tightness in his balls, his muscles tensing beyond endurance.

He had to choose: finger or cock. Cock won.

He pulled his hand out, captured her wrists again, and when he felt her heels on his hips, he goddamn exploded. The top of his head came off, the backs of his eyelids burst with colors, and she just kept squeezing him, her internal muscles sucking the life force out of him.

It seemed to go on forever. When he was finally dry, when there was nothing, not even breath left in him, he opened his eyes.

She was staring up at him with those wide blue eyes. With her auburn hair plastered against her skin, her cheeks blotchy and red. He couldn't imagine anything more beautiful. Not even close.

Too soon, his arms gave out and he had to crash beside her. She didn't speak; neither did he, but the sound in the room was loud enough to scare the fishes. Both of them gasping for air, cursing the world that made them need it.

"Holy cow," she whispered finally.

He grinned. "Yeah, that's just what I was gonna say."

She slugged him in the hip. It was a lackadaisical sock with only half a fist. But good for her. He doubted he could have done better.

"Sleep now," he said.

"Uh-huh."

"Tomorrow we'll figure out how to live through this."

"Okay," she said, and even in her breathlessness, her doubt came through.

He rallied himself to his side, so his hand rested on her belly and his gaze on her eyes. "You think I want this to be over?" he said. "You think I'm not going to fight for you?"

She blinked. Then she smiled. "Not anymore."

14

IT HAD BEEN DAYS—five days—since the kidnappers had disappeared with William Baxter's money and Tate. Sara, who'd never had a sister but had always had Tate, was sitting in her friend's bedroom, staring at the trompe l'oeil window on the wall. Through the painted window she could see a sandy beach, a brilliant ocean and a sky dotted with cotton clouds. It was so real that Sara thought if she moved closer, she would feel the breeze on her face.

But it, like the chances that Tate was still alive, was an illusion. There was a lot of trompe l'oeil throughout the penthouse, designed specifically to make the occupant feel as though she were living in an expansive world. The artist had done a superb job, but now Sara wondered if these fake paintings had been one more wall that had trapped Tate in her mental prison.

It wasn't fair. None of it was. That she should have been kidnapped at all, that she'd lived so much of her life in terror, that her cousin had been murdered in such a horrible way. Sara ached for Tate, but she also ached for William, who'd done so much to foster Tate's fear.

He'd aged ten years in these last few days. He couldn't sleep, wouldn't take the tranquilizers his doctor had prescribed and barely ate. Sara had taken a leave of absence from her job to be with him. To wait. But for how long?

Was Michael dead, too? Or was he, as William thought, one of the guilty?

Two days ago, she'd taken the bull by the horns. Despite her belief in Michael's team, she'd called the authorities. The FBI had swooped in, but they hadn't found much. She'd tried to believe them when they said they'd find Tate.

Sara stood up, knowing she had to go into the other room, face William as he waited another day by the phone. She had to keep things upbeat, if not for his sake then for her own.

She missed her best friend.

"ARE YOU SURE THIS is a good idea?" Charlie asked, trying not to sound too desperate. Jazz liked it when he could hurt people, and even though no one was gonna be beat up or anything, it was gonna be ugly.

"Just take the damn tray, would you? Jesus, you're such a whiny bitch."

"I haven't seen Mikey since—"

"I don't give a rat's ass. I'm busy."

Charlie sighed, but only after his back was to Jazz. He was so sick of this boat he wanted to scream. They'd already gotten the ransom money, so why in hell hadn't they just let him go? Why had Jazz given him that fix so he'd be out of it when they set out to sea?

He picked up the tray and headed to Mike's cabin. The cups rattled, but he couldn't help it. Mikey was gonna kill him, and Charlie already felt like crap. He knew there was some crack on board, but would they let him have any? Hell, no. They saw he wasn't doing so good, so it was just pure mean that made them act so shitty. And after he'd made them rich! The bastards.

"Well?"

Charlie jumped at Jazz's voice so close. He hadn't heard the dude walking, let alone opening the cabin door. "Shit."

"Do not piss me off, Charlie."

With as much indignation as he could muster, Charlie walked past Jazz into Mikey's cabin.

His brother stood up so fast he knocked an empty water glass off the bedside ledge. "What the hell?"

"Relax. I'm just bringing you something to eat."

"Get out of here, Charlie."

"I will. Just let me put this down." He went to the vanity, and as he was depositing the tray, the door to the cabin shut. It was Jazz screwing with him, making it easy for Mikey to wail on him. He turned, fast, but Mike was already in his face.

"How many people are on board?" Mike asked, his voice low, threatening.

"How should I know?"

Mikey's elbow bent and his arm went back. There was no mistaking the intent of his fist. "Count them."

"All right, all right. Me, Jazz, Martini, the cook, the pilot guy and some kid that cleans up."

"What are they planning?"

"You think I know? I shouldn't even be here. They was supposed to let me out when we brought the money. They tricked me!"

"Gee, I feel real bad for you there, Charlie."

"Look, I told ya—"

"I know exactly what you told me. And what you did. And what you're gonna do now."

Charlie shook his head, trying to inch toward the door. "I gotta go. They catch me talking to you, it's trouble all around."

"Don't you fucking move," Mikey said, pressing his body closer. "You tell me right this minute how many weapons are on board."

"I don't know."

"Charlie, I swear to God—"

"Mikey, I don't know. On Ma's grave, I don't know. They keep me in the dark."

"Then find out."

Charlie was sweatin' now. He could feel it dripping on his forehead, down his back. "I can't, Mikey. Don't ask me, 'cause I can't. You know I can't lie worth shit."

"You managed to lie to me."

"No, no I didn't."

"Find out, Charlie. Every single gun, rifle, harpoon, knife—you hear me? You find out and you get that information to me. If you try to pull something, I swear on Pa's grave, I will hunt you down and I will hurt you worse than you could ever believe."

"Yeah? Well, Martini will kill me. He's already threatened to throw me overboard."

His brother's arm went back, and Charlie flinched, but the punch never came. When he opened his eyes, he saw the woman behind Mikey, touching his shoulder. Shit, he hadn't even seen her when he walked in.

She looked different. Better. Pretty. No wonder Mikey liked his job so much. Must be sweet to get to work with a rich broad who looked like that.

"Get out, Charlie. Get out, and if you know what's good for you, you'll get me what I want to know."

"I'll try. That's all I can do."

Mikey spun around and Charlie wasted no time getting the hell out of there. Back in the saloon, Jazz was smiling like he'd been to the circus.

"Have a nice visit?"

Charlie almost told him what for, but he didn't. "No."

"What does he want you to do?"

He shouldn't say. Mikey was his brother, after all. His own blood. On the other hand, Martini had never liked him much. And Jazz? He was a goddamn psycho. "He wanted to know how many people were on board. How many guns."

"What did you tell him?"

"I didn't tell him nothing. I swear. I said I don't know, 'cause I don't."

Jazz gave him the once-over. "Watch your step, Charlie. It's a big ocean out there."

Charlie went out on the deck, staring at that ocean and planning how when Jazz wasn't looking, *he'd* be the one to go swimming. Next time he wouldn't tell Jazz a damn thing. He'd show them. Stupid rat bastards. Soon as he got home, he was gonna go to Len Taub's off-track parlor. Screw Ed. Screw Jazz.

TATE WASN'T SURE what to do. It wasn't easy watching Michael pace, so angry the vein on his forehead throbbed. But he also seemed to be working something out, at least from the bits and snatches of his mumbles that she caught.

Today was the first time she'd looked at Charlie. Jazz had brought them everything since that day she'd learned that Charlie and Michael were brothers. It had been upsetting, seeing them together, at least at first, but then, watching their interaction after spending so much time with Michael…she knew that she'd been right to believe him.

Michael might be good at his intelligence work, but he wasn't Olivier. He couldn't have made up his rage at Charlie. God, they were so different. Like night and day.

She decided she wasn't going to say a word. Let Michael pace, let him swear and plot and plan. While he was occupied, she took one of the sandwiches from the tray Charlie had brought, then she went to the bed and got the notebook she'd asked for two days ago.

It wasn't anything special, just an unlined notepad, but it was better than writing on the walls. Jazz had been reluctant to give it to her, too. Why, she had no idea. Who was going to see it? A passing sailfish?

Anyway, she curled her legs underneath her, got the pillow behind her back and turned to a new blank page.

"Dear Sara," she wrote, remembering where she'd left off. "Jazz brought a bunch of shopping bags into the room, then left us to sort through them. I was thrilled to find underwear—although, jeez, the slime-ball had gotten the most revealing things he could find. I swear, it looked more like he'd shopped at Frederick's of Hollywood than Victoria's Secret. Michael didn't seem to mind, but he played it cool.

"There's simply no way to forget why we're here. It's not a pleasure cruise, and there's no beach party waiting for us in Grand Cayman.

"I'm just grateful Michael is with me. He thinks he's failed, that he's responsible for what's happened. I can't agree. It wasn't his fault he had Charlie for a brother. But I can't seem to make Michael stop worrying about it and save his strength for when we dock.

"Personally, Sara, I think the real truth is that this whole thing was my fault. And before you say it, yes, I think Dr. Bay was more than idiotic. What I mean… You know the old saying 'You reap what you sow'? Well, I've been 'sowing' being kidnapped since Lisa. I know it makes sense that I was obsessed, but I didn't do near enough to get myself out of that insidious loop.

"I was given tremendous gifts and I squandered them to live in the land of what-if. No more. I am here, today. I am with Michael and he is with me. Together, we're strong. Even me.

"I—"

He sat in front of her, making her pen jolt like a lightning bolt up the page. "I should have killed him when I had the chance."

She hid her gasp as he said the words, his face showing her that it wasn't an idle threat. "Don't."

"Don't what? He got you kidnapped, Tate. He stole from me and he's probably going to get me killed. If I don't do something about it, we'll both die, and it'll be because of Charlie."

"It doesn't matter."

"What?"

"It doesn't matter that he did all this. You can't kill him. He's your brother."

"Not anymore."

"He'll always be your brother."

Michael stood up again. "No. I've done everything I could to help him. I've bailed him out of jail, I've given him money for his bookies, I've spent thousands putting him in rehab. He just wants more and more, and I have no more to give."

"Still—"

"Tate, if it was just me, I could see cutting him a little slack, although it wouldn't be for him but for my father. But to put you here? No. It's over. It stops. Now."

"I understand. I really do. But you'll have to live with whatever choice you make."

He smiled at her with a tenderness that made her melt. "I will do whatever it takes to keep you safe. Period. Now are you going to keep writing in that journal or are you going to take my mind off the rest of the universe?"

"Oh, you want to play charades?"

"Ha. You're funny." He slipped the notebook from her fingers and tossed it to the floor. The pen was dispatched next.

Then it got really interesting.

SHE SLEPT AS HE TORE a couple of pages from her notebook and found the pen where he'd tossed it hours before. The longer they remained on the boat, the more he worried that he'd never get her home.

The whole reason he'd come up with the idea of the Cayman bank was to give himself time. But had that backfired? Were there so many armed men on the boat that he couldn't take them?

The fact that he even thought that bothered him more than he could admit. Last year, would he have hesitated? Would he have given this motley crew a second thought?

He could take Martini and Jazz. As long as he knew where they were and no one jumped him from behind, there was no contest. But there were other people on board, and he had no idea where they would be at any given time.

He hadn't been a complete slouch. At night, when Tate was asleep, he'd done something in the way of recon. He'd only been out of their cabin twice, but he'd gotten a lot of information on both silent trips.

The first, he'd gotten a damn good idea about the saloon and the outer perimeter of the boat. He drew what he remembered now in a diagram that would help him put together the pieces he hadn't seen.

Charlie and Jazz had been asleep that night, the night before last. Charlie, snoring. Neither had stirred as he'd walked past them, and it had been harder than hell not to take the gun from Jazz's splayed hand and shoot him beyond recognition.

He'd held himself back. He might have been outside the cabin, but the boat was still mostly unknown. With Tate so vulnerable, he had to make sure. If he'd been killed, her chances for survival were slim. So he'd inched around quiet as a mouse as he'd used the full moon to check for possibilities.

Last night hadn't gone quite as well.

He'd made it halfway to the cockpit when Ed had come up from below. For what felt like an hour Michael had stowed himself in a ridiculously narrow gulley behind a couch. He'd learned nothing except that Ed Martini liked to cuss at televised sports.

When he finally got a chance to get back to the room, his leg had cramped and he'd missed being caught by a quarter of a second.

Tate had slept through it all, which was what he'd wanted.

He couldn't be sure when they'd reach Grand Cayman, but both of them had to be ready, starting tomorrow. He had to have plans made, with contingencies. The one he hated the most was where they would take Tate away, off the boat, alone.

She thought she was ready. That she could handle it. He knew better.

He finished the rudimentary diagram of the boat, but he knew if there was a cache of weapons on board, they would be below and they'd be under lock and key. But if he had a gun, any kind of gun, their chances of surviving this would be a lot better.

He turned to the bed. She looked beautiful with her hair in a halo on the pillow. Odd, a woman of such privilege and she never complained about the living conditions. He knew, far too well, all the things that made her life so different from regular folks'. She had a cadre of beauticians, aestheticians, nail people, wax people, makeup people who came to the penthouse on a steady schedule. He didn't know what half of them did except make her look great.

Aside from her looks, she had maids, cooks, him. She never had to get her hands dirty. Someone was always there to clean up her messes.

She looked better here, though. He'd never even known her hair was wavy. Or that she really liked peanut-butter-and-jelly sandwiches.

As he watched her sleep, he let himself think about after. Once they were back in New York, on her turf. Would she be embarrassed by the fact that she'd slept with her bodyguard? Would she pretend nothing had ever happened? Would he?

It wasn't as if they would ever be anything. Not a couple, that's for sure. William would have heart failure if such a thing were even suggested. Too bad. He'd liked her from the start, and being with her in this cramped cabin for all this time had just proved he'd been right in his earliest assessments.

Tate was an unusual woman, and not just because of her social standing. One thing he'd seen in his travels was that the children of the truly rich didn't understand the rest of the world. They made noises about helping out the disenfranchised or the handi-capped, whatever, but it was all posing. They lived in rarefied air, and those who weren't like them were as foreign as Martians.

Tate was the exception to the rule. She'd never made him feel as if he were the help. Not intention-ally, anyway. Hell, she hadn't even wanted to admit how badly he'd bungled things with her, even though his mistakes might cost her her life.

So what was a man supposed to do with a woman like that? Save her, that's what. Make damn sure she had the opportunity to find out what life would be like without her fear of being kidnapped overshadowing everything.

He had to find those weapons. Now.

15

THE FBI AGENT'S NAME was Webber, Nick Webber, and he called Sara at four in the afternoon on the ninth day. "We might have something."

"Go on."

"We think it might be her purse. There's no ID, but there's a GPS tracker sewn into the lining. The security people said that's where Caulfield hid his trackers."

"I'll know if it's hers," Sara said. "But let's meet somewhere. I don't want Mr. Baxter to know."

"Fine."

"Where did you find it?"

"In Jersey, by the GW Bridge."

"That could mean anything. They could have her anywhere."

"It'll help to know if this is her bag."

"Give me twenty minutes and meet me at Sarabeth's. You know where that is?"

"Yes."

"Twenty minutes." Sara hung up the phone, her heart so heavy she could barely breathe. Was this all they were to have of Tate? A purse washed up from the East River? Was Tate in that murky water right now with the punctured tires and the polluted fish?

William was withering away before her eyes. He wouldn't eat, and the only sleep he got was drug induced. She'd taken her fair share of tranquilizers, too.

How long was she supposed to hang on? She wanted to believe so badly. So when was the cutoff? Ten days? Twenty? Or were they always supposed to feel that jolt when the phone rang? A year, two years, what did it matter? A purse was not proof. It was simply a purse.

THE DOOR HAD BEEN unlocked for a good thirty seconds, but Michael didn't turn the knob. He pressed his ear against the door, trying to decide whether the noise he heard was just the television—which was on all the time, as far as he could tell—or actual conversation.

At one-twenty in the morning, he couldn't imagine who'd be chatting. Those first few days they'd made a point to keep themselves awake, guns at the ready, especially after his first attempt at escape. But the last couple of nights Jazz and Charlie had both been sound asleep and not even the louder-than-loud commercials from the satellite system had made them budge.

He couldn't tell whether tonight would be an exception, so he opened the door. Not wide—Jesus, no—but just enough so he could let his eye adjust to the light as he peered through the gap.

He didn't see Jazz, but there was Charlie, leaning back in the big man's favorite leather chair, mouth agape, snoring like a freight train. Even now, after everything, Michael's first instinct was to get Charlie out of that chair. If Ed saw him there…

It was just so goddamn typical. Charlie would never

change. If Michael could figure out a way to get him out of this mess, it wouldn't matter because there would be the next mess and the one after that. It made him sad—but not sad enough to forgive. That wasn't going to happen.

Another few seconds of absolute stillness, then he opened the door another inch. Still no Jazz. Surely they wouldn't leave Charlie on guard duty by himself? No one was that stupid.

Someone else had to be there. Or in the head or maybe getting something to eat in the galley. Whatever, it meant that tonight Michael wasn't going to make it below. He wasn't going to get a weapon, at least not yet.

He closed the door, locking it behind him, then debated the wisdom of getting into bed. Tate was hard to resist, but he wanted to check back in an hour to see if he could make it out. An hour of either sleep or something better wouldn't be prudent. He'd get too sleepy. Too satisfied.

"Are you just going to stand there all night?"

Tate's whisper scared the crap out of him, making him glad for the darkness. "What are you doing up?"

"Watching you be superspy. Like last night. And the night before."

He grinned as he headed to the bunk. "It's not nice to fool superspies."

"Hey, you're not the only one who can do that stealthy stuff. What's the matter? Someone's up?"

"I only saw Charlie. But they'd never leave him on his own. I'll check again in a while."

"Hmm," she said, scooting over as he sat on the edge of the bed. "How long is a while?"

He touched her cheek with the back of his hand. "It would be wonderful to climb in with you, but I don't think it's a good idea. We're getting too close to Grand Cayman, and either I get a decent layout of this boat or—"

"Or what?"

"Nothing. I'll get it. But I need to stay alert."

"I can do that, too."

"You should get some sleep."

"Because I lead such an active life? The only thing we do here that burns up calories is sex, and if you don't want to do that—"

"Who said I don't want to?"

She sighed. "I know. So what happens once we get there?"

"Ed's going to take you off the boat. You'll have to go with him to the bank."

"What about you?"

"I'll be taking care of business here. You don't have to worry about that."

She sat up, then leaned across him to turn on the light. She had on a T-shirt, which she wore most nights, and he wondered whether if they hadn't been afraid of Jazz barging in, she would have slept naked.

The thought of her long body next to his… Hell, they'd never get any rest.

Squinting against the light, she still managed to give him her "you're-in-trouble-now-mister" look. "I'll ask again. What about you?"

"There are things I can do once we're docked, once they can't use you as a shield."

"Like killing people."

"If necessary."

"Including Charlie."

"If necessary."

"They have weapons."

"I do, too."

"Where?"

He shrugged, wanting to reassure her as well as instill her with confidence. He wasn't sure he could do both. "I've been in a lot of situations where it looked as if I didn't stand a chance."

"But—"

He put his arm around her shoulder and situated them both more comfortably on the bed. "Let's talk about you for a while, okay? There are some things I want you to practice here, while we're alone, before you hit the bank."

"Like breathing? Not passing out?"

He shook his head. "You're going to be fine. You've been amazing, and there's no reason that shouldn't continue."

"Except that I won't be with you."

"Doesn't matter."

She looked into his eyes. "Are you kidding? Of course it matters. You're the only reason I'm not completely comatose. Or dead."

"You may have gotten some confidence with me nearby, but you've done so much on your own. You don't even break a sweat when they bring in the food."

"I do so."

"It doesn't show."

She sighed. "Not that much has changed, Michael. We're living in a bubble here where it's easy to pretend. But once I have to leave this room… If you're counting on me, you'd better rethink things."

"Don't worry about it. The plan is only viable if you think it'll work. There are too many unknowns to get too specific."

"Well, let's hear what it is. If I don't pass out now, then maybe I won't pass out in the bank."

AT TWO-FORTY, MICHAEL came back to the room. There was enough light from the porthole for her to see the foray hadn't been terrific.

"What happened?"

He came to the edge of the bed, stripping as he walked. His T-shirt hit the floor along with the jeans they'd bought him in Florida, leaving him in his skivvies. "Charlie lied again."

"Oh, no."

"Oh, yes. I thought I was home-free, everyone accounted for, and was just about to pick the lock where I'm sure the weapons are stored when that cabin boy he talked about—the one who was supposed to clean up—came walking out of the head. He's monster-size. Thank God he flushed or I'd have been very damaged."

"I'm very grateful you're not damaged." She threw the covers back and patted the bed. "But now you need to get some sleep."

"Let me get washed up. Don't move."

By the time he'd finished brushing his teeth she'd worked herself into a small frenzy of worry. "You can't do this anymore," she said as he crawled in next to her. "It's too dangerous."

"I have to get to the weapons, Tate."

"Find another way. I won't be able to stand it if something happens to you."

He pulled her close, putting his arm under her neck, positioning himself so he could look into her eyes. "I'll be here," he said. "I won't leave you."

She believed him as best she could. The closer they came to the island, the worse her fears were becoming. Michael tethered her to the earth, to sanity. If he were gone—

"Hush," he said. "Stay with me. Don't be anywhere else but right here."

She nodded.

He kissed her. It was long and languid and she touched his skin wherever her hand landed. In the days and nights that had sailed by, she'd learned the heaven of familiarity, the comfort of knowing she couldn't make a mistake.

She pleased him. She knew it, and it brought her an extraordinary confidence. If she could bring that feeling to her whole world…

"A little help?"

She looked at him, startled out of her reverie. "With what?"

"Panties."

"I don't think they would look that good on you, but, sure, give it a try."

"Oh, you're hilarious."

"Come on, Michael," she said, turning her head fetchingly to the side. "Haven't you ever wanted to try a walk on the wild side?"

"The masculine wild side, sure. Panties? That's a big no."

"What a chicken. You'd probably look adorable."

"The last thing in the world I want to look like is adorable."

"Right. You're a lumberjack and you're—"

"Hold it right there. You want to see some wild-side action? How does a little spanking sound?"

"Hmm. Your bottom all red and rosy?"

"Not mine."

"Oh, then no. It sounds terrible."

His mouth opened, but no sound emerged. Finally he just shook his head.

"Don't worry, Michael. You don't have to understand. Just smile and say, 'Yes, dear.'"

"Yes, dear," he said as he dutifully smiled. "But just for the record, this isn't over."

"No?"

"It's just going to take me a while to figure out my strategy. I'm thinking a surprise visit in the middle of the night. Something kinky but not too startling."

"All for me?"

He nodded.

She pulled his head down so her mouth was an inch from his ear. "Add some leather to that mix, big guy, and I'm all in."

"Oh, shit," he said as he got to his knees and pulled her into a kiss that went on and on.

He didn't have to remind her again about the whole panty situation. She got naked, fast, tossing her clothes somewhere away, and then she got him naked, too.

By that time he was hard for her, hard all over. She liked to run her hands over his chest and feel the hard buds of his nipples beneath her palms. He liked it when she tweaked him there, and she was happy to oblige.

He'd figured out a lot of her favorite things, too. Like now, when he used two fingers to get her ready for the main event. And how he nipped at the tender skin just below her ear until she shivered with pleasure.

Then oddly, his pace slowed until she pulled back to look at him. "What's wrong?"

He shook his head, but the look he gave her was as pensive as she'd ever seen him.

"Michael?"

"I would never hurt you."

"I know that."

"Maybe. But I want to say it anyway. I miss a lot about my old life—the pace, the adrenaline. It was good for me and I was good at it. But meeting you…"

She swallowed and held her breath, afraid to speak or even breathe lest he stop.

"Meeting you has changed every damn thing. But I want you to understand something."

He held her tighter, bruising her arm. She didn't care, not at all.

"I'm going to get you out of this. And when you go back to your real life, you won't be the same person. You'll be stronger. Better."

His eyes searched hers with amazing intensity, but he was starting to scare her now. This wasn't the speech she'd hoped for. She didn't know how she knew, but she knew.

"I'm going to miss you. But I want you to know I'll be rooting for you to have the life you deserve. You will. You'll be able to travel. It kills me to say it, but you'll have your pick of men. The world will be yours. All you have to do is take it."

"So you think I can have any man I want?"

"I know it. You're beautiful, and that's the least of it. Don't you settle for anything less than the best, you hear me? Any man—the goddamn princes of the world—would be lucky to know you, let alone love you."

She couldn't have stopped her tears if her life depended on it. His sincerity slipped into her heart, and she knew it would be there forever.

He was also telling the truth. Not about the men who'd line up for her but that he wouldn't be in that line. This was going to end. One way or the other, Michael was going to leave her. She didn't want it to be so, but even a woman who'd lived most of her life in the land of magical thinking could see that he couldn't continue as her bodyguard. Not after all this.

"Tate?"

She sniffed. "Hmm?"

"We still have right now."

There was something so sweet about his voice, about his face. "Thank you," she said. "Thank you for being my safe place. For seeing so much in me. I'll never forget you."

"You'd better not," he said as he laid her down, as he moved between her legs. As he entered her body as completely as he'd entered her heart.

16

THEY DOCKED AT FIVE that morning. Tate held on to Michael as she listened for new voices, a chance perhaps to get someone's attention.

He squeezed her shoulder and kissed her on the temple. She instantly calmed. Not Zen calm or anything, but she could feel the tension ease from her shoulders.

"I know it's wishful thinking on my part," she whispered after hearing nothing but Jazz's voice on deck, "but, hey, we have to try."

"We do, but I'd feel a lot better if you were off the boat. There's a much greater chance you can get away."

"I don't want to go."

"I know," he said.

"They're so damn secretive at the bank. We'll be taken into a private room. It's not like going to a bank in New York."

"Just do what we talked about."

"I'll try."

"You'll be great. I have complete faith in you."

"Well, that's just insane."

He laughed, then he tilted her chin up. There wasn't much light, not enough to make out every detail, and yet she could picture every inch of his face. She closed her eyes, holding the image still and strong so that when she was out there she could bring it back.

His kiss was gentle and sweet, a tender counterpoint to last night's urgency.

After the anchor went down, the boat rocked with a whole new motion. For two hours they lay entwined. Kissing sometimes, touching everywhere. She tried so hard not to think of this as the end, but she wasn't strong enough.

"Michael?"

"Yeah?"

"I know what you said last night makes sense, but I can't let it go. If… When we get back to New York, I want—" She felt him tense, and that made her stumble, but she really needed to say this now. "I want you."

His chest rose, but it didn't fall for too many heartbeats.

"Was that the wrong thing to say?"

He exhaled and pulled her closer. "No, not at all. I'm really flattered."

"Screw flattered. Talk to me."

"I'm going to resign," he said. "That's a given. But I doubt all will be forgiven. You're father's not going to be happy with me. And he's right. I was supposed to protect you and I put you in danger."

"You didn't."

"I did. Charlie is my fault. I should have cut him off years ago. I should have figured that he'd know how to break into my safe. I was stupid and you're paying for it."

"Okay, you have to stop that right now. I know you had nothing to do with Charlie's plan. You've put your own life at risk to take care of me. So don't even try to go there."

"Even if I don't, you're father already has."

"I'm not my father."

"And for that I'm most grateful."

"Michael. I'm not kidding around."

"I know you're not. And believe me, I'm goddamned amazed that a woman like you could want me. I just don't think you should make any promises. Not yet."

"I've run from promises my whole life. If I want to make one now, I will."

"Okay, then. Promise away."

"Please don't make light of this. I've never felt this way before. Not ever. You've been a revelation. Not just because you know how to make me tremble, but because—"

He didn't say anything. But he held his breath again.

"Because of how you see me. I had no idea this was even possible. All I can call it is simpatico. It sounds too fancy for what I mean, but—"

"No. I get it. I understand completely."

She allowed herself a little grin. "Told ya."

"Tell you what," he said. "When we get back, we'll take a look at how things stand. Just you and me. Okay?"

"Okay."

"Now try and sleep."

"Ha."

He kissed her temple one more time. "Rest, then. Rest."

FOR THE FIRST TIME since they'd kidnapped her, Ed came into the cabin. It was just past eight and she hadn't slept a wink. She'd been too busy thinking, not about the day ahead or what she'd have to face but about a future filled with Michael.

Of course, her father wouldn't approve, but that was too damn bad. She hadn't told him, not in so many words, but she loved Michael. Loved him in a way she'd never dreamed for herself.

"Get dressed," Ed said. "I want you ready in one hour."

He looked like an island millionaire. He wore an elegant Hawaiian shirt—which seemed contradictory but wasn't—khaki pants, deck shoes and a Panama hat to cover his bald spot. His tan was deep, his Rolex top-of-the-line, and the diamond on his pinkie could have been used as an anchor.

He turned to Michael. "Make sure she looks good."

Before Michael could say a word, Ed left, locking the door behind him.

She sat on the bed in her T-shirt. It was already starting. Her pulse pounded, her breathing grew labored. She closed her eyes so she wouldn't see the narrowing of her vision.

"Come on, kiddo," Michael said. "Don't project. One foot in front of the other. You need to shower, right? That's not scary. You've done that a thousand times before."

She nodded, then looked up at him as her thoughts took a right turn. "Michael, you have to promise me that you won't kill Charlie."

"What?"

"Promise me. I know you're going to fight and do all your spy stuff, and you can feed every one of these bastards to the sharks as far as I'm concerned, but you can't kill Charlie."

He straightened his back and flexed his jaw, and it was so easy to see the warrior in him. He'd been on his best behavior when her life had been at risk, but the moment she was off the boat… She tried to feel sorry for Jazz, but she couldn't. He deserved everything Michael would give him.

"Michael, please. If you do, you'll regret it forever."

"Don't ask me to make that promise, Tate."

"Why not?"

"I have no idea what I'm going to be facing once you're gone. Please don't tie my hands that way."

"All right. But will you try?"

"I will."

She stood and went right into his arms. "That's all I need."

He took her by the shoulders and looked at her with his green-gold eyes. "I need so much more."

There was nothing gentle about this kiss. She felt it to her toes, to her chromosomes. She needed to be strong for this. To come back to him.

He broke away. "Go on. Get ready. Remember, one step at a time."

It wasn't easy, but she managed to do just that. Shower, makeup, hair, the clothes Jazz had bought her in Florida. When she finally looked in the mirror, she knew she looked just as privileged as Ed. In fact, she looked as if she could have been his daughter.

It had been so easy to step back into the habits of

years. The hair not just curled but coiffed, after lessons from some of the most sought-after stylists in the world. The makeup might not have been hers, but she knew how to work it. Subtle in every way. Elegant and under-stated. To be flashy was to be vulgar. To be one of *them*.

And how would it be to live with—hell, date—one of them? A man who was her chauffeur, for heaven's sake? The talk would be incessant, the censure obvious at every gathering. She didn't give one solitary damn, as she'd never fit in anyway. But what about her father?

He cared so very much. His life was a monument to wealth and everything wealth brought. Including this.

While Michael insisted on blaming himself, she looked elsewhere. As much as she loved her father, her kidnapping now seemed inevitable. After Lisa, it had only been a matter of time.

He'd instilled in her a number of wonderful things: her social responsibility, her respect for hard work. But he'd also raised her to be a victim.

That she had spent so much of her time in captivity not feeling like a victim was a tribute to Michael. And herself. She couldn't forget that. She'd done re-markably well, considering.

There was a brief knock at the bathroom door. "Tate?"

This was it. She had to go out now, leave Michael behind, act her ass off. She had to be strong and there was no one to depend on but herself.

She took a deep breath and opened the door.

Ed was there along with Jazz. They looked her over

as if she were a prize pony. She felt the heat rush to her face, but she kept it together. Head up, shoulders back, an air of detachment. At least that part was easy.

"You look good. Now all you have to do is keep your mouth shut and sign the papers." Ed touched her hair and she didn't even flinch. "Make it look real, sweetheart, and you'll live to see another day."

Ed turned to Jazz and gave him a nod. Ed stepped closer to her and pulled a gun from the back of his waistband, while Jazz went to Michael's side, next to the bed.

"What's just as important," Ed continued, positioning the barrel of the gun in her side, "is that your boyfriend here might live, too."

Before she could even take a step or be scared about the gun, Jazz pulled Michael's right arm straight out, laid it palm up on the edge of the bedside counter and smashed it with the butt of his weapon. She heard the bone snap like a twig, followed instantly by Michael's sharp cry.

The blood drained from her head and she gasped for breath as she struggled not to throw up. She could see exactly where it was broken at the wrist.

She turned on Ed and slapped him across the face, the sound not nearly loud enough.

He lifted his weapon, his whole face red and furious. She knew he might pull the trigger, but all she wanted was to punish him for what he'd done, then turn her wrath on Jazz.

"Tate, no!" Michael, holding his arm tight against his side, stepped forward, his left arm out to pull her away.

Ed trembled as he stared at her and she could see

the war in his eyes. He wanted so badly to kill her, but it would cost him dearly. "You shouldn't have done that."

"You have no reason to hurt him. I've agreed to give you my money. That's what you're after. Not him."

Ed took another step closer, and now the barrel of the gun touched her temple, the same place Michael had kissed so tenderly. "If you try anything stupid again, I'm going to give Jazz here a call. He's going to break the other hand and then he's going to shoot out the right kneecap, then the left. By the time Jazz is finished there won't be a bone in his body that isn't broke. You got that?"

The thought brought up the bile in her throat, but she couldn't break down. Not now. "Yes."

"Good." He put the weapon back in his waistband, then covered it with his brightly colored Hawaiian shirt. "Let's go."

She looked at Michael's hand, already swelling. "He needs a doctor."

"When it's over," Ed said. "He'll get all the attention he needs. Come on."

He led her to the door, but just before she stepped through, Michael said, "Wait."

She turned.

"I love you," he said. "I think I have for a long time. Just know that, okay? Know it."

WALKING OUT OF THE room was like death. The sun shone warm on her skin, the water sparkled blue and the wind smelled of the sea—and it was all gallows.

She kept hearing that sickening snap over and over

in her head. All she wanted to do was kill Ed Martini and Jazz and, yes, Charlie, too, and get back to Michael. It hurt her that he was in pain, that Jazz could injure him so easily.

Too easily.

God, Michael had let that horrible man hurt him to protect her. Because Ed had the gun on her.

Her steps slowed, but Ed's hand on her back led her onto the small sea taxi, where he sat her down so close to him his aftershave filled her nostrils. She stared at the shore, at Seven Mile Beach, while Ed told her he was now her uncle Ed—Ed Martini, her father's best friend. That the money was being transferred to his account temporarily and that William would come soon to make different arrangements.

Then he made her repeat everything he'd said. By the time she'd done so for the fifth time, they had docked. As she stood, he touched her arm, her back, then her arm again, and it was all she could do not to slap him over and over until he took her back to the boat, to Michael.

She'd never felt this before, this rage so bright and hot that she knew without a doubt she could take his gun and blow him away. She'd never even guessed she had this murderousness in her. Her vivid imagination hadn't been enough. She'd always pictured herself as the victim, not the killer.

Although she hadn't been to Cayman in years, she remembered the soft white beaches here and how she'd enjoyed playing with the turtles and snorkeling. This memory would forever be overshadowed, however long forever turned out to be.

They walked, the two of them, past the seaside cafés

and shops, toward the center of town. Toward her bank. He held on to her each step of the way, hurting her as she passed one khaki-dressed police officer after another.

She said nothing. She obeyed and would obey. There was only one chance in a million she could get herself out of this, but she wasn't going to try even that. Not with Michael's well-being at stake.

He slowed her down as they crossed the street in front of Grand Cayman Bank. "Who am I?" he asked.

"Uncle Ed."

"Say it again—and smile this time."

She forced her lips to curve up. "Uncle Ed."

He walked into the shade on the right side of the street and took out his cell phone. With one push of his button he was on the phone with Jazz, and she was trembling. "Jazz, let's see what you can do to his left hand."

"No!" she said, but he yanked her back, close to a pastry shop window.

"Say it again."

She looked at him through a red haze of hatred, but she made herself smile, pretend this wasn't death, that Michael wasn't being hurt this very second. "Uncle Ed."

"Again."

"Uncle Ed."

"Better. Just don't forget I have the phone right here." He patted his pocket. "There's only one way he doesn't die, and die ugly."

IT HAD TAKEN MICHAEL too long to wrap his hand in the bathroom towel, to swallow half the bottle of aspirin. He knew Jazz would be coming back any minute, and when he did, there were going to be some changes.

Now that Tate wasn't directly in harm's way, he could do what he'd wanted to when Jazz had grabbed his wrist.

He went back to the bedroom. He could still unlock the door, even with his dominant hand out of commission. But that wasn't the plan. He needed Jazz to come in here.

Once he'd taken that prick out, he'd move on, but slowly. Each member of the crew had to be taken out before he'd blow the whistle on Martini.

On the one hand, he wanted Jazz to hurry the hell up. On the other, a few more minutes for the aspirin to take affect wouldn't hurt.

He cursed his luck for the hundredth time. Why had he bailed out Charlie so many times? Why'd he have to promise his father he'd watch out for that loser? And why the hell had he fallen in love with Tate Baxter?

There was no good outcome to this scenario. She didn't deserve any more anguish, not on his account. Goddamn, he was a fool.

He turned too sharply and pain radiated up his arm. Yeah, some more time for that aspirin would be just great. Was that Jazz? Shit, he had to be ready to do what needed to be done.

TATE SAT AT THE BANK vice president's desk, waiting for him to draw up the transfer papers. After 9/11, things had changed, even here, and there was a lot more red tape to tamp down on money laundering. If only they knew who Ed Martini really was. But they wouldn't discover the truth from her.

She'd smiled, answered questions, been attentive, but now she had to remember what Michael had told her. Even though it might be the wrong choice, she had to try. If she could stop Ed now, she could still get to Michael before Jazz had done too much damage.

She began with the breathing. Taking in larger and larger breaths.

"What are you doing?"

"I—"

He pinched her on the back of her arm, and she bit her lip so she wouldn't yelp.

"Stop it."

"I don't think I can."

He smiled broadly and leaned toward her, bringing his lips close to her ear. "First his right kneecap, then his left."

She breathed harder, deeper, faster, knowing she would hyperventilate and that would make her pass out. It was her only job, her only shot. To do what she'd done for years—have a panic attack, only this one had to be deliberate and it couldn't last hours. She had to faint, to be cared for by someone, anyone, except Uncle Ed.

He pinched her again. "Don't you fuckin' dare."

"Please, I can't help it. It's the agoraphobia. I have no…no control."

"You'd better find some, bitch. Or he won't have one—"

Mr. Granger, the vice president, reentered the room and Ed's face changed again. He looked up at the man with concern.

"Could you bring my niece a cup of water? She's not feeling well."

"Of course. One moment." He picked up his phone

and asked his secretary to bring fresh water. Before he hung up, he asked, "Is there anything else I can do?"

Ed shook his head. "No. She'll be fine."

Tate looked at him. Tried to smile. Then everything went black.

17

MICHAEL STOOD JUST to the left of the door, waiting. His right hand, immobilized in a towel, was strapped to his back with the aid of two torn pillowcases. It felt weird, but he couldn't strap the hand in front—it would present too easy a target.

He didn't think he'd be fighting long. Jazz would come in, Michael would knock the crap out of him using his three remaining limbs and get the gun. The gun would make the rest of his job simpler still.

His only worry at this point was Tate. She was out there by herself. Michael hoped that Ed had ditched his weapon before going to the bank. He doubted very much even an offshore bank would appreciate a customer coming in with a loaded Glock.

But even if he didn't have a gun to use on Tate, he'd have no trouble getting her to sign the papers. Breaking his hand was the smartest thing Ed could have done. Tate wasn't used to these kinds of tactics and she had no idea what Michael was capable of.

How could she? He'd been so afraid of getting her hurt that he'd behaved like a civilian this whole trip. He'd been knocked out—twice—caught behind a sofa, tripped up by his brother. She probably thought he'd made up his military training.

He should have kicked ass and worried later. Even with Charlie here, with Tate so vulnerable. He'd never behaved this stupidly before, not on any mission he'd ever had. He'd have been drummed out of the Army for this.

There was a noise outside, a thump, and it brought him right back into the room, into this mission right here. He breathed deeply and evenly, balanced himself to make optimum use of what he had to work with. Jazz was going down. And if it was painful on the way, so much the better.

The lock turned and the door swung open. Michael waited until Jazz walked in, ready for anything. Only, it wasn't Jazz. It was Charlie. He was crying like a baby, but his gun, silencer and all, was pointed straight at Michael's chest.

TATE OPENED HER EYES. She didn't know where she was, who the man standing in front of her was, what was going on, and fear shot through her. She scrambled back, barely realizing she'd been lying on a leather couch, and then she saw Ed.

He made everything worse. Her chest seized, her vision narrowed. And she was pretty sure he wasn't going to get his money because she'd be dead any second.

"I'll call the hospital," the man said, his accent broad and his face terribly worried.

"No, it's all right," Ed said. "Just give us a moment. She's disoriented, that's all. She had a rough night on the boat."

The man eyed Ed, then her. "It won't take them but a moment—"

"No, thank you. We just need a few minutes alone."

"Very well. I'll be right outside if you need me."

"I appreciate it," Ed said, his smile looking so genuine it made Tate's pulse pound harder.

The moment they were alone, Ed's demeanor switched to his true self. Malevolent, angry, brutal. He got right into her face, his arms on either side of her. If he'd been a lover, he'd have swooped in for a kiss, but there was nothing but hate in his eyes, in the way he sneered at her. "You have one more chance. You get out there and sign those papers. One more thing goes wrong, and your man is dead. You'll go back to a corpse, you got that?"

She nodded. "I didn't do this on purpose. Please don't hurt him."

"He's already hurt. Don't think I won't tell Jazz to kill him."

"I won't."

He smiled, stood up. "There, that's better. I knew you were all right. Let's go get this paperwork out of the way, then we'll go relax at the beach. How does that sound?"

"Great," she said, struggling to make her voice stop shaking and sound normal.

What she couldn't do was stop the rest of her from shaking. God, how she wanted to, but her body wouldn't obey. Even when they got back to the office where the papers waited in neat order, she couldn't hide the way her hand trembled as she picked up the pen.

"If you'd like to wait until you feel better," the bank executive said, "it's no problem."

She looked at Ed, then at the man. "Mr. Granger, I'm sorry. It's not going to be better later. I'm agoraphobic—do you know what that is?"

"A fear of being in public, yes?"

She nodded. "I know I need to sign these papers in person, but it's difficult for me. I'm just sorry to trouble you with my problems."

"There's no problem at all. In fact, once you've signed at the X's, there's no reason we can't do everything else for you and your uncle. We have his information, and I'll have Joseph give him the new account number right now." Granger picked up the phone.

While he made the arrangements, she signed each line following a red X. Fifty million dollars would be transferred from her account to Ed's, and that would be that. Even if he was convicted of all his crimes, she didn't think the bank could reverse the transfer. It was the Caymans after all, and from their standpoint everything was being done according to the law.

She didn't give a damn about the money, except that it would hurt her father to realize what had happened. He would have given the bastard the fifty million from his own funds given the choice.

As she signed her name for the last time, it was very clear to her that she was signing her death warrant. Michael was hurt. He wasn't going to be able to carry out his part of the plan, and she'd botched her part… What was left but for both of them to die?

All she could hope for at this stage was to stop Michael's pain. If she simply went along with everything Ed said, there was a chance they would be merciful. What a thing to wish for.

"CHRIST, MIKEY, I DON'T want to do this. You know that. You're my brother, for God's sake."

"Then put the gun down."

"I can't." Charlie wiped his nose with the side of his arm. "He'll kill me."

"He" was Jazz, standing in the doorway, his arms folded across his chest, his big teeth shining as he smiled like a child on Christmas morning.

"He'll kill you anyway, you idiot."

"No, no. You don't understand. I brought them this deal. I'm just clearing my debt."

"You know too much, Charlie. They can't let you walk away. What if you decide to blackmail them later?"

"Are you crazy? It's Ed Martini. No one double-crosses Martini."

Michael took one step toward his brother. "That's 'cause no one lives long enough. There's no way you're getting off this boat, Charlie. Not onto dry land."

"Shut up. You think you know so much. You didn't even know I could get into your safe, huh? You didn't know I watched you that night when I was sick. You thought I was sleeping, but I wasn't. I was behind the door and I watched you type in the numbers."

"That was pretty slick, there, Charlie. You sure had me fooled."

"Yeah, I know. You think I'm an idiot, but I'm not. I thought of this whole plan all by myself."

"Dad would be so proud."

Charlie lifted the gun and waved it at Michael's

face. "You don't talk about him. He trusted you. You were supposed to take care of me—and look what you did. You're the reason I got to pull this trigger. It's not my fault."

Michael felt so incredibly tired and he hurt so goddamn much that he almost wanted Charlie to pull the trigger. Only there was someone much more important he had to think about. Besides, he didn't want to give Jazz the satisfaction. "Charlie, put down the gun. I'll get you out of this. Alive."

Jazz laughed, but Charlie didn't see the humor. "You fucking liar. You just want to be with your rich girlfriend. Well, screw you!"

"It's not about her, Charlie. It's about Dad. About the promise I made him. I don't want to hurt you. And I don't want *them* to hurt you."

"I'm the one with the gun."

"You are, but Charlie," he said, his voice growing calm and quiet, "you've never been very good in this kind of situation."

"See? There you go again." He stepped closer and pushed the barrel of the gun into Michael's chest. "I am not an idiot!" he screamed, sending spittle and fear into Michael's face.

"Oh, Charlie," Michael whispered. "I don't know why it had to be so hard for you."

"What?"

"I'm sorry, buddy."

"It's too late now."

"I know, but I'm sorry anyway."

Charlie looked down at the gun, and Michael spun half a step back, then knocked Charlie's feet from underneath him. He grabbed the gun, turning it sideways, and as Charlie fell, Michael put a bullet right into Jazz's chest.

Charlie looked up at him with shock and hurt in his eyes. Michael pointed the weapon at his brother. "I'm sorry," he said again, but this time it was to his father. He fired once more.

"I'M SORRY, MS. BAXTER, there's one more thing we need to complete before we can let you go."

"That's okay," she said, trying not to panic. She looked at Ed and willed him to understand this wasn't her fault.

"What's the hang-up?" he asked.

"In order to transfer this amount of money, Ms. Baxter and you need to fill out statements that will go on record here. As a cooperating member of the international community, we have to have a signed statement that the money will not be used in money-laundering schemes or for any purpose that could be construed as terrorism or supporting known terrorists."

"Sure," Ed said. "We'll sign whatever you like."

"Excellent." He put the papers down in front of them, but Tate noticed there was a slight bulge under hers, toward the bottom. She looked up to find Mr. Granger staring at her. He glanced pointedly at the paper.

She moved the top sheet aside and saw a note in faint script. *Are you in trouble?*

She wanted so badly to say yes. She looked at him again, smiled as earnestly as she knew how and shook her head.

He nodded. She signed. It was over. At least this

part. She still had to make it back to the boat. To find Michael, to help him, no matter what condition he was in. Just thinking about his hands made her sick. What was she going to do if they'd done worse?

AT THE LAST SECOND he moved the gun. The bullet hit inches from Charlie's head.

Michael couldn't stop to figure out why he'd done it. He just had to make sure Charlie didn't call out to Danny or the other one. He dropped to his knees right next to his brother and pulled back his left arm. When Charlie hoisted himself up into the right position, Michael hit him in the temple.

Charlie went down hard. It probably was a good thing Michael's right hand was out of commission. There had been no kidding around with that punch. It was meant to silence. Sometimes it happened that the silence went on forever. He didn't think Charlie was dead and he wasn't going to check. Not right now.

He rose once more and looked at Charlie's gun. It was a Sig Sauer P-226, a gun Michael particularly liked. He had to use his teeth to check the magazine, which was full. He locked the mag back in the gun.

Jazz had fallen in the doorway, and by the time Michael got to him, he must have bled out—if the shot hadn't killed him on impact. Michael had wanted to do him slowly, to make him suffer, but he'd take what he could get. He stepped over the scumbag and went on the prowl.

He wasn't sure how long Ed would keep Tate in the bank, but he wanted everything completed when they returned. Maybe he could take his time with Ed. It would be good to let him know what happened to men who messed with Michael Caulfield's lady. On the other hand, Tate didn't need to have any more trauma in her life. Especially not from him.

No one was in the saloon. But there was someone in the wheelhouse. He was on the radio, and Michael figured he'd better get to him double time. It was the cabin boy, the kid Charlie had lied about. Michael got all the way across the saloon before he turned. The dude had a muscleman's build and a bullfrog's face. He seemed damned surprised to find Michael pointing a gun his way and made a foolish attempt to retrieve his own weapon from his underarm holster.

He fell across the seat, then tumbled to the deck. Michael picked up bullfrog's Walther PPK, but he preferred the Sig. He pulled the magazine out of the Walther and tossed it behind the saloon couch. The gun went into a fake potted plant.

Once he had the Sig in his hand again Michael went looking for Danny. The boat was anchored far from any neighboring vessels. There were people out there, but none of them would have heard the silenced gunshots. He doubted they would hear anything more than innocuous pops if he took a dozen shots off the port bow. It didn't matter. No one was coming to the rescue. It was all on him.

He headed down below. To his right was the galley, and he knew someone was inside from the whistling. "Alouette." He doubted it was Danny. Probably the cook, which sounded innocent enough until you thought about who he cooked for. No one on this boat was without a weapon—that much Michael knew. The cook, despite his ability to make a very excellent salmon steak, wasn't gonna make it.

With his right hand throbbing at nearly his pain threshold, Michael was more than ready to have this over and done with. If it was Danny in the galley, so much the better. If not, he couldn't be far.

Michael inched his way along the teak floor, the incredible interior of the boat showing just how much a bookie like Ed earned for himself. Of course now, with the fifty million in his pocket, he'd probably consider this a toy boat. Something convenient to take him out to his real yacht.

He stopped thinking about Ed. He was all about the whistler in the galley. Whatever the guy was making, there was some chopping involved. That's all that sound could be. So that meant a knife. Not a problem.

Moving as quietly as he could while keeping his balance, Michael made it halfway to the galley. He had to forget about his right hand, about that arm. If he gave it any attention, his instinct would be to pull it from the safety of his back. It was best to concentrate on the gun in his left hand. He listened carefully to the chopping and the whistling, figuring the size of the galley and where his shot should go. There was no room for error, so the second shot had to be close to the first but lower. Get him in the chest, then in the gut. That would take him down without giving him a chance to shoot back.

After a cleansing breath, he got close, a step away. He turned, aimed, adjusted two inches and pulled the trigger. The first bullet threw the cook forward, over his chopped vegetables. The second severed his spinal cord. At least that's what it looked like from the way the man fell.

Michael turned to move deeper into the boat. There should only be one man left on board, not counting Charlie.

Ed was gonna be so pissed.

Michael whistled "Alouette" as he continued the hunt.

THEY WERE OUTSIDE once more, in the bright island sunshine. There were so many people on the streets, mostly tourists with gifts in big bags and flip-flops on their feet. There were more cars now, too. And she wondered how many accidents there were here just because the American tourists had to drive on the left.

Ed had his hand locked on her upper arm, but he seemed a lot happier now that he was so much richer. She felt certain that all he wanted was to get back to the boat, wait till nightfall and make sure there was no one left to tell the tale.

He walked her across the street, making her wait for the light. Then they went toward the beach and the water taxis.

"There's no reason to kill us," she said. "Now that you have the money, there's no way for us to get it back."

"Shut up."

"Just let us go. We'll disappear. You won't hear from us again."

"I said shut up."

She did, but with every step her worry grew, and she kept picturing horror after horror of what she'd find on the boat. It was making it hard to see, hard to breathe, but she didn't want to worry Michael by showing up in a full-blown panic attack.

"Come on," Ed said, squeezing her arm.

"You're hurting me."

"Just get your ass in gear. I want to get back to the boat. We're celebrating tonight at the Ritz. Figure I'm gonna buy myself one hell of an expensive bottle of champagne." He tugged her again, practically pulling her shoulder out of its socket.

She stopped and tore her arm free, suddenly so filled with rage she forgot all about her constricted breath and pounding heartbeat.

He was celebrating at the Ritz? Over his dead body.

18

"I DON'T CARE WHAT evidence you have or don't have.
I know Michael Caulfield is behind this."

Sara bit her lower lip, trying hard not to react. Mr.
Baxter needed to have his say. She turned to Special
Agent Webber and he gave her a small nod. They'd talked
a lot yesterday, after she'd cried her millionth tear.

She'd recognized Tate's purse instantly. That the
wallet was still inside shut down the last of her hope.
It didn't matter that the money was gone. Tate
wouldn't have left that wallet. It had been a gift. From
Sara.

She'd debated long and hard about telling William
about the purse, but in the end she'd decided he had
to know. There was no choice.

He'd disappeared into the guest room, then
emerged this morning more angry than sad. He'd
called the meeting they were having now. Who knows?
His righteous anger just might pull him through.

"Sir, we're doing everything we can to find both
your daughter and Mr. Caulfield. We know his motorcycle is missing, but from the state of his apartment it
doesn't appear he planned a trip. There were no suit-
cases missing, all his clothing was in the drawers and

closets. Frankly we're much more interested in Jerry Brody than Caulfield."

"*I'm* interested in Caulfield. He was in military intelligence. I doubt very much he intended anyone to think he'd planned this. I didn't hire him because he was a fool."

"I understand, sir. Rest assured, we're leaving no stone unturned. We're currently investigating his brother, where there might be some connection."

"His brother."

"Charles. He has a criminal record. Theft, racketeering, drugs."

William stood so quickly he had to grab the edge of his chair to gain his balance. "I knew it. That's why they needed the five million—drug money."

"Mr. Baxter," Sara said, concerned now that he was working himself into such a lather. "I know it seems to make sense that Michael was in on this, but—"

"Enough," he said.

He'd never raised his voice at her before, and she didn't much care for it now. But the man was given a pass, at least for today.

"I know what I know."

"Excuse me, Mr. Baxter?"

Sara, as well as the men in the room, all turned as one to see three of the security team standing by the side wall. They all looked uncomfortable, as if they had thrown a baseball through a stained-glass window.

"Who are you?" Baxter asked.

The tallest one stepped forward. "I'm George Bryan. I work surveillance."

"I'm E. J. Packer, sir." Sara recognized him from

the scars on his face. "I'm ex-Army intelligence and I run night security."

They both turned to the only blond, a slender man with horn-rimmed glasses. "I'm also ex-Army intelligence, sir. Name's McPherson. Bill McPherson."

"What is it?"

"I served with Mike Caulfield for two years. He is not your man."

"What?" William looked from the men to Sara, as if she'd been behind this mutiny.

"I also served with Mike Caulfield." This from George Bryan. "I can't see it, Mr. Baxter. If he's involved, it's because he's trying to save her. I've never worked for a more honorable man."

"I agree, Mr. Baxter." E.J. nodded toward Sara. "Ma'am. For my money, looking at Caulfield is looking in the wrong direction."

"Get out of here, all of you," Baxter said, his face red with rage. "You work for him. Of course you're going to say he's innocent."

The three men, all with their military stance and utmost respect, took his fury like good soldiers. And when they were summarily fired, they didn't seem surprised.

But when Sara looked back at the FBI agent, it was clear attention had been paid.

"You son of a bitch!" Tate said so loudly the tourists in back of Ed stopped talking to stare. "You murdering bastard. You're planning on killing us before you have your champagne?"

He laughed as he looked around nervously. With his

left hand he pulled out his cell phone. "I'm warning you," he said, his teeth clamped together as he smiled.

"You're warning me…what? That you're going to hurt Michael? You're planning to kill us. What could hurt worse than that?"

"Stop it," he said. "These people are going to think you're serious."

She was serious. So serious that she didn't even stop to think, she just turned in front of him, grabbed his arms and kneed Ed Martini right between the legs.

He howled so loudly everyone on the street stopped, and when he fell to the ground, clutching his crotch, more and more people approached. But Tate wasn't done yet.

She circled around to his back. His piteous cries had the crowd murmuring, but she didn't care. She lifted his Hawaiian shirt above his waist and plucked the gun away.

Several members of the crowd backed up. Despite the hysteria she felt just under the surface, the gun in Tate's hands didn't shake at all. She moved around in front of the man and kept the barrel pointed at his head. "Someone call the cops."

She didn't hear any movement. "Someone," she said again, only a whole lot louder, "call the cops."

There were footsteps to her right and in back of her. Horns honked in the road, and she assumed the crowd had gotten so large that they were blocking the street. Hell, they probably didn't see a sight like this every day.

Ed Martini writhed on the sidewalk, holding himself like a child who has to pee. Martini, who hadn't blinked when Michael's wrist had been broken, who thought nothing of killing two innocent people, then drinking champagne. The pig deserved to die himself, but maybe it would be worse for him if he had to go to prison here. She didn't think the Caymans had extradition laws, but that didn't matter either. He wasn't going to kill Michael. Not now.

"Hey, hey. Put the gun down, miss."

She looked up to see two police officers standing on the road. "He's a kidnapper and a thief and a murderer, and I have proof of all of it."

"Put the gun down and we'll talk."

She didn't want to. She wanted to pull the trigger. But she didn't. She just bent, put the gun on the ground and backed away.

The cops, in their crisp khakis and black hats, split up, with one man shooing the bystanders away and the other coming toward her. Two steps in, Ed lunged forward and grabbed the gun.

She leaped back, cursing herself for not kicking the weapon as far as she could.

Ed got to his knees, then to his feet, the gun in his right hand pointing at her chest. His face was a red mess, with tears and more dripping from his nose and chin. He didn't look so smooth now. What he did look like was a man who didn't care about consequences. Not when he clearly wanted to kill her so damn badly.

"Sir, put the gun down. Sir…"

Ed didn't even glance at the cop. He just snarled at Tate. "You bitch. You're gonna pay—"

"I've already paid. Isn't fifty-five million enough? Isn't kidnapping and assault enough? You broke his wrists! All he was trying to do was protect me, and you've crippled him."

"He's long past caring," he said, lifting the gun. "And in one second you're going to be, too."

Tate closed her eyes, prepared for the impact of a bullet to send her crashing into the crowd. But it didn't come. She heard a scuffle, then a thunk, and she opened her eyes to see the two sturdy police officers on top of Ed, their knees planted on his back as they twisted his hands around for cuffs.

Tears filled her eyes and she laughed and wept as she realized it was over, that Ed was really in custody. And then it hit her, what he'd said about Michael.

Her legs didn't want to hold her up as she let the truth in. Michael was dead. They hadn't broken his other wrist, they'd shot him. Of course they had. Why bother to keep him around? She'd proved she would do anything for him, so all they'd needed was her own belief that she could save him.

Michael was dead.

LEAVING THE COOK IN the galley, Michael went back down the narrow corridor toward the master suite and the other berth. Danny, unless he'd taken Ed and Tate to the island, had to be there somewhere. Probably prepared, as the cook's death hadn't been all that quiet.

There was a head just before the smaller berth, and Michael slowed as he neared it. His arm and shoulder throbbed to the beat of his heart as he silently made his approach.

Gun at the ready, he kicked the door in, but no one was there. The room was too small to hide in, which meant Danny had to be in one of the bedrooms. If he was on board at all.

The berth, with a couple of beds and very little else, did have space to hide. Although a man Danny's size would have trouble.

If the roles had been reversed, Michael would have gotten behind the door, listening carefully for footsteps. He wouldn't wait for his assailant to show up, he'd shoot through the door.

With that in mind, Michael decided to lure Danny out. He still had a lot of ammo in the mag, so he got close, aimed his weapon at the master suite door and fired.

Despite the name, silencers never really silenced a gun. They helped, but for anyone below deck, the gunshot would have been heard. Just in case Danny had headphones on, Michael put the gun under his right armpit—which hurt like a bitch—unscrewed the silencer, then retrieved the weapon. Two more shots, and this time someone would have to be dead to miss the sound.

Michael crouched in the head doorway, waiting. It was tough to be patient. His mind went one of two places—Tate or pain. He had to keep bringing himself back to his target.

Three minutes went by and Michael saw the door to the master suite move.

Danny had ducked—at least that's what it looked like from the position of his gun. It didn't matter. He could have crawled out on his belly. For all his size and weight, there was nothing the man could have done to save his own life.

Michael put three shots into the door. Danny fell like a massive tree, his head cracking loudly on the teak floor.

Michael backed up until he could sit on the edge of the john. His whole body throbbed with pain, mitigated slightly by relief. Even that only lasted a minute. Tate was still out there. And Charlie.

He hadn't heard a thing from upstairs, but that didn't mean Charlie hadn't recovered. At least his brother didn't have a gun. He'd probably end up shooting himself if he had.

Michael stood, momentarily dizzy. Then, after a few deep breaths, he headed back to the saloon. The smell of death followed him, tainting the scent of the ocean. He felt pretty sure that the coppery taste at the back of his mouth would remind him of tropical islands for some time to come.

The saloon itself was in good shape. Michael's gaze went right to the big leather chair. The government would be selling off the boat once Ed was in prison, and it felt damn good to know the bastard would never sit in that chair again.

Michael needed Tate to get back. Looking toward the beach, he didn't see any water taxis—but then, they were pretty far offshore.

Shit, he couldn't put it off any longer. He turned to the small room that had been their prison for ten days. Jazz's body was still in the doorway, and beyond him, Charlie.

IT HAD TAKEN TOO LONG for the police to get their act together once the street cops had taken her to the station. She'd had to scream to get the right person's attention, but once Chief Eccles understood what was at stake, he made things happen.

In fact, she had to fill in the details as they sped to

a police boat. It was long and sleek and, according to the chief, faster than the speed of criminals.

He brought along six men, heavily armed, in what she assumed to be the British colonial equivalent of a SWAT team. As they flew over the water toward the *Pretty Kitty,* all Tate could do was pray. If only he could still be alive, she'd give more money to charity. She'd work in a soup kitchen. She'd trade years off her own life. Anything. Just not what Ed had said. Not that.

She stood up, too insane to be still, next to the captain. Wind and sea mist sprayed her face, ruining the makeup she'd so carefully applied this morning. Well, that and her tears.

CHARLIE HADN'T MOVED at all, and as Michael knelt next to him, his chest constricted with a stab of guilt and regret. He put his fingers to Charlie's throat, searching for a pulse. He thought maybe…but that could be his own heartbeat.

He bent down, putting his ear right over Charlie's heart. There, damn it. He wasn't dead. He wasn't in great shape, but he wasn't dead.

Relief made his eyes water as he sat back up. Now it was just a matter of time before Tate and Ed came back. Before Michael could finish taking the trash out.

He put his left hand down to steady himself as he rose.

The blow to the back of his head pitched him forward again, and for a second he thought Ed had returned to surprise him. But when he looked up, it wasn't Ed but the not-so-dead, very pissed off Jazz.

THERE IT WAS IN THE distance, the *Pretty Kitty*. She'd been brought aboard unconscious and she'd been taken under duress, so this was the first time Tate had really seen the boat. It was gorgeous. Sleek like a cheetah, it was an exceptional yacht in a harbor full of yachts. No wonder they'd gotten to the Caymans so quickly.

The beauty of the vessel paled as the thought occurred again, as fresh as the first time, that it was Michael's coffin. She chased the image away as quickly as it had come, but there was no more admiration for the boat.

She held on to the dash, willing this boat to hurry. To take her to the man she loved. To find him alive. Nothing else mattered. Nothing.

JAZZ STOOD UNSTEADILY on his widespread legs. His shirt—Hawaiian, like Ed's—was matted with blood. Blood that dripped down his fingers into the pale plush carpet.

He glowered at Michael with malevolent red eyes. "You're gonna die," he said. "You are gonna die slow."

Michael reached for his weapon, stuck into the folds of his pillowcase brace, but Jazz beat him to the punch with his own second gun at the small of his back. The Derringer was small, but it would kill just fine.

"Drop it," Jazz said.

"Like hell. It's over, Jazz. You're the only one left alive."

"Ed's still alive."

"He won't be—"

Charlie moaned. Of all the rotten timing… He moaned again and moved his head.

Jazz sneered and moved his gun so it pointed at Charlie. "You still think you can stop me?"

Michael smiled as he got to his feet. "With one hand tied behind my back, asshole."

Jazz took a step back, a hell of a lot more shaken than he'd been a minute ago. "Stop there or I kill him."

"Go ahead," Michael said. "You pull that trigger, it's the last thing you ever do."

"Fuck you, man." He jerked the gun up to shoot, but Michael was quicker. He dived over Charlie, knocking Jazz off his feet. Jazz lost his gun, but he still had his hands and he hit Michael, hard, in the right shoulder. The pain nearly knocked him out, but not quite.

The second blow hit his bad shoulder again. Michael had to get his left hand moving. He had to get his gun up, aimed at Jazz—and this time there could be no mistakes.

He could feel Jazz's knee come up against his stomach, his fist come down on his shoulder, then his other fist into his head. It was the most inelegant fight Michael had ever seen, but it was working. In another minute Jazz would be out from under him, and once that happened, adrenaline alone would carry him through.

With all the energy he had left in his body Michael pulled his left arm up, raised it above his head, stuck the barrel in Jazz's gut.

He almost lost it as Jazz bellowed and struck him fiercely in the head, in the shoulder, in the stomach. But Jazz didn't hit him in the left hand.

Michael pulled the trigger.

The sound of the gunshot filled his head as blood splattered his body.

He tried to move, to get off the dead man, but all his strength had gone with that last bullet.

He felt the dark close in on him. And he felt grateful.

"YOU HAVE TO STAY HERE."

"I can't."

Chief Eccles shook his head, even as he braced himself as the grappling hooks pulled the police boat up against the *Pretty Kitty*. "We don't have any idea who's up there and how many weapons are on board. You could be killed."

"I don't care. If Michael is alive, he'll need me."

"The ambulance boat will be here in a moment."

"Please," she begged. "I have to—"

"I know you want to see him. But I can't let you on board. I promise I'll let you see him as soon as it's safe."

She couldn't argue anymore. They were in position and ready to board. Numbly she watched as the men in their heavy armor climbed up into the yacht, quickly disappearing into the saloon.

She'd given the chief Michael's description, afraid that they'd think he was one of Ed's men. Even so, the thought scared her. Maybe scared was better than knowing. She could deal with scared.

The minutes ticked by. She heard no gunfire. There were shouts, but she couldn't understand the words. The ambulance boat pulled up, and as quickly as they could the EMTs climbed into the yacht, carrying heavy bags and a portable gurney.

If they could go aboard, that must mean that the

coast was clear, right? What kind of chief would let his EMTs walk into a gun battle?

There was only one cop left on the police boat. His job was probably to keep her from disembarking, but at the moment he was busy on the radio, his gaze on the ambulance boat.

That was all the permission she needed. With strength she didn't know she had, she jumped over to the ladder leading up to the *Pretty Kitty*'s saloon. She made it onto the yacht just as the cop assigned to watch her shouted out. But he was too late—she was going to find Michael no matter what.

There was a huddle of men just at the door to their room. EMTs crouched beside someone, but she couldn't see who.

She took one step, then another, dread and hope battling it out in her head. When she saw them lift Michael's body onto the gurney, her heart shattered.

She was too late. Ed had told her the truth. Michael—her lover, her hero, her friend—was dead.

They came toward her, one EMT pushing the gurney and Michael. Her horrified gaze took in all the blood, all the bruises on Michael's face. God, they'd tortured him. Tortured him, then killed him in cold blood.

"Miss?"

She looked up into the dark man's face.

"Why don't you come with us? I'm sure he'll feel better seeing you first thing when he wakes up."

Tate blinked. "What?"

"I said why don't you come with us?"

"No—that last part. You said when he wakes up?"

The EMT nodded. "He's gonna be sore as heck, but he'll be fine."

The words took their own sweet time sinking in. And when they did, when she finally got that she hadn't lost him after all, Tate fainted dead away.

19

THE PHONE RANG AT eight-forty, stopping Sara just as she was about to leave Tate's place. The day had been so horrible, starting with that dreadful meeting first thing, that she'd made an appointment to get a deep-tissue massage to work out some of her stress.

She turned, going toward the nearest phone, but William beat her to it. She smiled at him, then went back to the door. When he gasped, she stopped.

"My God, my God, it's really you!"

Sara's heart slammed into overdrive as she hurried back to the phone. She dropped her tote and held on to the living room wall as the truth sunk in. Even if there had been no words spoken, she would have known it was Tate by looking at William. He was pale as a ghost, far too thin and haggard, but the joy in his eyes was like a rebirth.

"Where?"

Sara wanted desperately to hear Tate's voice. She knew it was real, but she still needed more.

"I'll be there by morning. You don't worry about a thing. I'll come get you and we'll straighten everything out."

Sara watched as fat tears slid down the old man's

cheeks. Her own tears started then, and her chest got tight with a mixture of emotions too big to hold in.

"Yes, she's here. She's been here the whole time. She'll come with me."

Sara nodded happily, wondering a million things at once.

William's face changed and so did his posture. "We'll talk about him when I get there."

Michael. It had to be. Oh, thank God. He must be alive, too, and they'd been together. Finally the whole story would come out. Jerry Brody, the main suspect, had sworn the kidnapping had nothing to do with him, but now everyone would find out for sure.

She didn't care. Tate was alive. For the first time in ten days Sara could breathe.

When Mr. Baxter hung up, he grabbed her in a hug that would leave bruises tomorrow. It was perfect.

"You're up."

Michael turned at the sound of Tate's voice to find her sitting beside his bed. His hospital bed. "How'd I get here?"

"The cavalry showed up. Too late to be of much help to you, however."

"Doesn't matter. You're here."

She smiled, wishing now that she'd had a few more moments with a hairbrush and some makeup. She'd done little but cry since she'd been roused on the ambulance boat. Michael had still not gained consciousness at the time, and as she'd waved away the concerned medics, she'd asked them a hundred questions—all of them nonsense, really, because Michael was alive.

She'd ridden with him to the hospital, and while he'd had his wrist worked on she'd called her father. It had been so good to speak to him, to know that Sara was there and that she'd taken care of him. They would all be together in the morning, which was wonderful, but right now she needed to be with Michael. To make sure he was all right and that he wasn't going to disappear.

"How long have I been out of it?"

"It's ten. At night, just so we're clear."

He looked at his bandaged hand. "Is this all the damage?"

"To you, yes."

"They found all the bodies?"

She nodded. "There's going to be an inquest, but don't worry. You'll be cleared in a moment. Ed's in jail and he's not ever getting out."

"Charlie?"

"He'll live. He's here in the hospital. He has a concussion, that's all. But I'm afraid he won't be getting off so easily."

Michael looked away. "I'm glad he didn't die."

She scooted her chair closer to the bed and touched his arm. "I called my father. He and Sara are flying in first thing in the morning."

"Good. Great."

"You'll be released by then. But I'm afraid you'll be in police custody until the inquest. I was assured there would be no delay. When my father gets here—"

"I'll hand in my resignation."

"I was going to say he'll make sure you'll have everything you need. I've gotten us a room at the Ritz, so as soon as you're free—"

"Tate... I appreciate all of this. I do. But let's slow down a little. There's a lot to deal with, and my head's still too fuzzy to understand it all."

"Of course," she said, embarrassed at her own presumption. "I'll call the nurse."

"Thanks," he said. "I'm probably going to be knocked out till morning. I'll sleep better knowing you're getting some rest."

"I'm fine. That chair is really comfortable."

He shook his head. "Go to the hotel," he said too quietly. "Get a good night's sleep. We'll talk tomorrow."

His tone was gentle and concerned, but his message burned in her chest. He wanted her gone. What she didn't know was if he meant for tonight or forever.

Frankly she wasn't in any shape to ask the question. Better to leave it unanswered than to know for sure. "Okay. I'll send the nurse."

Michael nodded. His gorgeous face looked even more rugged with the dark bruises and his five-o'clock shadow. She hated that he'd been so badly hurt, but her prayers had been answered. He was alive. It shouldn't matter that he was sending her away. It shouldn't—but it did.

She stood, put the chair back, then headed for the door.

"Tate?"

She stopped.

"No kiss goodbye?"

She smiled as she went back to him. She bent over him and brushed her lips over his. He touched her arm with his left hand as he kissed her back.

When she pulled away, the look in his eyes told her everything. When he'd asked for a kiss goodbye, he'd meant it.

THE JET TOUCHED DOWN at seven-eighteen Caymans time. Tate had gotten to the airport forty minutes earlier and had too many cups of coffee as she'd waited.

The good night's sleep she'd promised Michael hadn't materialized. She'd lain awake in her very posh suite, thinking. The fact that she'd still felt as if she was rocking on the water didn't help, either, but mostly she'd just thought.

She'd wanted a kidnapping to change her life and she'd gotten what she'd asked for. She hadn't bargained on the close calls with death. But then, she hadn't bargained on Michael, either.

Bottom line, however, was that she would never be the same.

She'd faced off with Ed, and despite his gun and his cell phone, she'd come out the victor. She'd kicked her kidnapper's ass. That wasn't opinion, it was fact.

Would she ever have another panic attack? Yeah, probably. There had been that whole passing-out business when she'd found out Michael was alive. But the good news was she wasn't going to stop living. She wasn't going to hole herself up in her luxurious prison of a penthouse. She was a free woman. Forever more, if she did have a panic attack, she could think of the satisfying crunch of Ed's testicles against her kneecap. That would surely get her through.

The bigger question was what she was going to do about Michael.

There was no doubt in her mind that she loved him. That she wanted to be with him, and not just for a fling. But she also wasn't naive enough to think that scenario wasn't rife with problems. There was her father to deal with. And the money thing. Then there was his guilt about his brother. None of those issues was going to be worked out with a nice chat.

She was, however, not willing to let him go just because she wasn't sure about how things would work. They'd just have to take it one step at a time.

Assuming, of course, he was willing to try.

The glass door between the tarmac and the terminal slid open, and there was her father.

She ran to him and gave him a hug he'd never forget. Fresh tears came from that never-ending supply, but these were joyous, so maybe they didn't count.

He petted her head as he rocked her back and forth. She felt like a little girl again, safe in her daddy's arms.

Finally she pulled back, kissed him on the cheek, then jumped into another fierce round of hugs with Sara.

It took a while, but they all finally finished crying and hugging and went off to the hotel.

She talked the entire way, and after they'd checked in, she continued the tale in her father's suite. She emphasized that Michael had saved her life many times over, but her father could be the most stubborn man.

"Don't get me wrong—I'm grateful he saved your life. But if it wasn't for him, you wouldn't have been in that position in the first place."

"Stop," she said. "I know you want someone to

blame, so here's a really good solution. Blame Ed Martini. He's the one who kidnapped me, who threatened me. He was going to kill me that first night, after he got the ransom. Then he was going to kill me as soon as he got the big money. He tried to kill me in the middle of the street in George Town. That's who you can blame. And when you're done with that, you can go to Michael Caulfield and you can thank him for your daughter's life."

Her father looked at her for a long time, and while a stranger would have thought he was completely unmoved by her speech, she knew he had listened. More importantly, he'd heard.

"You care about him," Sara said.

She looked at her oldest friend. "I do."

"Is he really going to resign?"

"I believe he is."

"And?"

Tate sighed. There was no time like the present to let her father know exactly where she stood. "I don't know. I need to make some phone calls. Michael needs an attorney and I want to make sure the inquest is in motion."

She kissed her father on the cheek, did the same to Sara, then went for the door. "Get unpacked," she said, standing in the doorway. "I'm in 2720. I'd appreciate any help you two want to give me."

With that, she left the suite. On the one hand, she'd said what she needed to and felt stronger than ever. On the other hand, she was scared beyond words that Michael would disappear before she had a chance to figure out what to do.

MICHAEL SAT IN THE beach chair, staring out at the ocean as the sun rose in splendor. This was the fifth morning in a row he'd come out for the sunrise, coffee in hand—left hand—the day stretching achingly ahead of him.

He'd found this little bungalow a week ago, after all the legal maneuverings had ended and he was once again a free man. After he'd said goodbye to Tate.

Charlie was in prison, and Michael doubted he'd ever be released. It was hard justice, but there was nothing Michael could do to mitigate the circumstances. Charlie had made his bed. Michael supposed he'd feel guilty about it for the rest of his life—but then, that was *his* bed. His very lonely bed.

His hand was healing and his bruises were all but gone, but he couldn't stop thinking about Tate. She'd sounded completely convincing when she'd asked him to come back. To try and live a life with her. But he knew the score. Despite his thanks, he knew William blamed him. Hell, he still blamed himself. As for a life with Tate? She was just starting to live. She deserved the world, not him. God, not him.

Sara had come in to double-team him. But at least she'd understood when Michael had explained. Tate still would have none of it.

After many tears and a lot of heartache for both of them, she'd gotten on her father's private plane and gone back to New York.

So here he was, sitting on a beach, sipping coffee, unsure what he was going to do with the day, not to mention the rest of his life. Missing Tate Baxter more than he'd ever imagined. More than he could take.

TATE STARED AT THE foolish trompe l'oeil window in her bedroom. It symbolized so much. Her pretense of a life. Her false dreams of adventure and romance. Every precious moment she'd wasted in her fear.

She owed Dr. Bay an apology. In retrospect, the kidnapping had been a good idea—the fake kind, at least. Tate truly was a different woman now. Yes, she still suffered from nightmares and she wasn't going to give up on therapy anytime soon, but she no longer wanted to hide herself away. Life beckoned in the most alluring ways. Unfortunately her new dreams all centered around a man who didn't want her.

It occurred to her that she might not be thinking in the most rational terms. The experiences on the boat had been traumatic and profound. Perhaps, as her father had suggested, she'd gone through some sort or variation of Stockholm syndrome, where her beliefs about Michael were totally out of proportion to actual events.

But after a month back home of intensive journaling and visits to her new therapist, she didn't think so.

She missed him. So badly it ached, and not in a metaphorical sense. She yearned to be with him, to hear his voice, smell his scent. She couldn't stand that he was alone, that his hand wouldn't heal for a while yet, that he had to deal with the consequences of his brother's sentence. All alone. He'd put his own life at risk so many times for her. But it wasn't just gratitude or guilt that made her want him.

She'd become someone new with him. She'd seen herself through his eyes, and for the first time in her life she'd liked what she'd seen.

Michael believed in her. He'd convinced her of her own strength over and over again.

And, she had to admit, she missed making love to him. There was no doubt in her mind that the two of them were meant to be together.

Unfortunately there was a giant roadblock between them, and it wasn't the fact that he blamed himself for the kidnapping. It was the money.

"Knock-knock."

Tate turned to find Sara at the bedroom door. "I'm so glad you're here."

"Right back at ya," Sara said. She was in her workout gear, looking radiant, and she sat on the bed with a plop. "Come with me?"

"I will," Tate said. "But not today."

"You said that yesterday. I know you'll like my trainer. He's got the best ass in the five boroughs. Seriously. It's worth all the pain just to watch him bend over."

Tate grinned. "I missed you."

"I'm glad. It would have hurt my feelings if you hadn't."

"You're my sister, kiddo. So when I ask you something, I trust you're going to be honest, right?"

Sara crossed her heart.

"I can't let go of Michael. I miss him too much. I love him."

Sara's smile faded as she nodded. "I figured."

"I want to go to him. Do whatever it takes to make him see that we can be together. Except…there's the whole money problem."

Sara's head went down for a long time. Tate thought

of calling the kitchen for tea, but she didn't want to disturb Sara's thought process.

Finally her friend looked up. "It's a big problem, and I don't know Michael well enough to predict if he can get past it. But something that might help is the reward."

"What reward?"

"Your father offered a million dollars to anyone who was instrumental in finding you. Michael was instrumental, all right."

"He didn't tell me."

"Yeah," Sara said. "Go figure."

"Surely he'd have to agree that Michael deserves the reward."

Sara laughed. "Your father? Come on, Tate. He's going to blame Michael for a long time."

"But Michael deserves—oh."

"Exactly."

Tate grinned. "Do you think I'm crazy?"

"Only if you don't try. Tate, you haven't taken a risk in so long. I think taking this one will make up for it. The worst that's going to happen is he'll break your heart. And since your heart is already broken, it can't be that much worse."

Tate felt her pulse race and her heart pound. Sara was right. It would be scary to go to him—but then, she had faced scary. And she'd kicked scary's ass.

ANOTHER DAY, ANOTHER sunrise, and Michael wasn't getting better. His hand was healing, but missing Tate continued to get worse.

He didn't understand. Yes, he was depressed. He got

that. He'd made some big mistakes and there had been consequences. That wasn't what was making him nuts.

That had everything to do with Tate. Not Charlie, not the kidnapping, not the killings. Tate haunted his dreams, haunted his waking hours. He kept thinking about how she'd been so brave, how she'd fought so hard. He remembered, too vividly, the way her skin felt, the taste of her flesh, how he felt when he slipped inside her.

He took a sip of coffee, wishing she were there, wishing he could find a way to justify calling her. If he couldn't do that, he wanted a way to forget her. Perhaps now that Charlie was in jail he could go back to the Army. If his hand healed correctly. If they'd take him.

It would all be a lot easier if he would stop thinking he saw her out of the corner of his eye. Every woman with reddish-brown hair made his pulse race. Until he saw that it was just a woman and not Tate. Then he'd hear a voice, and the cycle would start over again until he saw it was a stranger.

The persistence of her memory had taken him over. Like a virus, she had spread throughout his system. Unfortunately there were no pills or shots to help him.

He felt someone next to his chair, but he didn't want any more coffee or a drink. He looked up, ready to send the boy away. But it wasn't a boy. And it wasn't a dream.

"Tate?"

She was wearing shorts and a T-shirt, with her hair down and wild, the way it had been on the boat. She wore no makeup and her eyes were puffy from crying. He'd never seen anyone more beautiful in his life.

"I tried, Michael. I did. I tried to see it your way and

I gave your argument all I could. But the only conclusion I could come to was that you couldn't be more wrong if you tried."

He couldn't help laughing at that, even though she looked damn serious.

"Don't laugh. I mean it. You're an idiot."

"I never had any doubts about that."

"Good, so we're agreed. And since you're an idiot and I'm tough and smart, here's what we're gonna do." She came around in front of him and pulled him up by his T-shirt. "We're going to figure out who we are and what we want and we're going to do it together. I have no idea if it's going to last a week or a lifetime, but I'll be damned if I walk away and don't find out."

"Really?"

"Yes. Any questions?"

"What about your—"

She put her fingers over his mouth. "This isn't about my father. So no questions about him. And it's not about money, because there was a million-dollar reward for my safe return, which you completely and utterly deserve, so you have money, I have money—and, dammit, money isn't the issue."

"Are you through?"

"No. I also want you to know that just because you saved my life doesn't mean I feel some kind of obligation toward you. I'm not going through a phase and I'm not here because you're the first man in years to make my toes curl. I'm here because being with you is the best thing that's happened to me. Ever. You're an amazing man and I admire every single thing about you. Of course, when we actually live together, I reserve the right to get cranky. But still, I think you're incredible and I don't want to spend another day without you."

"Are you through now?"

"For the moment."

"Good. Because I love you."

Her lips curved up in a wicked smile. "Yeah?"

"Yeah."

"All that other stuff?"

He shrugged. "We'll deal."

"I thought this would be harder."

He shook his head. "I can't get you out of my head. You've been driving me insane."

She sighed and closed her eyes. "Thank God. Because I love you, too."

He smiled as his whole body relaxed. "Thank God," he said. And then he kissed her.

* * * * *

Celebrate 100 years of pure reading pleasure with Mills & Boon®

To mark our centenary, each month we're publishing a special 100th Birthday Edition. These celebratory editions are packed with extra features and include a FREE bonus story.

Plus, you have the chance to enter a fabulous monthly prize draw. See 100th Birthday Edition books for details.

Now that's worth celebrating!

September 2008

Crazy about her Spanish Boss by Rebecca Winters
Includes FREE bonus story
Rafael's Convenient Proposal

November 2008

**The Rancher's Christmas Baby
by Cathy Gillen Thacker**
Includes FREE bonus story *Baby's First Christmas*

December 2008

One Magical Christmas by Carol Marinelli
Includes FREE bonus story *Emergency at Bayside*

Look for Mills & Boon® 100th Birthday Editions at your favourite bookseller or visit
www.millsandboon.co.uk

2 Books
and a surprise gift!

We would like to take this opportunity to thank you for reading this Mills & Boon® book by offering you the chance to take TWO more specially selected titles from the Blaze® series absolutely FREE! We're also making this offer to introduce you to the benefits of the Mills & Boon® Book Club™—

★ FREE home delivery
★ FREE gifts and competitions
★ FREE monthly Newsletter
★ Exclusive Book Club offers
★ Books available before they're in the shops

Accepting these FREE books and gift places you under no obligation to buy, you may cancel at any time. even after receiving your free shipment. Simply complete your details below and return the entire page to the address below. You don't even need a stamp!

YES! Please send me 2 free Blaze books and a surprise gift. I understand that unless you hear from me. I will receive 3 superb new titles every month, including a 2-in-I title priced at £4.99 and two single titles priced at £3.15 each. Postage and packing free. I am under no obligation to purchase any books and may cancel my subscription at any time. The free books and gift will be mine to keep in any case.

K8ZEF

Ms/Mrs/Miss/Mr .... Initials ....

Surname ....
                                                                    BLOCK CAPITALS PLEASE
Address ....

....

.... Postcode ....

Send this whole page to:
UK: FREEPOST CN8I, Croydon, CR9 3WZ